A Serving of Revenge

A Cubley's Coze Novel

R. Morgan Armstrong

By

R. Morgan Armstrong

First Printing

Copyright © 2020

Author - R. Morgan Armstrong

Publisher
Wayne Dementi
Dementi Milestone Publishing, Inc.
Manakin-Sabot, VA 23103
www.dementimilestonepublishing.com

Cataloging-in-publication data for this book is available from The Library of Congress.
ISBN: 978-1-7350611-6-0

Cover design: Rebecca Myrtle-Razul and Jayne Hushen

Graphic design by Dianne Dementi

Printed in U.S.A.

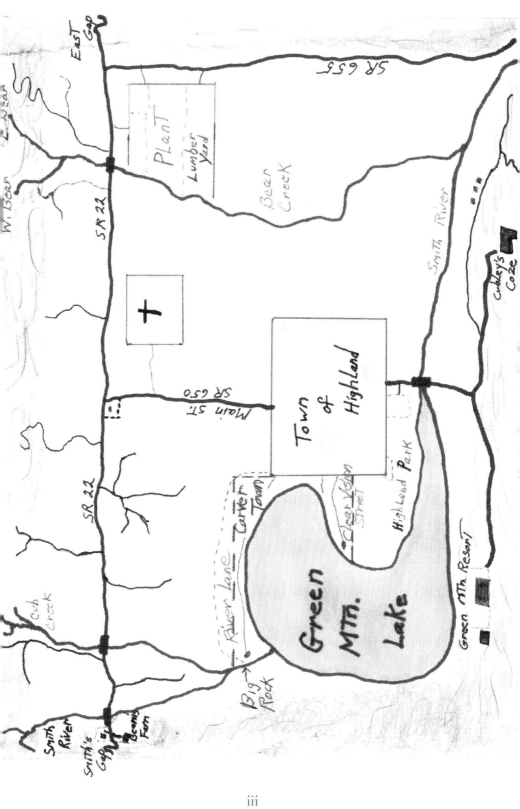

CUBLEY'S COZE MAP LEGEND
For The
TOWN OF HIGHLAND

Building #	Building Description
1	Frank Peters & Son Grocery
2	Highland Hardware
3	Top Hat Theater
4	Highland Furniture
5	Frank Dalton, Attorney at Law
6	Highland Five & Dime
7	Mountain Drugs
8	The First National Bank of Highland Ben Southwall's Law Office – Second Floor
9	Highland Volunteer Fire Department
10	Highland Methodist Church
11	Green Mountain Baptist Church
12	McCulloch Chevrolet Dealership
13	Black Panther Grill
14	The First Baptist Church of Highland

Town of HighLand

Guest check in

Parking

Veranda

Salon

Elevator

Banquet Room Stairs

Fire Exit

Fire Escape

Deliveries

Dining Room

Stairs China ↑

Lobby

Front Desk

Office

Kitchen

Car Wash Area

Fire Escape

Storage

Load. Dock

Cooker

ACKNOWLEDGMENTS

Thanks to the following family friends at Wintergreen Resort for critically reading the first drafts of this novel: Sue Carlson, Sally Singletary, and Terry Brooks, and to the first editor who helped tremendously with the storyline and grammar, Lynn Hilleary, of Nelson County, Virginia.

I am grateful to the artist, Rebecca Myrtle Razul of Staunton, Virginia, for her design of the book's cover and the little emblem of the tow truck, Blacky, which repeatedly appears to show a shift in time or location.

A grateful acknowledgment to the publisher's editor, Ariel Dantona, for all her hard work in getting this novel ready for publication. If this story flows and is fun to read, it's because of her hard work.

DEDICATION

This novel is dedicated to my wife, Jo Ann.

INTRODUCTION

During the summer of 1955, death came to town. Reporters circled soon after. Some would snatch tidbits and fly away; others would stay for the full feast.

The first body was embedded into the soil of a field of dandelions, grass, weeds, and stalks of volunteer corn. Hidden like a bug crushed by a rolling pin into soft dough. The earth, unlike dough, was more accepting of the intruder. It sipped from the offering before scavengers could deprive it of its due.

A herd of cows retreated to a more distant piece of their world of square corners and wire. The human, who provided them hay and a little treat of sweet feed, would become an occasional memory.

For now, the body was undiscovered. Not yet noticed by birds or animals, spectators or police. Just a corpse, partially buried in a field.

A Serving of Revenge

CHAPTER 1

A BAD TABLE SAW
1955

"Mr. Franklin, I hate to bother you, but I need to get a new blade out of the supply room."

"Why?" asked the foreman, Pete Franklin.

"I keep hitting nails in this batch of lumber. The logs must have come from a farmer's fence line or trees where hunters nailed in steps for deer blinds. This blade is dull and starting to get dangerous."

"Shiflett, ain't nothing wrong with that blade. Get back to work," ordered the foreman.

After lunch, Daryl Dean Shiflett screamed when the dull blade hit a knot, which caused the board to jerk suddenly forward, leaving two of his fingers on the factory floor.

He was taken over to Doctor Hill's office by the factory nurse. A janitor started to throw the fingers in the trash, but the foreman, Mr. Franklin, happened to be walking past and yelled, "Wait, give me one of those."

The janitor handed him one of the fingers. Grabbing a hammer and nail from a toolbox, Franklin nailed it to the factory wall as an object lesson for workers to be more careful. The digit, nailed above the McCulloch Wood Products calendar, oozed a drop of blood that dripped across the swimsuit of that month's pinup girl. She sported a brown sash across her swimsuit for the rest of March until that page was torn off for April's pinup.

Daryl Dean returned to work the next day despite the pain. His whole hand was throbbing, but the worker was desperate not to lose his job, which was necessary to support his wife and daughters. He clocked in on time, went back to the table saw, and turned it on.

Foreman Franklin saw him from the rough end office and yelled for him. Daryl Dean walked up to the foreman. "Mr. Franklin, where do you want me to work today?"

"Shiflett, we can't afford to have cripples working for McCulloch Wood Products because they slow down production. You shoulda' been more careful. You're fired! Get your family moved out of the company house by day after tomorrow. Don't wait for the Highland Police to make you leave. You won't like that. Nope, you won't like it one bit."

"Mr. Franklin, please give me a chance. I need this job. I have a wife and two little girls."

"Shiflett, you can leave now, or I'll have the police remove you. Now, get off company property. This is your last warning," demanded the foreman.

Daryl Dean walked out of the plant with his head down like a beaten stray cur. His final pay envelope was in his uninjured hand.

Pete Franklin looked around for a replacement on the table saw. He spotted a man coming out of the men's bathroom. It was one minute past time to start work by the company clock. Franklin yelled, "Hathaway, why are you late? We don't pay you to sleep in the crapper, get over here."

"Yes, sir. I wanted to avoid taking a break during the morning shift. I'll work a little extra over lunch," responded Maynard Donald "Doc" Hathaway.

"Do you know how to run a table saw?" asked the foreman.

"Ran one for six months on my last job."

"Well, you have Shiflett's job now. Catch up on that pile of oak. I need them all cut to sixty-five inches by lunchtime."

"Yes, sir. I'll get right on it," promised Doc.

He worked diligently for an hour, but the saw with the dull blade kept hanging on knots. The saw was jerking his fingers toward the spinning blade, just as it had with Shiflett. Maynard knew it was only a matter of time. He turned off the saw when he saw his foreman walking past.

"Mr. Franklin, may I please change out this blade. I can't afford to lose any fingers."

"What is it with you people? Who's running this plant, you or me? I told Shiflett the blade was fine. I'll tell you the same thing. That blade is fine. Now get back to work."

"Mr. Franklin, that blade is dangerous. Shiflett just lost two fingers, and what happened? He got fired. I need all my fingers and this job. If you won't fix that blade, I want to speak to the plant superintendent," demanded Doc, who was now angry.

2

The foreman's instant response was, "Shut your mouth!"

"Mr. Franklin, I don't have to take this. If you and the plant superintendent won't speak to me, I'm gonna complain to Big John. Maybe the owner of the company will let me change the damn blade," threatened the worker.

"Who did you say you wanted to see?" the foreman asked, and this time he wanted to be sure that he'd heard this jackass correctly.

"I want to speak to the boss, the real boss, Big John McCulloch. These conditions are just too dangerous. I need my fingers."

The foreman stood for a moment and then, with a smirk on his face, shouted, "Mr. John Louis McCulloch, Sr., has better ways to spend his time than listening to whiny-assed babies. Get back to work or get your pay and get off McCulloch plant property."

There was a pause as the other employees watched.

"Maybe it's time we started a union," Hathaway muttered.

It almost seemed the entire plant, which was ordinarily noisy, took a hesitant breath. The workers who were standing nearby pretended they had not heard that last statement. Men with brooms got busy sweeping, and everyone tried to get as far away from this troublemaker as they could get.

The foreman's face turned red. He began jabbing his finger at Hathaway's chest with spit flying from his mouth as he shouted, "I'm sorry! I know I did not hear you say that five-letter word. Not in this plant. I did not hear you say it. I'll show you where you can put your union! When I get back, you...are...done! You are damn dog done!"

After he had eyed the man with a cold stare for five or six-seconds, the foreman walked straight to the plant superintendent's office.

Mr. Franklin stormed past the surprised secretary and barged into the plant superintendent's office without even knocking. After five minutes, the plant superintendent, with the foreman in tow, came out of the office, walking hurriedly toward the main office building. Their destination was the office of "Big John," who presided over the plant, most of the Town of Highland, and half of Green Mountain County.

A tense thirty minutes passed. Franklin came back alone and said nothing. He just sat in his office all afternoon with his door closed. Everyone was shocked that Maynard Hathaway wasn't instantly fired. Whispered conversations began to take place all over the plant.

The next day, a few events occurred. Hathaway returned to work and a new employee, Billy Ray Bondurant, was hired to drive log trucks for the company. The union threat and lack of retaliation was the main talk of the factory. Even the new guy heard all about it. Some of the men were saying how the boss, Big John McCulloch, must be getting soft.

Billy Ray clocked out with the rest of the day shift at the end of that week, the plant's payday. All their money was held back. The workers were told to come for their pay on Saturday with no reasons given.

This was the first time that the plant had ever been a day late with the payroll. Some were worried, and others mad. Friday night was going to be a dry night for workers. Several of the men knew their wives would not believe that the employees had not been paid.

Three cops of the Highland Police Department stopped Doc Hathaway as he left the factory. The first was Sergeant "Little John" McCulloch, the son of "Big John." He grabbed Doc by the arm. Next, Officers Frank Younger and Roger Younger, look-alike twins, also grabbed him. The worker's lunch pail went flying as the three officers spun him in a half-circle and smashed him, face first, against the corrugated wall of the plant.

The officers handcuffed Hathaway and, without a word, dragged him back to his car, which was parked in the company lot. In the process of being dragged, Doc lost his left shoe. The police did not examine his lunch pail, nor did they search him. Sergeant Little John McCulloch went straight to the passenger side of the unlocked car and began to search under the front seat. He immediately pulled out four pay envelopes.

The town sergeant handed them to the plant superintendent who had just arrived.

"Mr. Spencer, would you read the names of the employees on these envelopes?" demanded Sergeant McCulloch.

Mr. Wesley Spencer read out the names in a loud voice. None of the names were Hathaway's. He asked Spencer to count the cash. Verifying the money was there, the plant superintendent handed the envelopes back to Sergeant McCulloch.

While everyone watched, the factory police carried Maynard Hathaway off to the county jail. The officers took no notice when the prisoner repeatedly denied stealing the pay envelopes, nor when he said he had no idea how the money had gotten into his car. The shoe and lunchbox remained where they had fallen.

Bondurant asked a couple of the older men who were standing near him, "Who are these Highland Police Officers?"

"Special police, company cops," announced one of them.

"What kind of police force is that?"

"New guy, the law says that certain factories can hire special police. They get paid by the factory, hired and fired by the factory, and to no one's surprise, controlled by the factory. These special officers have the same authority as any county sheriff. Here they wear a Highland Police Department uniform, are called town officers, but make no mistake; they are company cops."

When Bondurant asked, "How can that be?" He was told to shut up and stop being stupid. The older men moved on. Their lesson for the new guy was over.

Hathaway's wife went to court the next morning for the arraignment. She noticed her husband had a broken nose, a bruised jaw, a swollen shut black eye, and a split lip, and he walked with a limp and moved slowly, indicating that he was sore all over. The Highland Police added a charge of resisting arrest to the charge of theft. The officer told the judge that the plant employee had tried to escape and fought with Sergeant McCulloch. His injuries were from Officer McCulloch subduing the prisoner using reasonable force. No one mentioned the prisoner was handcuffed at the time of his attempted escape. He was remanded to jail until his trial because he had no money for a bail bond.

The Hathaway family lost their company rental house and had to leave town by Tuesday of the next week. While the wife and children cried, the Highland officer informed the wife, "Lady, the plant is being gracious in giving you two extra days to get out. Your man was arrested on a Friday; we waited until Tuesday. What more do you want?"

When the case came to trial a month later, the foreman, plant superintendent, and Sergeant John Louis McCulloch, Jr., testified against him. No one from the payroll office came to explain how he had gotten his hands on pay envelopes which were kept in a locked office under guard until it was time to hand them out. The state prosecutor asked for the maximum sentence of twelve months on each crime for a total of twenty-four months. The defendant had no lawyer and no witnesses to speak on his behalf.

The trial judge commented that his sentence of six months to pull with a year's probation was lenient because of the unusual circumstances. The police and plant witnesses stormed out of the courtroom upon hearing the light sentence. The wife and children cried upon hearing the harsh punishment. The defendant left the courtroom, claiming he was innocent.

Friday, June 3, 1955, Billy Ray Bondurant, who everyone now called the "new guy," had only worked for the McCulloch Company for about three months, but he knew all the details about Shiflett and Hathaway. Being a former coal miner from West Virginia, he believed he and his family were making out much better than when he had worked in the mines, despite his low wages at this plant. The McCulloch Company's rental house was cheap. The work was a lot cleaner and less dangerous than working shifts in a Hudson Company coal mine.

He was happy, it was Friday, payday, and this was his last trip from the Amherst Log Yard to the McCulloch Wood Products Plant. He planned to pick up his pay, go home, and surprise his family with dinner out at a local hamburger joint, the Black Panther.

His log truck was hard to drive, and he was more than ordinarily careful. The first problem with the truck was that it was overloaded, but since he had not met any Virginia State Troopers, he was almost home free. The Highland Town Police were on the McCulloch payroll and left the company trucks alone. The local sheriff was up for re-election, and his men were also not stopping any company trucks.

His second and more significant problem was a set of mushy brakes. They worked, but he had to pump on the brake pedal to get the most out of the braking system. He was worried that this load might be too much for them.

Billy Ray had known about the brakes on this truck for several weeks. But when he had reported the problem to his foreman, Mr. Pete Franklin had made it clear that if he wanted to continue with the company, he'd better not say anything else. Another log truck was in the shop for a transmission repair; therefore, his vehicle had to wait until the next quarterly budget cycle, which didn't start until July. Mr. Franklin promised him that next quarter, he would write him up a repair order. Until then, Billy Ray was told to keep adding brake fluid.

So, for the last two trips, he had kept his mouth shut and added brake fluid daily. He had even worked on the brake line himself after he almost rear-ended a car on his last trip into Amherst. Billy Ray tried to fix the brakes with some clamps and a three-inch section of small diameter hydraulic hose he found in a scrap bin at the plant and some gray tape he'd brought from home. Trained as a mechanic in the mine, he knew something about fixing things with wire, twine, and glue. Before leaving Amherst today, he'd poured in his last spare can of brake fluid.

Billy Ray wasn't stupid. He knew that keeping quiet and keeping his job made the most sense. His wife, Betty Sue, agreed, but she'd begged him to be careful when he left for work that morning.

"Please don't have a wreck. We need you."

"Don't you worry, I'll come home in one piece," he'd promised as he departed.

Billy Ray was keeping his word. Only one obstacle to go. Making it into Hidden Valley over Smith's Gap from the Amherst side required trucks to use lower gears. Prominent warning signs were posted at the top of the gap because on that steep downgrade, there were five sharp curves and a final long one. Once he made it through that last curve, he would be home free because the road was straight across the flats of Hidden Valley. It was so flat and straight that the high school boys ran drag races there. Truckers let their rigs run out of that last curve onto the flats—a good place to make up time.

Humming a tune, he crested the top of the gap and made sure his 1951 Mack log truck was in first gear. He used his brakes as little as possible on the steep downgrade and made it through the five sharp curves. When he got to the last long sweeping bend, he shifted the truck into second and then third gear. He let her run-up to just above the posted speed limit as he came out of that last curve. He could now stay off the brakes, let her run across the valley, and be back by quitting time. The truck backfired twice, but in third gear, his speed stayed in check, just under sixty miles per hour. He had left those wicked curves behind. He stopped worrying and began to sing.

An old 1942 Dodge pickup pulled out of a farm road fifty yards from the last curve before the log truck came into view. When Billy Ray saw the slow-moving pickup, he took a sharp intake of breath, opened wide his eyes, stopped singing, and started pumping the brakes for all he was worth. The log truck first slowed, then something popped under the hood. Instead of slowing, it gained speed. The harder he pumped the brakes, the faster the log truck went. He next tried to downshift into second gear. Once he got the speeding truck out of third gear, he could not get it to go into second or back into third. It was a runaway.

Oak trees lined the road on the right with a dirt bank on the left. The white-knuckled log truck driver saw one final chance to miss the pickup. He eased left to pass it. That's when he noticed the pickup's left turn signal blinking. The old farmer never looked back as he slowly, with all the time in the world, turned left for the field road to his tobacco barn.

What happened next was more of an explosion than a collision. The difference in speed and weight of the log truck versus the farmer's light, slow-moving pickup, resulted in the front end of the log truck smashing the bed of the pickup almost to the cab. The angle of the impact launched the pickup through the air sideways. It went high enough to clear the top of the bank and the four-strand barbed wire fence.

The old farmer died when his head slammed into the back of the cab. He never knew what happened because it happened faster than thought. His quick death was a blessing.

The pickup flew over the bank, landed sideways, and rolled side over side. During rollover number three, the body of the driver went up and out the driver's side window. It landed in the pasture just ahead of the rolling vehicle. The farmer's body was crushed when the pickup fell on it. The Dodge continued to roll, leaving the body partially hidden in the pasture. The smashed truck finally came to rest fifteen yards from the body.

The front end of the log truck was demolished. The damage was so bad it turned the long nose of the Baumis style Mack truck into a snub-nosed one. The front axle broke off at the frame. The motor was torn loose, ejected upward, taking the hood with it. The engine landed in the pasture to the left. The wreck, without the front axle attached, slid down the road on its frame, sparks flying. It swerved back to the right, hit a large oak tree at the edge of the right-of-way, and flipped over onto its left side. The missing front axle ground to a halt across the center-line. Logs and wreckage blocked the road.

All of the cows were up and on the move away from the wreck. Then there was silence. Dust, smoke, and steam drifted away. The only movement was the right rear wheels of the log truck turning until they finally stopped.

CHAPTER 2

BILLY'S MAGIC MIRROR
Friday, June 3, 1955

O n the first day of my summer vacation in 1955, by noon, I was bored. The next day, I made a wish because nothing ever happened in my hometown. Some older boys said it was a fact that by wishing on a mirror, your wish would come true. Things could not have been slower, so I stood in front of my bathroom mirror and gave it a try.

"Mirror, mirror, bring me a big adventure."

Okay, nothing happened. No smoke, no weird shadows, not even a spooky voice—no change in my mirror. Darn.

I began brushing my curly hair, which I hated, with lots of water to get the curls to flatten out. It was my same old reflection in the same old mirror. That's when Mom called me from the kitchen.

"Billy, breakfast."

My full name is William Boyer Gunn, but my parents and most adults call me Billy. My friends call me either Billy or BB Gun or just BB for short.

I've lived all my life in Highland, Virginia. Although I'm now fourteen and will start high school this fall, I remember all about the summer of 1955. I was twelve years old and had just finished the sixth-grade. My last exam ended, and school let out on Wednesday, June 1, 1955, at 3:05 p.m. I can remember important details like that.

I was reasonably confident that I'd made all A's. My teacher Miss Jones liked me. However, one could never be sure about grades, and besides, there was no use worrying about them until they arrived.

"Billy, you coming?" Mom yelled for the second time.

"Yes, Mom, be there in a minute." Working on my hair, I had one more call to go.

Right off, I should tell you that there arc two things I hate: an idiot and my curly hair. My dad hates idiots, and I agree with him,

10

except when he thinks I'm the idiot. I got my curly hair from Mom. She hates her curly hair, though I think it's beautiful. She claims to like my hair, but I think she feels guilty and is just trying to make me feel better.

Scotty, my little brother, was a little shy of three that June and starting to become spoiled. His only good quality that summer was that he was almost toilet trained. The main idea here being almost.

I did inherit one good thing from my mom, though: my brains. She was really smart in school, and, like her, my grades are all "A's." School, for me, is easy. I never got fussed at about grades, only talking in class, and being stubborn. Mom and Dad think I'm stubborn. Even Grandma calls me stubborn. I'm still not sure if being stubborn is good or bad, but I got being stubborn from Dad. It's not safe to cross him on certain things on certain days. When he gets stubborn, only Mom can change his mind and sometimes, not even then.

Mom is swell, most of the time. Wicked good, unless you do something terrible and she gets that funny frown that makes her nose wrinkle.

Now, when I was a little kid, I liked summer and being out of school. But when I was twelve, I started having mixed feelings about my summer break. You see, the summer before, I had learned to be afraid of my dad.

Most of Dad's days are okay, and then my days are okay. But some of his days that summer were what I called his "quiet days." Those days he didn't talk much, and I stayed out of his way. Mom was careful to stay home with Scotty when Dad was having a "quiet day." She or Grandma kept Scotty away from Dad on those days.

Even Scotty was starting to catch on to Dad's moods. He was a smart kid for being almost three (though intelligent and likable are quite different; the day of my wish for an adventure, Scotty was being a nosebleed).

Early that morning, while it was still dark, Mom and Dad got into a big fuss. I could hear them through the heating vent in my walk-in closet. They didn't know and still don't know about me being able to hear them that way. I was careful not to let on. I didn't want to lose my early warning system.

Before Mom and Dad bought our house, our closet used to be a tiny nursery. When my parents remodeled and added on to the house, it became a walk-in closet for Scotty and me. All our stuff was to be stored in there, and sometimes we did.

The day they had the big fuss, I was thinking that I might rather be in school. School could be fun. My sixth-grade year had been the best because of my teacher, Miss Jones. She was a teacher everyone liked. Not being married or having children must make it easier to be pleasant.

Miss Jones made stuff fun. Her school parties were something. We even had a party with cake and soda pop for no reason. She called it an end of year party. None of my other teachers had ever given us an end of year party. I heard my fifth-grade teacher tell another teacher the last day of school to come on over to her house for a teachers' celebration. I could only guess what a teacher's party was like because none of us kids were invited.

I also realized my fifth and sixth-grade years that I liked figuring out things—math and mechanical things. My dad let me help him fix things when I turned eleven. Gunn's Garage was his. He was the best mechanic in the whole world. He'd learned all about fixing trucks and jeeps in the Army. The year I was eleven, he let me work in the garage on his good days, and that was fun as long as I was careful to put his tools away.

Lost in thought, brushing my curly hair without making any difference, and thinking about summer, that's when I heard, "William Boyer Gunn, you get down here right now! Do not make me call you again!" This was Mom's last call for real.

"Coming Mom," I answered her in my most respectful voice.

One final look at my hopeless tangle, I hustled down the stairs and into the kitchen. Dad, Grandma Harris, and Scotty were already at the table. Grandma was playing the airplane game with Scotty.

Mom handed me a plate of eggs, bacon, and toast as I passed her on my way to the kitchen table. She also gave me a glass of orange juice that had been sitting on the counter by the stove. I took a sip and noticed it was warm. No way was I going to mention my juice was warm. I sat down to eat but didn't speak to my dad. I knew better.

"Here comes the plane into the hangar." Grandma had a spoon full of oatmeal and was making circles around Scotty's face. He had his mouth shut.

"Look out, here it comes into the hangar. Open up." She swooped the spoon toward Scotty, who opened wide. The spoon went into his mouth, and he clamped down on it. He bit down so hard, his face looked squished, and at the same time, he smiled. Now, he wouldn't let go of the spoon. Grandma was tugging at it gently, trying to get it back, but the little brat would not let go.

"Mom, I have asked you again and again, do not feed Scotty. He needs to learn to feed himself." Mom used her, "I mean it" voice. The same tone that she had used on her last call to get me to come to breakfast. It was apparent, to even the uninformed, that she was not happy. I guessed her rare bad mood was a carryover from her argument with Dad.

"Laura Jane, it never hurt you. Besides, he likes it," said Grandma, while still tugging on the spoon, but she was not getting it back from Scotty. The more she pulled, the wider his grin, and the tighter he held on to that spoon.

"Now, Mother!" Mom complained with a frown, but before she could fuss, Dad suddenly put down his fork and looked over his newspaper at Grandma.

"Matilda, I think you need…" Dad started to say, but then Grandma interrupted him. Oh, oh, that always made Dad mad. I tried to get smaller.

"John, you got in awfully late last night. You woke me up. I couldn't get back to sleep. So darn't you start in on me with your stingers and bouquets." Grandma looked at Dad and then at Mom, to see who was going to get drawn into a fight with her, first.

It had been about two weeks since Mom, Grandma, and Dad had gotten into what I called a "knock-down, drag-out fight." I knew that they were about due for another one.

When Grandma started telling someone not to give her "stingers and bouquets," which she called a severe insult, she was spoiling for a fight. The bigger the battle, the better she liked it. Mom started to say something when Dad folded his paper, stuck it under his arm, got up, picked up his coffee and cigarettes in the same hand, and started for the door to the back porch.

"Gonna drink my coffee outside, where it's quiet," he said to no one in particular. He kicked open the screen door with his foot and let it slam behind him.

I drank my juice and looked over the glass to see what would happen next. Mom and Grandma remained quiet. This meant they had either reached a truce or were building up steam for a major blow-up. I finished my breakfast in a rush while silence reigned. I took my dishes over to the sink, picked up the trash can from the corner of the kitchen, and headed for the back door.

Mom glanced at me but said nothing. I figured it would be better to take out the trash without her telling me to, thus earning me a position on her good side while things were pre-storm. I emptied the trash, took the empty can back into the kitchen, dropped it off, and fled out the back door, being careful not to let it slam.

I quietly worked on my chores by sorting out the car parts that Dad had ordered for some new jobs. I was careful not to drop them while putting them on the parts shelves. Later in the morning, I finished up by putting away his tools. So far, no explosions from the house. I was hoping things might settle down. Dad was quiet while I worked. I knew to stay quiet and out of his way.

Finishing up my chores, I looked for something else to do. That's when my best friend, Kent Clark, arrived on his bike. I think I was the only one who knew his middle name was Farnsworth. It was our secret.

Like every kid in this dumb town, he suffered from boredom. We both agreed there was never nothing to do. No, that's not right. There was never *anything* to do. I didn't much care how I said it unless Mom was around to hear my grammar.

I gave Kent the zipper sign. Now, he knew my dad was having a bad day. I pointed outside. We walked over to the picnic table on the side of the garage. Here, we were out of Dad's view.

Kent was my best friend, who stuck with me no matter what. We tried to be good, most of the time. Not like some other kids at our school. Even at twelve, I could figure people out pretty well, and I usually knew who was okay and who to avoid. However, some people could fool me. Figuring out what was wrong with a fuel pump or radiator was easy. I noticed early in life that some people, like cars that wouldn't run, were just broken. Unlike a fuel pump, they often could not be fixed because there was no way to figure out what was causing the problem. I learned as a little kid; it was best to stay away from certain people. My mom would tell me there were times Dad was not to be bothered. I knew when to be careful. I didn't want to get hurt again.

During the summer of last year, I got into a mighty big scrape with my dad. Scrapes are things a kid can study to try to avoid. Still, they happen. I had my share of 'em. Now at fourteen, it's easier to avoid them, well, most of the time.

When I started first grade, I had been an idiot. I had gotten into them all the time.

There were some scrapes in fourth and fifth-grade I hadn't tried to avoid. You see, I liked to annoy certain people. I was very good at doing that to the kids a year or two older than me. I knew how not to get killed. I learned only to annoy older boys when adults were close.

Superman—that's Kent's nickname—and I were running down the list of seventh and eighth-grade bullies. It wasn't wise to cross them, even when adults were close. We noted those in town for the summer and those out of town.

"Hey, Superman, are the Lockhart brothers here over the summer or are they going to stay with their grandparents in Blacksburg?"

"Last I heard, they're going to be in town all summer. As mean as they are, their grandparents probably took off for somewhere far, far away, like Baltimore or New York City. If I were them, that's where I'd go."

Kent gave me his sideways grin. The kind where one side of his mouth went up and the other went down just a little. He had hit a tree on his sled the winter before last and broke his arm and busted his mouth. Lucky for him no teeth got knocked out, but since the stitches got pulled from the corner of his mouth and cheek, one side of his smile didn't quite seem to match the other.

"Yeah, those Lockhart brothers are mean as snakes. One minute they're nice, and the next they're nothing but trouble," I agreed with him because it was true. They were broken, mean.

"Kent, we best stay away from them. I hear they're running with Lou McCulloch."

Kent made a finger into a gun and pointed it at me. "You know, someone needs to shoot Lou McCulloch. He stole my tennis shoes in gym class last December. I never did get them back. No way he could wear them on his big feet."

"He didn't need them. His grandfather could buy the shoe factory," I said with disgust. "He and that older Lockhart brother, Dickie, make a great pair. Then you add the younger brother, Carl, and you get triple trouble."

I picked up a stick from the picnic table and threw it over-hand to the ground like I was throwing a knife. "I think Carl is the one who let the air out of Miss Jones's tire."

Dickie Lockhart was a year older than his younger brother Carl, but since Dickie had gotten held back a year in school, he, Carl, and Lou McCulloch were now all in the same grade. Triple trouble times three was that bunch. Since Lou's grandfather owned the town, his grandson got away with murder. Even the teachers let slide a bunch of stuff for Lou that the rest of us would have been paddled for doing.

Kent and I agreed that we would try to avoid the Lockharts and Lou McCulloch for our own safety. I threw in not crossing several of the cranky adults in town, 'cause when they called Dad, that usually turned out bad. I couldn't afford to have Dad lose his temper again.

I looked over at Kent and asked, "Hey, Superman, what do you want to do today?"

"We could get our bikes and ride to town. Let's see what's going on," Kent said with that funny grin.

"Okay. We could check out the Top Hat Theater and see if what Mom was saying is true. She was fussing about the terrible movies that are coming here. Boy, did they sound good. One was *The Creature from the Black Lagoon,* and the other was *Bud Abbott and Lou Costello Meet the Mummy,*" I said, all excited.

"Doesn't get any better than that, BB. One of the eighth graders said *The Mummy,* the scary one, is coming over the Fourth of July. I can hardly wait," Kent said as he swatted at a bug. Movies were the most exciting thing that ever happened in Highland.

"Seen any summer girls, yet?" I asked Superman.

"Not a one. Still too early. Perhaps some will drift in this week," he said, hopefully.

Highland's population was quite small during the winter. But when the summer tourists arrived, the population grew. Visitors came to stay at the famous Green Mountain Resort. That resort is known for having wild parties, or so I'm told, and those families often had cute daughters with them. So, whenever girls came to town, Kent and I always checked them out.

The other resort in town was smaller, visited by some of the best families of Virginia, and was called Cubley's Coze. The guests there were old people. There were not as many cute girls at Cubley's Coze, but when one did arrive, they were often with their grandparents. Grandparents tended to be less strict, and the girls got to hang around with us more. Each resort was neat in its own way.

Kent and I were enjoying the sunshine, and I was thinking how beautiful today was. This morning, the red sunrise had been spectacular. We settled back to think and watch the clouds to see what shapes they were making.

Two broad valleys made up my world. One bigger valley ran east to west, the other smaller valley ran north to south, and mountains were all around. Beautiful but boring.

Driving from Charlottesville on State Route Twenty-two south and west toward Lynchburg, you drove over East Gap. State Route Twenty-two was the only way into and across Hidden Valley. Smith's Gap was how you left the valley to drive on west.

Hidden Valley, what a dumb name because it *wasn't* hidden. It was on the main highway. Once you were on State Route Twenty-two, there was no way to avoid Hidden Valley.

There was a big plant just as you came down off East Gap and drove into Hidden Valley—the McCulloch Wood Products plant. And, yes, Lou McCulloch was the grandson of the owner. A lot of folks worked at that plant. Many of my friend's dads worked there, and even some of the moms.

Sometimes that plant smelled up the whole town when the wind blew from northeast to southwest. Luckily for us, the wind usually blew the other way, so the stink headed away from Highland. It often hung over East Gap and welcomed visitors to Hidden Valley in a most unpleasant way.

Traveling west on twenty-two, you had to turn left onto Main Street to find Highland. If you missed that left turn, you zipped right on past Main Street and missed us entirely. One way in and one way out.

Main Street led to downtown Highland, which sat smack in the middle of Green Mountain Valley. This small town only had five main streets.

Find Green Mountain Avenue and drive south through Green Mountain Valley and you ran into Green Mountain. The first settlers dug the word "green" 'cause it was everywhere.

The town of Highland, like Hidden Valley, was named by an idiot. Highland was in the center of Green Mountain Valley, and there was nothing high about the town of Highland. Most people, who came to town, were not looking for Highland anyway and did not care what it was called. They were looking for one or the other of the two famous resorts, situated on Green Mountain.

To reach the two famous resorts, you had to pay attention to the directions. From Main Street, you turn left on any of the side streets, drive two blocks crossing Church Street, and turn right on Green Mountain Avenue. Main Street dead-ends at the courthouse. To get to the resorts, you have to turn off Main. Many of the tourists were idiots and ended up at the courthouse, asking for directions.

Green Mountain Avenue, passes by this big lake, south of town called, you guessed it, Green Mountain Lake. The road runs right over a bridge built on top of a dam—a great place to skip rocks or feed the fish or ducks.

Smith River feeds the lake, which lies in front of the Green Mountain Resort. The big hotel is easy to see from the bridge; you turn right at the neon sign at the end of Green Mountain Avenue to get to it.

To go to Cubley's Coze Resort, the smaller resort hotel, you turn left at the same intersection. There is a little sign for this resort, but few people miss it because they return year after year.

Why did they name this second resort Cubley's Coze? I'll save that bit of information for later.

That mirror thing, I'm not sure what it did. Most of my friends think I'm nuts, but I still believe that the mirror had something to do with what happened that summer.

A boy about to have a big adventure is like a sleeping dog on the road before the car hits it—not a clue. Kent and I never expected what was headed our way, and like the dog, we were going to find out.

CHAPTER 3

BILLY ALMOST LOSES A HAND
Friday, June 3, 1955

Superman and I sat in the sun behind my dad's garage with nothing to do. A bee was buzzing somewhere over my head. I had one eye open, trying to see if it was time to bolt or if the bee was passing by.

"Billy, I need you. Get off that picnic table; tell your friend it's time for him to get on home. You come here, right now. We got a tow." I moved a little faster than usual.

"What's up, Dad? Wreck or break down?" I asked, trying to be pleasant.

"Neither, Old Man Peters backed over a cement parking stop at his store. The idiot has his car stuck. Frank Junior wants us to fix things. Get the forty-foot chain out of the garage and throw it up on Blacky."

Blacky was Dad's 1941 Mack Diesel, Model B61 tow truck with tandem rear axles and a 237-diesel engine. The color was shiny black. It was a workhorse with six forward gears, and it could pull a house out of a mud hole. Mr. Peters' car was not going to be a problem.

I liked Old Man Peters as Dad called him. Frank Peters & Son Grocery had been my favorite grocery store for as long as I could remember. Mr. Peters, the dad, would give me candy cigarettes as a child. He gave me those free treats until I started first grade. I looked forward to going to his store with Mom and getting them. The candy Old Man Peters handed out probably got the grocery store more business than spending a hundred times that amount on advertising.

Frank Junior had gone off to college at the University of Virginia. When he returned home to run the store, he was all "dollars and cents," according to the locals. Great specials and something called Green Stamps took the place of free candy. Now, the only time the store gave free handouts of candy to the little kids was when Frank Junior wasn't looking.

Halfway to the garage to get the chain, I saw Kent hurrying to where he had stashed his bike. He knew better than to hang around when Dad told him to go home. I yelled, "See you later, Superman!" He threw a wave without looking back, picked up his bike, did a running mount, and was off.

Kent and I had talked a time or two about dads. Was it better to have a dad that was mean sometimes or no dad at all? Both Kent and I decided not having a dad, which was Kent's situation, was much worse.

My dad was a lot of fun at times, especially when he let me go with him on tow jobs. Tow jobs were fun to watch.

I pulled the heavy tow chain out of the garage and over to the rear of Blacky. I learned how to wrestle it up onto Blacky by myself when I was eleven. I would heave each three-foot section onto the truck bed while holding the chain in place with one hand and reaching for the next section with the other. I was doing good until the chain slid off before I could stop it.

Wham! I felt a blow to my shoulder. I went flying sideways. When I landed, it was on the ground on my right elbow. My dad was strong. He had given me a shove, a hard one.

The chain landed in a heap at the rear of Blacky. Dad was standing there, looking at the pile of chain at his feet. Me, I was on the ground, trying not to cry.

"I told you to get that damn chain on the truck. Use your muscles, boy!" Dad growled. "Ain't got all day."

My father grabbed that chain and, in one toss, threw all of it up onto the back deck of Blacky. Then, he rattled the tow cable, checked the hook and pulleys, but kept glancing at the house.

He finally turned his head to look at me, "You hurt?" he asked, just above a whisper.

"No, sir," I responded.

He checked the house a final time. When Mom didn't come to the kitchen door, he walked to the driver's door of Blacky and climbed in without a word.

I got myself up off the ground. With the palm of my left hand, I rubbed spit on my skinned right elbow to make it stop bleeding. It stung, but I knew better than to cry. I then brushed the dirt off my pants and rubbed my shoulder. Goodness, was he strong. It took all that morning for my shoulder to stop hurting.

Standing there, I heard a faint boom way off in the distance. It sounded like someone was blowing up a stump with dynamite.

"Stop picking your nose and get in the truck, boy!" Dad yelled from the cab.

I ran for the door on my side and climbed up onto the passenger seat. The interior of Blacky was an emerald green that matched the color of the mountains around Highland. Riding in Blacky was cool, 'cause you could look down on all the other cars. I was big at twelve, but I still had to sit on the front edge of the seat to see out of the windshield. The roar of the diesel often made people look our way.

Driving down Main Street, I saw my last year's teacher, Miss Jones, going into the hardware. She looked our way, so I waved, and she waved back. Her waving made me feel better.

The stick shift on Blacky was tall. It came up out of the floorboard, even with the bottom of the big steering wheel. When Dad changed gears, he did it quickly with his right hand to get both hands back on that big steering wheel. The gas and brake pedals were giant sizes. Big enough that Dad could wear his mud boots and drive Blacky without a problem. The clutch pedal was over to the left of the brake pedal, but for some reason, it was standard size.

"It takes a soft touch," as Dad would say, to drive Blacky with a heavy load and shift those gears without losing speed or grinding the transmission. I was looking forward to when I was fifteen and could get a learner's permit. Dad said he would teach me how to drive Blacky, but I would never be as good as him.

Everybody said my dad was the best wrecker driver in the county, maybe the whole state. He ran calls for the Virginia State Police, the Green Mountain County Sheriff, and many of the folks in town. The Town of Highland Police used the Chevrolet wrecker because Mr. McCulloch owned that dealership and paid the town cops. My dad got cut out of those calls unless their wrecker wasn't big enough to pull the tow.

Once, I saw my father pull a wreck that the Chevrolet tow truck couldn't even get to move. Blacky pulled that wrecked truck up a steep bank on the first try. Yep, my dad was the best.

Frank Peters and Son Grocery was eight blocks from our garage, making for a short ride. Dad pulled into the lot and made a half-circle, reversed, and backed up to the front of the stuck car. Dad glanced in his rear-view mirror and told me to forget the chain; he wouldn't need it. He pulled Blacky forward and off to the left to get the tow truck out of the way.

"Billy, get me four 4x4 blocks."

"Yes, sir." I jumped down out of the cab, went over to one of the side cabinets, and opened the swing-up door on its counter-weight. When that door swung up, you better be out of its way. I still have a scar on my chin from one time when I was slow jumping back.

That day, I opened it without any problem, reached in, and grabbed two of the 4x4 blocks of wood. I picked them up in both arms and ran them over to Dad.

"Four 4x4's dummy, not two," he said to me in a loud whisper as I dropped the first two beside the wheel.

"Yes, sir, coming," I answered and wasted no time getting the other two. I had learned being slow and making two trips was often better than dropping four. Dad had no patience with "weak-asses." I tried to never appear weak in front of him. Being a weak-ass was the reason he whacked me when I dropped the chain.

"Slow as molasses in January," he muttered, which was a standard response from him when he was in a bad mood. When he was not looking, I used to mouth that same phrase as he said it, but not that day—not worth the risk.

Mr. Frank Peters, Jr., and his father came out of the store, one after the other. They kept their distance, knowing Dad and hearing his tone of voice to me. Dad looked up and noticed them.

"Mr. Peters, how did this happen?" Dad asked, frowning. "You must have had some speed up to drive over this cement parking stop."

"Well, it was like this," said Old Man Peters, "I was parking the car, being careful, going slow, and I guess I was going too slow for some people. A car began blowing its horn. It startled me; I hit the gas instead of the brake. The car shot backward, and there you have it."

Dad shook his head but said nothing, which was a relief. He took the key from the ignition, popped the car trunk, and got out the jack.

Calling out, Dad asked Old Man Peters if the car was in park with the emergency brake set. Mr. Peters quickly responded, "Of course. I always leave it in park and set the emergency brake. Don't want it to roll off across the parking lot, you know?"

Dad said under his breath, so only I could hear him, "Yeah, well, putting the back wheels over the cement stop will sure keep it from rolling off."

I hoped Old Man Peters didn't have his hearing aid up all the way. Sometimes, he was able to hear quite well with it.

Dad set the jack under the back bumper in the middle and started to jack up the back of the car.

"Billy, listen up. Put a 4x4 in front of each cement parking stop in line with the rear tires. Once I jack the car up high enough, put two more to the rear of the parking stop under each of the rear wheels. I need those blocks placed exactly. I'll then lower the car down on the blocks, and the car can roll forward. This will make a bridge of 4x4's to get the wheels up and over those cement stops. Got it?"

"Yes, sir," I replied.

"Keep your hands out from under that car. I don't want to have to tell your momma you came back with your hands cut off. Don't need no more shit from her today."

Again, I said, "Yes, sir."

That day was a "yes, sir" sort of day. Dad had come in late, and Mom was not pleased. I heard it all through the secret vent. It was a bad day to be a kid of twelve in the Gunn household. That was why I got a little whack when I dropped the chain. A big whack would have earned me another trip to the hospital. I had learned Dad's limits. Sure, I got whippings with Dad's belt every once in a while, but I didn't count those.

I had just set the last block when, suddenly, the car rolled backward off the jack.

Crash went the car. It came down and the rear wheel just missed squashing one of my hands. I jerked both hands back, but that would have been a quarter second too late if that car had been over my way just a little.

Dad jumped back when the car fell. Lucky for him, it didn't roll backward very far, or he would have been under it. The jack just missed his foot.

He turned to face Old Man Peters and yelled, "I thought you told me you had it in park, dammit! You could have killed us!" It was then that Dad turned and looked at me.

"Billy, you got all your fingers?"

I held up both hands and began to wiggle all ten of my fingers. Dad looked like he might whack me for the second time, but he didn't. Instead, he took it out on the car. He reared back and kicked the tire with his boot — good thing he wore steel-toed boots.

Then, he marched over to the driver's door and jerked it open. He yanked it so hard, it sprung back out of his hand and latched closed. He grabbed it a second time, but this time he didn't jerk it. It stayed open. I watched through the window as he leaned into the car, set the emergency brake, and put the automatic transmission lever in park. No wonder the car rolled off the jack.

It was not unusual for dad to do dumb stuff after coming in late. Dad always told me, "If you want it done right, do it yourself." That day at the grocery, I was tempted to remind him of that piece of wisdom, but I didn't.

Dad looked back at the rear wheels. They were a good eight inches from the cement parking stop and were not on top of the 4x4's we had placed there. He looked around for me and yelled loud enough to be heard inside the grocery.

"Billy, bring me all of the 4x4's. I mean, right damn now!"

I ran for the other side cabinet and brought him two more 4x4's. I walked as fast as I could and tried not to drop them. I was lucky. I made the two trips without losing a single one. I hoped this would be enough because we were now out of 4x4's.

Dad jacked up the car and put all the 4x4 blocks under the rear wheels in a long line, end to end. He lowered the wheels back on top of the 4x4 platform that he had built. Then, he drove it forward across the 4x4 platform, over the cement parking stops, which were now only two-inch obstacles, and along the 4x4's on the other side. The rear wheels dropped off the end of the platform and the problem was fixed. He did it all without having to use Blacky.

Dad parked the car and walked over to Mr. Frank Peters, Jr. "That will be six for the trip and one to get it over the cement stops. You got a problem with that, Frank?"

"No, John, that's more than fair, and I'm sorry Dad got confused. He didn't understand how dangerous it was, not to set the brake and have it in park."

Dad had calmed and said, "Don't worry about it." He took the seven dollars and shoved the bills into the bib pocket of his coveralls. During this exchange, I put the 4x4's back into Blacky, put the car jack back in the Peters' car, and climbed into the cab on the passenger's side. Dad got in and started the diesel.

"Idiot!" He muttered. I didn't say anything. Neither my dad nor Old Man Peters were idiots, but they were indeed not at their best. I liked Mr. Peters just as much after that day as before. Candy cigarettes create a lot of "good-will" when you are a kid. Yep, a lot of friendship and a kid's memory lasts and lasts.

Leaving the lot, we passed a Town of Highland police car with its red-light flashing, going somewhere. Dad waved, but the two officers didn't wave back.

CHAPTER 4

THE BIG WRECK
Friday, June 3, 1955

B illy Gunn had heard the accident at his dad's garage. The locals would later refer to this one as the "big wreck." After the collision with the loud boom, there was silence. Bird calls returned as the smoke and dust drifted away.

A brand new, 1955 Chevrolet Bel Air, V8-350 came out of the last curve at the bottom of Smith's Gap. It was "swell" with its white top over a blue body and big chrome bumpers. A thirty-seven-year-old man was the driver. As he approached the scene, he slowed and stopped short of the first log blocking the road.

The driver was Charles Matthew Cubley, but he insisted on being called Matt. He had very blue eyes and dark hair in a crew cut, which was about due for a trim. His build was lean, average height, with a square jaw, and a bearing which left the impression he was former military. He wore blue jeans, a tan shirt, a summer sport coat, and ox-blood penny loafers. He got out of his car and just stood without moving.

When he spoke, he raised his voice in prayer.

"Oh God, please don't make me do this, not this!"

Matt stared down the road. He slowly walked toward the log truck but suddenly stopped after three steps. Would he stay or leave? Having made his decision, he returned to his car but passed the driver's door and ended his walk at the trunk.

"What am I doing?" he questioned himself.

Back in motion, he made it to the driver's door, leaned in, and retrieved the keys. Once again, at the rear of the Chevrolet, he reluctantly inserted the key, opened the trunk, and took out a large tackle box with "Roanoke Life Saving & First Aid Crew" painted on the lid. He carried it with him to the log truck.

Another car arrived on the east side of the wreck. It stopped, immediately turned around, and sped back toward Highland. Matt hoped the other car was going for help.

He hurried over to the front windshield of the log truck and looked into the cab through the spiderweb of cracks in the glass. The driver was unconscious and bleeding from his forehead and nose. His right forearm bent at an odd angle below the elbow.

The driver was breathing, which was the first good sign Matt had seen thus far. Since the truck was on its left side, the driver was also on his left side against the driver's door. This position would help drain the blood from his nose, away from his throat, and keep his airway clear.

Matt needed something to break out the windshield to get access to the driver. He spotted a club. Workers had been cleaning up a farmer's fence line by cutting brush. He pulled a tree branch that was three feet long and four inches thick from the pile alongside the road. Stripped of its twigs and leaves, it was perfect.

Matt climbed on top of the truck, leaned inside the passenger's window, and bashed out the passenger's windshield with the club. Most of the glass, the large pieces, fell outside the truck cab. The glass that fell on the injured man did not seem to do any additional damage. Matt carefully climbed back down the frame to the ground.

He was now able to finish the job. With the passenger side windshield broken out, he took the club, reached into the cab, and battered out the remaining windshield.

Leaning into the cab, Matt removed some glass from the driver's face and throat. He felt for a carotid pulse, found the driver had a good neck pulse and was breathing. The gash on the man's forehead continued to bleed freely, but the nosebleed had stopped. Matt got several compresses and roller bandages out of his first aid box. Using them, he bandaged the large gash on the driver's forehead.

Stepping back, he tried to figure a way to get the injured man out of the truck's cab. It was apparent he would need help, but no one else had arrived.

Matt was concerned about the man's broken arm, so he reached in and checked for a pulse, detected one, and left the injured arm as it was. He knew he had done all he could for the log truck driver until more help arrived. Closing his first aid box, he picked it up and carried it along with his battering ram to search for the pickup and more victims.

Matt scouted the dirt farm road and the land near the tobacco barn. Strewn across the meadow were an ax, a shovel, and a post-hole digger, clearly thrown from the bed of the pickup. He followed marks, bent vegetation, and debris across the field, dreading what he might find.

Matt recognized the make and model of the pickup when he saw it upside down in the pasture. A friend of his drove one similar. This wreck was a 1942 Dodge with front headlamps on the fenders that gave it the appearance of a face with bug-eyes. The nose of this model pickup was funny, rounded, and bulb-like with a Dodge emblem hood ornament. The grill was the mouth.

This wrecked pickup, however, bore but a slight resemblance to Matt's mental image of his friend's truck because the bed of this pickup had been smashed against the rear of the cab. The cab was intact, but there was no glass in either the left-side or right-side windscreen. The center metal piece that held the left and right windshield glass in place was missing. The roof was flattened four or five inches from where it should have been. It was clear the truck had rolled many times.

Matt looked for the driver, but he was not in the cab, around the truck nor under it. He backtracked, looking for the driver. Walking along the path where the vehicle had rolled over and over, he found the body.

The driver had been mashed into the ground. The body was tough to see because of the pasture grass, weeds, and bent over volunteer corn stalks. Matt knew the man was dead, but he checked anyway as his training demanded. His hand was shaking badly, but he was able to determine there was no pulse and no breathing. Matt stood quietly over the body, saying a prayer for this stranger.

He took off his sport coat and laid it over the corpse. This coat meant more to Matt than any other possession he owned. It was the last gift his wife had given him before her death. He knew all the spilled blood would ruin it, but he did it anyway. Janet would have insisted. Tears filled his eyes, and he wept.

There was nothing more he could do. He paused, took a deep breath, pulled himself together, wiped his face, and picked up his gear. He was drawn back to the log truck for the living, but his mind was on the dead. He could not help but remember the last time he saw Janet and Jack at the wreck that took them. He forced himself to stop thinking.

Arriving again at the smashed log truck, he tried to decide how best to remove the driver from the wreckage. He crawled partly into the cab and carefully took care of the driver's other minor cuts and abrasions. He did another check of his pulse and respirations and found no change.

Walking to his car, he got out a wooden splint from the trunk. Using his skill, he slowly, inch by slow inch, straightened the broken limb. Then, he splinted the arm. The pulse at the wrist was still good after the splint was applied. *This man must have a guardian angel.*

He finished by performing a detailed examination to see if there were any significant injuries that he might have missed. He checked the man's back and neck as best he could but found nothing remarkable. He added and secured more compresses to his head, where the blood had started to show through the first set. No changes in breathing or pulse, but he remained unconscious.

In the distance, Matt heard a siren. It got louder, and he could see red lights approaching. The siren wound down and stopped. Matt looked over to the east and saw a red 1951 Chevrolet pumper with a siren mounted on the roof. The fire truck was typical, with hydrant hoses on one side and a ladder on the other. Two men in turnout coats were making their way to him, having to climb over and around the logs. The fireman wearing a white fire chief's helmet introduced himself as Chief Bailey Danbury. Matt told him his name.

"What happened?" asked the fire chief.

"I saw the log truck rear-end the pickup as it tried to make a left turn into this pasture. The pickup driver is all busted up, quite dead. The log truck driver has a head wound and an angulated fracture of the arm that I splinted. He needs to go to the hospital as soon as possible."

"Are you a doctor?" asked Chief Danbury.

"No, but I used to work with the Roanoke Life Saving and First Aid Crew. We're going to need an ambulance or truck to take the driver to the hospital. The closest hospital is Waynesboro, isn't it?"

"Yep. I expect Koehler Funeral Home from Beech Grove, just west of here, will be on the way. They can use their hearse as an ambulance. I told dispatch a McCulloch truck was involved. Mr. Koehler's a cousin of the McCullochs, so that's who will get called. And their ambulance will be on the right side of this mess to get to the driver of the log truck. Might have to take the driver to Lynchburg 'cause the back way to Waynesboro through Vesuvius is steep and narrow. No one is getting to Waynesboro on this road."

A groan came from the cab of the log truck, and Matt turned to look at the driver. Time was running out to get him to a hospital.

A second fire truck, a utility truck, arrived on the other side of the wreck. Another fireman from this second fire truck was working his way through the logs to Chief Danbury.

A siren was heard coming from the direction of Smith's Gap. In just a few moments, a black hearse pulled into view. The vehicle was a 1948 Cadillac Meteor Hearse with two red lights on the front bumper and a big red spotlight in front of the driver's door. They all were flashing as the mechanical siren slowly wound down. Two men, one white and one colored, wearing dark suits, got out. Matt noticed the front seat was covered in plush, red velvet. New Orleans flashed across his mind.

He waved them over and gave them the same report he had just given to Chief Danbury. The white man in the dark suit introduced himself as Bill Koehler, the owner of Koehler Funeral Home. He pointed to the colored man and said, "This is my helper, Richard."

Mr. Koehler began asking Matt questions about the condition of the people in the wreck. Matt noticed that when he tried to tell Mr. Koehler about the medical issues of the log truck driver, Mr. Koehler went back to asking the exact location of the corpse. As the questions about the body continued, Matt got more and more irritated.

Matt squared up, looked Mr. Koehler in the eyes, and reiterated, "The man I found dead was the driver of the pickup truck. He's dead. We can't help him, and he will keep. This guy in the log truck is still breathing and needs some help, or you will have two to bury. So, who goes first?"

"Don't get all worked up, young fellow. We'll take your man first," said Mr. Koehler with a frown.

"He's not my man; I was just the first one here. Do you have a backboard or just a gurney?" asked Matt, raising his voice and matching frown for frown with Mr. Koehler.

"We have a gurney. We also have one tank of oxygen and a few first aid supplies. I run this ambulance stuff on the side. We're not a big outfit," Mr. Koehler offered in explanation.

"OK, I suggest we get the gurney, and with some firemen, gently pull the driver out of the cab. Watch his arm because it's badly broken. I splinted it, but we need to keep it quiet. I suspect he may have a broken neck or back after seeing how his truck is smashed." Matt looked at Mr. Koehler, who nodded and seemed to be in a more helpful spirit.

The driver was moved to the ambulance. Matt climbed in the back of the hearse-ambulance to make sure the patient was breathing, the oxygen was working, and the face mask was secure.

Matt heard Mr. Koehler tell Chief Danbury he was coming right back for the body, and not to let anyone touch it until he got back. He also gave Richard strict instructions on how to cover the body with a Koehler Funeral Home blanket. The light gray blanket had the name of the funeral home stitched on it in huge, gold letters. He told Richard he was not to leave the body for an instant.

"Richard, you make sure that outfit over in Waynesboro doesn't show up and take our man. You sit on it if you have to," said Mr. Koehler.

"No, sir, I'll stick right on it. Won't nobody move that body but you, Mr. Koehler. I'll make sure of it," exclaimed Richard.

Chief Danbury also promised to watch over the body.

Matt, hearing this exchange, climbed out of the back of the ambulance and spoke to Mr. Koehler. "Someone needs to monitor the patient, do you want me to ride in back with this guy?"

Mr. Koehler turned to Matt as if to give him a curt response, hesitated a moment, and then asked Chief Danbury if one of his firemen would ride in the back with the driver of the log truck. Danbury called to one of the younger firemen who had just arrived and told him to ride in the rear of the ambulance to Lynchburg.

The fireman wanted to stay where the excitement was, but finally, he said, "I guess so."

Matt started to tell Mr. Koehler that he was more qualified because of his first aid training. Thinking about it, he decided he had pushed Mr. Koehler to his limit, so he just turned and walked away as the ambulance left the scene.

Matt walked back to his car to watch and wait until the road was cleared. He had decisions to make about his future and this town.

CHAPTER 5

FACTS
Friday, June 3, 1955

Matt Cubley waited patiently at the scene of the wreck. The injured man was on his way to better care. He watched cars and trucks stop on both sides of the blockage. Some drivers turned around and drove away, but others pulled over, got out, and toured the scene.

Fifteen people were standing in a circle around the blanket-covered corpse. They looked at the blanket as if the body was a county fair side-show and the curtain was about to rise.

A police car arrived from the town of Highland carrying two officers. The first officer was over six feet tall with short blond hair. He was slightly overweight, and his belly slightly overhung his gun belt. Above the sergeant stripes were Highland Police Department patches. His biceps were so large that the short sleeves on the shirt looked like the seams might rip at any moment.

The other officer was smaller and leaner. He had the same uniform, but without the sergeant stripes, like the sergeant, he had massive biceps. Both officers took pride in lifting weights.

Despite the body being covered, it remained the center of a crowd. The sergeant pushed a slow-moving bystander out of the way, pulled back the Koehler Funeral Home blanket, and lifted the sports coat away from the victim's face. He took a look and quickly re-covered the body. One of the bystanders peeked at the crushed remains and threw up, earning a scowl from the sergeant, who put his hands on his hips, puffed out his chest, and ordered the crowd to move back. The crowd shuffled back a few steps, just enough to avoid the wrath of the big cop.

The two officers strode over to Chief Danbury for a conference, and Matt walked near to listen.

The sergeant took out a notebook and asked the fire chief, "What happened?"

"It's bad, Sarge, real bad! It looks like Old Man Beamis pulled out, and damn if he didn't get squashed by the log truck," said Chief Danbury.

The sergeant had started to write in the notebook but put it away after the fire chief's comment.

"Well, I guess it's a good thing Old Man Beamis is dead, or I would have to write him up for failure to yield the right of way. Dad's truck was in the right and Beamis messed up. Case closed," concluded the sergeant.

Matt's face clouded over at the cop's attitude. He moved closer to read the officer's name tag. He should have known: Sergeant McCulloch. The officer was called "Little John" by his peers, so as not to confuse him with his dad, "Big John."

Matt spoke up and said, "Sergeant McCulloch, that's not quite right."

Chief Danbury, with a shocked countenance, looked back down the road to hide his face from the officer. He concealed just a hint of a smile and waited for what he knew was coming.

The sergeant turned and gave Matt a cold stare. The other officer, Frank Younger, according to his name tag, took a step closer to Matt.

"And who might you be?"

"I'm the guy who saw the accident."

The sergeant took the 3x5 inch notebook back out, opened it, and with two fingers, pulled a pencil from the spirals at the end of the notebook. The pencil tip went in his mouth to wet it. He looked closely at Matt.

"I know most of the residents of Green Mountain County, but I don't know you. Where do you live?"

"Well, that's hard to say. I lived in Roanoke until recently, decided I needed to move on, and now I think I might live in Highland — for a while."

"You work anywhere?" said the sergeant with a suspicious tone.

"No, between jobs," Matt said in a matter of fact way without any hint of an apology.

"You looking for work around here? I know the plant is hiring good men, no troublemakers."

"Not particularly looking for work," again with an "I don't care" tone.

Sergeant McCulloch stopped writing and began conferring with the other officer as if Matt wasn't present. "No job, no residence, might live here for a while, but not interested in working, he says. Well, Officer Younger, this sounds like just another drifter to me. Never cared much for out-of-work drifters. You?"

"Can't say that I do," Officer Younger responded, but he knew the sergeant was not looking for a response from him.

The sergeant sighed, giving up on his conversation with his colleague.

"Name," the sergeant demanded rather than asked. He wasn't going to waste much more time on this tramp. Well dressed, but a for sure a tramp troublemaker in his book.

"Cubley's my last name. Charles Matthew Cubley."

"Charles? Where do you plan on staying for the 'while?'"

"I go by my middle name, Matthew, Sergeant. Right now, I plan on checking into Cubley's Coze. Do you know the place?" said Matt with a smile without warmth.

"Yeah, I know the place. You must be kin to T. J. Cubley. Only other Cubley I ever heard of around here. You his kin?" asked the sergeant, and his left eyebrow rose to punctuate the question.

"Yes," said Matt, answering the question, but not offering any other information. He just left it at that. He stood in silence, watching the sergeant.

"And?" the sergeant asked, now starting to get irritated without any effort to hide it. "How are you related?"

"Nephew."

"Well, sorry about the passing of your uncle. I never got on with him much; neither did my dad, but he ran a nice place. Now that he's no longer the owner, I guess the family will have to sell Cubley's Coze. Do you know anything about who might have inherited the place?" asked Sergeant John McCulloch with a dramatic change in his tone of voice, now that he wanted information. He was all sweetness. The dead and injured forgotten, and it was so evident to Matt that he almost told the uncaring officer that it was none of his damn business. Instead, he took a moment to get himself under control.

All of the things his Uncle TJ had told him about the Mc-Culloch family were true. His uncle had been gracious to almost everyone, but he had never liked this particular family.

"Don't know for certain. I'm headed over to see the Cubley family lawyer to find out." Matt answered with what he hoped was a good poker face.

The sergeant saw he was getting nowhere with this guy.

"All right, Mr. Charles Matthew Cubley, with no residence, what did you see and where were you when you saw it?" The sergeant poised the pencil ready to write.

Matt took a deep breath and let it out slowly before starting.

"I was up on the mountain, eating my lunch, enjoying nature when the log truck went by on the main road, headed down the mountain. He was going slow, real slow, almost walking speed. I lost sight of it behind the trees as he made the curves below me. I was watching for him to come out of the last curve when I saw the pickup pull out of a drive and head toward Highland. The pickup had not gone far when the log truck came into view, barreling out of the last curve. It was picking up a load of speed. The log truck went left and tried to pass the pickup just as the pickup made a left turn into the pasture. Then bang! Nothing but dust and smoke. That's when I tossed the sandwich I was eating and came on down to see if I could help."

"And you claim to have seen all of this from that overlook?" Sergeant McCulloch pointed to the top of the mountain.

"Yes, I did."

"And the log truck tried to pass the pickup when the pickup turned left in front of the log truck?"

"Yes, it did," Matt repeated.

"You been drinking?" the sergeant suddenly asked, giving Mr. Cubley another stare.

Now, it was Matt's turn to look surprised. "No, I haven't been drinking. Do I look like I've been drinking?" And with that last question, Matt's demeanor stopped being amused and swung to angry.

"Just checking," said the sergeant. He waited, looked at Matt for a few seconds, and then added, "So just before the pickup turned in front of the log truck and cut him off—I assume the pickup gave no turn signal, right?"

"No, Sergeant, that's an incorrect assumption. The pickup gave a left turn signal right after he pulled into the road, prior to the log truck coming around the curve. The log truck was going fast when the pickup made his turn. The log truck plowed him in the back end. The pickup driver never had a chance."

"Sir, you are a gol' darn liar. There's no way in hell you could see a turn signal from that overlook."

"Sergeant, please don't call people liars when you don't know what you're talking about. I was watching a vixen and three kits with my binoculars when that log truck passed by me. I was curious about the loaded truck and watched for it as I ate my sandwich. I could see the pickup's turn signal quite clearly through my binoculars," Matt reported with his words clipped, his blue eyes drilling into the brown eyes of the sergeant.

Matt and the sergeant stared at each other for a good ten seconds. The officer finally looked down at the pad in his hand, the one he had stopped taking notes on right after Matt said the pickup was giving a turn signal.

"OK, let me be sure I got this all down correctly." The sergeant then pretended to read notes that were only partially there.

"You were way up there on that overlook, clear at the top of Smith's Gap, eating your lunch?" Before he could answer, the officer kept right on talking. "And you claim you had nothing to drink. You think you saw the pickup give a turn signal from way up on the mountain, and when it turned at the last second in front of the log truck, the log truck had nowhere to go, and they collided. Right? Glad we got that all straightened out."

Sergeant McCulloch put the pencil back in the spiral rings of the notebook, folded it up and put it in his pocket. There was a pause that got a little awkward as Matt stood staring at the sergeant in amazement. Matt started to say that the turn signal shifter was still indicating a left on the wrecked truck; in fact, he even opened his mouth to speak, but then in a split second, he changed his mind.

"I want to thank you for all you did here today. I have everything I need, and we will be in touch if we need any further information. The facts are clear. You can go."

Resigned, Matt's said, "That might be a little hard."

"And why is that?" asked the sergeant leaning into Matt with his upper body. The sergeant's hands were on his gun belt with his thumbs tucked inside of the leather.

"Well, the road is still blocked with a wrecked truck and logs."

"Oh yeah. Well, as soon as we clear up this mess, you be on your way. Just don't go too far and don't leave town without my permission."

Matt had suffered enough; he raised his voice by half again. "Why do I need your permission to leave town? Am I under arrest for something?"

"No, you are not under arrest, but don't leave town unless I say so."

"Sergeant, let me get this straight: I am not under arrest, but confined to town? I think you have been watching too much *Dragnet*. This is Virginia, not Los Angeles, and you are a town cop, not Detective Joe Friday." He turned before the sergeant could respond or make a grab for him.

Several firefighters saw the red-faced sergeant think for a few seconds, and it was obvious to them that he was not sure who this fellow might be. He decided he better not push things too far. Even the firemen knew the sergeant had no reason to detain the man or force him to remain confined in town.

The sergeant turned on the other officer and began spouting orders to regain face. "Officer Younger, tell dispatch to get Gunn Towing out here, right now. I hate to use them, but the damn dealership tow truck is down for repairs. Also, tell Judy to call Dad's office and tell them we need a mule with a boom and bring me another log truck to get this mess cleaned up. Find out when Koehler Funeral Home will get back out here and have Judy tell whoever is driving to haul freight! I want that body moved."

Frank Younger looked pained and hesitated, but then came out with the following in a rush, "Uh, Little John, I'm clear on telling Judy what you need her to know, but you know we have to get permission from Dr. Hill before we can move Old Man Beamis."

Sergeant McCulloch burned through a half-second fuse and exploded.

"This is the last damn straw! I might have to put up with bullshit from drifters and civilians but not from you. Frank, just do it! Of course I know we have to call the medical examiner before moving a body. Damn, think for yourself and get it done. Also, remind Judy to call the chief, or he will be pissed if we don't fill him in. I think he drove over to Waynesboro to pick up a birthday present for his wife."

"OK, Little John, I'll get right on it."

"And Frank, stop calling me Little John; it's Sergeant McCulloch, you stupid oaf!" Sergeant McCulloch stomped off to yell at Chief Danbury and some of his firemen to get organized and start moving the rubberneckers back from the body.

Little John was mad. Really mad. He had nothing but ill thoughts going through his mind. Those damn Cubleys. Nothing but trouble. That blame uncle had been stubborn as a mule, and this upstart, smart-mouthed drifter was going to be more trouble—*Dragnet,* my ass.

CHAPTER 6

BILLY, CLEANING UP MESSES
Friday, June 3, 1955

When we got back to the garage, before I knew that the big boom I had heard was a wreck, I was disappointed. Not one adventure for me that day. That dumb mirror legend was not working, or so I thought. The biggest excitement that had come my way today was Mr. Peters' car falling off the jack. Not a big deal since I had all my fingers and the car was not damaged. Still, I never told Mom about that little mishap.

I went to my room and counted the money I had saved from my allowance, which was in a cigar box stashed in my sock drawer. During my sixth-grade school year, Dad had paid me fifty cents a week for doing Saturday morning chores around the garage and taking out the garbage. Excitement for me had been taking out two bags rather than one—no kidding.

Now that my summer vacation was here, Dad had promised to pay me a dollar a week. It sounded like a nice raise, but in addition to taking out the garbage, I had to add mowing the grass and helping Dad every day in the garage. That man could think up all manner of stuff for me to do. Some of it was fun, like when he was showing me how to fix motors and transmissions, but most of it was grody. Sweeping out the place or putting parts away was dullsville. I earned an extra fifty cents a week for three times the work. How was that fair?

Don't get me wrong. A dollar a week was a lot of money. Movies cost a quarter, popcorn was a nickel, and you were still able to get nickel Cokes and Pepsis. Some of the older kids told us that when they went on a field trip to Washington, DC and Cokes and Pepsis there had cost ten cents. No one could believe pop was selling for ten cents after those same kids claimed to have seen Communists holding up signs on the steps of the Capitol.

Later, I did believe it when the news reported Communists were in Washington, New York, and California, and Mom found ten-cent Cokes in Roanoke.

Not that working for my dad allowed me to drink pop all day. He was a slave driver. Take sweeping: the handle on the garage broom was too long for me, but he made me choke up on the handle, and make short pushes. I could get by okay, but it was hard.

It was obvious I needed to grow up, then Dad's tools and stuff would be my size.

On the day of the big wreck, I was almost finished sweeping when the phone rang. I didn't know it, but my first adventure was about to begin. Dad picked up the phone.

"Yeah, I can come out. What happened to the Chevrolet wrecker? Oh, that's too bad. Okay, I'm on the way."

Even though I was only across the garage, Dad yelled like I was across the car yard. "Billy, we got a mess out on State Route 22, west of town." He saw me a few feet away and he got softer. "A log truck just ran over Mr. Beamis. The Chevy dealership tow truck is down for repairs, and the Highland Police dispatcher called us to come. I may need you to help me but you gotta stay out of the way and do exactly what I tell you. Got it?"

Of course, I said, "Got it." I hung the broom up on the wall by the toolbox, and we both hurried over to Blacky. As we drove out of the yard, Dad blew the air horns twice to let Mom know we were headed out for a tow. They had worked out this signal, except Dad couldn't use it between three and four-thirty. He was under orders not to wake the baby.

When I saw what folks later called the Beamis Wreck or the "Big Wreck," I knew it was the worst wreck ever. To this day, folks in town still talk about it and compare other wrecks against it.

Firetrucks, two Highland police cars, a sheriff's car, and two Virginia State Police cars were all there, plus a crowd of spectators with their vehicles parked every which way. The state police cruisers were pulled over behind the sheriff's car. I knew this was going to be something to tell Kent about.

I saw a bunch of logs blocking the road, and a log truck had turned over on its side. Cleaning up this wreck was going to be a big job, even for Blacky.

All of the cops were in a bunch around a red-faced Little John.

Dad and I walked over to the policemen to get our instructions. My dad was more interested in what was happening between the police than watching me. I got up close to listen and knew right away that this job might be more than I wanted to see.

"What do you mean, you have jurisdiction?" Sergeant Mc-Culloch complained to one of the state troopers.

This trooper had the same kind of stripes on his sleeve as Sergeant McCulloch. I figured out right quick that this trooper was a sergeant. I knew all the local troopers from working wrecks with my dad, but not the sergeants; they didn't work many wrecks. This sergeant must have been over at the courthouse in Highland to have gotten here so fast.

"Sergeant McCulloch, I don't care whose truck was involved. This is a fatal wreck on a state highway. The Virginia State Police will handle the investigation. Trooper Mike Quinn will work it, and that's that," demanded the trooper sergeant.

Goodness, someone is dead. I wonder where the body is?
"No, that is not that, Sergeant Oliver!"

Sergeant McCulloch stomped over to his car, leaned in, grabbed the microphone, and started yelling into his radio. I pitied whoever was on the other end. He then sat down in his car, slammed the door, and glared at the dashboard as if it were a movie screen showing a lousy movie that was out of focus.

Trooper Quinn walked over to his state police car, which was a typical 1948 Ford. It was blue and gray with the top and fenders painted dark blue and the side body gray. They looked neat. Trooper Quinn got stuff out of his trunk.

I noticed that the state police sergeant's car was different. It was one of the newer 1950 Fords that looked streamlined next to the 48 versions. This one also had the red-light smack in the middle of the front grill in a chrome holder. All of them could run down speeders, but this sergeant's car looked fast, parked

While I was admiring the police cars, I noticed Sergeant McCulloch reach for his mike. He talked for about a minute and then got out of his car with a smile on his face. He walked over to the other sergeant and Trooper Quinn, who were taking measurements near the log truck. He said something to the sergeant. That sergeant got a funny look on his face like he didn't believe what he was hearing. The state police sergeant walked over to his car and got inside. He closed the door and began a conversation on his two-way radio.

When he got out, he had a very hard face. The sergeant walked over to Trooper Quinn, and after just a couple of words, Trooper Quinn rolled up his tape and closed his pad, and they both walked back to where Sergeant McCulloch was standing by my dad.

"Well, you straight now, Sergeant B. T. Oliver?" Sergeant McCulloch said.

"I am," said the other sergeant. "Your daddy called the governor, so I guess this accident is all yours. We are to offer assistance if needed." Oliver waited. The two sergeants stared at each other for a few seconds.

"Sergeant Oliver, you and Trooper Quinn may resume your duties. You are relieved," Sergeant Little John McCulloch declared with a smirk on his face.

If those troopers had pulled their guns and shot Sergeant McCulloch right then and there, it would not have surprised me at all. Troopers were often at Dad's garage, but I had never seen one this angry. Perhaps irritated at times, but never like this. These two troopers were fighting mad.

Dad turned and asked, "Little John, what was that all about?"

Sergeant McCulloch turned to Dad. "That's how a McCulloch gets things done. Now stop wasting my time, Gunn, and start dragging those logs out of the road. I want to get this mess cleaned up. The medical examiner gave Koehler Funeral Home the okay, and they've already taken the body away. You need to get moving and get this damn road open."

Dad got red in the face, not as mad as those troopers, but close. He walked back to Blacky taking long strides and went to work without a word to any of the policemen. I was sure glad.

I never got to see the body. It wasn't until the end of the summer, when sweet corn came in, that I realized Mr. Beamis was gone forever. He would never sell us any corn, ever again.

My dad quickly set up a system for the logs. He had three five-foot logging chains with hooks on the ends. More firemen had arrived, and he had them divide up into three groups, each taking one of the five-foot chains and wrapping it around a log, forming a choke chain. Again and again, Dad backed up Blacky, attaching the free end of one of the chains to the truck's tow cable, before lifting it and dragging the log up the road to be deposited in the pasture. I was tasked with running each chain back to its respective team of firemen while Dad backed up to the next log.

One group of idiot firemen kept placing their choke chain near the middle of their logs, rather than closer to one of the ends, which caused the log to whipsaw back and forth when Dad pulled it. I watched them do it a third time before speaking up.

"Mister firemen, sirs, you need to attach the chain near the end of the log, so it pulls straight," I told them this as respectfully as I knew how.

"Mind your own business, boy." One of them called back to me and darn if he didn't lay it out in the same place.

Another fireman said to the one that had given me grief, "Listen to the boy, I think he's right."

"I know what I'm doing. Roll the damn log."

I moved off to pick up another chain from Dad, and, as I walked past a man standing on the side of the road, he spoke to me. "Hey, kid, what's your name?"

"Billy Gunn, sir."

He smiled at me. "You know, you're right, and that fireman is doing it all wrong. It's a shame when people don't listen to someone who knows what they're doing, eh?"

I had to smile but made sure the firemen didn't see me.

"Thanks, Mister, but I gotta go," I said, and ran to get a chain that was ready for me to take back to the next group of firemen.

When we were halfway through pulling the logs out of the road, two trucks from McCulloch Wood Products arrived. One old relic had been rigged by the plant mechanics with a crane to lift logs onto other trucks. They pulled into the pasture and began loading the logs that we had pulled out of the road.

Once the logs were cleared, Dad went to work on the wrecked log truck, pulling it across the east-west road with the front end facing south. Then, he hooked one chain to the rear end of the truck bed and another to the bed, next to the cab, and fixed the two chains together using the forty-foot one I had dropped. Dad backed Blacky up about fifteen feet from the log truck, hooked on the chains, and reeled in his tow cable to lift the bed just high enough. Then when he gave Blacky some gas, it jerked that log truck over onto its wheels without tipping it over.

Dad quickly unhooked from the log truck, pulled up the road, and hooked up to the axel. In less than a minute, he towed the front axle to the pasture before going back and hooking Blacky up to the front end of the log truck. The road was now ready to open and the town cops started yelling at people to move their cars.

After we hauled the truck to the garage on its rear wheels, we returned to the scene to collect the front axle, and carried it to the garage. I thought Dad might take a break, but not him. He had more work to do.

When we came back the third time for the pickup, it was dark, the storm had arrived, and it was pouring rain. The crowd, the police, and the firemen were gone. We had the place to ourselves.

I was pulling a piece of fender over to the pickup when lightning suddenly lit up the ground, followed instantly by a loud boom of thunder. I jumped and dropped my load like it was on fire. Dad was brave and didn't even notice it. He went right on gathering up damaged pieces. I continued to help but I was very tired.

The pickup was rolled onto its wheels in one try.

We were soaked, muddy, and it was late when we finally arrived home. It had taken us a long time to secure the wrecked pickup with wire and clothesline to keep all the damaged parts from falling off. We had towed it backward with the front wheels on a dolly since the rear wheels and bed had been smashed to smithereens. I had had to watch it the whole way back, in case something came loose but nothing did. Even Dad said this tow had been one of the hardest he had ever seen.

It was great that Mom had kept our supper ready; I was starved. She made me and Dad take showers before she would let us eat, and sent me back upstairs to wash my hands twice because I still had mud and grease on them.

Still, despite being hungry, I had a hard time eating, trying to tell Mom and Grandma everything I had seen. Mom kept interrupting me, telling me to eat.

After we all went to bed, I heard Mom and Dad talking. That closet vent was great to have, especially when my parents were trying to keep secrets from me.

"John, you know Billy's only twelve. I don't think you should take him to wrecks where people have died."

"The body was gone when we got there, and if he knows about that stuff now, maybe it'll make him more careful when he gets older. I've got to be hard on him, or he won't grow up strong," Dad said in a husky voice.

"Billy thinks the world of you, but sometimes you're too hard. Tonight, not many grown men would have stuck it out with you. Just remember he's twelve," she said.

"He did work hard today, and he watched what he was doing."

"Did you tell him you appreciated what he did? He came in all worn out and covered in mud. Well, did you?" She asked.

"Laura Jane, you know I don't hand out compliments."

"Well, you should. He's your son, not some hired hand," Mom said in a softer voice.

"Yeah, maybe you're right, but my dad never gave me anything but a hard time."

Then I heard what sounded like a kiss. That was the last I heard 'cause the rest were just bed noises. Dad must have had a hard time falling asleep. I didn't have that problem. I was tired and fell right off.

CHAPTER 7
MATT VISITS HIS LAWYER
Friday, June 3, 1955

After the tow truck cleared the road and traffic began to move, Matt started his car and drove toward town. He was watching for State Route 650, the turn for Highland, when he saw a new billboard for Green Mountain Resort that had not been there on his last visit in the fall of 1950. This new sign was large, gaudy, and ugly. It visually shouted at visitors to turn right at the next intersection in bright orange letters. The green mountain painted on the sign was outlined with green neon lights that flashed on and off. A tasteful white and black sign, almost hidden by the neon one, directed visitors to turn right for the Town of Highland.

Uncle TJ had not tried to match his competitor's advertisement. His uncle had had no interest in joining a sign war.

Even though everyone in Highland called Thomas Jefferson Cubley "Uncle TJ," Matt was his only nephew. Uncle TJ used to laugh and say all these other people are imposters. There had never been any problems between his dad and his uncle. The two men had simply not been alike and were, thus, never close. However, Matt had formed a special bond with his uncle and now felt an obligation to take over the old hotel because there was no one else.

Now, he was alone. He wished his Uncle TJ, his mom, or his dad were still alive. Most of all, he prayed for one last visit with Janet and Jack.

Matt stopped the car in a gravel turnout beside a billboard for Gunn's Garage. It was a simple billboard, not too large, and no neon lights.

Thinking about the boy helping his dad at the wreck, he remembered Jack helping him work in the yard or trying to hand him a hammer that was too heavy. Generations had followed each other in his family until now. His Grandpa Cubley had built Cubley's Coze and left it to Uncle TJ until he had died at the age of seventy. After Matt, there would be no one. His boy, his hope, was gone.

Today, seeing another death was almost too much. He was not afraid of death but was worried he had become too fond of it. Death for him was a seductress. Matt feared he might commit the unpardonable sin. Several times he had placed the barrel of his pistol in his mouth, but each time he had feared that the act of suicide would cut him off from heaven, from being with his wife and child for eternity.

He believed in God, but God, to him, was not a loving father. God did not show mercy. Not being with Janet and Jack would be his hell. People told Matt, life would go on, but going on was not living.

Then, he took a deep breath, shifted the car into first gear, pulled out into the road, and hit the steering wheel with his hand so hard that he had to drive with his other hand.

He turned onto State Route 650 or Main Street at the famous Liberty Bell Gas Station. He forced his mind from his despair onto an old story told by his uncle. The landmark used to be an inn with a large bell in front—an easy way to explain to strangers how to find Highland. Since the automobile had become a way of life, the original inn became a more profitable gas station. The old bell had been moved from the front to the side of the station to make room for the gas pumps.

Some people swore the old bell was from a church, burned down during the Revolutionary War and brought to Highland by a preacher patriot as he fled from the British.

Others said that the Revolutionary War version was total trash, that the bell had been cast for a wealthy farmer by a foundry in England. It was ordered by the farmer to still his wife's complaining, as she had wanted a way to call her husband in from the most distant field in case of an Indian attack. The fact that for years there were no reports of Indians anywhere in the valley did nothing to appease her. The farmer, desiring peace over silver, bought the bell that was the size of a church bell. Thus, the size of the bell matched either version of its origin and provided no solution as to which was the truth.

Matt liked both versions. It taught him something about the opposition of truth when it came to people. Uncle TJ used to tell him,

"When the people are in a state of confusion, both sides will swear they're right and what is the truth is often lost within the puzzlement of history." As a prosecutor in Roanoke, he was all too familiar with how proficient liars could add to the puzzlement of history.

Whatever the truth, the old bell still rang. It survived being stolen by some college kids as a prank. Later recovered, it was protected now by a wrought iron fence with a big Master padlock on the gate. Picnic tables added outside the enclosure were an added appeal for folks to stop. A big sign on top of the shed roof over the gas pumps now proclaimed the traveler had arrived at the Liberty Bell Gas Station of Highland, Virginia. More signage than was necessary for the small gas station.

Feeling slightly better with some distraction, he slowly drove on and passed Gunn's Garage. This had to be the place where the little boy lived. He had heard the Gunn family moved here and started the business after the war, but that was all he knew of them. He saw a neat two-story residence and large auto-repair garage, both inside a tall fence.

Down Main Street, he arrived at the dead-end in front of the courthouse. He pulled into a small parking lot between three buildings.

Matt noticed only small changes since his last visit. None in the old courthouse. Even the painted sign out front seemed original.

The Lewis and Clark Building, which historically had housed the county offices, now contained the administration offices for both the county and the town and had "Green Mountain County Administration Building" painted across the front facade. The name on the building itself had not changed, though, and it was a little misleading.

Painting "Green Mountain County and Town of Highland Administration Building" would have been too expensive, and the front of the building was not long enough. The locals felt if you couldn't figure it out, you didn't need to conduct town business anyway.

Next to the Lewis and Clark building, Matt noticed new paint on the Green Mountain County Sheriff's Office and Jail. It looked much nicer this visit. The Town of Highland Police Department was located on the corner of Lake Street and Court Street in a building that had been a feed and grain store for many years before the McCulloch Company bought it. It was now the plant's special police department, but one could still make out the faded, feed and grain store sign at the top of the building. Everyone in town knew there was a weight room in the back of the police department in one of the old storerooms. Mice still enjoyed the bounty under the floorboards, while the department officers lifted weights.

Way down toward Green Mountain Avenue was the Jeremiah McCulloch School Administration Building, named after the founder of McCulloch Wood Products and father of Big John McCulloch. The family gave money to the school system, but not too much. The school budgets were always austere. Jeremiah and now his son, Big John, wanted factory hands, not "swell heads," as was often heard at the yearly budget meeting of the school board.

Matt parked in Frank Dalton's Law Office parking lot and went in for his appointment. Carol Martin, the receptionist, greeted him with a warm, "Hey, Matt, good to see you."

Carol was one of the prettiest girls in town, single, and the object of some hot pursuits by several local bachelors. She was a green-eyed brunette with a figure that stopped conversations. Any pool hall gossip about Frank Dalton's interest in Carol was just gossip. He was happily married to a pretty woman named Samantha— Sam, to her friends—who was known as a crack shot with a pistol, and had only hired Carol for her expertise as a legal secretary.

Matt greeted Carol and took a seat on the wall opposite.

"How was the drive up from Roanoke?" Carol asked, giving Matt her full attention.

Matt tried to smile but failed. He responded to her in a soft voice with, "It was okay until I got near town. There was a bad wreck at the foot of Smith's Gap. One of the McCulloch log trucks ran over a farmer by the name of Beamis. He didn't make it."

Carol looked shocked and said nothing for a few moments. "That's awful. My dad always bought his corn and steaks from Mr. Beamis. I still go out and get his silver queen corn when it comes in. He always seemed to be quiet and gentle. Hard on his boys, but quiet and gentle with everyone else. That's just terrible!"

She turned in her swivel chair, walked over to Mr. Dalton's office door, and knocked. She stuck her head in the door when Mr. Dalton answered the knock, and she informed him of Matt's arrival. She also asked if he had heard Matt tell about the wreck. Mr. Dalton said he had overheard their conversation. The doors in the office were thin. Matt surmised not much got past Carol, or Frank, for that matter.

Mr. Dalton came right out with, "Hi, Matt. Sorry to hear you had a rough time getting into town. Mr. Beamis is, I mean was, an occasional client of mine. I'll miss him. Are you sure he didn't make it?"

"Yeah, the wreck was a bad one. I was, unfortunately, the first one to find it. I tried, but there was nothing I could do for Mr. Beamis. I was able to do a little for the driver of the log truck. He should make it," Matt concluded somberly. His posture and his shoulders sagged as if weighed down by a heavy burden.

Frank saw this, looked at Carol, back at Matt, and then, to his relief, the legal documents caught his gaze. He held them up for Matt to see.

"Well, the documents are all ready for you to review. I appreciate you letting me finish up the estate, but I'm sure you could have done it easily."

"Well, Frank, I've had to finish so much. After dealing with Janet and Jack's stuff, dealing with another death was about more than I could stand. I almost turned around when I saw the wreck at the foot of Smith's Gap."

"Matt, I'm not sure I could have helped out at that wreck if I'd been in your shoes. Are you sure you're up to finishing the paperwork on your uncle? We could do it later," Frank Dalton asked with more than a little concern in his voice.

"No, let's get this over with."

"All right... Carol, would you get the documents, and spread them out on the conference room table for Matt?"

Carol got up without a word, picked up three six-inch thick file folders, and walked into the conference room. The two men followed. She immediately began spreading out the papers into three groups. Everyone in town knew that while Carol Martin was not the lawyer, her expertise allowed her to go over financial and legal details for her boss with ease.

"Matt, this first group is the will and the first of your uncle's estate papers. You are now the sole owner of Cubley's Coze Hotel and Resort. Due to Uncle TJ's death, the hotel was in a bit of turmoil during the late spring season, but Chuck Tolliver is a heck of a manager. He's kept things running. The hotel lost two early summer bookings of regulars, and Chuck isn't sure why. The monthly profit and loss accounts are also at the end of the first group of documents along with the bank statements. I'll send the signature cards over to the bank once you have signed them, and the signed originals of the estate papers will be filed with the court."

Mr. Dalton picked up the next group of documents. "Matt, were you ever shown the lease your grandfather and Jeremiah McCulloch signed?"

"Yes, when I was in college, but I never took the time to read all of it. Is there anything I should be concerned about?"

Frank smiled. "No, your grandfather was one of the very few people in Green Mountain County that bested Jeremiah McCulloch. He did it rather well. Your grandfather refused to sell to Jeremiah, but he did offer him a long lease for the land Jeremiah needed for his Green Mountain Resort and Hotel."

Matt took the lease and studied it for a full fifteen minutes. He looked up, "I own Cubley's Coze *and* Green Mountain. That amounts to over ten thousand acres and includes Green Mountain Lake."

"It sure is," responded Frank Dalton. "Here is a second lease between your grandfather, the McCulloch family, and the Highland Town Council. The Town of Highland gets to use Green Mountain Lake for a dollar a year as long as it builds, maintains, operates, and assumes liability for the park, dam, and bridge."

"That's a good deal." Matt laid down the second lease and picked the first one back up.

"John McCulloch doesn't pay much rent for such a large tract. I was shocked until I read that he has to make his amenities available to the owners, guests, and employees of Cubley's Coze. It includes horseback riding, boat rental, and all swimming facilities. And he has to share the big lake in front of his hotel with the town."

"No wonder he wants to buy us out," Matt said. "Our people using his facilities for free must irk the daylights out of him."

"Yes, these two leases are golden for you and the town." Frank Dalton replied.

"A very sweet deal," agreed Matt.

"Your uncle turned down four offers from Big John to buy him out. The last offer was a large sum of money, but I think Uncle TJ enjoyed holding onto his upper hand. Not many can claim that. Not to say Big John hasn't caused your uncle trouble from time to time. Still, your family remains on top," Frank Dalton said with a chuckle.

"Well, I ran into Sergeant McCulloch out at the wreck, and he kept asking questions about Cubley's Coze. He wanted to know who would inherit and wasn't the family going to sell? I got irritated at him and his attitude, so I let on like I knew nothing. Now, I can expect Big John will be visiting me when he finds out I'm the new owner. If he acts like his son, I'll have to hold my temper."

"He can be trying," responded Frank.

Carol interrupted the men. "I know some wives who would like to try the McCulloch men for paying cheap wages and on how locals get treated by the plant cops."

Frank laughed and added, "I would hate to be the lawyer who defends them before that jury."

Matt sat up straight. "So would I." Looking down he added, "What's the third pile of papers you have for me?"

"Your Uncle TJ was very frugal and while he maintained the property to a very high standard, he bought bonds and certificates of deposit over the years with the profits from the hotel. He also was quite good at picking stocks. This envelope contains your stocks and bonds. Look them over at your leisure. I suggest you keep them at the bank in Waynesboro. Big John seems to know quite a lot about what goes on at the First National Bank of Highland." The attorney then gave Matt a large briefcase that would hold all the documents.

"Frank, you just told me that my uncle has made me rich. You don't have to give me your briefcase. Heck, I can afford to buy a dozen," Matt said with a wide smile, the first one, since his arrival.

"That was your uncle's, and I know he would want you to have it. Chuck found it in his room after he died and brought it to me. Your Uncle TJ carried that briefcase with him every time he visited me. Also, the combination to the hotel safe is in the zipper pocket. He left written instructions with me to give you this special sealed envelope if anything ever happened to him."

Frank handed Matt a manila envelope that was not only sealed but had an honest-to-goodness wax impression on the flap.

"This looks like something important. What is it?"

"I have no idea," Frank answered. "It's yours now."

Over the next ten minutes, Matt signed all of the documents necessary to transfer the ownership over to him and transfer the bank accounts into his name. He placed his copies in his uncle's briefcase.

"I think this wraps up what I have for you today. I'll keep working on the estate, but anytime you want to take over, just let me know and I'll back out," Frank said.

"No, I want you to handle it." Matt's face clouded over, but he quickly shook it off and smiled back at Frank, adding, "You are doing a great job, and Carol is wonderful. I might just hire her away from you."

"Be careful, some things are justifiable homicide in this state, and that's one of them." Frank laughed, thankful that some of Matt's sadness had seemingly lifted.

Matt left the office with the heavy briefcase. Miss Martin saw him place it in the back seat of his car and drive out of the parking lot. Suddenly, there was a crack of thunder from an approaching storm and it began to rain.

CHAPTER 8
A NEW OWNER
Friday, June 3, 1955

M att drove in the rain from Frank Dalton's Law Office to his hotel. That sounded odd to him, "*his* hotel," but it was.

Where Green Mountain Avenue dead-ended, Green Mountain Resort had erected another gaudy sign. This one added flashing orange bulbs to the right turn arrow under a green neon mountain. Forty feet beyond that awful sign was a very sedate sign for Cubley's Coze Hotel and Resort. It was white with black lettering, telling guests for this resort, turn left. A flash of lightning lit this sign, which naturally outshone his competitor's for an instant. A boom of thunder followed.

Matt turned and followed the entrance road for one mile as it gradually climbed upward through pines onto a small plateau. Nestled on the south side of the plateau and against the rising mountain was Cubley's Coze Hotel. The entrance drive made a half-circle around the front, past the broad steps that led to the hotel's veranda.

Four parking spaces were out front and Matt pulled into the second one. Each bore a dark green sign with bright gold letters that said, "Guest Check-In" without any time restrictions. A subtle example of the old hotel's gracious, Southern hospitality and non-rush atmosphere.

Matt paused and then got out of his car as the rain diminished to a few sprinkles. Childhood memories warmed his spirit as he looked first at the magnificent old hotel and the grounds, and finally, north where he could see the valley and distant mountains. The storm was moving away in that direction.

Turning back to face the hotel, a grand "U" shaped structure, Green Mountain sat behind the hotel. A pine forest grew on the lower mountain with hardwoods taking over as the elevation rose. The trees on top had stubby branches from the high winds that often swept across its upper four-thousand-foot crown.

Up broad stairs to the veranda, the front facade was as he remembered. He pulled open one of the two massive double doors at the center of the front porch and entered the large lobby. It extended two-thirds across the front of the structure. The main staircase went up to a small mezzanine and met two staircases, one to the left and one to the right that connected to the second-floor front hallway.

On the left side of the lobby was the front desk with the hotel office behind it. The kitchen and dining room occupied the rest of the first floor.

The west wing of the "U" did not reach the rocky slope but stopped short. A service road left the entrance drive and went around this shorter wing, which allowed trucks to back up to a loading dock for the kitchen. The delivery area was hidden so well by screening white pines that it was not unusual for new delivery drivers to come to the front desk to ask for the loading dock. Employees parked in a small lot, hidden behind that same row of screening white pines.

The hotel's second floor over the lobby contained the office for the head of housekeeping, storage closets for the maids, and two apartments. Uncle TJ had occupied the largest and the hotel manager, Chuck Tolliver, the other. There was a banquet room over the dining room, but it could only be reached from the first-floor dining room by a private staircase.

The remainder of the second, all the third, and all of the fourth floors were guest rooms. The two side staircases at the east and west end of the front hall and the Otis elevator served all the upper floors except one.

The fifth-floor was attic storage and was reached by a private locked stairway from the fourth floor. The attic had no elevator service because the elevator machinery was there. Matt had played as a child among the holiday decorations and antiques stored in this attic. An attic bedroom and bath had been added just for Matt when he turned eight.

The east wing had more rooms and space than the west side because it intruded into the mountain and contained underground storage rooms on the lower floors. Spooky places to a child, where the temperature was always cool. The third and fourth-floor end rooms on that side were mountainside ground floor suites with exterior doors and small patios cut out of the mountain. Each terrace was protected by a stone wall to prevent children from venturing onto the steep slope.

A pleasant aroma coming from the kitchen as it suffused the lobby caught Matt's attention. Vivid memories flooded his mind of the great meals served from that kitchen by Maddie Johnson, the hotel's chief cook for the past twenty years. Her French father had been the hotel chef before her and had trained her in the French tradition. Not having graduated from a formal culinary school, she would not refer to herself as a chef, but her meals were of that quality. Maddie spoke French would translate dishes into French for Uncle TJ to give a little class to the menu. Her mother, born in the South, had also taught her cooking in the Southern style, making her very versatile in the kitchen.

After Maddie's husband died, Uncle TJ had invited her to move into one of the cottages down by the river. They used to be guest rentals, but now they were rented, very reasonably, to staff. Maddie could be heard singing French songs as she walked back and forth to work. Walking had not reduced her size, which was a visible testament to her culinary skill.

Matt noticed cut flowers on each of the lobby tables. He knew without looking there would be cut flowers on each of the dining room tables, as well. The hotel manager, Chuck Tolliver, always made the arrangements himself. The perfume of freshly cut flowers and the delicious smells from the kitchen drew guests into the lobby well ahead of the opening of the dining room.

Guests enjoyed the lobby in the afternoons for another reason. Afternoon teas were served at four, during which Chuck would frequently give concerts on the piano. He had been a concert pianist once but gave it up, though no one knew why.

Over the dining room within the very private banquet hall was where local clubs had their dinner meetings. Despite the availability of dining facilities at the Green Mountain Resort, it was not able to provide a secure room, nor food of equal quality. Thus, many of the social clubs met at Cubley's Coze.

The size of the hotel might give the impression that it was too small to feed all the hotel guests plus a large crowd in the private banquet room, but the kitchen and staff were more than adequate.

The longer east wing, which contained the kitchen, extended into the side of the mountain.

Matt smiled to himself because he knew the reputation of this hotel's dining room over the one at the Green Mountain Resort had always been an irritant to the town boss. Big John often referred to Cubley's Coze as that "damn other resort," despite the fact that he often dined at Cubley's Coze when he attended the private and very secret meetings of the Highland Business Owners Association. Those secret meetings went back to the eighteen hundreds when the hotel first opened, and when certain community matters had to be kept from Yankee outsiders.

Big John's wife also forced him to dine at Cubley's Coze on her birthday and their anniversary each year. She loved Maddie's spice cake, and Uncle TJ made sure it was on the menu whenever she reserved a table. Big John grumbled a lot on these occasions, but he usually cleaned his plate and ate two desserts.

Maddie's spice cake or her chess pies were favored by the townspeople when a special dessert was required at home. The chess pies were cupcake-size pastry shells filled with chess pie filling. Incredible on the palate of children and adults.

Matt recalled how Maddie would crack a knuckle with a spoon if she even suspected a waitress, waiter, or Cubley child was reaching to snatch a chess pie or piece of spice cake that was promised. On the other hand, Maddie always made a mistake on the count when she made her unique desserts. Those mistakes were left for the staff as a motivation. Maddie could not tolerate waste, and Matt fondly remembered all the times he was included in the miscount.

Matt was so lost in thought as he crossed the lobby that he was startled when Chuck Tolliver loudly banged open the fold-over section of the front desk and made his way to Matt to give him a big hug. He then held Matt at arm's length, looked him up and down, and gave him a second hug.

"Well, well, Matthew Cubley, it is wonderful to see you. You've been sorely missed. We have your second-floor apartment all ready."

"My apartment? What happened to my room?" Matt asked with dismay. He feared a fire or leak in the roof had damaged his old room.

My special room where I could sneak out to meet summer girlfriends by using the fire escape. The room that I almost set on fire by smoking in bed. Lucky for me, I had a Coca-Cola handy before I burned down the place. No one knew about my close call because I buried the sheet behind the hotel.

Chuck interrupted Matt's thoughts with, "Matthew, we can't have you sleeping in the attic. My goodness, your Uncle TJ would skin me alive. I'm sorry, I've totally forgotten myself: I mean Mr. Cubley," Chuck concluded in a frenzy.

"Chuck, Mr. Cubley sounds like you're talking to my dad. Call me, Matt. Even Matthew sounds pretentious. Okay?" Matt finished in a slow, steady voice, hoping to calm Chuck down.

Chuck sure hasn't changed. Uncle TJ would speak almost in slow motion to get Chuck to calm down; his frenzy triggered whenever something went wrong. When that guest's car caught fire, Uncle TJ had had to grab the phone and give the fire department the address while Chuck yelled hysterically in the background.

"Yes, of course, Mr. Matt. We have you in Uncle TJ's apartment—the one your uncle used to have— I mean *your* apartment, the *owner's* apartment; it's all ready," Chuck said, somewhat calmer, but still flustered.

"Chuck, has Uncle TJ's stuff been stored somewhere safe?" Matt tried diplomatically to see if he could face staying in his uncle's room.

"Yes, yes, we carefully placed all of his things in cardboard boxes, labeled each one, and stacked them in the storeroom at the end of the hall. He didn't have a lot. His books we left on the bookcase in his— er, your room. Is that acceptable?"

"That's fine. I've just had trouble sleeping lately. My insomnia might give me a chance to read a few of my uncle's books," Matt answered gently.

"Matthew— sorry, Matt, may we retire to the office, I need to sit down and compose myself. If I may, if it is not too soon, perhaps not too much trouble, may I—would it be okay?"

"I think I know what you want to ask me. Let's go into the office for a chat."

Chuck turned and started to walk around the front desk and into the office. He stopped and stepped back from the office door to let Matt enter first, pick a chair, and sit down. Only then did he seat himself.

"Sir, Mr. Cubley, this is rather…" but before he could finish his sentence, Matt interrupted him.

"Chuck, there is no better hotel manager than you, and the answer is 'yes' and yes.'" Matt looked at Chuck and continued. "I intend to stay here in Highland. After recent events, I need to keep busy or I just—well, let's say I need to stay busy. My problem, I know almost nothing about running a hotel. The legal stuff I can handle, but the day to day operations, well, I would be lost."

Chuck's face went from concerned, to relieved, to almost joyful. Then he caught himself and backed his demeanor down a notch or two in light of Matt's recent loss.

"Chuck, Uncle TJ not only left me the hotel but stock and income from a lease. I plan to run it as he would have. So, yes, I'm staying, and yes, I want you to stay on as my hotel manager. That is, of course, if that's what you want?" Matt asked.

"Oh Matthew, I want—you have made my day, no, my month, no, my year. I want nothing more. It's been my life since your Uncle TJ took me in and gave me this job. I love the guests and know every one of the regulars. Thank you. Oh, thank you. This is wonderful!" Upon concluding this outpouring of emotion, Chuck sank back in his seat and partially deflated. Well, for a few seconds.

"Call me Matt, and you didn't ask me about the pay?"

With a look of sincerity, Chuck said, "I understand completely how hard things have been. Whatever cut in pay you require, I certainly understand."

"I don't want to cut your pay; I want to give you a ten percent raise. You deserve it after running this place after Uncle TJ died. You and all the supervisors. We need to tell Maddie Johnson and Rose and Richard Baker right away because if they're thinking I came here to shut the place down or reduce their pay, that would just be wrong. Please, go call them."

"We all knew your Uncle TJ was tight with money. Now, that's not to say he wasn't fair. Can you afford a raise? One this extravagant? I know you have had some unusual expenses with the hospital and funeral bills. You know you don't have to do this.

I'll stay on at my current pay as will Maddie, Rose, and Richard," Chuck said in a bit of a rush.

"Chuck, I'm alone; I have no one—only this hotel. I have a settlement from the wreck that I don't want. Uncle TJ left me stock and the income from the lease. I'm not sure how much I'm worth, but I think even old tightwad Uncle TJ would join me in this decision. Anyway, I've made up my mind."

Matt called in Maddie Johnson, the chief cook, first, for the announcement.

She was round, and her face, body, arms, and legs all plump. She was dark-skinned, even for her race, but her smile was brilliantly white and went clear across her face. She was happy most of the time and spry despite her age and weight, but cross her ,and the staff told the newcomers to expect a knife-throwing cyclone that was a deadly wonder to behold. In truth, she had only threatened to throw knives, choosing instead to fling a spoon or rap a knuckle.

Maddie had taken off her apron and was holding it balled up in her hands when she came to see Matt. She was wiping hands coated in flour on it repeatedly as she patiently waited for the new owner to speak. Matt said with nostalgia, "Maddie, it's good to see you, and much too long since my last visit."

Maddie looked into Matt's face and said in a loud voice, "Mr. Matthew, it's good to see you, too. I knew you were coming. I fixed black pot chicken, special, for supper—the kind you like so much. Law'd child; you have gotten to be nothing but skin and bones. You got the sorrow in your eyes, and I know exactly how you is hurting. I hurts with you. Mr. Chuck told me you need to see me. If it has to be bad news, then I'll take what God says I must. Don't you worry about ole Maddie; you got troubles enough. I have my daughter Rose and her man, Richard, the best son-in-law anyone could have. They'll take care of ole Maddie."

Matt almost laughed but stopped himself. Maddie was fluent in French; she could teach English grammar to most of the English teachers in Green Mountain County; so, Matt was wondering if she was putting him on just a little with her, "Law'd child" and "I hurts" stuff. Perhaps she was so used to speaking that way in the kitchen, in case the guests were listening, that she was now talking that way all the time. He hoped not. Racism took many forms, and Maddie knew when to be careful and play the colored servant. There was at least that one group who met in the private banquet room with ties to the KKK.

"Maddie, thank you for your kind words. They mean a lot, but I bring no bad news. I'll tell you what I just told Chuck: I'm moving to Highland, and I intend to operate the hotel the same as Uncle TJ. I want you and Richard and Rose to stay on with a ten percent raise in your pay. Would you?"

Maddie's face broke into a big grin and she said in a quiet voice that only those in the office could hear, "Matthew, I can speak for all of us when I say we would be delighted to continue to work here. Thank you. May the Lord bless you and give you peace."

Maddie departed with the apron still in her hand and in her loud kitchen voice, shouted, "We gonna have black pot chicken, mashed potatoes and gravy, collard greens, and I am gonna do up a spice cake, right this minute. You just bring me your appetite, and we's gonna eat high on the hog tonight. Make that high on the chicken. This week's Sunday fixings is gonna come twice."

Matt shook his head. *"Parlez-Vous Anglaise?"* he whispered to himself.

Later, Matt confirmed to Rose, Maddie's daughter and the Housekeeping Supervisor, and Richard, Rose's husband and the Grounds Supervisor, about keeping the hotel open and informed them of their raises.

Richard was tall, lean, and much stronger than he looked. He had a long-legged gait that could eat up distance even when he looked like he was just ambling along. The two men went out to Matt's car to move his belongings into his new home.

While Richard got Matt's suitcase, Matt carried the briefcase with the legal documents and a suit bag up to the second-floor apartment. When they returned to the car, they each carried a large box of Matt's family mementos. These boxes would remain sealed. The last two trips were boxes of Matt's personal items and a few law books.

Matt's apartment consisted of a sitting room, a large bath, and a bedroom. One wall of the sitting room was a bookcase, and on the other side, large windows faced out the front of the hotel. The view went clear across the valley and included Smith River, where some ducks were swimming among the reeds.

Moving in took about fifteen minutes. When alone, Matt took the briefcase, opened the pocket, and looked at the combination to the office safe. The combination his uncle had used was easy. It was his birth date, only backward. The pack of documents with the wax seal, he opened, and much to his surprise, the first and largest document looked like a treasure map.

The map showed Matt the location of a second, secret, fire-proof safe in his apartment with its combination in the margin. The safe was hidden behind a section of the bookcase. Uncle TJ had identified several other secret places in the hotel on the map and explained their details in other collateral documents.

Matt's grandfather, he read, had several secret places built during the construction of the hotel. There was a brief history of the hotel and a detailed map of an abandoned copper mine which was located on the property. The mine had been closed down long before the hotel was even planned.

Matt reviewed the stock certificates his uncle had left him. Once all of the stock certificates were transferred into his name, he would be rich. He was glad he had decided to give those raises.

He took all of the documents and placed them in the apartment safe. It was a rather large safe with plenty of room for more stuff.

Compartments in the bottom half of the safe carried labels with his father's name and some with Uncle TJ's. What he found in each were sacks of gold coins—a lot of gold. His grandfather's generation did not trust banks, so people had hidden their gold in their mattresses. The Cubley family just had a better brand of mattress. So, everything of value, he now locked in the safe. He swung the door-like section of the bookcase back over the front of the safe to hide it. Matt left his apartment to look the place over in more detail.

Would he be able to take over and run this hotel? He worried that he might not be up to the task. He had the funds, but could he make himself do it? If he failed—old friends—good people... He better not fail.

CHAPTER 9
BILLY'S SATURDAY MORNING
Saturday, June 4, 1955

"Scotty, you poke me again with that toy gun and you die!" I wanted to sleep in since it was Saturday and there was no school. Then, it came to me. Heck, no school at all for the whole summer. Scotty got in another poke with his gun.

"Scotty, you are going to get it—now!" Growling and faking a move like I was going to jump out of bed and grab Scotty, he ran.

"Momma, Billy is going to hit me!"

"William Boyer Gunn, do not make me come up there. You be nice to Scotty." Mom's voice from the kitchen rang out.

Throwing my pajamas in the closet and out of sight, I dressed for the day by donning a t-shirt, shorts, and tennis shoes without socks. It was summer after all. Then, downstairs for some eggs and pancakes.

"Hi, Mom; Morning, Dad," I said, sticking my tongue out at Scotty who was sitting at the table like the little angel he was certainly not.

"Morning, Billy," Dad said as I sat down, which was a bit unusual for Dad. He generally read the paper and ignored Scotty and me at breakfast unless we were in trouble. "What are your plans today?" he asked.

Now he had my attention. He was speaking to me, not fussing, but *talking* to me.

"Oh, nothing. I think there might be a western on at the Top Hat if I can track down Kent," I responded with the minimum so as not to get yelled at or whacked.

"Sounds good." Dad's reply was typical of a parent who was trying to sound involved to impress his wife but who was not, you know, *interested*.

"Oh, by the way, I wanted to tell you that you did a good job yesterday, helping me on Blacky." He even looked up at me as he finished the compliment.

Wow, that came at me from left field—a compliment from Dad. Then I remembered what Mom said to him last night and realized I needed to give her more credit when it came to him. She had, after all, gotten him out of one of his quiet moods and into a good mood. Wonder what she did?

"Thanks, Dad," I responded. Mom placed a plate of eggs and pancakes in front of me. I reached for the syrup, being careful to pour as much on the eggs as on the pancakes. I learned in school that it was essential for young athletes to eat a balanced meal and I wanted to be sure I balanced the syrup on both the eggs and the pancakes.

I put the open bottle back on the table as far from Scotty as possible. That little monster could hit a target five feet away by tossing a bottle of Log Cabin, and I didn't want to provide him with sticky bomb practice. I knew he was looking for a way to get me.

I was planning on how to get even for something he might do when the phone rang. Mom got it but only said, "Yes, I'll get him for you," and handed the phone to Dad.

"Hello… yes, I am… yes, I could come on up and do that, no problem, be there in about twenty minutes. Bye."

Dad slowly put the phone back on its base and put the whole thing back on the kitchen counter. We had a long extension cord for Dad to be able to take the phone out of the kitchen for privacy.

"Was that a job?" Mom asked as she began doing the breakfast dishes.

"Yep. Mr. Tolliver wants me to come to Cubley's Coze and jump-start one of the guest's cars. He thinks it's the battery, not that Mr. Tolliver would know a battery from a fuel pump."

I looked over at Dad. He was grinning like he had just told a joke, but I missed it completely.

"Now John, be nice. Business is business. You can't believe everything you hear," Mom cautioned, giving him a warning look that was not lost on me.

"Don't have to hear nothing, Laura Jane, I got eyes. Speaking of eyes, where's your mother?"

"John, please don't start in on Mother. After the argument we had yesterday, I'm guessing she wants to let sleep late and let things cool off," Mom concluded with a sigh.

I knew it was easy to get a good fight going between Grandma versus Mom and Dad, but never with me. Grandma and I never fought. Well, almost never, except that time I hid her false teeth. I got a spanking for that one, but a spanking from Grandma was nothing like a whipping from Dad.

"Billy, how about you helping me jump off that car? I can trust you to hold the cables; that Mr. Tolliver gives me the royal pause. He doesn't have a clue about mechanical or electrical stuff. I would put him and Old Man Peters in the same boat."

"Will we be finished by noon? Kent and I sorta made plans." I asked, watching Mom to see her reaction.

"Don't see why not," Dad answered, folding his paper and tossing it on the table as he rose.

"I hope Kent can keep you out of trouble," Mom said, knowing full well when we were together stuff happened.

"Come on, Billy, or you won't get back by noon," Dad observed as he pushed open the screen door and walked across the yard. His long strides were putting distance between us, though he didn't look like he was walking fast. I had to run to keep up.

Blacky fired right up. The tow truck was easy to start in the summer. But when it got cold, sometimes I had to wait and wait for Dad to heat up the engine. Today, it started on the first try. Dad let her idle while he made sure the jumper cables, spare car battery, and his travel box of tools were all on board. He kept both his box of tools and the cables in the first compartment on the driver's side. The battery for jump starts was on the back deck of his truck in a wooden box. Satisfied he had what he needed, we left in a cloud of smoke from Blacky's stack. Mom knew we were going; no need for the horn.

Pulling into the hotel, we stopped right out front. Dad was smart. No sense having to back Blacky around if you guessed wrong about where the car was parked. Dad no sooner had gotten out of the cab of the truck when Mr. Tolliver and two other men came down the steps from the veranda to the gravel drive.

I knew Mr. Tolliver. The second man, I had never seen. The third one looked familiar, but I could not think where I had seen him; I figured he must be one of the regular guests of the hotel.

Mr. Tolliver started to speak to Dad, but man number two beat him.

"My car won't start. It must be a dead battery," he said to my dad. "It's the green, 1946 Plymouth Special Deluxe parked over in the side lot there." The car was a dull green, four-door sedan with a spotlight side mirror combination. I sure would have liked one of those spotlights for my bike.

Dad picked up his set of jumper cables and was about to pick up the spare battery when the man who looked familiar turned and spoke.

"Hello, Billy. Good to see you again," and he smiled at me.

"You know each other?" Mr. Tolliver asked.

Dad was giving me a cold stare, and I was trying my best to remember where I had seen this man.

"This young man and I met at the wreck yesterday. Billy is one smart kid. He was telling a fireman how to place a logging chain to pull a log out of the road but the guy wouldn't listen. If he had listened, he would have gotten things done a lot faster."

"Well, well," said Mr. Tolliver. "In that case, may I introduce you to the new owner of Cubley's Coze, Mr. Matthew Cubley."

"Pleased to meet you, sir," I said, looking Mr. Cubley in the eye and holding out my hand. Mom had taught me the proper way to greet an adult, and I wanted to make a good impression. Mr. Cubley shook my hand and smiled at me.

Dad picked up the cables, the spare battery, and left with the other man. He watched me over his shoulder to be sure I greeted this adult correctly.

Mr. Cubley asked me some questions about how Dad had cleaned up the logs and the wrecked vehicles. I explained I was Dad's assistant on Blacky and filled him in on the way things had gone.

"Billy, it looks like your dad had no trouble getting that car started. Here they come, back already," reported Mr. Cubley.

Dad and the hotel guest returned with my dad in the lead.

"Much wrong with the car?" Mr. Cubley asked Dad as Mr. Tolliver also leaned in to listen.

"Not much at all. Someone left the spotlight on all night, and that's what ran the battery down. It fired right up when I hooked on my spare battery, and if it runs for fifteen minutes, everything should be fine."

Dad did not look at the owner of the car when he said this. He was in a good mood today because he didn't add some idiot left the lights on all night and ran the battery down.

The guest asked how much it would cost for the jump.

Dad answered the man but looked and spoke more to Mr. Cubley.

"Well, it's like this. Uncle TJ, the former owner of Cubley's Coz, and I had an arrangement. When a guest would have trouble, he would call me, and in exchange for the repeat business, the charge was half the normal rate. My normal fee is six dollars, so I think if the new Mr. Cubley thinks this is fair, I'll charge you three dollars."

Both the guest and Mr. Cubley responded, "More than fair," and then they both laughed.

Mr. Cubley spoke up and said to my dad, "You know if we are going to be using your services on a regular basis, may I call you John and you call me Matt? I think that would only be fair."

"Sounds fair to me," Dad said. "Sounds like we are going to be having a lot of fairs around here. Always liked fairs." Both Dad and Mr. Cubley smiled at that, and even I understood the double meaning. Dad was making a joke. What did Mom put in his coffee?

While the guest was paying Dad, Mr. Cubley started speaking again.

"You know, John, we have been having a problem with our ice cream at the hotel. It seems some of it has been going to waste. Perhaps you and Billy, if your son likes ice cream, might help us out with our waste problem. Would you two like some now?"

I looked at Dad with a "could I" expression on my face, but Dad shook his head no. His face went from happy to dark in a split second.

"Thanks, Matt, but Billy and I just had breakfast. We wouldn't want to spoil the boy more than he already is. Perhaps we could take a raincheck on the ice cream?"

Dad then gave me a distinct look that even an idiot could read, "Keep it to yourself if you want to live."

What a disappointment, and here I thought Dad was in a good mood. On the other hand, we *were* offered a raincheck. Things might turn out okay. Kent and I often rode our bikes out here to check out the girls and free ice cream would be super. This summer was beginning to show some real possibilities. Funny how a day can change.

Dad thanked Mr. Cubley again for the business and the offer of ice cream. We both walked to the cab of Blacky and climbed in. As we left, I waved at Mr. Cubley, and he waved back at me. Well, I think it was at me, or maybe it was at my dad. No matter what, things were looking up.

Riding back to the garage, I was thinking of all the things I had to tell Kent, and that reminded me; I needed to call him about seeing a movie this afternoon.

Pulling into the garage lot, Dad pulled up near the house and then backed Blacky behind the garage.

"Dad, can I use the phone to call Kent?"

"First, I need you to take Scotty upstairs and keep him occupied for about ten minutes. There's something I need to discuss with your mother. I'll call you when you can bring him back downstairs, and then you can use the phone. After you make your call, though, you have to put away those parts for the Dodge job that came in yesterday."

Together, we walked to the house, and when we got to the kitchen, Scotty was in the living room playing with some cars. I picked him up and told him there was a surprise for him upstairs. He smiled and off we went. I gave him an old comic book of mine to look at the pictures and sat down under the hanging clothes next to the heating vent in my closet to eavesdrop on my parents. Some things are on a need to know basis, and I needed to know.

I heard Dad say to Mom, "Yeah, things went fine."

"You don't sound like they went fine. What's the matter?" Mom was good at picking up on Dad's moods, even when he said things were okay.

"I met the new owner, and I got a bad feeling about him. Mr. Tolliver introduced us. He's the nephew of TJ Cubley. Do you remember him? I noticed him when he visited there years ago with his family. Anyway, I don't think the man has a wife or family, and Mr. Tolliver seemed to be happy he's running the place. What really got me worried was when he asked Billy and me into the hotel for ice cream. Of course, I said no."

Dad got quiet, and I knew he was done talking. Grandma jumped right into the middle of the conversation that Dad was trying to have with Mom. Out came one of her sarcastic remarks.

"Good Lord, John, anyone who would offer you and Billy ice cream must be a Russian Communist. Let's call the feds and have the whole bunch carted off to jail."

Grandma Harris could not resist getting Dad all riled up when she thought he was off on one of his "pipe dreams" as she called them.

"Mother, you need to hush and let John and I talk. Why don't you go into the living room and watch your soap? Isn't it about time for it?"

I could hear Mom moving around the kitchen, and I could just see her moving Grandma into the living room to get rid of her.

"Stingers and bouquets, that's all I get around here, stingers and bouquets. Besides, it's Saturday; no soaps on Saturday. Today is the day there is nothing on but junk, just cartoons and kid shows."

The TV turned on downstairs. Grandma pretended not to like kid's shows, but she often watched them with Scotty, which gave her the excuse she needed.

I wiggled closer to the vent to hear over the noise of the television.

"John, what's wrong with being nice and offering the two of you ice cream?" Mom asked.

"I think the man wears white bucks," Dad said with a strained voice.

"What in the world do shoes have to do with ice cream?"

"Laura Jane, don't you know anything. Guys who are gay wear white bucks. You know, so the girls stay away, and the boys, the ones who…well…they just wear them. Everyone knows about white bucks. I got real uncomfortable when he started to ask Billy over for ice cream. I don't like that one bit. We need to tell Billy never to go up there without you or me."

Dad was talking and walking around the kitchen, and then I heard a chair creak. He sat down on it a little too hard.

I was confused. Now I'm fourteen; it's still confusing. Why was it bad to wear white shoes if you were happy about something? None of the girls I know have even mentioned that girls don't like guys who wear white shoes. Adults make no sense most of the time, and then, they'll go clear off the tracks.

Mom went on talking. "My goodness, John, you got all of that out of the new owner asking you both for ice cream? That nephew of TJ Cubley was a nice kid. His parents were nice people, as I remember. All the girls at the beauty shop thought the world of Uncle TJ. You know he never got married because he got wounded in World War One. When he came home, his girl had run off and married a dentist, and Uncle TJ never got over it. A retired nurse also told me his war wound not only made him walk with a limp, but fixed it so he couldn't have children. The Cubley family has always been kind and the men gentlemen. No one has ever said anything bad about T. J. Cubley, and neither should you speak ill of his nephew. If this new owner is not right, as small as Highland is, we'll know it soon enough. Now, don't you go spreading rumors! Not about a good customer."

Mom was trying to put Dad back on track.

"Well…" Dad started to say something, but Mom interrupted.

"Well, nothing, John. Leave it alone. I hope you didn't make the new owner mad, causing us to lose his business. We get a lot of business out of that hotel."

Mom was on a roll now and Dad better get out of the way.

"Mr. Tolliver is a perfect gentleman. He runs that hotel like a Swiss watch. Much better than the Green Mountain Resort crew, who only call us occasionally to give us work. You know it as well as I; they use the McCulloch Chevrolet dealership garage for almost all of their business. The only time we get called is when the job is too big for the Chevrolet wrecker."

Dad was saying not a word.

"Now, enough said. Besides, I need to run down to the beauty parlor to get my hair done. You are about to make me late. Give me the keys to the Buick. I'll be back in a couple of hours."

And with that, Mom left. Grandma was still watching TV. I got out of the closet because Dad was about to….

"Billy, your Mom and I are done. You and Scotty can come back downstairs. Don't forget to put those parts away before you get tied up with Kent. You hear me?" Dad yelled.

"Yes, sir, I promise to put them away as soon as I call Kent."

Scotty was finished with his comic and looking to get into something. I took him by the hand and said, "Let's go see Grandma."

I dropped Scotty off with Grandma, who was pretending not to watch *Death Valley Days*. Scotty liked the horses and mules, so he climbed up on Grandma's lap and started watching it with her. I looked in the kitchen and found Friday's paper. After checking the movie section, I called Superman on the kitchen phone. I told him about the big wreck, and we made plans to meet for the movies. Then, it was back to my chores. I had forgotten all about the wish, but my mirror had not forgotten me.

CHAPTER 10
BILLY'S SATURDAY AFTERNOON
Saturday, June 4, 1955

I finished my chores except for one box, which held a transmission and was way too heavy for me to move. I left it for Dad when he got back from a job.

What a great day it was for a movie. I told Grandma that I was going downtown with Kent to the Top Hat Theater. We had a stop to make along the way, but Grandma didn't need to know that.

Grabbing my green Schwinn Hornet, I rode out of the gate and turned left on Main. A dog was crossing the street, so he got a blast from my bike horn. Well, maybe it was more like a toot. The dog ignored me.

I rode over to Green Mountain Avenue, where Kent was waiting astride his red Columbia bike. The one his mom got him for Christmas—well, it was from Santa Claus, but we all knew how hard his mom saved up for Santa to give him that bike. Not many moms who were raising a son by themselves could afford a new $39.99 bike for their boy, so he thought the world of it.

I got my Hornet when Dad took it in trade for some work he agreed to do on a truck for one of the loggers over near Piney River. The logger's boy had gotten a new bike for his birthday from his uncle, but his dad traded it in on the bill. Dad then sold it to me for $10.00. I had saved up my allowance and hated to see most of it go, but my bike was worth every penny. I felt bad for the birthday boy, but it was boss of my dad to let me have it for half-price. Mom may have had a hand in the deal.

"Hey, Superman, you ready to get scared to death?" I yelled and gave Kent a grin plus a toot on my horn.

"Naw, BB, nothing scares Superman except kryptonite. Do you think the *Creature from the Black Lagoon* can scare me? No way." Kent gave me that crooked grin of his from his sledding accident and a return toot.

"Race you to the dime store. Loser buys the peas," he challenged and stood hard on one of his bike pedals to get a jump on me.

"You're on, but not even Superman can beat the Gun," I replied and pedaled off as hard as I could go. Kent beat me by a foot because I almost clipped a car backing out of a drive near Dogwood Street, but losing the bet was no big deal. The peas were free.

The dime store was a ritual for us. A peashooter with a bag of peas for the movie only cost a nickel. Next on the list was a nickel Charm sucker, which was advertised as an all-day sucker. That was close to being true. We hid our purchases under our clothes, stashed our bikes behind the furniture store on Church Street, and walked down to the theater.

After we got in line, two of the girls from our class joined the line behind us.

"Hey, Laura, hey, Judy. How's your summer been?" Kent asked which took me by surprise. Since when did Superman have the nerve to begin a conversation with girls?

"Oh, that's funny," said Laura smiling at Kent. "Well, let me think of all the things I've done since the day before yesterday. I would have to say it's been going pretty well."

Both girls laughed. Kent blushed redder than the red on his Columbia bike. Before I could say something to try and save the day, Dickie Lockhart, his younger brother, Carl, and Lou McCulloch broke in line in front of us.

"Hey, watch it," the two of us said in unison as we got pushed back.

Mr. Stone had been waiting on two colored children on their side of the concession stand and didn't see what happened. When he turned to wait on us, he remembered the four of us had been at the head of the line.

"What's going on? You three boys can't just break in line," Mr. Stone remarked with a frown on his face.

"We certainly don't want to hold up important people like the Lockharts and Lou McCulloch," Judy said with a frown on her face that matched Mr. Stone's.

"Yeah, we certainly don't," added Laura.

Now, girls can say that sort of thing and not get a beating. Guys—well, for us, it's different.

Dickie Lockhart turned, never looked at the two girls, but stared first at Kent and then me for a chilling second. He slapped down his quarter on the counter and spat out, "Pay up, boys. Let's go before I have to hurt a couple of crybabies."

The other two boys tossed down two more quarters, and all three picked up some paper 3-D glasses from a box that had a creature on it. They strutted toward the theater door like they owned the place.

"Wow, what bad manners. Someone ought to teach those bullies a lesson," Laura said loudly enough for the three to hear.

"Listen," said Mr. Stone, "we don't want any trouble, but if you have any problems out of them, come let me know. I had to throw them out of here two weekends ago. Darn if I won't do it again. Makes no never mind to me, who their fathers are."

Mr. Stone picked up the three quarters off the counter and put them in the till.

"Now, what can I get for you ladies and gentlemen?" he asked with a smile replacing his frown.

Kent and I, taking the hint, yielded our place in line to Laura and Judy. We got a smile from each of them.

The girls each bought a ticket, a nickel Pepsi, and a nickel bag of popcorn. Thirty-five cents for a full afternoon of two movies, four cartoons, a serial and sometimes two, plus popcorn and a drink. This sure beat the price of movies over in Charlottesville. Can you believe they charged fifty cents for a Saturday afternoon matinee for kids—what a rip.

Laura and Judy left with their stuff. We did a repeat of what the girls bought. I started to like Laura that summer and Kent thought Judy was swell, but we never mentioned it. Guys don't do that. Besides, girls usually like older boys.

Mr. Stone gave us our drinks and popcorn. We picked up our 3-D glasses and, juggling our booty, walked into the theater. The house lights were on and we quickly found two seats down front. We made sure to pick our seats away from the bullies who were sitting in the back row.

The Top Hat Theater was old when my mom was young. She told me she had attended plays, vaudeville nights, and minstrel shows there. She and Dad had heard Floyd Mills and His Marylanders, the Frankie and Johnnie Orchestra, and other famous bands give concerts there when she was in high school. The stage was wide and deep, but when the movie started, the screen lowered, and the curtains closed in on each side of the screen. When the lights went down, this place was scary, even without monster movies. Then, a pea hit me in the back of the head.

"Kent, why does Mr. Stone like the coloreds better than us?"

"What do you mean, BB?" he mumbled while munching on popcorn.

"Well, I look at it this way. Every Saturday, while we watch the movies, we get peashooter shots from the balcony, right?"

"Yeah. Peashooter fights are part of the fun. Been that way since we've been coming here. Why?" Kent asked me.

"Okay, the coloreds have their own special entrance, they order from their side of the concession stand, never a line, and they get to sit in the balcony. Right?" I asked, knowing the answer.

"Yeah, but what's your point? The movie's about to start."

"Superman, it's obvious. They get to sit in the balcony, which is the high ground whenever we get into a peashooter fight. They fire down; we have to shoot up. So, why can't we sit in the balcony sometimes? It sure would make it evener. Never has happened, never will. He must like them better than us." I concluded as the lights dimmed.

"BB, you're nuts. Shut up; the movie is starting."

All of a sudden, three shadowy figures blocked our view.

"Get out of our seats!" Carl said to me with his face about three inches from mine. He then grabbed my shirt by the front, lifted me out of my seat, turned me a quarter of a turn, and let go before I could get my feet under me. I sat down hard on the floor, trying to save my popcorn. He reached down and grabbed it out of my hand. Some had spilled when I fell, but he got almost a full bag. The drink that had been between my legs was spilled. I found myself in the aisle with a sore butt, and my left leg and sock were sticky-wet. Dickie did pretty much the same to Kent. He was some better; his drink missed his leg. There was Dickie, Carl, and Lou, sitting in our seats with our popcorn. Suddenly, we had nothing.

"Losers, beat feet before you get hurt." Carl snarled at us. I almost threw a punch at his face, but Kent pulled me away.

"Come on, Billy, leave them be. Let's go."

Superman pulled me up the aisle, back toward the concession stand. He was out of money, so I had to pretend to loan him a dime for popcorn and a drink.

When we ordered replacements, Mr. Stone gave us a questioning look. He didn't say anything; neither did we. Back we went into the theater and sat as far from Dickie, Carl, and Lou as we could. The first feature had started.

Every once in a while, we would fire a volley from our pea-shooters at the three bullies. Once I even heard Lou shout, "I better not find out who's shooting peas at us, assholes!"

The responses from the crowd came quickly. "Shut up down front—hush up—watch the movie!" Judy and Laura even joined in with a couple of shouted comments. Kent and I said not a word. We made sure our pea shooters were tucked out of sight.

We waited for a night scene when the movie theater would be very dark. We had our aim all worked out and fired five or six rounds at the bullies. Some must have scored hits because all three began to yell insults. There was so much noise that Mr. Stone came into the theater with his flashlight. He went straight to the bullies. A couple of high school boys who were juniors or seniors ratted on the three trouble makers and Mr. Stone escorted them out of the theater.

We tried not to laugh, but I think Lou spotted us. He said something to Dickie as they were leaving.

Kent and I watched the rest of *Colt 45* starring Randolph Scott, four cartoons, and an action serial called *King of the Rocket Men*. Finally, what we all had been waiting for, *The Creature from the Black Lagoon* in 3-D, began. What a great movie! There was so much screaming, that, well, if kids were dying from fright, no one would have noticed.

I remember how that day, some of the junior and senior boys had dates. Those girls were screaming right in their ears. I know now at fourteen why they pretended to be frightened: so they could hide their faces in the necks of their dates. The boys had their arms around the girls and didn't care how much they yelled. A lot of hugging was going on. I even saw one couple kissing. When I was twelve, I wondered why anyone would kiss during a monster movie. Now, I know why.

It was late afternoon when we got out of the show. We were out of peashooter ammunition; the second round of popcorn and drinks were long gone. The Charm suckers were down to the sticks.

We said goodbye to Judy and Laura. Laura smiled at me. I think they were both too hoarse to speak.

We picked up our bikes from behind the furniture store and took a right onto Seventh Street, but saw trouble looking our way. A block down Seventh Street at the corner of Seventh and Green Mountain Avenue, the two Lockharts and Lou McCulloch were sitting on their bikes, waiting like vultures.

"Kent, beat feet the other way. Ride for leather up to Highland Hardware," I said taking off.

"Cut out, I'm with you!" he yelled and began pedaling hard for Lake Street. We turned right on Lake Street and flew north toward the hardware. We figured the Lockharts might hesitate to start a fight near the hardware store since their father managed it. Well, we were wrong, because that's where they caught up with us.

"Hey, if it isn't Stupidman and his sidekick, Big Butt Gunn, king of the dummies," Dickie said, trying to be funny as he cut us off.

"You guys lost?" Lou McCulloch snarled, dropping his bike. He came at us with his fists balled up.

Alone he was half mean, but when he was with Dickie and Carl, he was full mean and crazy.

Kent, trying to keep an even voice, yelled, "Leave us alone, we haven't done anything to you!"

"Hey, Stupidman, it's not a question of what you did to us; it's a question of what we're going to do to you. The way I see it, you are 'cruisin for a bruisin'!" Carl shouted.

"I got this one. BB, here's a knuckle sandwich just for you," said Dickie pointing at me. "Carl, you and Lou pound on Stupidman. First one who draws blood wins the prize."

All three dropped their bikes. We were surrounded. If we tried to hop on our bikes, we would get clobbered. If we dropped our bikes and ran, they would destroy our bikes and track us down before we could get home. Either way, we were in for a beating. If we stayed and fought them, we might save our bikes. Kent and I dropped our bikes, stepped away from them, got back to back, and got ready for a pounding. Three against two with the three being older and bigger. Things did not look too good for the home team.

"Hey, Billy, what are you doing?" A man's voice called from the direction of the hardware store.

I looked around and darned if it wasn't Mr. Cubley. You know, when you're scared the strangest thoughts come into your mind. I looked at his feet to see if he was wearing white shoes. Well, he wasn't. In fact, he was wearing big boots. Big enough to stomp some kids if he wanted.

"I told you to meet me here to help me load supplies for the hotel. You can play with your little friends another time. Now get to it." He moved toward us like he was mad. He even gave Kent and me a mean look.

"Uh, that's okay, mister, we gotta scram. See ya, BB. See ya, Superman. Goodbye, sir," said Dickie, just as nice as you please. Off the three went on their bikes in a hurry.

"Billy, who's your friend?" Mr. Cubley asked me. He had a look on his face like he recognized Kent from somewhere.

"Wow, Mr. Cubley, it sure is good seeing you here. This is my best buddy, Kent Clark. We were on our way back home from the movies when we ran into the Lockhart brothers and Lou Mc-Culloch. Whew... that was a close one! Kent, this is Mr. Matthew Cubley." I explained how I met Mr. Cubley and caught myself rattling as Mom would say. Also, this was as great an introduction as I had ever given in my life.

"Pleased to meet you, sir," Kent responded. He also extended his hand. I noticed his hand was shaking; just a little, not a lot. Mr. Cubley took it and shook it.

"Well, you boys going to be all right if I go in and pick up my supplies?" Mr. Cubley asked.

"Oh, we should be okay now. Those bullies lit off toward town. We'll be heading north and home. Can we help you with your stuff?"

"No, I think I can handle a box of screws and a light fixture," Mr. Cubley said laughing.

"Well, thanks for showing up when you did. You saved us from a scrape. Really!"

Mr. Cubley turned, waved a farewell, and headed toward the door of the hardware. Kent and I picked up our bikes, dusted them off with our hands, and rode north, away from the bullies. We took a right onto Beechwood, I dropped off at Main and pedaled for the garage. Kent rode on home, which wasn't far.

When I got home, Dad met me at the back door.

"Hey Billy, was the show good?" he asked.

"Yes, sir, the movie was like wow." I left out the part about the scrape with the bullies—also, no mention of Mr. Cubley or his shoes. I knew fighting my own scrapes was part of growing up, but was mighty glad Mr. Cubley showed up when he did. We sure seemed to be running into each other a lot for him just arriving into town. Some things seem to work out that way.

I also could not for the life of me figure out what was wrong with white shoes. Even today, I'm careful not to buy any and would never wear them on a date.

Mom had supper ready and on the table as soon as I walked in. She sent Dad and me to wash up. Grandma and Scotty were already at the table waiting. After Dad said grace, Mom informed us she had learned a whole lot of stuff at the beauty parlor.

"What?" Dad asked.

Mom smiled at Dad, but there was something odd in her smile.

"You were so wrong about Mr. Cubley. I found out all about him."

"Oh yeah, who from?" Dad asked as he took a helping of pot roast.

"A most reliable source. You know Frank Dalton, the lawyer who did the closing on this place after the war? Well, his secretary, Carol Martin, was in the beauty parlor. She told me all about Mr. Matthew Cubley. It is quite sad what happened to him."

Mom filled Scotty's plate and told Grandma to let him eat without help. Grandma ignored her, but Mom got busy telling Dad all about Mr. Cubley, so she didn't notice her feeding Scotty, who was trying to decide if he wanted to pick his nose or eat the meat.

"Well, Matthew Cubley was married. He had a little boy, Jack; a little younger than Scotty. His wife's name was Janet. She and Mr. Cubley were the perfect couple. They lived in Roanoke. He's a lawyer, of all things, and he worked for the City of Roanoke, Commonwealth's Attorney. She told me a drunk driver killed his wife and child. Isn't that just terrible? After the funerals, poor Mr. Cubley quit his job. His friends weren't sure he would make it or even where he was for a short while." Mom drank some tea and continued. Dad stopped eating to listen.

"Then, when he started to recover a little, his Uncle TJ died. His parents died about five years ago. He's all alone. I just don't know how a body could stand that much tragedy. Well, he was coming to take over the hotel here when he ran into the big wreck." Mom took another drink of iced tea and paused to watch Grandma do the airplane thing with Scotty. Least he was not picking his nose. She shrugged her shoulders and started back, telling Dad her news. Dad returned to eating his pot roast and potatoes.

"Well, Carol told us, here he comes to Highland; darn if he doesn't run smack into the worst wreck in years, right at the foot of Smith's Gap. He was the first one at the scene and to hear her tell it, he may have saved the life of the driver of the logging truck. He most certainly saved his arm, according to one of the firemen who rode to the hospital in the ambulance."

"I thought you said this guy was a lawyer. How did he manage that? I mean, how did he know what to do for that truck driver?" Dad asked, and he had stopped eating again to listen.

"Mr. Cubley was a member of the Roanoke First Aid and Life Saving Crew. Carol said it was a rescue thing in Roanoke like the Waynesboro First Aid Crew, only older. He even was on the call where his wife and boy were killed. They say several of the rescue men almost had to fight him to get him to stay away from the car. When he found out his boy was killed right off, he really broke down. The police knew him from work, so they took him to the hospital right behind the ambulance, or he would have fought them for sure and gotten right in the back of the ambulance. Can you imagine how hard it must have been for him to help that truck driver? He even tried to help Mr. Beamis, but there was nothing he could do. Now, aren't you ashamed of yourself for talking ugly about that poor man?"

Mom was staring at Dad.

"Laura Jane, I didn't know. I guess I had him figured wrong."

Dad looked ashamed, which was unusual for him. He usually just retreated to the garage. Grandma looked like she might say something, thought better of it, and went on another round of airplane landings.

I said not a word but took it all in. My favorite person in the whole world, apart from my family, was Miss Jones. But that day, I added Mr. Cubley to my list. He had lived a sad life, but he still managed to be nice.

Supper ended when Scotty threw his cup of milk across the table, knocking over Grandma's ice tea.

That summer, I loved it when Scotty got into trouble. I still do.

CHAPTER 11

LEARNING THE LAY OF THE LAND
Sunday, June 5, 1955

Matt was learning that Sundays were not days of rest in the hotel business. No, Sunday was often the busiest day of the week. Matt hadn't slept the previous night. He'd dreamt about his wife and little boy being lost on the other side of a raging river. He hadn't been able to get to them and fell out of bed in a sweat.

Billy's friend reminded him of Jack. His manner or the way he moved, something. He had given up on sleep, began his uncle's first edition of Hemingway's *The Old Man and the Sea,* and read until dawn.

Today, he was making an effort, despite being tired, of learning the hotel business. What he desired to do today was walk off into the mountains and never come back, but he had this hotel to run. Good people depended on him.

Sunday was the usual day for guests to check-out and check-in, and many of the guests who were leaving looked forward to Sunday lunch as a special ending to their stay. While guest check-out time was eleven o'clock, many hung around for lunch. Sunday lunch at Cubley's Coze was also a big attraction for the after-church crowd.

Both the religious and non-believers loved Maddie's black pot chicken and mashed potatoes covered in gravy, along with her fresh fruit, vegetables, cakes, and pies. Sunday usually meant the dining and banquet rooms were full except when the factory closed for the summer vacation week.

The first week of June was when they hired and trained the new staff for the summer season. Matt was trying to learn names, learn the business, and stay out of the way, all at the same time. Guests had also been dropping hints that they wanted to meet the new owner, and Matt realized it was to size him up against his Uncle

TJ. All this activity was keeping his mind occupied and his body moving.

The senior lady who usually supervised the dining room was with her brother, who was having an operation. A real godsend was the waitress everyone called "Boo." Her real name was Beverly Olivia Skelton, but Boo had been her nickname since first grade. She was a university student who had worked for Uncle TJ as a summer waitress for the last two years. Boo was both smart and mature, and Chuck placed her in charge of the dining room the day she returned from school. She agreed to fill in during the absence of the normal supervisor, and, despite her young age, had things under control.

Matt's attorney, Frank Dalton, arrived for lunch with his wife, Sam. The three chatted in the lobby until their table was ready.

Chuck then introduced Matt to a local trooper, Bobby Giles, and his family, and the two men instantly took a liking to each other. They conversed until all too quickly a line formed to meet the new owner. Chuck was doing his best to introduce him to the regulars, but Matt felt overwhelmed. Many names were forgotten in the rush of people.

After lunch, Matt joined several guests on the veranda, a convenient place that granted the hotel guests and locals an opportunity to meet him more leisurely.

A lady with a little girl of six appeared on the veranda. They looked around, hesitated, and finally walked into the lobby. Matt noticed their clothes were worn, they had no luggage, nor did they walk toward the dining room. No car or taxi had driven up in the last ten minutes. He wondered how they had arrived.

Chuck walked onto the veranda with the mother who had the daughter in tow. When he spotted Matt, he brought the pair over.

"Mrs. Betty Sue Bondurant, I would like to introduce you to Mr. Matthew Cubley, the new owner of Cubley's Coze. Matthew, this is Mrs. Bondurant and her daughter, Bonnie Jane. Mrs. Bondurant's husband was the driver of the logging truck. She would like a word with you."

Chuck, after making the introduction, glanced at the lobby to hint to Matt that he might want to take this conversation to his office. Matt took the extended hand of Mrs. Bondurant and suggested,

"Mrs. Bondurant, please come into the hotel office where things are a little quieter."

He whispered something else to Chuck as he started to usher them into the lobby. Chuck smiled and said to the mother and daughter, "Bonnie Jane, do you like vanilla ice cream with chocolate fudge over the top? If that's okay with your mother?" Chuck looked at the mother for a response, but Bonnie Jane was ahead of him and her mother.

"Mom, may I? That would be so nice. I haven't had ice cream in ages. May I?" The little girl was almost jumping across the veranda rather than walking.

"Bonnie Jane, stop jumping. If you are quiet while Mr. Cubley and I have a conversation, you may have some ice cream. Not too much, you know how sugar gets you all in a dither," her mother said with a smile.

Once in the office with Bonnie Jane enjoying her ice cream, Matt asked, "How is your husband?"

"He's doing better, at least physically. He's home, but can barely move. We don't know when he'll be able to get back to work. Since he can't come in person, he asked me to come by to thank you for all you did. I also want to thank you because the doctor said your care saved his arm. God sent you. I thank you and the good Lord." She then reached over with a handkerchief and wiped the child's face.

"Momma!" Bonnie Jane fussed at being interrupted while eating the treat. She went back to spooning in the ice cream.

"Bonnie Jane, slow down, or you'll give yourself a headache," her mother scolded while placing the handkerchief on the child's lap.

"Mrs. Bondurant, you said he was doing better at least physically, does that mean he's having some other kind of problem?" Matt looked at the lady to see her expression.

"He feels terrible. He blames himself for the death of that poor farmer. That deputy, who's related to his boss man, came by the Lynchburg hospital to talk to him. When he left, Billy Ray—that's my husband's name, Billy Ray Bondurant—he was all tore up."

"Sergeant Little John McCulloch, I believe, is the deputy's name. I, too, had a run-in with him. He struck me as not being overly concerned with people's feelings. Did he threaten to arrest your husband?"

As Matt was asking, he took out a couple of sheets of paper from a side drawer of his desk. On the top sheet, he wrote a quick sentence, stood, and walked over to a pass-through where he put the note in the box. He knocked a couple of times on the little door on the other side. It was immediately opened and the paper was removed. Matt walked back over to his chair and sat down. Then, Mrs. Bondurant began answering Matt's last question.

"No, just the opposite. When Billy Ray told him the brakes failed on the truck, the officer got angry. He told Billy Ray to keep his mouth shut because there was nothing wrong with the brakes. My husband told me this officer demanded he swear that Mr. Beamis pulled out in front of him, which isn't true. That officer is trying to make it look like that poor farmer was at fault. He's forcing my husband to lie."

Mrs. Bondurant looked like she was about to cry. She took a deep breath and continued. "Mr. Cubley, may I share something with you? Please don't get mad at me."

"I promise not to get mad. What is it?" asked Matt.

"Officer McCulloch told Billy Ray you saw what happened. That officer told him that you saw the farmer pull out right in front of his log truck. But, now you're saying there was nothing Billy Ray could do."

Before Matt could answer, Mrs. Bondurant added, "Perhaps my husband is just confused. Billy Ray is insisting his brakes were bad. Been bad since the day he started driving that truck. But when he reported it to his foreman, he was told the brakes were fine, that they just needed a little fluid. What that foreman then said, makes no sense. That foreman claimed a plant rule required him to wait to replace the brakes. How is that right? The other drivers told my husband he better keep quiet about it, or he would lose his job. Billy Ray said he didn't know what to do. He had to have his job. He even tried to fix the brake line his self, but his fix may not have held."

Mrs. Bondurant looked over at Bonnie Jane. Matt started to answer her, but he decided to wait until she had finished all she had to say.

"Mr. Cubley, Billy Ray is scared. Real scared. He's afraid of what might happen to him. He's heard stories about what happened to a man who tried to cause trouble over some broken saw—that man's in jail. So, Billy Ray is going to keep quiet for the sake of Bonnie Jane and me, but he thinks the wreck's his fault. What are we to do?"

It was as if a flood of words had come through the office, but now the force of it was exhausted, and all that was left were puddles.

Matt saw tears in her eyes. She had a pleading look on her face.

"Mrs. Bondurant, that officer is lying. I told him what I saw, but I don't think he even wrote it down. The pickup pulled out and was driving down the road when the log truck came around the final curve into sight. Your husband's brake lights went on as soon as he saw the farmer. That log truck did not slow down one bit. I didn't know whether the brakes were bad all of a sudden or not. Now with what you just told me, it looks like he was put in a bad spot by his foreman."

Matt sighed, paused, and finished with, "You know, I think your husband is going to have to wait this out. Tell him his version is the way I saw it. He should stick to it because he's not confused. It would be wrong for him to lie, no matter who says he must. I have to warn him; the truth could also cause him trouble. I can't tell him otherwise. The law makes the driver responsible for the truck he's driving. You'll have to support him and help him work through this. I know how death can weigh on a person, but he has you and Bonnie Jane."

Mrs. Bondurant smiled and thanked Matt for his time, for letting her know the truth, and for the ice cream. The timing for them to leave was perfect. Maddie Johnson came into the office carrying three large paper sacks from the kitchen. She put them into a burlap sack that thirty pounds of beans had come in and handed the burlap sack to Matt.

"Mr. Matthew, here are the three dinners you wanted. I also put in some extra biscuits and three slices of my spice cake."

Matt handed the sack to Mrs. Bondurant.

"Ma'am, you take these dinners home. I want all three of you to have a nice supper. I know when trouble comes, the last thing you want to do is cook."

Matt saw her start to say no, but change her mind. She looked at Bonnie Jane and took the sack with a quiet, "We owe you, you don't owe us. Thank you."

Taking Bonnie Jane's hand with her free hand, the two walked back out into the lobby. Matt walked out behind them and asked, "How did you arrive here?"

"We walked," responded Mrs. Bondurant.

Just then, Matt saw Frank Dalton and Sam about to leave.

"Frank, could I have a word? Mrs. Bondurant, wait here just a moment."

Matt took Frank and Sam into the office, where he gave Frank a summary of what had just happened. He then asked Frank to drive the mother and child back into town if he didn't mind.

"Of course we don't mind," said Sam for Frank.

Then, the three returned to the lobby, and Matt introduced the couple to Mrs. Bondurant and Bonnie Jane. The four departed in Frank's car.

That couple might need a competent attorney, and my little introduction will allow both parties to get acquainted for the Bondurants' future benefit.

Shaking his head about how quickly a stranger could get into the middle of so much, so fast, he retreated to his apartment to study the papers left to him by his Uncle TJ. A good hour passed when he was interrupted by a knock on his door.

"Just a minute," he called out. He quickly put the papers in the briefcase, put it in the safe, locked the safe, and closed the bookcase. Matt opened the apartment door and there was Chuck.

"Sorry to bother you, Matt, but you will not guess who is at your door now."

"Okay, I give up. Who is it?"

"Sergeant McCulloch of the Town of Highland Police Department," Chuck said with a look showing that he was thinking, *oh boy, trouble is in the lobby.*

"I guess I better go see what he wants," said Matt, locking his apartment door. He rattled the doorknob a second time to be sure it closed and followed Chuck down the stairs to the lobby.

"Sergeant McCulloch, nice to see you again. What can I do for you?" Matt asked as he extended his hand to the officer.

The sergeant looked like it pained him to take the offered hand. He gave it only a quick shake.

"We need to talk, right now," McCulloch demanded.

"That's why I came down here to meet with you. How about stepping into my office?" Matt decided to act overly polite since the officer was still acting like a jerk. He also decided to stop using his title of sergeant, but to only use the title "officer," and over-emphasized, "my office."

Once seated, Matt looked at the sergeant with an expectant expression and a raised eyebrow.

"Mr. Cubley, I hear you are the owner of this hotel. That right?" The sergeant squinted at Matt and leaned toward him.

"Yes, Officer. I officially found out from Attorney Dalton, right after—yes—right after the wreck on Friday. I presently enjoy being the owner of this hotel. Did you come here to congratulate me? That is so nice but unnecessary."

"What? No! Now you listen here. What we need to discuss is much more important." Sergeant McCulloch was not smiling.

"Okay, Officer, I'm all ears. What's on your mind?" Matt said with a benign smile on his lips, but his blue eyes grew colder.

"Mr. Cubley, it would be in your best interest—your very best interest—not to discuss the Beamis wreck with the general public. In fact, you should not be discussing the facts of this case with anyone who is not a police official."

Sergeant McCulloch folded his arms and leaned back into his chair as if this would conclude further discussion on the matter. He peered at Matt with a raised right eyebrow like a punctuation mark.

Matt dropped the smile and turned a steely stare on the sergeant.

"Interesting comment, Officer McCulloch. May I ask by what authority you are placing a gag order on me? More specifically, what court issued this order of yours? May I have my copy?"

Matt asked, almost sure of the answer, but waiting with interest for Sergeant McCulloch's explanation of this blatant fabrication.

"Court order! Court order! What the hell do you mean court order? I told you, and that is all you—I need. You want me to lock you up? What are you, a damn Red? Court order my ass; I'll show you a court order!" Sergeant McCulloch turned red in the face.

"Officer McCulloch, without a court order, you have no authority—none! I will decide with whom I might want to discuss the Beamis matter until a court of law orders me not to discuss it. It has been my experience that courts are very reluctant to issue gag orders, even as a jury trial approaches, and to my knowledge, no one has even been arrested, yet."

"Listen here! Don't you play the two-bit lawyer with me! You run your mouth about this wreck, you'll find out whose boar ate the cabbage."

Sergeant McCulloch started to rise, but Matt waved at him to sit down in his chair. Matt was a little surprised when Sergeant McCulloch did sit back down.

Matt changed his tone slightly. "Officer, I have no intention of running my mouth about that wreck, and… I do not want a fight with you or your department. I hope you don't intend on having one with me. I don't plan on picking a fight with anybody over something that doesn't affect me one way or the other. As for playing a two-bit lawyer, well, I plead guilty to the lawyer part. The two-bit part, I might argue over that one. My fees run slightly higher than two-bits," Matt replied with a shadow of a smile, but his eyes, they were glacial.

"Lawyer, humph!" responded the sergeant.

"If you want to see my license to practice in the courts of Virginia, it's in my apartment upstairs. I'll be glad to show it to you if you doubt my credentials. I know the law, and without a court order, police do not have the authority to make up gag orders, let alone enforce them. Now, is there any other subject you would like to debate with me? I find a good debate is most refreshing. This last little intellectual exercise has been delightful. I would love to engage you in others." Matt grinned like a fox and waited for an explosion.

Sergeant McCulloch's face went livid. He looked like he might be a candidate for a full-blown heart attack or stroke. His jaw was set and his hand went to his pistol. Matt was not sure how much adjusting of the gun was an actual threat and how much was bravado because this officer was used to people cow-towing to him.

"Cubley, I see talking to you is a waste of my time. You better watch your *P's* and *Q's* if you know what's good for you."

Sergeant McCulloch started for the door to the office, and Matt hurried around the desk to escort him out. The visitor was not waiting for his host.

"Officer, I'm glad we had this little discussion, and we were able to enjoy a meeting of the minds. Come back anytime; coffee and dessert are on the house whenever you visit."

One of the guests crossing the lobby and hearing this last comment said to his wife, "Isn't that nice; this hotel honors our men in uniform."

Sergeant McCulloch gave the man a withering glare and barged out of the lobby. When he drove off, he sprayed gravel into the yard of the hotel from the spinning rear wheels of his patrol car.

Matt walked back to the front desk. Chuck smiled at Matt and quietly said, "That went about as well as I expected."

"Were you able to hear our conversation?" Matt inquired, smiling at Chuck.

"I did and hoped you didn't mind. Somehow, the letterbox pass-through was accidentally left open."

"Chuck, that man just makes me mad. I normally don't bait police officers, but I can't help it with Little John. I guess you noticed; I kept calling him officer rather than using his rank of sergeant. I overheard at the wreck that he's sensitive about his rank."

Matt chuckled and returned to his office.

He called out, "Is that pass-through okay for mail, or is it only to be used to listen in on my conversations?"

"Well, both, I guess, but listening in is usually more fun," replied Chuck.

"Who cut the hole in the wall?" Matt asked.

"Your uncle cut it and installed a mailbox inside the thick wall with a door on each side. He did it so the desk clerk could retrieve letters he was mailing, and later discovered it allowed eavesdropping from either side. He thought it was ingenious and guests would not notice it."

"Did Uncle TJ add some other improvements to the hotel?" Matt asked Chuck to see if Chuck knew about some or all of the secrets shown on the family map.

"Your grandfather did. When the hotel was built, your grandfather hired workers from Germany. No local laborers built it, which caused resentment, but all the secrets remained secret."

"My family is full of surprises," Matt said.

"After I close up tonight, I'll show you the false wall in one of the storage rooms. You can slip behind this sliding wall, watch and hear what is going on in the banquet room. Uncle TJ told me his dad listened in on the secret meetings of the Masons. He was able to make some shrewd investments from the knowledge he gained from his hidey-hole. There were rumors of KKK meetings, but your uncle wouldn't talk about them. I've only been in there once. I'm certain we are the only ones who know about the little secret room," whispered Chuck to Matt.

"I never knew my grandfather and uncle came from a long line of devious hotel owners. Perhaps I should write a spy novel. Better keep this to ourselves, or we may find ourselves carted off to Washington to appear in front of the House Committee on Un-American Activities. They scare me more than the KKK," Matt contended with a frown.

"I watched news reports about some of the hearings on TV. I agree. They scare me more than the Reds they're investigating," Chuck quickly concluded when he saw a guest approaching.

Matt stood in his office beside the letterbox cubby hole to hear how the thing worked. He learned he could listen to everything that was said at the front desk. He noticed a knob on the inside of each door as well as on the outside of each one. This allowed one to close both doors from either side and cut off eavesdropping.

When the guests all retired, Chuck took Matt up to the linen closet on the second floor near Matt's room. He showed him how the latch worked on the false wall and how one could slip into the secret space. There was a tab on the wall that opened an eye hole. A vent in the wall allowed the eavesdropper to listen to what was being said in the banquet room.

Matt wondered if the Cubley menfolk might have been spies. He doubted he would ever use these unusual features because this was Highland, Virginia, not Washington, Germany, Japan, or Moscow. He watched Chuck return the wall to its original position, and they both retired for the evening, failing to appreciate the value of this secret room.

CHAPTER 12

BILLY AND BUSINESS
Monday, June 6, 1955

The day was cloudy, and it looked like rain. Dad got me up early because he said there was a lot of work to do and he could use my help. We no sooner started to work in the garage when a Virginia State Police car pulled into Dad's lot. Dust from the tires settled where he stopped.

Trooper Giles got out and walked up to Dad with a friendly, "Good morning, John; hello, Billy."

This trooper was the nicest of them all. Everyone in the county said so. Heck, he was even kind to the criminals he arrested. He learned my name when I was a little kid, and he always greeted me.

"Bobby, how's it going?" Dad asked and smiled at Trooper Giles.

"Can't complain, John. How about yourself?"

"Busy, but I guess that's good," Dad answered while wiping his hands on a rag. Only then did he shake the trooper's hand.

"How's the sergeant? The last time I saw him, he was hot. I thought he was going to shoot one of the town officers." Dad asked this with an apologetic look. I was wondering how or if Trooper Giles would answer.

"Well, John, between you and me and that post over there, he was just about as mad as I've ever seen the man. When the governor tells a sergeant that he can't investigate a state highway fatality, you can bet the farm you have one mad sergeant on your hands."

"Been hearing the same thing all over town."

"None of us liked it. To rub salt in the wound, telling the Virginia State Police to hand a fatal wreck investigation over to a town police department—a couple of bridges got burned that might not get replaced anytime soon."

Trooper Giles was almost whispering as if he was afraid someone might be listening beside the three of us and the post he mentioned. Of course, me being a kid, I was invisible. I knew that as long as I stayed silent, I could learn all kinds of secrets from adults. I remained as quiet as a mouse.

"I don't blame the sergeant. Having the Highland special police, who we all know are nothing but puppets for Big John, investigate a wreck involving one of his trucks is bad business."

The trooper blurted out, "John, it stinks."

Dad went on. "Based on what I saw, that log truck might have been overloaded. It took me longer than it should have to clean up a single load of logs. The Highland Police were not even counting the logs as they removed them. I guarantee they didn't weigh the load at the plant."

"First thing, I would have called out the scale boys to check the weight," stated the trooper.

"Bobby, it took them two trips to get those logs to the plant. Poor old Mr. Beamis never stood a chance, and that log truck driver is lucky to be alive." Dad was also whispering, trying not to be overheard.

"Well, enough said. John, my blue and gray is acting up. I was on a blood run the other night. Had to get three units from Lynchburg to Charlottesville. Whenever I got her above a hundred, she seemed to hesitate. Gas mileage is down a little, too. Could you take a look? No hurry. I'm off for two days and can leave her with you. Mike Quinn will be by in a minute to pick me up if you have the time?"

Trooper Giles always asked Dad if he had time, even when Dad was sitting in the garage, taking it easy, and listening to the radio.

"Bobby, I'll make time. I know you take care of that state car better than your own. Hell, the money you put into her, they ought to transfer the title into your name. Go ahead and pull into the garage; park over on the left. I'll start on her this afternoon," Dad answered and pointed to an empty space.

"Need any money upfront?" asked the trooper.

"Not yet. Once I know what I have, I'll give you a call on the damages. I'll get Billy to wash her. No charge. You got all your guns out?" Dad asked, glancing at me.

"Yeah, John. Cleaned them out this morning before I came over. I left my new radar unit at home too. I would hate to get that thing stolen. I might never get the state paid back for that piece of equipment."

"You'll have to show me how that new contraption works. I hear it's something. Boys down at the SFW were talking about it," said Dad.

I knew he was talking about the men's club called the Soldiers of Foreign Wars. Mom hated the place. She refused to go to what she referred to as that beer hall for drunks.

Dad then asked, "You got any idea what might be wrong with your blue and gray?"

"Glad you asked. I think the timing is off, but I'll leave it to the expert."

"Bobby, everyone knows you're the best wheelman in the Third Division, and most say in the state. If you think the timing is off, I'll check it first. It's either that, a bad spark plug, or a bad contact in the distributor. Whatever it is, I'll find it."

Trooper Giles pulled his car into the garage and bumped the siren for me. He was cool like that.

When the trooper got out of his car, Dad asked, "How do you like the new headquarters over in Appomattox? I hear it's something."

"It's first-rate. Stop by sometime, and I'll give you a tour."

"Can I come, too?" I asked, earning a look from Dad that could go either way.

"Why sure, Billy, you have your dad bring you. I'll give you a special tour. The one we reserve for good friends of the Virginia State Police." Trooper Giles gave me a big smile.

We all heard Trooper Quinn pull in on the gravels. It took a moment for the dust to settle. He waved to Dad. I waved to the trooper, but guess he didn't see me. Trooper Giles got in on the passenger side, they backed out onto the street and drove toward town.

No sooner did they leave than Matthew Cubley pulled into the lot in his 1955 Chevrolet Bel Air. It was a beauty with a white top, blue body, and white trim on the rear fenders. He got out and called, "Hey, John, how's your Monday going?"

"Well, it's going fine, Matt. What brings you by this morning? Your guest leave his spotlight on all night again?" Dad must be in a good mood because he omitted the word idiot.

"No, the guests don't seem to be tearing up anything on their cars today. I'm here for an oil change."

"When do you need it?" Dad asked and smiled at him.

This time, Dad was a lot warmer toward Mr. Cubley. I noticed Mr. Cubley was not wearing white shoes.

"How about I drop it off tomorrow?"

"Sure. You gonna wait?" asked Dad.

"No, I'll get someone from the hotel to follow me down, and I'll leave it. I have to admit; it's a little overdue but not by much. Does that sound okay?"

"Sounds good to me," Dad said.

"Say, was that the state police I just saw pulling out of your lot?" Mr. Cubley asked Dad. "One of the troopers may want to talk to me."

"Yeah, Trooper Giles dropped his car off for me to check out. He's as particular about that car as an old lady. He won't let the state police mechanic touch it. Pays me to work on it out of his own pocket. He keeps it in perfect shape. Very few around here can outrun Trooper Giles. He isn't after you, is he?" Dad joked and laughed.

"No, nothing like that. I saw that wreck happen out on State Route 22. I was wondering if one of the troopers might want to talk to me. The town police sergeant already did, but I was not impressed. That man was more interested in burying the facts than finding them." Mr. Cubley shook his head in disgust.

"What did you expect? His father, Big John, owns the factory, several stores in town, and the Green Mountain Resort, so he thinks he runs the world. The guy has brass. He called the governor and got the state police taken off the wreck investigation. His son and the Younger boys are now in charge."

"It's a fact then, they are doing the whole investigation," responded Mr. Cubley.

"Cover-up would be more like it. I heard part of the conversation when the state police were pulled off, leaving those troopers hop'n mad. You say you saw the wreck happen?" Dad asked and moved closer to Mr. Cubley.

"Yeah, it wasn't good." Mr. Cubley told my dad all about what he saw. He finished with, "I found out the log truck driver's name is Billy Ray Bondurant. Do you know him?"

"Don't think I do," Dad answered thoughtfully.

"Well, his wife and daughter came by the hotel. She seems like a nice person, and the daughter was well behaved. Her husband sounds like he is honest because he told her that his log truck had bad brakes. The wife is worried about what the local cops might do to him if he doesn't lie for the company," concluded Mr. Cubley.

"I would be, too," agreed my dad.

"Sergeant McCulloch is not helping. That puffed-up toad came by the hotel yesterday and told me to keep my mouth shut about the wreck or else."

"Typical for Little John," Dad added.

"Well, that didn't sit well with me. I had just talked with Mrs. Bondurant. His attitude got me steamed, so I gave that officer a short course on the law. So much for making new friends in high places." Mr. Cubley said with a sinister laugh.

Mr. Cubley seemed relieved that he was able to unload all of this on someone. I guessed since Dad and I were at the wreck and knew a bunch, he felt he could confide in us. Wow, did I have a lot to tell Kent.

My thoughts were interrupted by Dad warning Mr. Cubley, "Well, the McCullochs run things here in Highland and Green Mountain County. They don't own me, but they think they can tell everybody what to do. That's the cloth they're cut from. You better watch yourself."

This was confession day for adults. I never heard my dad say anything like this to anybody but Mom. Here he was, telling this stuff to Mr. Cubley.

Mr. Cubley's next statement changed my life. "Thanks, I'll be careful. I'll bring my car in first thing tomorrow. Oh, I have a question about some business for you and Billy to consider, if you have a minute?"

Dad turned around and came back to Mr. Cubley.

"Shoot," my dad responded. "Always interested in business."

Mr. Cubley looked serious and began with, "Good, and I don't need an answer today. I expect you will need to talk this over as a family."

"Not interested in selling, got too much invested in the place," Dad stated with a shake of his head.

"No, nothing like that. I got more than I can handle, running the hotel."

"Matt, I bet you do. I bet you do," my dad agreed.

"This is for Billy. The guests at the hotel want someone to wash their cars. Richard and the maintenance crew don't have the time, and the rest of the staff are inside workers. I was wondering if Billy might want a summer job? It won't be every day, only when we need him. If he does a good job, we might be able to collect fifty cents a car. The hotel will provide the supplies. Think it over and let me know what you all decide. If he can't, I understand but thought I would give him first refusal. If you say no, I'm interested in the names of other kids who might want a summer job." Matt looked at Dad to see if he could detect a reaction.

"Let me give this some thought," Dad said and then added, "I've been using him around the garage, but I'm getting to the point that I need a man full time. His mom will have to say okay, but we will sure give it some thought. My only concern will be if I need him here on a day you need him, that might be a problem."

"Dad, can we include Kent in this? If I have to work here, he can cover for me at the hotel. Also, with two of us working, we might be able to do a better job and do it faster." When I finished, I looked first at Mr. Cubley, who was smiling and then at Dad, who was not.

"Well, just speak right on up and interrupt anytime, son. Just anytime." Dad let me know my suggestion was about to earn me a bit of trouble.

"John, that doesn't sound like a bad idea. Sometimes our guests want a rush job and having two workers might be helpful. Is this the boy that I saw you with at the hardware?"

"Yes, sir."

"Is he dependable, Billy?" Mr. Cubley asked, looking at me like I was all grown up.

"Oh, he's very honest and very dependable, Mr. Cubley. He and his mom could also use the extra cash," I added, hoping that this would lessen the frown that had started to form on Dad's face.

"Boy, don't you go jumping the gun. Your mom gets the last word on you working." Dad turned back to the garage, signaling this discussion was over.

Mr. Cubley smiled at me, got in his car, waved, and drove out of the lot.

I could hardly wait to call Kent with all this news, but I knew better than to push it. I followed Dad into the garage, and for the rest of the day, I tried to be good, work hard, and not say much.

A little after dark, Dad got a call for a tow. He took Blacky and headed over to Highway 151 to pick up a car that had gone into a ditch. Since it was about my bedtime, I didn't get to go with him. It really messed things up because I was going to listen in on the conversation that I knew he would have with Mom about the hotel job. I tried to stay awake until he got home, but like Christmas, my eyes got heavy. The next thing I knew, it was morning. When Mom called me for breakfast, I was almost dressed. I was down those stairs in a flash. Scotty was the sleepyhead today. Grandma had to go upstairs twice to get him up.

Over breakfast, Mom and Dad said they thought, with the emphasis on thought, that if Kent's mom agreed, they would let Kent and me try out this hotel job for two weeks. If things worked out and we did a good job for Mr. Cubley—we better, if we knew what was good for us—we could work for him over the summer. Dad also told Mom he was going to hire a man to help him in the garage. Provided, he could find someone decent, who was not an idiot.

Mom called Mrs. Clark with the news about working at the hotel. We drove over to Kent's house before eight-thirty. Kent's mom was just coming out the door.

"Laura Jane, glad you caught me before I left for work. The bank president has been on my case lately. He had me working extra hours twice last week," complained Kent's mom.

While Mom and Mrs. Clark talked, I filled Kent in on the offer. We both thought it was great. Working at the hotel, getting paid, seeing who might be staying at the hotel, and if all that ice cream was going to waste, well, we would do our best to help them with that problem.

Mom and Mrs. Clark then gave us the bad news. They expected us to save half of what we earned for college. Well, there went our riches right into a dumb old savings account at the First National Bank of Highland.

Kent and I began to figure our finances. If we worked hard, we could do at least five cars a day, seven days a week. That let us clear fifty cents a car, totaling two dollars and fifty cents a day. Then, multiply times seven, so that was seventeen dollars and fifty cents a week divided by two. That meant I could take home eight dollars and seventy-five cents a week. And while I had to give Mom half of my hard-earned money that still left a whopping four dollars and thirty-seven cents a week. Did I carry over the…well, who cared? We were going to be rich. I told Kent the total and explained the math.

"Hey, BB, you got that figured wrong," Kent said with that half-grin on his face. "Let's be realistic about this. First, neither my Mom or your parents are going to let us work on Sunday. Second, the hotel guests have to ask us. I doubt we get five cars a day. Still, several a week will keep us in baseball cards, candy, and a movie on Saturday with no trouble. Maybe we could start a bank. Let's loan kids money and collect interest."

"Kent, now look who isn't being real. You know how much trouble you had with percentages in Miss Jones's class this past year, and you want to open a bank. I just want to spend what I get. I don't plan on there being any leftover. I hope we get to start this week."

"Me too," Kent said, but he had a vacant stare, thinking about how he would be spending his loot.

"Gotta go, Mom's leaving." I hurried over and got in the front seat of our Buick. "Mom, are you going to call Mr. Cubley when we get home? Think we can start tomorrow?" I was dying to know.

"Billy, if you pester me with this hotel business, then you can just forget it. I'll let you know what I decide. I don't want you bothering me every five seconds, you hear? Now be quiet and let me drive."

Backing up was not my mom's best skill. She put the car in reverse, backed out into the street, and nearly hit a garbage can. I remained quiet. Nope, not one word from me. Besides, she missed it by a good three inches.

CHAPTER 13

WHO'S POLECAT?
Tuesday, June 7, 1955

Matt got up early to check on several hotel matters and get his car to Gunn's Garage. It was cloudy and had rained, and the ground was damp. The sun was now peeking through the clouds.

Richard was going to follow him over to the garage in the 1947 Ford Club Wagon, which served as the vehicle for guests of the hotel. It was dark maroon and freshly washed and waxed, and looked like a vehicle at a big city hotel rather than a country resort. Uncle TJ had always said, "If you make the guests feel important, they will return." Matt liked that philosophy and intended to adopt it. Most of all, he liked the look of the Ford wagon.

He entered the kitchen to get breakfast and speak to Maddie and Boo. Everyone was in a rush, preparing food and picking up orders. Matt knew to stay out of Maddie's way, so Matt waited on the waitresses' side of the counter for her to serve up what she wanted the help to have. If the staff was behind doing eggs for the guests, not even the owner would get an egg. One got much better food with less danger of being scolded if one was patient.

This morning his being patient earned him French toast, two strips of bacon, and a sliced fruit medley with heavy cream. Maddie pointed a long-handled spoon at the orange juice canister in the corner that was full of fresh-squeezed juice. Matt carried his fare over to the staff table next to the storage room and sat down to eat. Chuck came in as he was about to finish and got a cup of coffee for himself.

Matt noticed a bum standing at the kitchen's screen door that led out to the loading dock. He leaned over to Chuck and whispered, "Who is that at the door?"

"That's Polecat. But don't ever call him that to his face. His real name is George Washington Smith. He prefers G. W. or just Smith, but everyone in town knows him as Polecat. He delivers the *Highland Gazette* to the hotel and about every business in town."

"He's dressed like a hobo. What's his problem?" Matt asked.

"That's his way. The man is brilliant. Some say he went to Harvard, got bored, and left. Others say he worked for a professor at Princeton, got his education by simply listening to classes," stated Chuck.

"That is strange," whispered Matt.

Chuck went on, "If you want to know about the news, ask Polecat. He reads the paper from cover to cover every day and remembers everything he reads. You can ask him who got shot last December sixth, and he'll tell you all about it—who did the shooting, why, and what happened in court. The man will recite the family tree of the victim and the defendant and tell you all about the relatives. He also listens to the town gossip on his newspaper route, and not much ever gets past him. You cheat on your wife and Polecat knows all about it. Embezzle from your boss and Polecat will be at the residence long before the police arrive to make the arrest.

Your Uncle TJ always treated Polecat to free breakfasts. If we need extra papers for our guests, we get them. I think he shorts the Green Mountain Resort on papers in our favor. He has no love for the Green Mountain Resort because Big John told Polecat to stay out of the lobby because he smelled bad and he's very sensitive about insults. And, yeah, he might not bathe as often as he should, but we never mention it because if information is what you need, he's the person."

During this long monologue, Matt saw Maddie fix a plate and watched Boo carry it out to Mr. G. W. Smith. Matt cleaned his plate, finished his orange juice, got a cup of coffee, and joined Chuck on the loading dock to be formally introduced to this Polecat.

Chuck greeted Mr. Smith; then, he began an introduction as if he were introducing Matt to royalty. "Mr. Cubley, may I introduce you to Mr. George Washington Smith, a well-known member of the *Highland Gazette* staff. Mr. Smith, may I introduce you to the new owner of Cubley's Coze, Mr. Charles Matthew Cubley. Mr. Cubley is the nephew of the late Mr. T. J. Cubley. Mr. Cubley goes by his middle name, Matthew or Matt."

Polecat quickly placed his plate on the loading dock and rose from his seat. Wiping his hand on a much-soiled pants leg, he extended it to Matt and announced in a deep voice, "So pleased to meet you, Mr. Cubley. I thought your rescue of Mr. Billy Ray Bondurant was heroic. Of course, old man Beamis's death is tragic—most sad. There's a rumor that Mr. Bondurant is suffering from the malady of depression over the incident. It's quite regrettable that the state police were removed from the case by the governor because it was done in a most unorthodox manner, and I predict some serious political repercussions for our governor. Justice, I also fear, will not be served by the intervention of Mr. John Louis McCulloch, Sr., into the matter."

"Mr. Smith, I see you are very well informed," Matt responded after a pause, trying not to sound shocked, though he was amazed. Here was a brilliant mind in someone who most folks would dismiss as a dirty bum. Polecat truly was an invaluable resource.

"Mr. Cubley, I fear that trouble may be on the horizon for many. The Joshua Beamis funeral will be conducted this week at his church near Carlisle Falls. His deeply religious family will be arriving for the funeral." Polecat concluded his speech, took a seat, and picked up his plate. He then motioned for Matt and Chuck to be seated as if they were his guests on the loading dock.

Matt and Chuck pulled over two chairs. Chuck placed his off to one side, and it was then that Matt noticed, too late, a slight odor drifting downwind from Polecat.

Polecat resumed his discourse while eating. "I fear Beamis' two sons, Jacob Beamis and Joash, will not be pleased with this turn of events. They were never close to their father, who was harsh with them as children, but rumors are rife that when a Beamis is harmed, these Old Testament sons might return to town to extract retribution from everyone involved, however slight that involvement. The fact that the state police have been removed from the investigation will exacerbate the situation. I fear trouble looms for all concerned."

"Oh my, I hope I haven't caused them to come after me," Matt said with a worried look. "I tried to help Mr. Beamis, but there was nothing I could do. I had to help the log truck driver who had a chance to live."

This was not something he had experienced while serving with the Roanoke First Aid and Life Saving Crew, but mountain folk sometimes saw things differently. When death was involved, sides were drawn, and feuds were born.

"Mr. Cubley, the actions you took align with the good Samaritan parable in the New Testament. I imagine the Beamis family will pass over you. They are God-fearing and, as such, will view your conduct in a Christian light. Others, however, may not be so fortunate."

Polecat was talking and finishing his food at a rapid rate. Often holding the food between his teeth on one side of his mouth and speaking without unclamping his teeth. Often at the end of a sentence, he would chew vigorously and swallow. A quick pause for a sip of coffee, then, he would stab a morsel with his fork, pop it into his mouth, clamp down on the food, and speak again without slowing.

The conference was interrupted by Maddie yelling from the kitchen, "Mr. Smith, you hurry up and finish. I need my dishes. Can't do lunch until I get breakfast out of the way, y'all hear?"

Polecat wasn't perturbed in the least and quickly responded, "Yes, Ma'am, Mrs. Maddie, dishes will be right in. Mr. Cubley is holding me up with a plethora of questions, but I'll finish as quickly as I can."

This bum had just diverted Maddie's complaint from himself to Matt as slick as a Philadelphia lawyer. While Matt was turning red, Chuck was struggling to smother a laugh.

Polecat rose and knocked on the screen door to the kitchen. A waitress retrieved the plate and silverware. Polecat returned and sat down to finish his cup of coffee. Chuck was enjoying the show of Matt getting bested.

"Mr. Smith, was your breakfast to your satisfaction?" Matt intentionally asked, changing the subject. He wanted to assure Polecat that his free breakfasts would continue.

"Mrs. Maddie is a chef of world-class skill. Will meals continue as a gratuity, or am I to expect a debt will be incurred?" Polecat asked the critical question quite bluntly and saved Matt the trouble of broaching the subject.

"Mr. Smith, your presence here is always welcome. In fact, if your schedule would allow it, I'd be happy to chat again sometime."

Matt hoped this did not sound condescending. He was navigating uncharted waters.

"I'd be happy to adjust my schedule to accommodate your request. I look forward to talking with you again. Now, could I trouble you for a dollar until Friday? One of my customers has failed to honor his mercantile obligation to me."

"Okay," Matt said as he handed him a dollar, knowing it might never be repaid.

"I look forward to our next meeting, Mr. Smith."

Matt retreated to the kitchen, holding his wallet tightly in one hand with Chuck following behind. Matt smiled at being conned so easily out of a dollar, but as a former prosecutor, he knew the value of an informant. A good informant was worth his or her weight in gold, so breakfast plus a dollar now and then was a cheap price to pay.

Matt noticed Chuck was trying not to laugh as they retreated into the safety of the noisy kitchen.

"He is slick," Chuck said, laughing when he knew the noise would drown out his laugh. "You know that was not a loan but a gift. You will never see that dollar again."

Maddie looked at Chuck and frowned. There was nothing funny about her kitchen.

"Well, I guess I got bamboozled. Bet you've been his victim on more than one occasion," Matt said.

"Actually not. He panhandled your uncle on a regular basis but left the staff alone. I know he's never approached me for a handout. Guess the boss is fair game. You better watch out. Uncle TJ used to keep some change in his desk, just to pay off Polecat. Uncle TJ once pulled out a five-dollar bill since that was all he had on him and darn if Polecat didn't end up with it. After that, your uncle would never pull out anything in front of Polecat that he couldn't afford to lose." Chuck went behind the front desk and picked up some papers.

"Do you think Polecat is right about the Beamis family? Is trouble brewing?" Matt asked with a slight frown as he propped himself up by leaning on the front desk.

Chuck was reading the document in his hand, but he still answered, "Yeah, Polecat is right a lot more than he's wrong. The trouble with the Beamis clan—one never knows if or when they might serve up a helping of revenge. Might be tomorrow, might be next year, or never. You just don't know. And who, you might ask, needs to be worried? My guess is the log truck driver. One better not forget Big John McCulloch. If Big John wants to stay clear of trouble, he might want to send an emissary over to talk to the Beamis family before things get out of hand. If the Beamis boys find out what really happened, they might pay him a visit. Won't matter how rich Big John is if he's gifted a bullet." Chuck set the paper down, picked it up, then put it down again.

"And another thing, Big John better keep that boy of his away from the Beamis brothers. Little John can go to a prayer meeting, and within five minutes, he'll have the deacons fighting the preacher and the choir attacking the ushers. Over half his arrests include a charge of assault on a police officer with the defendant in the hospital. Meanwhile, Little John seldom shows a scratch."

Matt rubbed his temple and thought. *Well, one thing about Cubley's Coze: there are some interesting folks to meet. Maybe this is the place for me to forget my own troubles. Seems there's a lot for me to do and, so far, not a dull moment.*

"Well, look at the time, I must get over to Gunn's Garage. Have you seen Richard around?" Matt asked Chuck.

"Yeah, he's out by the loading dock sweeping up some corn that spilled. Want me to go fetch him?" he asked.

"No, I will, and I need to give Maddie back this coffee cup before she skins me alive."

"You know her bark is worse than her bite," Chuck said as he returned to his papers.

"If I return with a knife in my back, you'll know your predictions aren't as reliable as Polecat's. Maybe I should ask Polecat to give me a prediction on how much danger Maddie poses?" Matt joked.

"Well, Polecat never enters the kitchen when Maddie is on one of her tirades. Might take a lesson from that." Chuck's voice faded as Matt left the office and went into the kitchen. He was worried Maddie might have heard Chuck, but if she did, she did not let on and he passed through the kitchen unscathed.

He found Richard out back on the loading dock, taking a

smoke break.

"Richard, mind following me over to Gunn's Garage? I need to run my car in for an oil change. I'll get my keys and drive around to the dock. We can leave from here."

"Yes, sir, Mr. Matthew," Richard said, making no move to stop his smoke break. He had the keys to the hotel's Club Wagon in his pocket, having just cleaned the windshield. Bugs hitting the windshield were always a problem since the lake and the river were close. He tried his best to keep the windshield clean, but he found it hopeless once the bugs arrived with the summer heat.

Richard ended his smoke break and had the Ford ready by the time Matt drove past the hotel on his way to Gunn's Garage. He followed at a relaxed pace.

Neither man saw the Highland Police car backed into the trees at the foot of the hill. As the two vehicles drove out of the hotel drive and down Green Mountain Avenue, Sergeant John McCulloch wrote down the license number of Matt's car, folded up his pad, and proceeded on up to the Green Mountain Resort.

Polecat was watching the sergeant watching Matt, and after the sergeant drove away, he mounted his old bike and followed the police car to the Green Mountain Resort Hotel. He was on his way to deliver the leftover papers of the *Highland Gazette* to this second hotel. No free meals from this kitchen. In fact, the manager had made it clear: he was to deliver the papers to the back door entrance beside the janitor's room and was prohibited from ever entering the lobby.

Full of Maddie's breakfast, Polecat hummed a hymn as he pedaled his bike up the hill to that other hotel. He would drop off his remaining papers and depart. He was three short. Too bad if they ran out—he just didn't care.

CHAPTER 14
BILLY HAS A SCARE
Tuesday, June 7, 1955

K ent and I were hired on the first Tuesday of my summer vacation. Mom took the call from Mr. Cubley. Afterward, she called Kent to ride his bike over to the garage because Mr. Cubley wanted to explain some rules to us.

Like all kids of twelve, we thought we were going to get rich. I had dreams that summer that I might even buy a jeep and fix her up, just like Nellybelle on *Roy Rogers, the King of the West.* That show was something with Roy Rogers, Dale Evans, Trigger, Buttermilk, Bullet, and Pat Brady. Nellybelle was keen. If I had a Nellybelle, well, I could go anywhere and get away from anybody.

"Billy! Stop staring off into space and put those tools away," Dad yelled from under the hood of Trooper Giles' state police car. He determined that the timing was off, just like Trooper Giles guessed. When Dad called him with the price to fix it, he told Dad to go ahead and install a new timing chain. Dad warned him it would run close to sixty dollars, but Trooper Giles told him to do it. He needed the fastest car in the county for a job that might be coming up.

Dad was in a good mood and happy about the money he was going to earn. He told Mom at supper the night before all about his conversation with the trooper. He even mentioned that he and Trooper Giles were going to head on out to the flats on State Route 22 and try her out.

Man, did I want to go with Dad on that trip but I knew what the answer would be without asking. I heard Dad tell the trooper over the phone that he thought he could get it to run close to one hundred twenty miles per hour, maybe one-forty, once he adjusted the carburetor.

Going a hundred miles an hour in a police car. Wow! Imagine that!

Replacing a timing chain was a big job. First, Dad had to

take a lot of stuff off the engine to get the old one out. Then, he had to put all the parts back. Working until ten last night had left Mom none too happy. Dad had explained that he was behind and promised Mom he would get serious about finding another mechanic to help out around the garage.

Just then, Kent came flying into the garage lot on his bike.

"Yo, BB Gun, where are you?" Kent yelled as his bike slid to a stop with the back end, cutting a half-crescent in the gravel.

"In here, Superman. Hold your horses! Mr. Cubley ain't even here yet," I yelled at him as I put three of Dad's screwdrivers in the screwdriver drawer. Suddenly, Mom's voice reached me. I didn't know she was even around.

"Billy! Ain't is not a word. Don't let me hear you use that word again, young man, or you will be spending the summer studying proper grammar. That job that you're so excited about will go to some other boy who knows how to speak properly."

Mom had heard me as she walked into the garage from the house. Sometimes I thought she had super-hearing.

I responded quickly, "Yes, Ma'am. I mean, No, Ma'am. I won't use ain't—not never again."

"Billy, are you trying my patience?"

"No, Ma'am, I'll leave your patience to you," I said in a panic. What had I said?

"John, you need to stop using double negatives around Billy. I hear you using them in the garage and he's picking them up." Mom had crossed her arms and was tapping her foot on the cement floor of the garage.

"Yes, Laura Jane," Dad said as he kept on tightening bolts under the hood.

Lucky for me, Mr. Cubley pulled into the lot in his Chevrolet to leave it for repairs. The hotel wagon followed and parked near him. Mr. Cubley got out, waved at Kent and me, then walked over to the driver's window of the wagon. I heard him tell the driver to go ahead down to the wholesale grocery to pick up supplies. He said, "By the time you finish, I expect I'll be through." The driver, Richard Baker, nodded and drove off.

"Well, Kent, Billy, I see things are a little calmer today than when we last met." Mr. Cubley grinned at the two of us.

"What? Calmer? Have they been causing you trouble?" Mom asked.

My mom did not miss a thing. Mr. Cubley looked like he wanted to take that last sentence back, but it was too late.

"No, just kidding around, Mrs. Gunn. The last time I saw them was after a movie, and they were hot from riding their bikes. Billy and Kent have not caused me any trouble. Just the opposite." He looked like he hoped she bought it.

"Well, they better behave if they want to keep this nice job you're offering. First trouble and Billy won't sit down for a week. I'll turn him over to his dad, and that will be the end of that. I know Kent's mom; she won't stand for any funny business, either. Isn't that right, Kent?"

"No, Ma'am. My mom don't stand for no funny business," Kent said, looking real proud of himself.

"Kent Clark, you two have got to stop using double negatives, and I mean right now. You are starting to sound like white trash. I won't put up with it." Mom was starting to get that frown with the crinkles in her nose, not a good sign.

Mr. Cubley saved the day. "Mrs. Gunn, you know this job might just help with that problem as well. The guests at the hotel are from the best families of Virginia. The atmosphere at the resort might help them pick up a little better use of the King's English. What do you think?"

"I think anything would be an improvement over what Billy hears around this garage," Mom remarked while her nose crinkles smoothed out. She half-smiled at Mr. Cubley.

Dad kept his head under the hood of the police car.

"Well, young men, are you ready to hear the rules of your employment?" Mr. Cubley asked with a smile.

"Yes, sir," we both said, almost in unison.

"Okay. Here is what I have in mind, Mrs. Gunn."

He added a little louder, "Mr. Gunn."

I guess he wanted Dad to hear him, "Anything you want to change, you just let me know. I want you both, and of course, Mrs. Clark, to be happy about this arrangement."

"Good!" Mom said.

Dad responded with, "I'm leaving this up to my wife. I better not hear of any shenanigans, not from either one of you boys. You hear?"

"Yes, sir," we both said again, but this time Kent was a little slower on the response.

"Kent, Billy, it's crucial that you are honest, dependable, work hard and treat the vehicles you are cleaning better than your own—no messing around. The tires will be scrubbed until the white walls are white with all the scuff marks off. Soap and elbow grease will be liberally applied. Clean the hard-to-see parts, like under the fenders and on top of the roof. Each car will be cleaned and dried, and I don't want to see a single soap or water spot when you're done. Can you do all that?" Matt looked at us for an answer.

"Yes, sir," I said first.

"Yes, sir," Kent joined in a second later.

"Each of you will have a separate money box at the front desk. If only one of you washes a car, then all the payment goes into that boy's box. No money goes into the box until the owner approves the work. Is that clear?"

We both said, "Yes, sir." This time together and with no eye-rolling.

"Now, each time you are asked to clean the inside of the car, you will inform the owner all valuables are to be removed. The hotel will store them in the hotel safe at no charge. A wash, wax, and good cleaning will cost fifty cents, which is expensive. The finished product must be up to snuff. The hotel will furnish the water from the spring that supplies the hotel. Do not leave the hose running. If you let the cistern run dry, each of you will be held responsible. I will not accept the excuse; the other guy did it." I glanced at Kent, and he looked at me.

"Finally, I will post a sign in the lobby explaining the cost is fifty cents per car. The guest will pay the desk clerk, and you will pick up your money at the front desk. Let's talk about tips. All tips will be shared equally, regardless of who does the work. I have seen friends fall out over tips, and I do not want to see that happen. Now, any questions?" Mr. Cubley looked at Mom first.

"That sounds good to me if you think fifty cents a car is not too much." Mom answered his questioning look.

"No questions," said Kent.

"I do have one question," I said.

I glanced at Mom, and she had that look of oh, no, what now?

"Go ahead, Billy."

"Why is your hotel called Cubley's Coze?" I asked.

"Billy, we get that one a lot. When Grandpa Cubley built that hotel many years ago, he was going to name it Cubley's Cozy Inn and Tavern. His son, my uncle TJ, was just a little kid and couldn't say all that. All he could get out was 'Cubley's Coze,' spelled 'c-o-z-e.' Like doze with a 'c.' Grandpa Cubley liked the sound of it; it was easier to pronounce. He had all of the signs changed and people from that time to this have called the old hotel just 'Cubley's Coze.' Guests frequently ask us what the word 'c-o-z-e' means. Well, other than being part of the word cozy, it has no meaning," Mr. Cubley ended with a smile.

"Wow, that's a neat story. I think I like the sound of Coze. Guess your grandpa invented a new word." I smiled at Kent, who rolled his eyes at me and mouthed, "Brown noser," so only I could see. That was twice he gave me the rolling-eyes thing. He was so going to get it, double.

All heads turned when someone turned into the garage lot off the main road. It was a black 1947 Ford Super Deluxe Sedan with a long nose and equally long front fenders. It had chrome trim down the side. If a car could look mean, this one fits the bill. There were two couples in the car. It rolled to a stop near Mr. Cubley's car, the engine was turned off, but no one got out of the car. To me, it looked like a car that public enemy number one would drive.

Kent and I moved a step or two closer to Mom. Not that we were scared or anything—it was to protect her.

Finally, the driver's door and the passenger's front door opened. Two men got out. Each wore a black coat, black pants, black shoes, a white shirt, and a black hat with a round brim. Neither man had on a tie, but each wore the white shirt buttoned up to the top button. The men did not speak but moved to open the rear doors on each side for the ladies. The ladies stepped out without help and did not talk or even look directly at the men, but kept their eyes on the ground. They wore full-length black dresses that went from their necks to the ground. Those dresses looked hot in this weather. It was hard to tell the age of the ladies because they wore black bonnets and no makeup or jewelry. I would guess they were old, probably twenty-five.

"John, would you come out here... please. You have some customers," Mom called to Dad. She turned toward him and repeated it to be sure he heard her.

Dad looked out from under the hood, saw the four new arrivals, and immediately advanced to greet them. The men took slow, even steps. The two women walked five steps behind the men. I thought it very odd since they had all arrived together in the same car.

"Can I help you, folks?" Dad inquired as he walked past Mr. Cubley, Mom, Kent, and me.

"Are ye Mr. Gunn, the proprietor of this garage?" the older of the two men asked Dad.

"I am, sir, and, please, call me John. Everybody calls me John." Dad smiled and wiped off his right hand in preparation for a handshake if the other man was so inclined. It only took a second to be clear to me, and everyone else, that guy was not.

"My name is Jacob Beamis, and this be my brother, Joash. We understand it was ye who brought our father's pickup truck here, Friday last, the third of June. We seek permission to view it. We shall make arrangements, not to be beholden to ye." Neither Jacob nor Joash cracked even a hint of a smile.

I suddenly thought of Captain Ahab of the *Pequod* from the novel I had been required to read in Miss Jones's class. For some reason, the older Mr. Beamis, Jacob, reminded me of that stern and unforgiving ship's captain. When Dad spoke again, I was lost in thought and almost jumped at the sound of his voice.

"Mr. Beamis, your father's pickup is stored under a tarp behind the garage, over near the southwest corner. Are you sure you want to see it? It was a rather bad wreck, and the pickup is well— wrecked." It was clear Dad was uncomfortable and struggling for the right words with the Beamis family.

The two men never changed expressions. Nor did they respond; they just stood in silence.

"No hurry on the six-dollar tow bill. Also, I'm not charging any fee for storage—leastwise, not for thirty days. Follow me; I'll be happy to show you where it is." My dad turned to Mr. Cubley, "Matt, if you will excuse me for just a moment, I'll be right back."

"We are so sorry about Mr. Beamis," my mom added to try to say something to the family that was friendlier than just giving them the price of the tow.

"Thank ye, Ma'am. Now, if ye will excuse us." Jacob motioned for Joash and the two ladies to follow, but then he suddenly stopped. He stared at Mr. Cubley as if trying to decide if he wanted to say something or not.

"Mr. Gunn called ye Matt. Would ye be Matthew Cubley, the same man we be told was present at the wreck?" Jacob Beamis looked Matt over as if he was sizing him up for a fight or a coffin.

"Yes, Mr. Beamis, I was there," Mr. Cubley stated, and he looked somewhat worried. His eyes would travel from one Beamis brother to the other.

What in the world was going on here, I thought to myself. If this were a movie, a gunfight would be next.

"Where do ye reside?" the elder Mr. Beamis asked, and I saw the younger Mr. Beamis staring at Matt.

Mr. Cubley hesitated for a moment, seemed to resolve an issue, and he looked at the elder Mr. Beamis with the same stern expression he was getting from the two brothers.

"I reside at Cubley's Coze Hotel and Resort. Since my uncle passed away, I'm now the owner. Just ask anyone at the hotel, and they'll tell you exactly how to find me. Is there something I can help you with?"

"Mr. Cubley, Joash and I have something to settle with ye. We will not postpone our next meeting longer than necessary. As soon as arrangements are made for our pa, ye may expect us."

Dad had stopped to listen. Mr. Jacob Beamis walked past Mr. Cubley and motioned for Dad to continue. Dad resumed walking, and he, along with all four members of the Beamis family, disappeared around the corner of the garage.

Mom turned to Mr. Cubley and whispered, "What in the

world was that about? Do they have business with you?"

"I'm not sure," Mr. Cubley whispered back with an eye on the corner of the garage. "Mrs. Gunn, I was told that the members of the Beamis clan are, let us say, hard-line, no-nonsense, old Testament types, and I believe it after seeing these four. I may have gotten on their wrong side when I helped that log truck driver. I guess I'll find out because they don't seem to be the types to let things slide."

Matt's face showed a distressed look for an instant, then a flash of anger, and then he smiled at me. Adults could be so confusing. When I grow up, I won't never be that way.

The hotel wagon pulled slowly into the lot and Mr. Cubley looked relieved, saying, "Well, Richard is back, and not a minute too soon."

Dad returned to where we were. He told us that the Beamis family was praying in the back by their dad's truck and he thought it better to leave them to it.

"Matt, did you do something to make the Beamis family mad at you?" Dad asked as Matt handed him the keys to his Bel Air.

"Not anything I could help or change now. If the brothers say anything to you about me, would you let me know?" Mr. Cubley requested, climbing into the wagon.

"Will do," Dad said as the hotel wagon started to back around to leave.

I waved to Mr. Cubley. He waved back.

Kent and I went into the house to see what might be in the refrigerator. No luck. Next, we tried to panhandle Grandma for the stash of chocolates she kept hidden from Mom. She told us she was out, but would get some next time she went to the store.

Kent and I were reading comics in my room when Dad came into the house. We heard him tell Mom that the Beamis brothers gave him three dollars on the six-dollar tow bill and told him to keep the pickup for the rest. Dad said he figured the scrap was worth about four dollars, plus he was sure he could get another two dollars for two tires off the front.

"I never expected them to be that generous."

"Three dollars more than the bill, rain from heaven," Mom countered.

I heard Dad add, "I hope Matt stays close to the hotel until after the funeral. Maybe things will blow over. I hope so. I heard one of the women, not sure which one, tell Joash that the Cubley matter must be settled before they left town. Both Joash and the older brother said it would be done. I'll give Matt a call to warn him."

Kent and I stayed busy with the comic books, but I began to worry about what Dad said. It seemed bullies came in all shapes and sizes.

CHAPTER 15
BILLY HEARS ABOUT A SPY
Friday, June 10, 1955

K ent and I rode our bikes to the Coze for our first day of washing cars. I had marked the date on my calendar—my first real job!

That day, it was a pleasant 68 degrees and washing a car or two at the hotel sure beat cleaning up around the garage or mowing the grass. Dad had been up early working on a fuel pump, and I'd felt guilty leaving him until I thought about the money I was going to earn, which helped ease my guilt.

Mr. Cubley called the previous afternoon to let Mom know Kent and I were needed the following day. Our money was going to arrive just in time for us to splurge on the movies.

We parked our bikes at the rear of the hotel and found Polecat sitting on the loading dock with a full plate and a cup of coffee. All the kids in town knew him, but we knew better than to call him Polecat to his face.

I greeted him, "Hi, Mr. Smith."

Kent joined in with, "Good morning, Mr. Smith."

Polecat responded with a raised eyebrow. "Boys, I hope you have been directly invited to peruse these premises, or are you flagrant trespassers?"

Kent spoke up to defend himself and puffed out his chest. "No, sir. I'm not sure what a fragrant tea passer is, but we're official hotel employees. Honest."

Just as he finished, Mr. Cubley came out with a breakfast plate and a cup of coffee. He sat down on one of the chairs that was upwind of Polecat.

"Mr. Smith, are you acquainted with Billy Gunn and Kent Clark? I hired them to wash cars for our hotel guests, so, yes, they are permitted on the premises." Mr. Cubley smiled and added, "Oh, by the way, boys, 'flagrant' means conspicuously offensive. And a trespasser is someone who is on the property of another against the will of that owner, in violation of the law. I told your mother, Billy, working here might improve your language skills. Pay attention to Mr. Smith because you can learn a lot from him. Now, Billy, you and Kent go just inside the kitchen door and politely ask Maddie, our cook, for a breakfast plate, provided it's convenient." Mr. Cubley pointed toward the kitchen screen door, then turned to talk to Polecat."

Kent and I did as we were told. Sure enough, in a moment, we each had a plateful of scrambled eggs, bacon, and a buttermilk biscuit. A waitress came into the kitchen and asked the cook who we were and Maddie told her we were the new car wash boys. The waitress introduced herself to us as Boo.

She also told us to help ourselves to the jam jar on the counter, becoming our instant friend. This place was getting better and better.

Kent and I returned to the loading dock, moved two chairs upwind of Polecat, but not so far we couldn't eavesdrop. Polecat often had news to tell that no one else had heard. Mom would sometimes give him a sandwich or change and, afterward, she would tell Dad Polecat's gossip. So I ate and tried to listen without being obvious.

Polecat was in the middle of telling Mr. Cubley the local news.

"Wednesday's paper contains the obituary for Joshua Beamis. It details the traffic accident as the cause of his demise. Some of the facts are suspect."

"Did he have family here?" asked Mr. Cubley.

"Mr. Jacob Beamis is the elder son. His wife's name is Sarah, both of Charleston, West Virginia. Mr. Joash Beamis is his younger son. Both he and his wife, Lucinda, hail from Roanoke. The elder son runs a religious printing business in Charleston. He must be well to do because he drives a black 1947 Ford, Super Deluxe Sedan. When he pulled over to my paper corner and asked for directions to Cubley's Coze, I gave him the directions gratis. I inquired if he desired a paper, but he declined. I thought the patriarch was tight, but his older boy is more austere than him. He seemed mighty eager to know exactly how to locate this hotel. Mighty anxious." Polecat took a sip of coffee and adjusted himself in his chair.

Mr. Cubley responded with, "Since the funeral is over now, I guess I can expect a visit from one or more of the Beamis clan. I still don't think I have anything to be concerned about."

Mr. Cubley sounded to me like he was trying to convince himself, more than merely telling Polecat what he was thinking.

Polecat came back with a warning. "Well, that clan has always been inscrutable, and you should be cautious in opposition to being sanguine."

I looked over at Kent, who had a blank expression. Neither of us had the slightest idea what Polecat had just said. I was wondering if he was from some foreign country where the language only sounded a little like English.

I took a big bite as Polecat mentioned something about a Doc Hathaway getting released from jail.

Kent looked at me and mouthed "jail?"

Polecat continued. "This guy's family was tossed out on the street until a church housed the family at the General Wayne Hotel in Waynesboro. The church pastor has access to a couple of spare rooms on the top floor because of a fire escape problem. The hotel could let staff use them but not paying guests. The wife, in exchange for free rent, did some cleaning for the church and the hotel while her husband was incarcerated."

I figured that her being an employee of the hotel, she could have the room and not violate the fire code.

Mr. Cubley said he knew all about fire escape problems, and his old attic room on the top floor of Cubley's Coze had the same issue. This is how I learned that fire codes protected hotel guests, but it was okay if relatives and staff burned up—something to remember.

Polecat explained to Matt how several of the men from the plant were giving Doc's wife a little money because of the frame job. I understood she must be a carpenter to be framing houses for the men at the plant. I wondered about that frame job work because most of the plant employees lived in McCulloch company houses and tenants weren't allowed to make changes. So, how was this lady doing frame jobs? Then I heard the people in town were slipping her money in secret to keep the McCullochs from finding out. That explained it. She did it on the sly, and they had to pay her in secret. Yep, Polecat knew some stuff.

Boo came out and asked Mr. Cubley did he need anything else from the kitchen? The cook was ending breakfast. He told her he was fine. As she went into the kitchen, Mr. Tolliver came outside with a worried look.

I'd seen that look before. Once, I saw a little kid break a vase in the lobby when my family was here for Sunday lunch. Mr. Tolliver had gotten his worried look over that broken vase. Then when the kid had begun screaming because he got a little cut on his finger, Mr. Tolliver had gone from his worried look to a panicked one. He could be one nervous individual when things went wrong or got broken.

He eased up to Mr. Cubley and whispered loud enough for me to hear him, "Mr. Cubley, we have a problem with one of the staff. Might I have a word with you in private?"

"Sure thing, Chuck, I'll be right with you. Billy, you and Kent finish up your breakfast. I'll have the owner of the green 1938 DeSoto come on out. He can tell you what he needs. You boys will find the cleaning stuff on the other side of the hotel, and the hose is already hooked up to the faucet. Be sure you both do a good job now, ya hear?" Mr. Cubley got up and started for the kitchen with his plate in one hand and coffee mug in the other.

"Yes, sir," I said as I jumped to get the screen door for him.

Polecat reared back in his chair, pulled a Zippo lighter from his shirt pocket, and lit a cigarette. His shirt had a stain on the left sleeve, and I noticed his black tennis shoes had different colored laces. One was white; the other was brown. I was relieved to see he was not wearing white shoes.

"I'm ready," Kent said, "You ready?"

"Yeah, I'm ready. More than ready. Don't think I'll want food ever again. If we eat like this all summer, we'll gain ten pounds," I joked, but sort of meant it.

"Maybe then we can fix the Lockhart brothers and old snooty-nose McCulloch," Kent said with his crooked grin.

Polecat came instantly alert. "You boys stay away from those three. They are incorrigible and best left to their own devices, you hear?" he lectured.

He blew a cloud of smoke, followed by a giant smoke ring. He had a self-satisfied look on his face because the smoke ring went right through the cloud and out the other side. I'd never seen that done before.

Kent answered him. "Uh, yes. We'll stay clear of them, Mr. Smith."

Kent looked at me like he was not going to be able to hold his laugh inside. But he knew if it slipped out, Polecat might give us both a thrashing.

"We'll be careful," I said as I pushed Kent toward the kitchen door with my shoulder while trying not to drop anything. "Have a nice day, sir," I said as we escaped into the kitchen.

Maddie told us to scrape our dishes, but there was nothing to scrape. Then she had us rinse them in the big sink and stack them on the side to be washed later with the other dishes. We both left by the back door and crossed the loading dock. Polecat had gone while we were in the kitchen and Boo was cleaning up his dishes.

Kent and I walked around to the wash area on the other side of the hotel. We saw the hosepipe right under the office window. The guest had not arrived to show us his car, which gave us time to sit down in the grass with our backs against the wall to wait. That was when we heard Mr. Tolliver's voice through the open window.

"Matt, I caught him making a copy of the names and addresses of our guests. I surprised him when I came downstairs at three a.m. to get a glass of milk from the kitchen. I had on my bedroom shoes, and he didn't hear me until I was right by the front desk. He jumped when he saw me and shoved the copy he was making into a drawer. That's what made me suspicious. I didn't let on, but kept on to the kitchen."

I could tell Mr. Tolliver was nervous because his voice was high pitched. He sounded like a woman.

"I made sure I was at the front desk when he left, to keep him from removing whatever he'd been working on. After he left, I looked in the drawer and found the copy he made of our reservations for this month. Then I remembered two of our regular guests commented when they checked in that they had received a letter from the Green Mountain Resort inviting them to stay and receive one night's free lodging. I asked several more regulars this morning as they came down to breakfast if they had gotten similar letters. Every one of them said they had. They mentioned they thought it was funny they had gotten those letters this year and never in the past. I bet if we ask, more of our regular guests have gotten those letters. I checked our house count for this year against last year's count, and we've had more than the normal number of cancellations."

Mr. Tolliver rattled all of this off so quickly, he was out of breath when he finished. He had to stop to take a couple of breaths, which gave Mr. Cubley a moment to ask a question.

"Chuck, do you think Big John would stoop to hiring a spy? Their guests and our guests are quite different. Ours are the upper crust of Virginia. I would think that type of guest wouldn't be all that interested in a free night's lodging in a hotel that's more of a party hotel than a quiet, genteel establishment. Also, most of our guests come back year after year. My uncle always said they were more like family than guests. Could you imagine the Lankfords wanting to drink cheap beer or dance past eight o'clock in the evening, let alone three or four in the morning?"

Mr. Cubley sounded like he was thinking out loud. I heard someone walking across the office floor, then a squeak when the person sat down in a chair near the open window.

Kent looked at me and held his finger over his lips.

I nodded to tell him I understood.

"Why else would our night clerk be copying down our guest list? You know the McCulloch family has been after this place for years. Knocking off our reservations for a season or two could pave the way for them. Even your Uncle TJ couldn't afford to run a hotel with no guests." Mr. Tolliver moved closer to the window and a chair creaked as he sat down.

"Well, Uncle TJ always liked Cliff Duffy, but if he's a spy, I guess we better fire him. What a shame. I hate to show up to take over the hotel and then start firing people. What does that say to the other staff? Heck, I need to hire a few more, not fire the ones I have," Mr. Cubley said with a sigh.

"I don't see how you have a choice, Matthew. We can't have a spy selling off our guests' information to the highest bidder." Mr. Tolliver's voice climbed an octave higher in pitch.

"Where is Duffy, now?" Mr. Cubley asked.

"I asked him to come in this morning to talk with you. He should be here at ten. He thinks it's to discuss changes you might want. He has no idea I figured out he's a spy."

"Chuck, I just had an idea. Let's confront him with what we know and find out why he's in cahoots with Big John McCulloch. It has to be something more than money. If it's what I think it is, we might be able to use this to our advantage."

"What do you think it is?" Tolliver asked in a lower tone and softer voice.

"I bet he has some kind of leverage over Duffy. Does Cliff gamble? I've always heard the Green Mountain Resort runs a little casino in the basement."

Mr. Cubley got up and paced the office floor. The boards in the middle of the room creaked every time he crossed over them.

"I know Cliff. If he gambles, I'm going to be shocked. He's a good family man. I bet it's something else," Mr. Tolliver said and then added, "You know, I think his wife might work for Big John, doing books. Come to think of it, I've seen her a couple of times going in and out of the Highland Hardware and the little grocery owned by Mr. McCulloch with a ledger in her hand, but I've never seen her with groceries or hardware items when she had the ledger."

"Well, we'll know soon enough, it's almost ten," Mr. Cubley said as they both walked out of the office.

"Wow, BB, a spy! Right here at Cubley's Coze. Could he be a Russian?" Kent asked, getting up and brushing off his shorts, which were old jeans cut off. The seat of his shorts was wet from a small leak where the hose had dripped.

"Why would he be a Red?" I asked as I checked to see if my seat was wet. It wasn't. I went over to tighten the hose on the faucet.

"Well, the McCullochs could hire Russians if they wanted to. They have the money. Everyone knows the Russians won't be taken alive if they get caught. Sounds like something Big John would do!" Kent ended and smiled his crooked smile.

"Naw, Kent, there can't be no Russians here. Even if they were here, Mr. McCulloch would be too scared to hire one. The Russians would have to kill him and probably his family if they got caught. I've got a comic at home that tells all about communists."

A man with white hair wearing a white suit with a Panama hat walked our way with a set of keys in his hand. He got in and drove his 1938 DeSoto over to our wash area. This old man told us twice that he wanted the works. We answered him both times and saw his car was old like him but in perfect condition.

He took a small toolbox out of the trunk and carried it into the hotel for Mr. Tolliver to keep behind the front desk. I guess he thought we were Gypsies who would steal anything not bolted to the car. We didn't care. The rule was no valuables, and I guess he thought his little box of tools was valuable. The only thing we cared about was our fifty cents for the wash.

The car was washed, and we were drying her off when we heard several people enter the hotel office.

"Cliff, take a seat. You know Matthew Cubley, our new owner. You met him the last time he stayed with his uncle. Isn't that right?"

"You are correct, Mr. Tolliver. It's nice to see you again, Mr. Cubley. I'm sorry for the loss of your uncle and your family tragedy. My wife and I prayed for all of you. May I say, I look forward to working for you. This is the finest hotel in Virginia, in my opinion."

The man we heard talking had to be Mr. Duffy and, boy was he a smooth talker. Kent and I wiped down the car and tried to be as quiet as we could. We wanted to listen in on a spy getting caught. There could be real trouble before this day was over.

"Cliff, I need to ask you something. It's important. Now before you answer, think about it carefully. Okay?" Mr. Cubley's voice was louder.

"Sure, Mr. Cubley, what is it you need to know?" Mr. Duffy responded, but his voice cracked.

"We know you've been copying down reservation information, then giving it to Big John McCulloch. My question is, why?"

Kent and I waited for an answer, but all we heard was silence. I didn't think the man was going to answer. Finally, Mr. Duffy spoke.

"Mr. Cubley, I had to do it. My wife works for Big John as an accountant. She handles the books for four of his businesses and we need the money. She earns twice what I do, so losing my job would hurt, but losing her job… I don't know how we would make it. I'll get my stuff and go. I'm very sorry. Your uncle was always good to me, but I can't fight Big John."

As Mr. Duffy finished, we heard a chair slide on the floor.

Mr. Cubley raised his voice and said harshly, "Sit down, Cliff. There's more to this than you just walking away."

Can a hotel owner shoot a spy? I was beginning to wonder. Kent looked at me and his eyes got bigger.

"Mr. Cubley, I'm ruined. Big John told me if I got caught, my wife and I better disappear because there would be no work here for either of us. We don't have much. If you want to lock me up or take what little I have, I don't blame you. But please, don't hurt my wife." Mr. Duffy was about to cry. You could hear his voice quiver.

"Cliff, what you did was wrong. It was a breach of trust, and I can't abide disloyalty."

"Mr. Cubley, I understand. I'll take whatever I must, just leave my poor wife out of it. She knows nothing."

Mr. Cubley was silent for a few moments. Then he spoke in a gentler voice. "On the other hand, Big John is the culprit here. Threatening to fire your wife the way he did is inexcusable."

"Mr. Cubley, if he hadn't involved my wife, I would never have taken those names—not in a million years."

I listened to another silence. Mr. Cubley began in a firm voice but no longer harsh voice, "I know what you can do to make it right. Are you willing to hear me out?"

"Yes, sir," Mr. Duffy squeaked.

"If you agree to my terms, you get to keep your job," Mr. Cubley announced.

"What? Keep my job? How?"

"Yes, keep your job. Here's how this is going to be possible: I'll give you the names to give to Big John. They will not be the names and addresses of our real guests but others of my choosing. Now, you tell Big John that the new owner has taken the guest book to review for three or four days, and you won't have access to it. That'll give me time to get the special names and addresses ready for you to feed to Big John. Can you do that?" Mr. Cubley asked.

"I guess so." After a pause, he ended with, "Sure, I can do that."

Mr. Cubley's tone of voice turned serious. "Will you promise to be loyal to me? If we pull this off, Big John will think he's getting our guests' names, and your wife should be safe. Should he ever discover what I'm doing to him, play dumb. You tell him you've been getting the names out of the same book you always have, and if there is something wrong with them, you don't have a clue." Mr. Cubley seemed to be warming to the new plan he had hatched.

"Okay, I can play dumb. If you keep me on, I promise to be the most loyal employee you have."

Mr. Cubley continued, "Now, from time to time, I will also be throwing in some of the names of real guests. The ones who don't pay their bills or who leave owing us money or leave a damaged room. We don't have many of those, but the few we have, their names will go to Big John. Those real names will add a little credibility to our fake guest list. But if we find out you aren't loyal, I'll throw you out the front door."

"And I will add a boot as you go out," Mr. Tolliver added.

I couldn't see Mr. Tolliver booting anyone out of anywhere. Whacking a flower would be about as violent as I could imagine him getting.

"I'll do as you ask and try to restore your trust in me. Do I need to tell my wife? She doesn't know anything about this."

"No, I see no reason to bring her into this. In fact, not knowing will prevent her from leaking something by mistake. Cliff, why don't you go on home and try to put this behind you," Mr. Cubley concluded.

I heard the chairs move on the wooden floor as everyone got up. This meeting was over.

After Mr. Duffy left the office, a few moments passed. Someone walked back into the office and came over to the window.

"Kent, Billy, did you hear everything, or is there something I might need to repeat?"

I looked up. Oh, no! Right above me, Mr. Cubley was looking down on Kent and me from the window in his office. Neither one of us said a thing.

"You boys come on into the office! Now!" Mr. Cubley said in a very stern, no-nonsense, kind of voice.

"I think we just blew it, Superman," I said.

"Oh, darn it, BB. Our moms are going to kill us for getting fired the first day on the job," Kent moaned.

"Kent, last big scrape I got into, Dad gave me a belting so hard I had trouble sleeping for two nights. Sitting down hurt longer than that."

We both walked back around to the front entrance into the lobby, walked into the hotel office, and stood like condemned men at the foot of the gallows. Mr. Cubley was standing there, frowning. I thought he was going to hit us, 'cause he raised his right hand. Kent and I both flinched.

"Repeat after me, and raise your right hands," he said. We looked at each other, but despite having no idea what might happen, we did.

"I solemnly swear or affirm that I will not repeat the conversation I heard about Mr. Duffy and Mr. McCulloch to anyone other than Mr. Cubley or Mr. Tolliver on pain of a horrible death, so help me God." Mr. Cubley stood there, waiting.

"I do!" we both said with our right hands in the air.

"Now, I mean it. The both of you get out of here and get that car finished. Go!" I thought I heard him chuckle as we both beat feet out the front door as fast as we could go.

"You boys, stop that running!" Mr. Tolliver yelled as we crossed the lobby, went down the steps, and around the corner of the hotel, not slacking our pace one bit.

"Do you think he would kill us?" Kent asked.

"What? No. If he killed a couple of kids, he would go to jail forever and a day," I replied.

"You sure?" Kent asked.

"Don't intend to find out. Remember, if one of us talks, we both get it, so double swear and double die; deal?" I added.

"Yeah, I double swear on two deaths, the second worse than the first. Now, grab that towel. Let's start on the windows," Kent ordered as he bent over to grab a clean towel. He was close to getting whacked.

Matt closed his office window and moved to the front desk. Chuck and Matt checked but saw no one in the lobby. They began a whispered conversation.

"If those boys heard all of that last conversation, think they will talk to their buddies?" Chuck whispered to Matt.

"I hope not, but other than scare them, I didn't know what else to do. I didn't see them listening until I stood up as we finished. We'll find out if they can keep a secret. Those boys may turn out to be more mature than we think." Matt cleared his throat and picked up the guest book Chuck had just laid on the counter.

"Where will you get the bogus names?" Chuck asked.

"There's the plan, Chuck; there's the plan. I know the prosecutors in both Roanoke and Richmond. I worked in the Roanoke office, and one of my friends moved to the Richmond office. I will have my old colleagues send me the records of those convicted of petty theft, forgery, fraud with a few con artists, and anyone who has been convicted of taking money under false pretenses thrown in for good measure. Those convictions are public records. I can get the information I need, and it's all legal. Those are the names we will feed to Big John McCulloch. Let's see how he likes the spy business after he gets a few of these special guests. I won't send him anyone dangerous, other than dangerous to his pocketbook." Matt grinned as he walked back into his office.

"Remind me never to cross you, Matt. You have a mean streak buried under your mild manner," Chuck jested.

"Maybe, but spying is a dirty business, so now, Big John gets what he deserves."

Chapter 16

Billy and Kent Hear Shots
Friday, June 10, 1955

After Kent and I finished cleaning the DeSoto, two guests, having seen seeing us do the first car, hired us for their vehicles. We got lunch from the kitchen after our hard morning. It looked like things were going to work out for us—we even got apple cobbler for dessert.

Mr. Cubley came out to chat with us right after lunch. Just like a typical grown-up, he reminded us how important it was not to reveal what we had heard, and we promised that we would never tell.

The day became warmer than was forecast, and washing cars turned out to be an excellent job to have because we could cool ourselves off with the hose.

Two people came by the hotel looking for work. Mr. Cubley hired the first as a maid to work for Rose, but refused the second lady a job. At lunch, we later heard the kitchen staff talking about how the one who was not hired had refused to work for a colored person. The word Kent and I heard was a bad one. My Mom would have washed my mouth out with soap if she had caught me using it. We overheard the waitresses in the dining room talking about how mad Mr. Cubley had gotten when he heard it, but I figured a lot of folks in town would have taken the side of the maid he didn't hire.

Mom would have taken the side of Mr. Cubley. Dad, I'm not sure which side he might have chosen. It's not that he's against whites or coloreds; he's just against idiots. To him, it depends on who's the bigger idiot. Dad has colored customers and he's courteous to them. So, all in all, better to steer clear of the idiots.

At about one o'clock, Mr. Cubley left to check the mail and run some errands. Not long after he'd left, that black 1947 Ford Super Deluxe Sedan pulled into the side lot not far from where Kent and I were washing a car. I recognized it at once. The Beamis brothers got out, looked at us, nodded without speaking, and walked toward the front of the hotel. Both men had on black coats and pants, white shirts, and odd black hats. I noticed that once again, despite the heat, their shirts were buttoned to the top button.

"BB, did you see the body?" Kent asked all of a sudden.

"What body, Superman? You mean Mr. Beamis?"

"Of course, Mr. Beamis, who else would I mean?"

"No, the funeral home took it before Dad and I got to the wreck," I answered.

"Did you see any blood?" Kent asked, but in a lower voice so no one else could hear him.

"Superman, I don't know. I saw brown stuff where he got smashed in the ground. I'm not sure if it was blood or oil from the wreck. Mostly I was busy helping Dad get the logs out of the road. Dad had me running chains to the firemen, and I didn't have time to wander around, looking for blood."

I stopped talking because Kent had just given me the zipper sign across his mouth. He was facing the front of the hotel, so I looked over my shoulder to see what was what. The two Beamis brothers were walking back to their car. While I looked in their direction, they both nodded at us for a second time. They never spoke. They just got into the Ford, sat there, and talked.

"Wow," Kent whispered and dropped his wet rag in the bucket of soapy water.

"They don't look very friendly, do they?" I whispered back as I dipped my rag into the same bucket to get more soap on it. We were washing down a '51 Dodge. It looked like it drove through a hog pen at forty miles an hour. Near the back-left tire, it smelled like a hog pen, too.

"Do you think they're going to do something to Mr. Cubley?" Kent whispered.

"Well, they do keep showing up. It seems odd that they're just sitting there," I whispered back.

"You remember that movie with Roy Rogers when the bandits thought they would shoot Roy in the back, but he saw them in the mirror and shot them both? If I was Mr. Cubley, I would buy ten or twenty mirrors and put them up all over the hotel," Kent said in my ear as he dipped his rag. He moved over to the bumper of the Dodge.

133

We both jumped when the Beamis car started up. It drove slowly out of the guest lot and on down the drive toward town.

"Kent, what good are a bunch of mirrors going to do if you ain't got a gun?"

I thought that was pretty smart, but then I remembered what Mom said about using the word ain't. Still, I'd made a good point. I was waiting for Kent to get out of that one.

"Wasn't he a prosecutor down in Roanoke? I bet all of those guys carry guns. Otherwise, the bad guys would be shooting them down in the street. Yeah, I bet he has a whole *roomful* of guns." Kent grinned at me as if to say, "Got out of that one, your turn."

"Well, I never saw him with any gun. When we get to know him better, let's ask him." I smiled back at Superman. Just then, we heard a faint bang in the direction of town.

"What was that?" I asked.

"Sounded like a gunshot! Do you think the Beamis brothers shot Mr. Cubley?"

"Wow, there go two more! Those are gunshots! Let's run and see if Mr. Cubley's back," Kent shouted.

"Come on! He parks over by the loading dock. Run faster," I urged.

We both flew around the hotel to the loading dock. The hotel's wagon was parked over by the woods, but Mr. Cubley's 1955 Chevrolet was still gone. Mr. Tolliver came out of the kitchen and caught us not working.

"What are you boys doing?" he asked.

"We just heard gunshots coming from town. We wanted to see if Mr. Cubley was back. He ain't." I said.

"No, he isn't." Mr. Tolliver answered. I wasn't sure if he was correcting my grammar or if he just agreed with me. Since ain't wasn't important, I ignored it.

All three of us could hear sirens off in the distance. They were getting louder and sounded like they were coming toward town: no more shots, but plenty of sirens.

"Have you boys finished that last car?" Mr. Tolliver asked, but his eyes were looking toward the entrance drive.

"No, sir, we're worried about Mr. Cubley," Kent said.

"Yeah, you know those Beamis brothers just left. After what they said at my dad's garage, I sure wish Mr. Cubley was back."

I looked at Mr. Tolliver, hoping he knew something that would tell us Mr. Cubley was not shot.

Instead, he ordered, "Go on back to work."

Superman and I went back to the wash area to finish our last car of the day. We sped up the process and hoped we were doing an okay job on it. Twenty minutes went by, and we had just finished when the owner came out to look over our work. He pointed to a spot on the windshield, and Kent wiped it again. The owner grunted, left us, and walked toward the lobby. We checked the car over a final time, and it looked passable to us.

Kent and I both checked the hose to be sure it was off. I put up the buckets and he took the rags around back, washed them out in the sink in the maintenance shed, and hung them on a clothesline strung between two trees in the woods.

We heard a car and saw the Bel Air turn into the drive that led to the loading dock. Just as soon as Mr. Cubley parked the car, we ran up to him.

"Are you okay?" I asked.

"We heard shooting coming from town!" Kent said, even louder.

"Mr. Cubley's back! Mr. Tolliver, he done come back!" Maddie yelled from the kitchen so loudly, I knew any guest taking a nap anywhere in the hotel was now awake.

We heard the kitchen door slam as Maddie came rushing out onto the loading dock with Mr. Tolliver five-seconds behind. Then Boo and several waitresses came rushing out with dinner plates in their hands. They must have been setting up the dining room for supper. Mr. Cubley was looking at us, surprised.

"Hey everybody, I'm fine. Someone shot at Chief Smith but missed. No one shot at me. I'm fine."

"What happened? Tell us the details," Mr. Tolliver blurted out.

"Well, Chief Smith was about to get into Big John's car when someone shot at him. They missed the chief; he was lucky. All three shots went high and wide; only the courthouse was hit. A window on the second floor got shot out, which scared a judge's secretary."

"Where were you when all this was going on?" asked a waitress.

"I was coming out of Mr. Dalton's office when it happened. After I heard the shots, I ducked back inside his office until it was all over."

"Did they catch the shooter?" Kent asked.

"I don't know, but the town is crawling with town police and deputy sheriffs. It looks like a hornet's nest got kicked over with the way the police are swarming."

"Wow, I wish I could have seen the shoot-out," Kent said.

"No, you don't," Mr. Cubley answered him right back, scowling at Kent. "Someone could have gotten killed. You're too young to leave this world. Don't *ever* say you want to see something like that. Understand?" Mr. Cubley looked at Superman and me. He looked more hurt than mad.

"Sorry, I didn't mean anything by it," Kent apologized.

"No, I'm sorry, Jack," Mr. Cubley answered him.

Kent and I looked at each other. We remained silent about the name mix-up.

"Listen, everyone into the kitchen. Let's dish up some ice cream to help us forget about all the mean stuff in the world. Everybody follow me."

Mr. Cubley shook Kent by the shoulder and pointed at the kitchen door.

"Jack, Billy, I'm going to drive both of you home today. Don't leave on your bikes. I'll call your moms and let them know. We don't want them to worry. Now, let's go eat some ice cream." Mr. Cubley smiled at each of us, but his eyes were sad.

"Okay, Mr. Cubley, it sounds like a good plan to me," I said.

"Yeah, I can eat my weight in ice cream. You might need a truck to get me home," Kent said with a laugh, not bothering to mention Mr. Cubley kept calling him by the wrong name.

While the ice cream social began at Cubley's Coze, Trooper Mike Quinn parked his police car in front of the courthouse to investigate the shooting. He was doing his best to hold his temper. It looked like half the town had turned out to see the show without any regard for ruining possible evidence.

"Chief, if it's not too much trouble, how about we set up a crime scene perimeter. This is not a circus. We don't need civilians trampling all over the evidence."

The trooper was doing his best to move people back, but since he was the only one doing anything, he was not having much luck. Chief Smith was pale and his hands were shaking. He kept licking his lips. Every time he tried to move toward the trooper, he would lean back against Big John's fender.

Big John's car was a black Cadillac and not just any Cadillac, but a brand new Fleetwood Sedan. The boys at the McCulloch Chevrolet dealership had it polished to perfection. Everyone who walked past the Caddy, which was parked in the courthouse no-parking zone, could see themselves in the finish.

The driver's door was flung open and Big John got out. The man was over six feet tall, bald on top with gray hair on the sides. His face was round but not jovial. His eyes were cold and calculating; his face bore the mark of a driven man who judged others as either prey or predator. The predators, if he considered them a business rival, were usually ruined financially with cunning.

His suit was white Egyptian cotton, his shirt a pale blue, and his dark blue tie was silk. A Panama hat was on the back seat, and he pulled a handkerchief from his coat pocket with which to wipe moisture from his forehead.

"Obie, get off my damn car before you scratch it."

If Chief Smith heard the boss, it didn't register.

Big John's focus shifted to the trooper and he was angry. He was mad at almost getting shot and mad at the inconvenience. Now a Virginia State Police trooper was working the crime scene because Chief Smith was in shock and doing nothing.

To make matters worse, his son, Sergeant McCulloch, came flying up the street with his siren on and lights flashing. He slid to a stop, almost striking the open door of his dad's new car. Despite his arrival at breakneck speed, he got out of his patrol car and began strutting like a general reviewing the troops. Gawking like a tourist, he was in no hurry to take control of the scene.

Every special police officer of the Highland Police Department knew that Big John McCulloch paid them to do his bidding. The boss was generally not too concerned about them enforcing the law unless it happened to be a law that he or his company needed enforcing. Today, his boy was not picking up on the situation but was more interested in making an appearance than performing some useful function. Big John became furious.

"Smith, get your fat ass off my car or you're fired!"

Chief Smith jumped away from the Cadillac. He stumbled about four paces to the courthouse steps, turned, and collapsed in a heap on the hot marble. Sweat was dripping from his pale face—corpse pale. He kept making gestures with the two fingers of his right hand as if directing imaginary traffic.

"Sergeant McCulloch, would you please take this yellow rope over to that railing, move those people back, and rope off that side of the sidewalk from the railing to the lamppost? That would help a lot," Trooper Quinn asked, and he started to hand the rope to the officer.

This task would have allowed one side of the crime scene to be cordoned off so the trooper could do the same with the second piece of rope on the other side. The sergeant made no move to take it.

"I don't work for you," Little John said with a sneer on his face.

Before the trooper could react, Big John stepped up on the sidewalk and yelled, "Goddammit, Little John, get your sorry ass in gear and help the trooper. Find out who took a shot at Obie and scared the shit out of me, or I'll..."

Big John just left the sentence hanging as he became aware that he had an audience. The trooper, Little John, and several members of the crowd were staring at him with their mouths open.

Rethinking how his conduct looked to these bystanders, he began again in a different tone of voice with, "Sergeant, go help the trooper restore some order here."

"Yes, sir, right away," Little John answered.

Officer Frank Younger, who had run to the courthouse from the police department, stopped right in front of his sergeant. Little

John McCulloch now had someone upon whom he could vent his anger.

"Frank, get those people back. Anyone who doesn't move fast enough, shoot 'em!"

Little John was smart enough to whisper this, so only the trooper and Frank heard it. The cop looked around for someone else to bully. Seeing no one nearby, he grabbed the yellow rope the trooper still had in his hand and started to tie it to the railing.

The trooper gasped and watched for Frank to pull his gun. What the heck have I turned loose on the town of Highland now? He shook his head and started politely asking the people on his side of the street to move back so that he could rope off the area.

Next to arrive was Officer Roger Younger. At the same time, a Green Mountain County deputy sheriff's car came up the street from the other direction. They both stopped in front of the court-house, nose to nose, causing the road to be blocked in both directions. The deputy reported to the state trooper, but the town officer walked past the trooper to Sergeant McCulloch. The trooper called to Officer Younger, "May I have a word with you?"

The officer hesitated, looked at Little John, who motioned for him to go see the trooper. Only then did Officer Roger Younger turn and walk back to the trooper.

Trooper Quinn gave orders to Officer Younger and the deputy in a hushed voice. "Gentlemen, I know for a fact that the one place this sniper is not going to be is here. Officer Younger, please go out to the intersection of twenty-two and six-fifty. Set up a road-block. The next officer that comes through, stop that officer and ask him to help you. Check every car for firearms and write down every car plate plus the name of each person who comes through your roadblock. If we act quickly, we may nab the sniper."

It looked for just a moment that Officer Younger was about to say something smart to the trooper.

"Roger, move your keister," Little John yelled with a face that said it all.

Roger got back in his car, slammed it in reverse, backed up four car lengths, stopped, then drove around the police car blocking his way by driving over the sidewalk. Several bystanders jumped to avoid being run over and Officer Younger swerved back onto the street and roared off like the hounds of hell were overtaking him.

Trooper Quinn gave his next orders to the deputy. "Deputy, cruise the back streets. Let me know if you see anyone walking alone. Be careful! If you see someone with a suitcase, bag, or even a coat wrapped around something, call for backup. Don't be a dead hero. This guy may get lucky. Despite being the worst shot in the world, he might just hit something next time. Don't let it be you. Okay?"

The trooper went to his car, took out a case from the trunk, and began to photograph the scene. He and Sergeant McCulloch processed the scene and located the bullet holes in an attempt to retrieve the bullets.

While this work was going on, Chief Smith had gotten up and gone into the courthouse. He made his way into the office of the Commonwealth's Attorney and took a bottle of medicinal whiskey from the bottom drawer of a file cabinet.

Trooper Quinn soon found him asleep on a couch with the empty bottle in his hand. The trooper had wanted to talk to him about who might want to kill him, but drunks made for terrible witnesses. He postponed the interview until the chief could sober up.

While the streets returned to calm, the people were not. They locked their doors and windows. Those with guns loaded them and kept them close at hand. Not a single child was allowed outside once word got around, and word traveled fast over the town's gossip grapevine as dusk descended.

The hotel guests at the Green Mountain Resort and Cubley's Coze also stayed inside. No one strolled the grounds, and not a single boat was out on the lake at sunset. Kent and Billy were driven home by Mr. Cubley, their bikes piled in the back of the hotel wagon.

The boys returned home to find their report cards had arrived in the mail that afternoon. Billy had gotten all *A's* with good teacher comments, though she had indicated that he needed to work on not talking in class, a comment Kent had also received.

Kent did good for Kent. He got two *A's,* three *B's,* and a *C* in math, not his best subject. Billy was allowed to use the phone to talk with Kent for a full fifteen minutes as a reward for his good grades.

The family spent the evening trying not to talk about the shooting, but the phone kept ringing until after ten o'clock. The gossip grapevine was working late.

Billy's wish for an adventure was being granted, but it was turning mean.

CHAPTER 17

BILLY AND KENT BECOME WITNESSES
Saturday, June 11, 1955

I awoke to the smell of pancakes and bacon. Mom often made a special breakfast on Saturday. Today would be a good day to eat at home.

I checked the clock and saw it was 7:30 am, jumped out of bed because I knew Kent and I had at least one car to wash this morning and was surprised that Mom had let me sleep in, since she knew I had to work at the hotel. On the way to the bathroom, I glanced outside; darn, it was raining. No cars to wash today.

I took my time washing my face, brushing my teeth and skipped my hair because my curls had curls. Rain meant curls. Today was not going my way.

Scotty wandered into the bathroom, moved his little two-step stool in front of the toilet, stepped up, and just stood there looking down at the water. His right thumb was in his mouth. His left hand was winding a couple of strands of his straight hair around a finger. Today, I hated my brother and his straight hair.

"Scotty, you gonna pee or just look at the toilet?" Being almost three, I was not about to help him—a number two, perhaps, but a number one, no way.

I startled him. He jerked. It was not a full jerk like when you almost fall into a creek from the bank and you save yourself in the nick of time. It was about half that.

He looked over at me, stuck out his tongue, pulled down his pajama pants, and let fly with a stream similar to what one might see from a firehose at a three-alarm blaze. How does such a little kid hold that much water? He finished, pulled up his pants, and as he ran from the bathroom, he stuck out his tongue at me for a second time. I came close to whacking him. I just missed him as he cleared the door jamb.

"Momma, Billy is trying to hit me," he yelled as he went down the steps too fast. He made it without falling, but just barely.

"Am not!" I yelled in response before Mom could fuss at me from the kitchen.

"Stop it, you two! Billy, come downstairs for breakfast."

Mom used a voice that hinted she was tired from a bad night's sleep. I could tell she didn't want to talk to either of us, but she knew she had to yell something to keep up appearances.

"Yes, ma'am," I called and ran down the stairs to get to the kitchen before Scotty could tattle tall tales on me. When I entered the kitchen, out the back door, I saw puddles in the yard. Dad told me the obvious.

"Billy, it's raining. No cars to wash today. Besides, I have a tow job this morning, and I need your help. Eat up; we have to go," Dad ordered as he got up with an empty plate and took it over to the sink.

"John, you work that boy too hard," Grandma complained as he passed behind her on his way to the sink.

"Matilda, that boy doesn't know the meaning of the word. When I was his age, my father would have had me up at daybreak doing chores. Here he's just now getting out of bed, and the day's half gone. I refuse to let him lie about. I don't want him growing up lazy and good for nothing like some of our relatives."

Mom gave Dad a little punch in the arm, but she didn't say anything. I wasn't sure if it was a teasing punch or an angry punch for his remark about our relatives. It turned out to be a warning punch.

"John, there you go criticizing me. No matter what I say, you hand me stingers and bouquets. I get so tired of it. You're never happy until you criticize every word I say. I can't say a single thing that you don't yell at me. You treat me like a dog. Just like an old dog. I'm nice to you, but look what I get in return!" Grandma was going after Dad this Saturday and it was going to be a bad one.

Scotty began to cry. Mom turned to Grandma, clearly about to jump into the fray.

"Mother, you're the one causing trouble. You're never happy until you get something going. Leave John alone and mind your own business. How we raise our kids is our business. You need to remember who's the guest. I don't want to hear another word."

Mom had on her frown with the crinkle in her nose. I just looked down at my pancakes and ate as fast as I could.

Scotty went from crying to stage two screaming. I leaned over, picked up a truck he had left on the table last night and tried to get him interested in it. He grabbed the toy truck and threw it across the room, hitting Dad in the back.

"Scotty, stop that right now!" Dad shouted and picked up the truck and looked for a place to put it. Before he could do anything with it, Mom turned on Dad.

"John, don't take your spite out on Scotty. He's just a child."

"Laura Jane Harris Gunn, I've had it. I'll raise my boys as I see fit. Scotty better mind, or I'll give him something to cry about."

Dad threw the toy truck down on the floor so hard it bounced into the living room. He stormed out of the house through the rain to the garage.

"Billy, get out here now!" he yelled from the yard.

I dropped my fork, left my breakfast half-eaten, and went outside. As the kitchen screen door slammed, I heard Mom and Grandma going at it in one of their famous knockdown drag-out fights.

Now, here is how most of my family fusses go: Grandma will start a fight with Mom that lasts for about ten minutes. Grandma retreats upstairs to her room for the rest of the day, refuses to eat lunch, and Mom cries on and off. That night, Mom leaves a supper plate on the hall table. Grandma tells her she is not going to eat it, that Mom is just wasting food because she will never eat again.

Grandma will moan and sob and mumble, "I will lie down and die since that's what everyone wants me to do. Just lie down and die. Then the Gunn family will be rid of me once and for all."

Around nine o'clock, Grandma will sneak out of her room and take the plate, clean it, drink the iced tea, and leave the dirty dishes on the hall table. The next day, Mom and Grandma will have a good cry, makeup, and everything will be good for about two, maybe three weeks when it will happen all over again.

Dad will sulk for a day or two. That's when I have to be careful. After two or three days, Grandma will do something nice for Dad, and all will be forgiven until the next blowup. Predictable. Not pleasant, but very predictable.

I made it to the garage, only half soaked, and watched Dad fuss and fume about how things had better change. I got busy, swept out the garage, put away his tools, unpacked a bunch of parts and put them away. A little before eleven, Dad finally cooled down enough to talk to me about us meeting a trooper to pull a car out of a creek. The trooper had asked Dad to wait until eleven because he had been up most of the night and wanted to go home to get a few hours of sleep.

"Was the trooper working that shooting in town yesterday?" I asked, trying to get Dad's mind off the fight with Grandma.

"Yeah, Trooper Mike Quinn is the lead trooper on the shooting, and Trooper Bobby Giles is helping. Quinn's not sure if this car is connected to the shooting or not. One of the town officers tried to pull this car over last night and it ran on him. The officer tagged it in the quarter panel, spun it out, and put it in a creek. We gotta pull it out so the troopers can check it. Get your rain gear; it's time to go," Dad announced as he reached for the keys to Blacky.

Dad drove Blacky out to State Route 22, turned left, and headed west toward where the big wreck had happened. We turned right on an old road about a half-mile short of the Beamis farm. The road turned from gravel to mostly mud as it wound up the holler along Cub Creek. Lucky for us, the rain stopped. A mile up the holler, I saw a Virginia State Police car with its red-light flashing. The trooper was pulled over at a wide place in the road. Dad eased Blacky past the trooper's car and stopped. Trooper Giles got out and waved as we both climbed down from Blacky.

"Hey, John, thanks for coming out on a rainy Saturday. We need a Studebaker pulled out of Cub Creek." He was pointing in the direction of the creek.

"Morning, Bobby. What model?" asked Dad.

"A nice 1954 Studebaker Champion," answered the trooper.

Trooper Giles greeted me and then continued to tell Dad the car belonged to one of the guests at the Green Mountain Resort who happened to be downtown when the shooting started. The guest got curious and decided he wanted to see the excitement. He walked six blocks down toward the courthouse, and when he returned about thirty minutes later to get his car, it was gone.

"Let me guess. The idiot left his keys in the ignition?" Dad asked, but I knew what the answer was going to be, and so did he.

"You guessed right, John," Trooper Giles told us and gave me a wink.

"One of the town officers spotted this car with its lights off, engine running about dark last night. This was thirty minutes after the roadblocks were taken down. When the officer tried to check it out, the Studebaker took off. The officer chased it out here, and he did a good job of stopping it. He hit it in the quarter panel, spun it out, put it over the bank and into the creek. The officer got out with his flashlight to investigate when all of a sudden, the shooting started. He dropped his flashlight, which I think might have saved him. He jumped into his patrol car, slammed it in reverse, and backed into a tree about a hundred yards down there. You can see his rear bumper is still at the base of the tree." Trooper Giles pointed down the road and, sure enough, we could just make out a chrome bumper at the base of a tree.

"Idiot. I guess they don't teach the Highland Police how to back up," Dad said unkindly.

Trooper Giles then added, "Well, he was able to pull forward, maneuvered around the tree, and back all the way out to Route 22 without getting shot or hitting any more trees." Trooper Giles kicked a rock with his foot. It splashed in the creek dead center. "Trooper Quinn got here with a bunch of officers, but when they checked the woods, no one was around. The rain washed out all the tracks and messed it up for the dogs, as well. I need you to tow it to your garage for me to search it and process it for fingerprints. If it's not too much trouble?"

Dad didn't answer the trooper but walked over to the bank's edge and looked over to see how he was going to pull her out. He started talking to himself.

"Based on how it's angled in the creek, I best rig a block and tackle on that big oak that's on the far side of the road from the creek. If I take my wrecker cable through the block and tackle, I can get a right angle down to the car. The only way is to pull it straight up the bank and onto the road; Blacky will be out of the way. If I try to pull it up the bank with my truck, the angle is all wrong; I might roll it. Okay, Bobby. It's a ton of trouble, but I think I got it figured."

Dad looked at me.

"Yeah, Dad, that's how I figure it, too," I said with my hands on my hips.

Trooper Giles started laughing, "Well, John, you and the boss agree, so let's see if we can get her out without tearing her all to pieces, right?"

Dad said not a word, never cracked a smile, just stared at the car over the bank.

The trooper added, "Far be it from me, a mere trooper, to tell the experts how to get this job done. Right, Billy?"

I knew Trooper Giles was making fun of me, but that's what those troopers did when they were joking with other troopers or when they liked you, so I didn't get mad. Well, not much. Dad never said a word for half a minute. He just kept looking down the bank until he made up his mind for good, and then he turned and looked at me.

"Billy, you stay up here with the trooper. This one will be tricky, and if my cable snaps, I want you up here by the trooper's car. You understand?" Dad asked in a no-nonsense voice. I also saw by the look on his face, he meant business.

"John, I'll keep Billy up here safe and away from that cable. You don't have to worry about that. You just watch yourself," Trooper Giles warned and rubbed the top of my head. Usually, anyone who messes with my curls would get a punch in the stomach, but since it was Trooper Giles, I felt proud and let this one go.

Dad had to back Blacky down to a side road, turn around, and drive in reverse to where the car was over the bank. My dad knew how to back Blacky about as good as he could drive her forward. He would not have backed his police car into a tree—not my dad.

While he worked at rigging the block and tackle, I thought I would see what I could find out from the trooper about the shooting downtown.

"You close to catching the guy who did the shooting yesterday?" I asked.

"Not yet, Billy, but we're working on it," Trooper Giles replied and paused, not giving out anything else.

This was going to be harder than I thought. I was going to have to be smart about getting the trooper to talk.

"I heard the shots clear up at the hotel. Must have been a shotgun, right?" I asked, knowing I was totally wrong.

"Not likely, Billy. The shooter was too far away for a shotgun to be any good. According to the witnesses, the noise was sharp like a high-powered rifle. The sound a shotgun makes is more of a boom than a crack. I'm betting a 30.06 or something close. We found single bullet holes in the walls of the courthouse, not a spread that a shotgun would make." The trooper grinned at me, and I think he knew what I was doing, but he was still giving me the facts I wanted.

"Well, Mr. Cubley said Chief Smith was plenty scared," I said and added, "when he told us all about it. He said Chief Smith was shaking like a leaf. An inch closer, and he would have been dead."

I knew this was also not true but hoped to get the trooper talking again.

"Billy, anyone would be a fool not to be scared if someone was shooting at them with a rifle. But I can tell you, those shots missed the chief by a mile. One even went through a second-floor window. It missed the judge's secretary by two feet, but it came closer to her than to Chief Smith," the trooper concluded.

"Who did Chief Smith say might be mad at him?" I asked, looking as serious as I knew how. One had to look that way when one was talking man-to-man with a state trooper.

"We are trying to find that out from Chief Smith. Unfortunately, he has not been available for us to talk to him. We think he may be able to talk to us by this afternoon."

"Do you think one of the Beamis brothers might have had something to do with it?" I asked, proud of myself for taking the clues I knew and putting them together.

"What do you know about the Beamis brothers?" The trooper was suddenly interested.

I told him all about seeing them at the garage, how Kent and I were afraid that Mr. Cubley was the one who might have gotten shot because the Beamis brothers were at the hotel just before the shooting started in town.

When I finished, Dad had the Studebaker back up on the road. What was left of it, anyway. The front end was smashed from going nose-first into the creek and the back quarter panel was badly dented where the police car had slammed it. Someone was going to be sick over their new car being wrecked.

Trooper Giles called Trooper Quinn on the radio and asked him to meet us at the garage. He said I had some information that might help in the investigation. Boy, did I feel important. The trooper told my dad what I had revealed to him. My dad was not mad; at least I don't think he was. He gave me a worried look, and I began to wonder what I might have gotten myself into. Perhaps more trouble than I knew.

The rain started to come down in a steady downpour again, so the trooper got in his car and I got in Blacky. Lucky for my dad, he was hooked up and ready to go.

When we got back, Trooper Quinn was in the lot waiting for us. Both troopers took me into the garage and talked with me for about thirty minutes.

I told them about the Beamis brothers coming to the hotel on Friday afternoon and how, when they couldn't find Mr. Cubley, they had sat and waited for him. I knew when they left; it was only two, maybe three minutes until I heard the shots. It was such a short time that I had thought they might have met Mr. Cubley at the foot of the drive to the hotel and shot him. Now, I knew those shots had been fired in town at the courthouse.

Trooper Quinn asked me to go over everything at least four times. He asked me over and over about the time. How much time passed between when the Beamis car had left and when I had heard the shots. I told him Kent and I had watched the time because we were worried about Mr. Cubley meeting up with the Beamis brothers, since we could see the Regulator clock on the wall of the office from outside. If they didn't believe me, I told them to ask Kent; he would say the same thing.

They both said they would, and that's how Kent became a witness.

The troopers talked to my dad afterwards. When they finished, Dad told me I was not to leave the house. When I told him I had plans to go to the movies with Kent, he simply said, "No."

When he went into the house, I heard Mom start to cry. This witness thing was not turning out like I had thought it would. Then things got even worse. Dad came out and told me Kent was not going to the movies either because the troopers were over at his house asking him questions. I had messed up his Saturday as well as mine.

Thirty minutes later, Mom came out to the garage, and while her eyes were red, she was no longer crying. She told me if I wanted, I could spend the night with Kent. His Mom had asked me over. The deal was if we had a sleepover, we had to agree not to fuss about missing the movies. I said, I will, like it was painful, but this was not all that bad. I just didn't want Mom to know how I felt.

All afternoon it continued to rain, so I spent it reading comic books in my room. I heard Dad talking to Mom. He was trying hard to calm her.

"Laura Jane, Trooper Quinn and Trooper Giles don't see how the Beamis brothers could be directly involved in the shooting based on what Billy and Kent are saying."

"I hope they're right. John, I'm scared. I don't want Billy in this mess."

"Those troopers both think if there's a threat, it's against the chief because his department is covering up the accident. They know of no threat against us. The Beamis brothers now have an alibi based on what the boys know, so it would be foolish for them to want any harm to come to Billy or Kent. It's just the opposite."

"Well, I hope someone tells them the boys can clear them. I want my boy safe; Kent, too. Will the troopers tell them that?" Mom asked.

"Laura Jane, they should, but if the brothers didn't do the shooting, why would they be mad at us? Our only connection is I towed in their dad's pickup. Their kin will only have it in for people who work for Big John."

"John, several of the ladies are telling—how it's all over town—those brothers got into it with the chief after their father's funeral. When the chief told them that their dad pulled out in front of the log truck, well, both Beamis brothers told him he was crazy."

"Yeah, Shorty told me the same thing when he stopped by the garage for wipers. Those brothers told the chief in no uncertain terms: they know the log truck would not have even been in sight when Mr. Beamis pulled out. Their dad was way down the road from the driveway when he got hit."

"The girls at the beauty shop said the same thing," added Mom.

"I heard something else at the VFW. Now don't go getting mad—I only had one beer, but I was there and heard it straight. One of the town officers has a big mouth; he told us the two Beamis wives asked the chief why the Virginia State Police weren't investigating the accident. The chief told her that his office was in charge, and that was just the way it was going to be. One of the wives made a comment that the Highland Police were bought and paid for. Well, that sent the chief into a rage. Words passed back and forth, and the two husbands jumped into the argument. Anyway, it ended up with the chief throwing the Beamis family out of the police department. Imagine that."

"I can't imagine the victim's family being treated that way. How inconsiderate," Mom said.

"Laura Jane, it gets worse. The big mouth town officer told us that Jacob turned as he left, pointed a finger at the chief, and yelled, 'Unto ye I charge thee, ye better heed the word of God and follow first Kings, 8:32 or a terrible vengeance will descend upon thy brow,' and those were his exact words." Dad was moving around the kitchen. He does that sometimes when he's trying to think or work something out.

"Oh, my Lord in Heaven. Laura Jane, let's pack up and go to my sister's place up in West Virginia. We can't stay here with a threat like that. We're all going to be murdered in our beds," Grandma said with panic in her voice.

"Matilda, we are not going to get murdered in our beds. The Beamis brothers have paid half of their bill in cash money, and I scrapped their dad's truck for more than the rest, plus these boys can help clear their names. Why would they be mad at us?"

"Mother, please, let John and me talk. John, what does that Bible verse say? Are you sure you remember the book and chapter?" Mom asked.

"Yep. I copied it down on the back of a parts bill. Everyone knows the Beamis clan is religious. Matilda, may I use your Bible?" Dad asked.

"Let me get it. I know we'll need it handy for all the burying that we are going to be doing. I just know it." I heard Grandma go into the living room where she usually kept her Bible, and then return.

Dad began to read, "Here it is. '…then hear thou in heaven, and do, and judge thy servants, condemning the wicked, to bring his way upon his head; and justifying the righteous, to give him according to his righteousness.' It sounds to me like it's simply saying punish the guilty and let the righteous or innocent be rewarded. Not much of a threat. The way I figure it, Chief Smith, Big John, and that log truck driver might need to look over their shoulders, but our family is in the clear."

"Can't we keep the boys out of this?" Mom asked with concern in her voice.

"Maybe. Trooper Giles said that based on what the boys know, there's no way the Beamis brothers had time to get to town to do the shooting at the courthouse. Might have had it done, but it's not possible for one or both of them to have done it themselves. So, I think things should settle down. If they don't, you say the word, and I'll get you and the boys out of here."

"Oh, now, I see—no mention of Matilda. Well, I guess you'll just leave me to get shot and rot in the sun. No thought for me, not one," Grandma said in a voice much louder. Startled, I jerked back from the vent.

"Oh, Mother, no one is going to leave you to rot. We're a family, and John will look after all of us, including you. Stop your worrying." Mom sounded like she was back to normal.

Things got quiet, and I went back to reading my comics, but I stayed near the vent. Six comics later, I heard my name.

"Billy, you got your bag packed? It's time to go to Kent's," Mom called from the kitchen.

"All packed," I yelled back as I scooted out of the closet and back into my bedroom. I was all ready for a sleepover. Little did I know, this sleepover was the start of something horrible.

CHAPTER 18

BILLY'S WILD SUNDAY LUNCH
Sunday, June 12, 1955

Kent's mom was crazy nice. She let us make a tent out of blankets in Kent's bedroom, and we were able to sleep nice and dry in our tent while we listened to the rainfall outside. During the night, I rolled over on my Daisy BB Gun, which woke me. I thought it wise to take it to Kent's house in case we had to protect his mom. Other than that mishap, though, the night went fine.

The next morning we got up and had breakfast, and Kent's mom drove us to church. She went to the Highland Methodist Church, while my family went to the Green Mountain Baptist Church, but that day I went to church with Kent. Both of our families were going to meet at Cubley's Coze for Sunday lunch, as we had been invited by Mr. Cubley.

When Mr. Cubley had called last night to invite Mrs. Clark, she had at first said she didn't think she and Kent would be able to join the group for lunch. I knew why. Kent's dad had died in the Korean War and Kent had confided in me that while his mom had received some money from his life insurance, as the government sent a check each month, they still did not have a lot of money. Her job at the bank did not pay well. Superman said his mother called not spending money being frugal. I wondered if she heard that word from Polecat?

I think Mr. Cubley guessed what was happening because he asked her to reconsider her response. He repeated that he wanted both our families to be his guests, adding that Kent and I were doing a good job, and he wanted to get to know the families of his employees better. When he put it that way, she said okay.

I liked to go to the Methodist Church service because they got out earlier than the Baptist Church. We got to the hotel at least fifteen minutes before Mom, Dad, Scotty, and Grandma. Just as we entered the lobby, Mr. Cubley came over and asked Kent to introduce him to his mom.

Kent got all flustered, and it came out, "Mr. Cubley, may I introduce my mom. Mom, may I introduce Mr. Cubley."

Just as he finished, Kent realized what he said and immediately got red in the face. "Uh, Mom, I mean Mrs. Clark, this is Matthew, er… I mean Mr. Cubley."

Kent looked at me. I rolled my eyes at him to tease him about his dumb introduction.

"Mrs. Clark, it's a pleasure to meet you. You have such a nice young man, and he's a hard worker. And please, call me Matt."

"Thank you, Matt."

Mr. Cubley then stated, "I'm so pleased you could join us for lunch. Maddie has outdone herself today. We're serving fried pork chops." Mr. Cubley smiled, but his eyes were sad. Still, he seemed sincerely glad to see us.

"Mr. Cubley— I'm sorry, Matt, please call me Sally Ann. This is a special treat for Kent and me. He's been bragging about the wonderful food here and how you've been letting him eat from the kitchen. Though, you better watch both Kent and Billy, or they will eat up all your profits." Kent's mom also had a sad cast to her eyes, but she smiled up at Mr. Cubley and put her hand on Kent's shoulder.

"Aw, Mom, I don't eat that much," Kent said and shrugged off her hand.

"Kent and Billy have helped me more than you will know. It's nice to have them around the place, and I promise not to work them too hard." Some of the sadness returned as he spoke.

"Well, you keep an eye on them, and if they slack off or give you any trouble, you call me." Kent's mom gave Kent a warning glare as she finished this last statement.

They then talked about the town and the recent shooting as other people started arriving from church.

"Well, well, here comes your family, Billy. Would you introduce me to your Grandma?" Mr. Cubley watched Grandma leading the procession into the lobby.

I got through the introduction without messing up too much. Grandma told Mr. Cubley that he had a spider web in the top corner of his front door, and I thought Mom would pass out from embarrassment, but Mr. Cubley laughed.

"Mrs. Harris, I see you have a keen eye. I'll get that taken care of today. Thanks for letting me know."

Mom's face was pink.

"Who's this fine young man?" Mr. Cubley asked, kneeling and looking Scotty in the eye. Scotty immediately ran behind Mom to hide his face in her dress.

"This shy young man is Scotty. Scotty, can't you say hello to Mr. Cubley?" Mom urged my brother, and I could see her embarrassment was now compounded. Scotty was not cooperating as Mom's face blushed to a deeper shade of pink.

"Well, no matter. I bet we'll be good friends by the time we get to dessert," Mr. Cubley said with a wistful look at Scotty. He then turned and glanced into the dining room.

"Let's go to lunch. I hope you all like pork chops, fried apples with cinnamon, sweet potato casserole, cabbage, corn on the cob, and cherry pie for dessert."

Mr. Cubley led us into the main dining room, stopping at a large table for eight. Even Scotty had his place at the table with a high chair and everything. Mr. Cubley motioned to Boo, who came right over and asked us for our drink orders.

Both Kent and I said Dr. Pepper at the same time. That lasted about two seconds because both our moms changed our drink orders to milk. I started to protest until Dad gave me the "don't you dare if you want to live" scowl. I got busy with my silverware, instead. Even Kent, who was often slow to pick up on such things, saw the warning from my dad.

Boo and another waitress brought us our food right away and left us to it, and there was only a little talking during the meal. Mom told me twice to chew my food and stop rushing. We had just finished when Boo came over to the table and whispered something in Mr. Cubley's ear.

"Are you sure they said their names were Beamis? Out back on the loading dock, you say?" Mr. Cubley looked a bit startled, and before he could move, Mr. Tolliver came rushing up and shouted.

"Matt, they're parked out back as big as you please. I think they brought a gun with them. It's in a bag. Should I call the sheriff? Maybe the state police? I'll keep them busy while you leave by the front and hide in the woods."

Mr. Tolliver was gaining momentum and passing through his flustered stage on his way to twitchy panic by leaps and bounds. The dining room went silent with everyone trying to see and hear what was happening.

"Chuck, calm down. I'm not running out the front or any-where else. That would be rude. I don't even know for sure what they want. I'm going to go out and talk to them. You stay here and keep these nice folks company while I get to the bottom of this."

Mr. Cubley rose from the table and walked quickly into the kitchen. He had only been gone for a minute when someone in the kitchen dropped several plates with a crash. We all jumped.

"Oh lord, we're all going to be killed," Grandma said loud enough for the tables around us to hear her. The guests smiled and some laughed outright, much to the embarrassment of my mom. All they knew was someone dropped a plate, and here this ridiculous old lady was afraid of being killed.

Mom's face was back to red, and then I saw her frown with the crinkle in her nose. She turned on Grandma with, "Mother, you hush, and I mean it. Hush, right now!"

Dad spoke up. "I'm sure everything is fine. I'm going out to check on Matt. Be right back."

Dad tried to get up, but Mom grabbed him by the arm to stop him.

"John, don't you go out there, you stay right here," she said with a look that said more clearly, "don't cross me on this."

"Laura Jane, I'm just going to look out the back door. If I don't like what I see, I'll come right back here, and Mr. Tolliver can call the police. Matt's our friend and we are his guests. The least I can do is check to see that he's all right." Dad gently removed her hand from his arm and took the same path that Mr. Cubley had into the kitchen.

The next five minutes were long and tense. We all sat and just looked at each other, with only Scotty continuing to eat the last of his lunch. Mr. Tolliver was in a nervous fidget, walking between our table and the door to the kitchen and back again. Grandma kept muttering to herself. Scotty finished and tried to get out of his high-chair, so Mom clamped down on his arm until he started to cry. I was hoping he wouldn't stop crying until he got a good spanking, but he stopped just in time.

Dad and Mr. Cubley returned to the table together, and both were laughing.

"Everything end up alright?" Mr. Tolliver asked, looking both worried, confused, and relieved at the same time.

"Better than all right," Mr. Cubley said.

"We'll talk about this misunderstanding for years," my dad said with a grin.

"What happened? For goodness sake, tell us what happened," Mr. Tolliver demanded.

"When I went out back, I half expected to get shot because of all the speculation about the Beamis family and what they might want with me. Well, that goes to show, jumping to conclusions is stupid. Yeah, they wanted to see me about unfinished business. They brought me a sport coat to replace the one I ruined at the wreck. The brothers said they could not rest until they paid their debt to me. Ordered it from the same men's shop where my… where the other one had been purchased. They found the store's name inside it. That coat meant more to me than…getting it back, well, means a lot." Matt looked like he might have something in his eye. He wiped it.

"They gave me a second gift. Something special that belonged to their dad. He used it on the farm, and while they didn't feel one brother could keep it over the other, they thought the best solution was to give it to me. Since I had given their dad a final gift, they wanted me to have his prized possession. It's a 12-gauge shotgun. The one old Mr. Beamis won in a competition against Uncle TJ many years ago in a contest that was so close that it had to be decided based on the width of a horse's hair. Now, that takes some shooting. They told me of my uncle and Mr. Beamis and how they were the best shots in the county and good friends. I'll keep it as a reminder of my uncle and Mr. Beamis, and why I should never jump to conclusions without the facts." Matt smiled at everyone at the table.

"Well, looks to me that it wouldn't have hurt you to at least have asked them in for dessert," Grandma blurted out.

I didn't know whether Mom was going to slide under the

table or just drop dead. Her face went from normal to beet red in two-seconds, which was starting to be her standard color today.

"Mrs. Harris, I asked them in for a meal first and then tried for dessert, but they declined both. I see where Billy gets his sharp eye for details and honest approach to life."

Mr. Cubley laughed. I admired the way he turned an awkward situation into a compliment.

"The brothers said they're late picking up their wives, who are waiting for them at the farm. The two couples need to meet a cousin who's going to take over running the farm, and leave for home. The men are both needed back at each of their businesses," Mr. Cubley told us and smiled.

"What took you so long?" asked my mom.

"They wanted to speak to me about the wreck. I told them what I knew and what I saw. They took it better than I expected. Joash even said he didn't blame the truck driver as much as he did the company for not repairing the truck. Jacob said vengeance was in the hands of the Lord, not man. They both believe in the New Testament that punishment is the Lord's and the courts to deal out, not man. Well, they said Caesar, but they meant the government. So, whatever's going on, the Beamis family has no part in it," Matt finished, and the table was quiet for a few seconds.

Conversation then revolved around the events of the past week and how you could never predict how things might turn out.

Grandma interrupted the conversation with, "Mr. Cubley, you better be careful with that shotgun. You just might shoot your foot off with it if you aren't careful."

Even Mom had to laugh at that one.

While guests were finishing their Sunday meal at Cubley's Coze, Jacob Beamis and his younger brother Joash left the hotel for the farm. Neither brother noticed the Highland Police car on Court Street, watching and waiting.

Frank and Roger Younger were in the Highland squad car about to doze off when the Beamis car drove past the intersection.

Frank saw them, punched Roger in the ribs, started the car, and made a U-turn.

Roger, now awake, immediately asked, "What in damnation are you doing? Those were the Beamis brothers that just went down Green Mountain Avenue. You're going the wrong way!"

"Do you want them to know we're tailing them? Gosh, Roger, sometimes I wonder if you weren't dropped on your head as a baby," Frank contended.

"Wasn't neither."

"I'm certain the doctor dropped you; I seem to remember it," Frank teased his brother with a grin.

"Where are you going, dummy?" Roger demanded to know.

"I'm going to shoot down Main and park at Gunn's Garage. Once we see for certain the Beamis brothers are headed for the farm, you call the chief and tell him we're on the way. With any luck, maybe the brothers will make a play for it."

Frank braced himself on the steering wheel as the police car slid to a stop on the gravel in front of the garage gate. Since the entrance was recessed, the police car was all but hidden. Sure enough, the Beamis car made the right turn from First Street onto Main Street and drove slowly out of town toward State Route 22.

"Make the call, Roger, and be sure the safety is on that shotgun you're holding. The chief is madder than hell at the car you banged up last night," cautioned Frank.

"I'd like to see you do any better with shots flying all around. Tarnation, I was lucky to save my skin. The chief would have done no better," Roger responded on the defensive.

"Only a dummy would drop his flashlight in Cub Creek. You better replace it because the Chief is sure as shoot'n' not gonna," Frank teased his brother.

Roger was having trouble keeping the shotgun from banging against the dash, rear-view mirror, and himself.

"I can't handle this shotgun inside the car," Roger complained as he put it on the backseat.

"Make the damn call, or we'll be there. Stop sitting on your thumb," Frank fussed as he followed the Beamis car.

"I'm calling, keep your shirt on. Car three-three to car one," Roger said into the microphone.

"Car two here, one's tied up, go ahead with your traffic, three-three." Little John's voice came through the radio loud and clear.

"The Beamis brothers are about to turn onto Route 22. We should be there in ten. Will keep you informed. Three-three out."

Roger Younger replaced the mike on the dash of the car, pulled out his Colt 38 caliber revolver and checked to be sure it was fully loaded. He then rolled down his side window from halfway to down all the way. A few minutes later, the Beamis car, which was about a hundred yards ahead of the patrol car, turned left off State Route 22 and drove at normal speed along the farm road that led up to the main house.

Roger Younger grabbed the radio mike and yelled into it, "He just turned, he just turned! He's coming up the farm road; get ready, he just turned!"

Frank Younger then floored the accelerator and the patrol car surged forward. He also reached over and hit the dash switch that turned on the red roof light. The patrol car swerved hard into the dirt road, and Frank tried his best to catch up to the Beamis car. He was going thirty-five on the dirt road and the car bounced every time he hit a rut, root, or pothole.

Roger stuck his arm out the window and tried to bring the sights of the gun to bear on the Beamis' car. It was still a distance ahead of them and slowing to a stop in front of the main house. As the police car came out of the wooded lane into the clearing for the main house and barn, they hit a deep rut. Officer Roger Younger's gun went off with a loud bang. The right front tire of the police car went flat, and the patrol car veered to the right and stopped. Roger jerked the gun inside the car.

"Oh God, I shot our car. Our tire is flat. Oh, no, the chief!" Roger looked at Frank, who looked back in dread, knowing that every officer stationed around the farm was about to open fire on the Beamis' car.

CHAPTER 19
CHIEF SMITH MAKES TWO ARRESTS
Sunday, June 12, 1955

Sarah and Lucinda Beamis, the wives of Jacob and Joash, had just finished cleaning up the lunch dishes at the farm. They were all packed and ready to put the suitcases in the car as soon as Jacob and Joash returned from Cubley's Coze. Repaying the debt owed to Mr. Cubley was of such importance that the brothers were doing it on Sunday. While such a matter would have ordinarily been postponed until Monday to avoid the Sabbath, Jacob and Joash had decided that repaying Mr. Cubley for his kindness was not work.

The ladies were sitting patiently on the porch swing, waiting for their husbands, when they heard several cars approaching. Two Highland police cars and five sheriff's vehicles drove into the graveled area between the house and the barn. Suddenly, armed officers were everywhere. Chief Obie Smith and two town officers ran up on the porch with their guns drawn and handcuffed the two women.

"What be this? What do ye want?" demanded Sarah.

Chief Smith pushed Sarah toward the barn and barked, "Shut up. We're here to arrest your husbands for attempted murder. One word out of you, and you'll join them."

The other officers took over, roughly pushed and locked the two ladies into the back of a police car, which was parked behind the barn. Officer Larry Sparrow and Officer Zeke Barnes of the Highland Police Department, who usually worked the night shift, were ordered by the chief to watch the ladies. They had been called back to duty for the raid. Usually, they hated extra duty, but not today: these arrests would be the talk of the town for months, and they were right in the middle of it.

Besides having the entire Highland Police Department there, ten additional deputies had been added from Nelson and Green Mountain Counties. The chief had called for the extra help to capture the "armed and dangerous" Beamis brothers. Extra deputies hid in various positions around the farmhouse, barn, and behind trees at the edge of the woods.

Officer Sparrow watched the two women while Officer Barnes peeked around the corner of the barn, waiting for the action to start. All the police cars had been moved into the woods or behind the barn.

When the Beamis sedan pulled into the yard and slowed to park, everyone thought this arrest was going to be easy. Suddenly, a police car came out of the lane swerving and bouncing over the rough road. Then, without warning, a shot rang out, and all the officers ducked. The police car slid sideways to a stop in the yard.

Jacob Beamis put his car in park when he heard the shot. He began looking behind his car to find the noise's origin. He recognized a Town of Highland Police car with its red roof light blinking and heard the driver yelling.

"Don't shoot, don't shoot! Hey, everybody, don't shoot," Officer Frank Younger screamed and waved his arm outside the driver's window like he was swatting at bees.

Four deputies, two on each side of the Beamis car, ran up to the Beamis' car with their guns pointed at the faces of the two occupants. Adding to the confusion, screams of two women could be heard coming from behind the barn.

Joash was the first to react. He opened his door and started to step out when he saw the deputies with their shotguns pointed at his face. He threw up his hands and fell back onto the car seat. Jacob looked first out the passenger side of the car and then out his driver's window, but wisely sat without moving.

"Are ye mad? Why are ye pointing guns at us? Where is my Sarah? What have ye done with my wife?" Jacob yelled. Before he received an answer, a deputy jerked his door open with one hand while trying to hold the shotgun in his other hand. Since the man's finger was on the trigger and the safety was off, it was a miracle the gun didn't discharge its load of buckshot.

This officer, with his one free hand, grabbed Jacob by the lapel of his coat. The shotgun was waving and wobbling as he put his foot on the sedan's running board and pulled Jacob out of the car and onto the ground.

On the passenger side of the car, Joash was leaning backward with two shotguns about four inches from his nose.

"Where be my wife, Lucinda?" Joash bravely demanded.

No one gave him an answer. Putting his shotgun on the ground, one officer pulled Joash from the car and pushed his face into the dirt. Both were handcuffed with their hands behind.

The women continued to call for their husbands as the brothers were pulled to their feet by their captors.

"Where be my wife?" Jacob yelled again at the deputy nearest him. He got the butt of a shotgun in his chest for his effort. Down he went onto the ground, gasping for breath.

"Why are ye about the devil's work? Unhand us," Joash yelled. He was struck with a lead sap on the left side of his head behind his ear. When he fell to the ground, he didn't move.

Chief Obie Smith came out from behind his patrol car, which was hidden behind the barn. Once he saw the Beamis brothers were down on the ground, handcuffed, and that it was safe, he walked from behind the barn.

"Good work, men, we captured them alive. Good work. Find out which one of these black hearts shot at Frank and Roger. By God, I'll add two more counts of attempted murder to their charges, and enjoy watching them fry in ole Sparky," Chief Smith boasted and began giving orders all around.

"Okay, Frank, I want you to get me all the guns out of their car. Sergeant McCulloch, take some men and search the farmhouse. Bag and tag all the hidden guns you find. Also, see if you can't find boxes of shells to match the bullets they fired at me at the courthouse. Roger, you take the barn with the rest of the men. Watch out for tripwires; I bet they have bombs all over this farm. Find me all the ammunition they have stored around the place." Chief Smith's voice was getting a little hoarse, and if he had been a frog, he would have been all puffed up.

The officers and deputies began to go off in different directions to try to do at least some of what Chief Smith was asking. The chief never slowed up, spewing orders.

"Larry, cut those women loose and tell them to shut the hell up, or I'll charge them with disturbing the peace. Zeke, as soon as

Larry gets them to shut up, you and Larry take these two before the justice of the peace. I want these bastards charged with attempted murder on me and that secretary, attempted murder on Frank and Roger, use of a firearm while they attempted to kill everybody, and failure to stop for a police car."

The chief reared back, snuffed in a big chunk of air through his nose, hawked up a big one, and spat it on the ground. A big smile was on his face.

"By God, the people of Green Mountain County will know the kind of police they have in this here county. We sure as hell captured these two."

"Uh, Chief," Officer Frank Younger said, and he looked like he would rather be anywhere else in the world than where he was.

"What is it, Frank? Nice work. You chased them right into our ambush. Did you or Roger get hit when they shot at you?" the chief said, becoming worried.

"Uh, Chief... You see, here is how it went down: I don't think they shot at us. It was an accident," Frank Younger explained while keeping his eyes on the ground. He moved his foot around in the dirt like he was putting out a cigarette.

"Accident! Accident! How the hell could it have been an accident? Those two tried to run from you and tried to kill you to get away. How in Sam Hill is deliberate murder an accident? What's wrong with you?"

The chief had gone from talking to yelling and from a charming smile to a scowl.

"Uh, Chief, I was trying to catch up to them when I hit the rut, and the car bounced," Frank mumbled, still looking down at the ground.

"What rut? Who bounced?" the chief yelled, looking around. He was beginning to believe that his officers had gone mad.

"Chief, I'll just tell you like it is," Frank said, and he saw out of the corner of his eye Roger, sliding up to listen and looking sick.

"I was coming in hot, really fast, so Roger and I could be here to back you all up. That's when I hit that rut, and the car bounced. Well, Roger was drawing down on that Beamis car because we knew how dangerous these religious nuts can be, right?" Frank took a chance and looked at the chief to see how things were going so far.

"Okay, I follow you, but what difference does that make. They did shoot at you, didn't they?" asked the chief.

"Chief, the Beamis brothers didn't shoot at us. Roger's gun went off accidentally when I hit the rut and the car bounced. Roger shot out the tire when he put a bullet through the front fender of the car. It was an accident, just an unfortunate accident," Frank concluded with a sigh of relief.

"And they were running from you. Weren't you in hot pursuit? At least we can add a charge of failure to stop for a patrol car. Ain't that right" The chief was pleading.

"Chief, I wish I could. They never sped up, and I don't think they knew we were behind them. I laid back a distance so they wouldn't see us. When they turned into the farm road, that's when I floored it to get up here in a hurry. That bullet hole in the fender is back to front, not front to back," Frank maintained his position as his brother tried to look invisible.

"Do you realize this is the second police car your brother has put out of commission in just two days? Who in tarnation is going to pay for this? I sure as hell am not, and I bet the town isn't either. How do you shoot your own police car? Tell that idiot brother of your's to get over here."

Not only was Roger standing right behind the chief listening, but so were six deputies. No one was laughing at the moment, but several were moving off before they did.

During the time Chief Smith was yelling insults and threats at Officer Roger Younger, the night shift officers left to take the Beamis brothers into town. They wanted to get away from Chief Smith before he turned his wrath on them. They also wanted to get a jump on getting the charges drawn up by the justice of the peace, since going home for supper before their night shift started was on their minds. When the chief calmed down, he saw that Sparrow and Barnes had left with the prisoners. Chief Smith called them on the radio to tell them to wait up. The charges would have to be modified.

Things got even worse for Chief Smith before he left to catch up with the prisoners. No guns were found in the Beamis Ford, in the house, barn, or any of the outbuildings. No ammunition was found. There were no tripwires and no bombs. The most dangerous weapon on the farm was a rusty pitchfork hanging in the barn.

The chief left the farm and drove into town fuming. Suddenly, he slammed on the brakes. A puppy was in the middle of the road. The chief hopped out, picked up the dog, and gently placed it on the front seat of his car. He looked along the shoulder and saw its mother had been hit by a car. No other pups were in sight.

Dropping the pup off at his office, he told the dispatcher to give the dog a bowl of milk.

"What's this?" asked the lady.

"A puppy," responded the Chief.

"What are you going to do with a puppy?"

"Keep it. His name is Oliver, after my favorite Dicken's book. I'll be back in thirty."

The Chief had walked over to the office of the justice of the peace and was working on the warrants when Trooper Mike Quinn of the Virginia State Police walked in to get a warrant for a hit and run driver. Officer Sparrow, who was outside guarding the prisoners and had a big mouth, gave the trooper a full account of the capture of the Beamis brothers. The trooper walked in and greeted the court officer and Chief Smith.

"Chief, I hear you brought in the Beamis brothers. I saw them out in Sparrow's car. Joash doesn't look so good. What are the charges?" Trooper Quinn asked.

"Not your case any longer, and no need to try and weasel your way into taking credit for these arrests. My department is getting full credit for solving this one," the chief boasted and never attempted to answer the trooper's question.

"Oh, I wouldn't think of even asking for a mention on your arrest reports. Officer Sparrow told me all about it. I want you to get everything that's coming to you. I was just a little curious… professional courtesy, one officer to another," the trooper said with an amused smile.

"We are writing up both Jacob and Joash Beamis for two counts of attempted murder and two counts of use of a firearm while attempting to commit murder. Sound about right to you?" said Chief Smith with a smug smile of his own.

"One is for you, and one is for the judge's secretary, right?" asked the trooper.

"You got it right. Right on the money. This case is open and shut," gloated the chief.

"Did you recover any guns, Chief?" asked the trooper.

"Not yet, but we will. My boys are out at the farm and should have a suitcase full any minute," he lied.

"Well, I talked to the Beamis brothers last night, and they even showed me their father's shotgun. They assured me it was the only gun at the farm."

"Father's shotgun? You have it? Quinn, you need to turn that over right now!" demanded the chief.

"Chief, I don't have it. They said they were going to give it to Mr. Cubley along with a sport coat they were replacing. I believe they were going to give both gifts to him today. I'll be surprised if you find any guns at the farm."

"Trooper, those brothers tricked you with their smooth-talk-ing, preacher ways. I want that shotgun. Besides, no farmer just has one gun," Chief Smith proclaimed, and he sounded more and more determined.

"Chief, my experience is that many farmers *do* only have a single shotgun. My investigation shows our shooter used a rifle. I'm positive about that. I retrieved three bullets. One is deformed, but the other two I dug out of a door jamb and the wall of the judge's office. Those last two are good enough for a comparison. My bet is on an M-1 military-type weapon. Might even be the MC 52 sniper rifle, but if this shooter was a sniper, then he's the worst shot I've ever seen. Sorry, Chief; I meant it's lucky for you that he was a bad shot. What evidence have you got on the Beamis brothers?" asked Trooper Quinn.

"I know damn well they did it. We had to throw them out of the police department. They came around demanding this and demanding that and acting all snooty a few days ago. Wanted us to charge a McCulloch employee, some foreman, for their dad's acci-dent, like we would do that. They were spouting scripture and making threats. Then, next thing you know, I get shot at right in front of the courthouse. They're mad 'cause of the... well; they're just mad. We'll find the gun they used, just you wait and see."

Chief Smith seemed to pause, and Trooper Quinn thought his tirade was losing steam. Smith was not done, however.

"I see the look you're giving me. You take me for a fool? I know those Beamis boys are guilty. Don't think I'll even need to find their gun to get convictions. You can come by anytime and get my final report. Don't waste any more time trying to solve what the Highland Police Department has laid to rest. Case closed."

The chief finished and waited to see what the trooper's response was now.

"Chief, now I told you that the state police want no part of this arrest, and my sergeant and lieutenant will back me up on that 100 percent. I am obliged to tell you that I stumbled on some information just yesterday that sheds a different light on the Beamis brothers. Let's sit down and go over this new evidence. I think it clears them."

Trooper Mike Quinn motioned for Chief Smith to follow him out of the hearing of the justice of the peace.

"Clears them, how can you have evidence to clear them? If they didn't shoot at me, then who the hell did?" he demanded.

"I wish I knew. I'm still trying to figure that one out."

"Figure all you want, sonny boy. I got all the evidence I need. So, thank you very much."

Chief Smith made no effort to leave the office of the justice of the peace. Mike Quinn's blood pressure was at the top of the scale. He took a deep breath and told the justice of the peace he would come back later for his warrant.

Trooper Quinn marched down the hall toward the front door. As he left the courthouse, he began to whistle the theme song from the movie *The High and the Mighty* with John Wayne. He had recently seen it with his wife in Charlottesville, and the tune had just popped into his mind for no apparent reason.

He waved to Officers Sparrow and nodded to Officer Barnes as he walked by the Highland police car with the Beamis brothers in the back. One brother was upright, but the other was still slumped over with blood down the back of his head.

The chief of police for the Town of Highland had pulled out all the stops on this one. Getting the night crew out for a daytime arrest was rare. Rare, indeed. Later, he would find out that two other departments had joined in the arrest. The state police, however, had not been invited to the party and would be spared what was coming.

On down the street, he slowed his steps to an amble, but that darn tune would haunt him for the rest of the day.

Chapter 20
BILLY AND KENT EAVESDROP
Monday, June 13, 1955

Highland was buzzing with news of the arrests of the Beamis brothers for the attempted murders of Chief Obie Smith and Linda Carlisle, the court secretary for Judge Harland. Polecat was selling the *Highland Gazette* so fast he had to hide the Cubley's Coze and Green Mountain Resort's papers. The fifty extra ones he got over his regular order went in a flash.

It also took him longer to finish his regular paper route because of the people stopping him to buy his extras. Folks were out and about, now that the sniper danger was over, they were hungry for the news. Polecat, however, was not convinced the town was safe.

Kent and I rode our bikes up to the Coze, but Dad followed us in the car. We saw Polecat doing a brisk business on a street corner, and I waved, but he didn't see me. We arrived at the hotel and began dining on a plate of French toast with a big glass of orange juice five minutes before Polecat arrived.

Superman and I had started skipping breakfast at home on the days when we worked at the hotel. Dad was glad because our food bill was going down. Mom's feelings, however, had been hurt, so, whenever I ate at home, I bragged about her meals.

We currently had our hands and mouths full with five slices of fried ham Maddie added onto a third plate for Kent and me. As we left the kitchen, she yelled at Boo to lock the back door to keep the riff raff out.

Boo answered, "Maddie, the young rats are worse than the old ones; you need a bigger butcher knife to cut off their tails." And she laughed as she rushed into the dining room with a large order balanced on a tray over her shoulder.

After leaving the kitchen for the loading dock, juggling our plates, and trying not to spill our juice, we had settled down to eat breakfast when Polecat arrived and parked his bike at the loading dock steps. I noticed his paper bag was almost empty.

"Good Morning, Mr. Clark. Good Morning, Mr. Gunn. I see you two are enjoying an abundant breakfast this antemeridian," Polecat said with the expectation of sharing in the bounty from Maddie's kitchen.

I whispered in Kent's ear, "*a.m.*"

Kent nodded and then said with a grin, "Hi, Mr. Smith. Boy, is this good! You better get you a plate before it's all gone."

"Good morning, Mr. Smith. Isn't it great things in town are back to normal? Mom even let us ride our bikes to work."

I then recounted, in spurts, a recent history of how strict our parents had been, as I paused to work small bits of French toast from between my teeth with my tongue. Kent had powdered sugar on his nose.

"So, you think we are back to normal? Well, at least I see you are following the rule of proper nutrition. One should eat like a king for breakfast. I shall attempt to join you."

Polecat slowly opened the screen door to the kitchen and peeked in, waiting before he carefully stepped inside. He looked as if he were stepping onto an ice skating rink. He slowly eased the screen door shut behind him, stood without moving, and waited patiently for someone to notice him.

We quickly heard, even as busy as the kitchen was this morning, a yell from Maddie telling one of the waitresses to fix up a plate for Mr. Smith and be sure to put on extra slices of ham. The waitress was Teresa Long, a local high school student who was last year's homecoming queen. Whenever she walked away from a table in the dining room, the male guests watched her on the sly. It was said, despite her getting numerous requests for dates, that she ignored all the boys, except for one, and even he only got the occasional date. The town gossips unanimously reported that she was a very good girl. The boys, who she turned down, said other things.

Having seen the size of her dad, everyone understood why her date was never late getting her home. Kent and I felt special because she spoke to us in the kitchen. We both had a crush on her. If only I were a college boy with a jeep, I would ask her out.

Boo Skelton came in from the dining room and greeted Polecat. She told him to help himself to the coffee and that the new pot was on the left. Polecat was often permitted to help himself so that the kitchen staff could keep their distance. Boo had counseled the other waitresses to stay out of "the zone," as she called the area near him.

Polecat came back out with his plate piled with French toast and ham. Some of it was in danger of toppling over the side, but he was able to manage his balancing act and get seated. Mr. Cubley came out behind him with a cup of coffee.

"Good morning, Mr. Smith, Maddie has exceeded my expectations for a Monday morning breakfast. Looks like she made sure you got a good quantity," Mr. Cubley said and smiled at Kent and me. "You boys have two cars waiting when you finish your breakfasts, and there's a new box of soap powder in the maintenance shed. Richard left it on the second shelf; you'll see it as soon as you open the door."

"Thanks, Mr. Cubley, we'll be sure to get it. We're about out," I replied and looked over at Kent, who was in the middle of chewing off a piece of ham with his teeth rather than cutting it with his knife.

Mr. Cubley spoke to Polecat. "I see from the headlines the chief thinks he's caught the snipers. What's your opinion, Mr. Smith?"

"I believe he made a mistake. Time will provide full verification."

"I also think the chief's wrong. I've met plenty of mean people in the courts of Roanoke; these two brothers don't fit the profile."

Mr. Cubley took a sip of coffee as Polecat continued talking and eating.

"It appears a miscarriage of justice is occurring in our metropolis. Even the *Highland Gazette* has an editorial warning of paranoia skewing factual determinations in notorious criminal cases," lectured Polecat as if we were students in a classroom. He paused briefly for a bite and continued. "Old Mr. Beamis was a good man who raised two good sons. He was never one to spare the rod. Some boys would have rebelled, but those two, while hard to the core, were always known to be honest and law-abiding. They seem to have done well for themselves in their respective trades. And, with such clean records, this alleged conduct does not comport with the police theory of criminality."

Polecat stopped talking and stuffed an entire slice of rolled-up ham into his mouth, but I noticed his eyes never left the face of Mr. Cubley. He was looking for a reaction.

"Agreed. If I were handling this investigation, I would be looking more deeply into the facts and would have held off making these arrests. I'm scared the real sniper is still out there, lurking in the shadows. Chief Smith better be cautious," Mr. Cubley stated with confidence. "Speaking of Chief Smith, are you related to him? Mr. Tolliver, who loves to look into the history of Green Mountain County, says Chief Smith is a distant relative of Smith, the explorer who named Smith River and Smith's Gap."

"We do not share a genealogical history to my knowledge. My family moved here a long time after the events that led to the naming of the gap and tributary," stated Polecat as he looked over at our third plate, which still had a slice of untouched ham on it. One neither Kent nor I could eat without risking it not staying down. We were both stuffed.

I picked up the plate, looked at Kent, who shook his head no. I offered it to Polecat, who didn't hesitate but took the slice of ham and put it between two leftover slices of French toast. I noticed that he had left off the syrup. A French Toast, ham sandwich; I would have to remember that one. He wrapped it in one of the hotel's linen napkins and put it in his coat pocket—a sport coat which had not been cleaned in years. I was thinking, not a very suitable food container, but hey, what does a twelve-year-old know? I saw Mr. Cubley glance at what he was doing.

"I shall return the linen, clean and ironed, with your permission?" Polecat inquired with a smile.

"No need to clean it, just bring it back. Give it to Boo, and she'll see it gets in the laundry hamper," Mr. Cubley said as he began to scan one of Polecat's papers.

"I have reserved five papers for the hotel lobby. This edition has been very popular," said Polecat. "Truth be told, I was offered a dollar for the one you are reading."

I saw Mr. Cubley reach in his pocket and pull out a shiny silver dollar. He flipped it to Polecat, who snagged it out of the air like Stan "The Man" Musial of the St. Louis Cardinals catching a fly.

"I bet this edition was flying off the shelf," Mr. Cubley concluded with a laugh. "Everyone is talking about the wreck and its aftermath. Biggest news in some time, isn't it?"

Polecat agreed with, "People are divided over the turn of events. Several firemen are talking about the wreck scene not matching with how the police are portraying it. Rumors abound regarding Mr. Bondurant's confession about his brake failure, which I think caused the crash. Many believe him. One of the nurses overheard the trucker explain to the police how the foreman ignored him asking for the truck brakes to be fixed. When Sergeant McCulloch saw her listening, she reported that he slammed the hospital room door. Bondurant's version is all over the Lynchburg hospital and the town of Highland."

Polecat finished off the ham, took a sip of coffee, and leaned back in his chair to light up a cigarette. Taking a draw and puffing two perfect smoke rings, he continued with his conversation.

"Dribs and drabs of information are leaking like a sieve from the investigative structure that the Highland Police have attempted to build. People are concerned that the governor removed the state police from the investigation, which reeks of corruption and cover-ups. This information must remain between you and me—and Mr. Kent and Mr. Gunn, who I assume are pillars of discretion. Right, boys?" Polecat asked and gave us a stern stare.

"Uh, yes, sir, we don't say nothing about what we hear around this hotel," Kent said with a cross your heart motion.

"Mr. Cubley, Kent and I promise not to say anything. I'm not sure what a *pillow* of destruction has to do with things, but I'm happy to swear an oath on it."

I was quite proud of myself for correcting Kent's little grammar problem.

Mr. Cubley and Polecat both laughed. "Billy, that word is *pillars,* like great big columns that hold up a church, not *pillows* you sleep on. Discretion means you don't reveal private information that should be secret, or at least not spoken of when it would hurt someone's feelings. Working at a hotel often means you have to be mindful of keeping some information to yourself, like what we spoke about a few days ago. Think you and Kent can do that?"

"Yes, sir, I'll be a pillar of discretion and not reveal any secrets," I said

"Yes, sir, what he said," Kent joined in with his chest all puffed out like he was president.

"Any news on who might represent the Beamis brothers, Mr. Smith?" Mr. Cubley asked after draining his coffee cup.

"Nothing's been reported in the *Gazette*, but I did hear something from Officer Sparrow this morning. He informed me that the Beamis wives were allowed a visit with the brothers. I would surmise it was to acquire legal counsel." Polecat stood to stretch, pocketed the silver dollar, and moved toward the kitchen with his dishes.

"I wonder who they might contact?" Mr. Cubley pondered out loud.

Kent and I stood up after Polecat and followed him into the kitchen with our dishes.

We passed Boo at the waitress counter and smiled at her. She poked each of us in the ribs. We both were beginning to like Boo. Kent thought she was cute. Okay, I thought so too.

"You boys get outta my kitchen; I got work to do. Now get, you rascals!" Maddie was laughing, so we knew she was just being Maddie.

We did hurry it along. Out the kitchen door we went, passed Polecat on the dock, and hauled freight down the steps to the drive. We raced each other around the hotel and pulled up where we washed cars.

Kent asked me in a whisper, "Should we tell Mr. Cubley about the Beamis brothers being here just before the shooting started. How they didn't have time to get to town and shoot up the place?"

"After all that speech about being a pillar of discretion, we better keep quiet about it. The troopers will fix things," I said.

An older model Buick was waiting for us. Just as I reached for the faucet, I turned to Kent and called out, "Hey, stupid. You forgot the soap."

"I didn't forget the soap; you forgot the soap," Kent countered.

"Okay, flip you for it," was my response.

I pulled a spare quarter out of my pocket. Since we got our car wash jobs, we were always carrying around at least fifty cents, sometimes a dollar, in change in our pockets. Unless, of course, we were headed into Lockhart-McCulloch territory, then we hid our money in our socks.

Well, I flipped, Kent called it, and he lost. Off he went to get the soap. I started washing off the dust, getting the car ready for a good soaping. The office window was open, and I heard several people enter the office.

"Have a seat, ladies. What can I do for you? How about a cup of tea? We have both hot and iced," Mr. Cubley was telling someone.

"Thanks, but no. We must ask of ye a favor. We are beside ourselves over the arrest of our husbands. 'Tis not possible they be part of this courthouse matter. Jacob and Joash never betook themselves to town on Friday. They never left our sights until they departed for here. We four observed the Sabbath at the farm and made preparations to receive Cousin Josiah. He will abide there and farm our land for a fortnight or more; God be willing. Our men did depart from us to travel to this inn, but now affirm to us they never ventured into town." A lady was speaking, but I was not sure which one.

"I'm sure your husbands will be able to clear their names. My short acquaintance with them has convinced me they're innocent," Mr. Cubley stated with conviction.

"Truth is blessed over lies. Our husbands require us to hire ye. Lucinda has read much in the Roanoke paper, and ye are known as a fair and honest prosecutor. You defending our husbands would give us great comfort. The local police seem to care not where truth abides. We may offer any reasonable sum for thy services."

"Mrs. Beamis, I'm honored, but I have a hotel to run. I don't intend to open a law practice here. Besides, I was a prosecutor, not a defense attorney. I also might have a conflict in this case. I saw the wreck. I know for a fact that your father-in-law didn't pull out in front of that log truck. The log truck wasn't in sight until after the pickup pulled out onto the highway. There was plenty of distance for that truck to stop. I suspect his brakes were faulty."

There was silence for a few seconds, and then Mr. Cubley added something. "Ladies, my suspicion was confirmed by the wife of the log truck driver when she told me how her husband tried to get the company to fix his brakes. They refused. The company put him out on that road with a defective truck. Being a potential witness, I must decline your request." Mr. Cubley sounded uncomfortable, having to turn them down.

Kent came around the corner carrying the box of soap. He started to say something, but I put my finger over my lips, he saw me, and immediately walked up on tiptoes.

"Listen!" I whispered.

"This tragedy is Satan's work. We repent having taken thy time, Mr. Cubley. Lucinda, shall we depart? God bless, sir."

I heard chairs scrape.

"Mrs. Beamis, I said I might have a conflict, and while I can't help you, I think I know someone who can. A law school buddy of mine who's an attorney in Roanoke. He and I have fought many a battle in the courtroom against each other, so I know he loves a good fight. I think Charles Parks of the firm Powell and Parks might be just the lawyer for your husbands. With your permission, I'll call him right now."

"Oh, Mr. Cubley, if ye would favor us so. If it's not God's will for us to hire ye, we would gladly accept a godly man on thy recommendation."

This was the same voice as before.

Kent and I were trying to wash the Buick, listen to the conversation, and not make too much noise. We did pretty well with washing the car but missed the phone conversation. We only heard Mr. Cubley say goodbye.

"We're in luck. Mr. Parks had a case settle, so he can drive up and see your husbands this afternoon. He would also like to meet and talk with the two of you. So, if you could meet him out in front of the jail around three, things can get started. He also has done work, both for and against Frank Dalton, my attorney in town. Mr. Parks is going to call Mr. Dalton to see if he can use his conference room.

I also invited Mr. Parks to come to the hotel to have dinner with me. Would you two ladies care to join us, or do you have plans?"

"It would be a privilege, Mr. Cubley, but it would not be proper to attend such a dinner. Our menfolk would not approve. Ye have been truly kind. We will share these tidings with our husbands."

"Ladies, my help has been minimal, but I think your husbands will be in good hands with Mr. Parks. Also, I seem to have crossed the path of the Beamis family several times lately. I think the Lord may have played a hand in this. Please call on me if you need anything else, and thank your husbands again for the gifts. That sport coat was a gift from my late wife, and I will cherish the replacement." Mr. Cubley sounded like he had gotten up.

"Thanks be, and may the Lord walk with and guide you, Mr. Cubley," one of the ladies said.

"Yes, and may peace dwell in thy heart," another female voice said. This one was softer.

"Wish we could go to the trial," Kent said.

"Yeah, like what? Those Highland Police would toss you and me out the back door so fast, not even Superman could catch us," I replied.

"Superman could so catch us," Kent argued.

"Stop looking at that whitewall and start getting the black marks off. I think we have another car when we finish this one," I said to Superman.

"BB, you ever think about getting a job as a guard on a chain gang? You would be good at it," Kent said as he threw a wet rag at me and missed.

It was time to get a move on. I thought I had heard a rumble of thunder in the distance.

CHAPTER 21

DINING WITH BIG JOHN
Tuesday, June 14, 1955

I t was a beautiful day in the mountains of Virginia. Not too hot and not too cold, but just right with a very blue sky. The afternoon remained clear. Kent and Billy were on their fourth car of the day, and Matt thought those kids would own the town, fifty cents at a time if they kept up their pace. They were doing good work, and more and more guests were asking for them.

Usually, one of two things brought the boys business. A guest who was staying for two weeks would tip off the newcomers, and that would bring in business. Or a guest would try the boys out, based on the flyer at the front desk. There had been a day last week when the boys had to stop taking orders because business was too good.

Matt was growing fond of BB Gun and Superman. Boo had tipped him off about their nicknames. It seemed nicknames abounded at Cubley's Coze.

In less pleasant news, though, Big John's spy network was still costing his hotel some bookings, and Matt was ready to get him back. Today, the mail had included a letter from his friend in Roanoke with the list of names for Cliff Duffy to pass on to his contact at the Green Mountain Resort. It was going to be interesting to see the end result.

Matt saw a regular guest coming into the lobby and decided this would be an excellent time to see if this guest had received an offer from his opposition.

"Oh, Mr. Carlton, might I have a word?" Matt requested with a smile for the old gentleman.

"Good morning, Mr. Cubley, how are you this fine day?" Mr. Carlton also smiled and extended his hand in a firm handshake.

The guest followed Matt into the hotel office, and by his ease in doing so, Matt understood this was not his first visit within. He and Mr. Tolliver greeted each other and Chuck immediately asked, "Sir, would you prefer tea or coffee?"

"Tea, please," Mr. Carlton responded.

"It would be my pleasure. Earl Gray with one sugar and lemon, not milk, right?" Chuck Tolliver asked, knowing full well what the answer was going to be.

"Perfect, Mr. Tolliver, that would be perfect," Mr. Carlton replied.

"Mr. Carlton, since I've taken over from my Uncle TJ, has your stay with us been satisfactory and up to the same standard?" Matt asked, hoping for a positive response.

"It has not diminished one whit, Mr. Cubley. Your uncle would be quite proud. And I like the new car wash idea you have implemented. Those two youngsters did a bang-up job on my Bentley Continental. I was a little hesitant to let them near her until I saw the work they did for Mr. and Mrs. Grayson. They were careful. I was so impressed, I tipped them a whole dime."

Mr. Carlton took out a cigar and lit it, and Matt noticed he was looking for an ashtray. He grabbed one from behind some file folders and handed it to him. Boo arrived with the tea, placed it on a table next to the chair that Mr. Carlton was occupying, and asked would he like a side of biscuits or scones? He thanked her and said no, as he was about to join his wife for lunch as soon as she returned from a little shopping trip in town.

"Mr. Carlton, it's good to hear things are up to my uncle's standards, and might I impose upon you for an additional inquiry?"

"Quite all right. What's on your mind, son?"

"My competition, the Green Mountain Resort, has started sending out letters to my former guests. In their letter, they offer a free night's lodging in exchange for a reservation with them. It seems they intend to lure away our guests to their establishment. In your opinion, should I be worried?" Matt asked the old gentleman.

"Are you serious? Cancel here to go to that place of loud music and drunken parties?" Mr. Carlton asked, startled. "Mind you, we do enjoy their horses for our grandson, as well as the occasional boat ride on their lake, but we'd never stay there. You have the proper atmosphere. Does that answer your question?" Mr. Carlton flicked his cigar into the ashtray.

"It does, thank you. I just wanted to be sure that you were happy here. Now, if it's not too much trouble, I would deeply appreciate it if you would let me know if you ever get such a letter. I would be happy to match their offer," Matt said.

"I thank you, but no need, if you'll excuse me, I hear my wife has arrived." Mr. Carlton rose, picked up his teacup in one large hand, stuck his cigar in his mouth, and strode out of the office and into the lobby. He greeted his wife with the cigar still firmly clenched between his teeth.

Matt called Chuck in to share the details of the conversation he had just had with Mr. Carlton and instructed him to deduct one night from the couple's bill. Then, he gave him the list of names and addresses for Cliff Duffy to pass along.

When Matt returned the tea service to the kitchen, Boo told him that Carol Martin and Judge Harland's secretary, Linda Carlisle, were in the dining room at table six.

"It might be nice for you to say hello. Mrs. Carlisle is the judge's new secretary. And a war widow. Have you met her yet?"

"I can't say that I have. Any reason you mention it?" Matt asked.

"Oh, no. I just thought it might be good business to meet her, since she and Carol eat here often," Boo related and headed off to watch over the dining room.

Meanwhile, Maddie was giving one of the waitresses, Teresa Long, a scolding for not picking up her ready orders fast enough. Teresa rushed past Matt, banged the exit door with a hip, and was gone in a flash without spilling the soup she was carrying.

He had started to follow her into the dining room, when he spotted Carol Martin sitting at table six with a pretty brunette woman. Teresa set their food down in front of them, and Matt thought, seeing those three women in one spot, that these three could stop the heart of any man. The brunette was laughing at something; her face was captivating.

A sudden memory of his Janet, sitting at a similar table at the Hotel Roanoke, rushed into his mind. It was the evening Janet had insisted they go out to the most expensive hotel in town for dinner. She had made the reservation without asking him, which was unusual for her since dining at the Hotel Roanoke on his salary was a rarity. He had gone along, however, since it was so out of character for her. He knew something was up.

It ended being a very big something: they were having a baby. Those had been the happy days, him and Janet and Jack, living like they had a lifetime to enjoy together.

He felt a hollowness in his chest.

"Mr. Cubley?"

One of the waitresses nudged him. He was blocking the kitchen exit, and the waitress was trying to leave with a tray of hot food. With Maddie on the warpath, he was about to cause a real ruckus.

"Uh, I'm sorry," Matt said, immediately moving into the dining room. He held the exit door open for her. She cranked up a head of steam as she passed him and proceeded to her table, full speed ahead.

Carol glanced in his direction and began to wave him over. Realizing it was too late to retreat, and feeling guilty for staring at the ladies when he should only be having thoughts for his Janet, Matt slowly walked over to table six, trying to compose himself.

"Hello, Carol, welcome to Cubley's Coze. So glad you could join us for lunch. Was Frank nice for a change by actually letting you out of the office? I hope the practice doesn't collapse in your absence."

Matt tried to smile at his joke but couldn't quite get it to work. He thought at least he was able to get something out in the form of a conversation that was not totally stupid. Well, maybe it was stupid.

"Hi, Matt. Yeah, the ogre is letting me out on an hour furlough. Let me introduce you to my friend, Linda Carlisle. She's Judge Harland's new secretary," Carol said with a smile.

Matt collected himself and responded with, "A pleasure to meet you, Mrs. Carlisle."

Linda answered, "A pleasure to meet you, Mr. Cubley. Carol has told me a lot about you. I think you might know my boss, Judge Harland?"

Matt paused and finally spoke. "Uh, yes, Judge Harland, I do know him. He came down to Roanoke on a special appointment when our local judge received a threat from a defendant. I doubt he remembers me; I was second-chair on that case and a newly-minted Assistant Commonwealth's Attorney." Matt was trying not to stare, but she was so pretty. Something more profound was holding his attention.

Mrs. Carlisle looked into his eyes and said, "Actually, when we heard about the wreck and how you helped, I asked my boss if he knew you and he said he did. You must have made an impression on him."

She gave him that endearing smile again.

Matt awkwardly asked, "By the way, how is your lunch?" He turned his attention to Carol to avoid staring at Mrs. Carlisle.

Carol came to his rescue by answering. "Delicious, same as always. I eat here a lot, and I figured I'd invite Linda to join me."

"Now that you are running the place, I expect we will see you from time to time," Linda said with a subtle smile.

"Thank you. Keep me informed on how you like the food," answered Matt.

Carol looked at Matt and grinned. "And the service? Don't forget the service. Boo is doing a fine job running the dining room. She really picked up the slack with Mrs. Longwood being off."

Carol was laying it on pretty thick. She must have noticed he was blushing.

"Well, ladies, enjoy your meal. I need to go," which was a total lie, but Matt felt it was time to retreat. As he left, he heard laughter from table six.

Crossing the room, it hit him like a slap in the face: here he had just met Judge Harland's secretary for the first time and he'd been too dumb to ask her how she was doing after her shooting scare. How could he have been so dense?

He passed Boo at the Maître D's stand and, on impulse, told her to cancel the bill for table six.

"Yes, sir," Boo said with a smile that she hid from Matt. "Not a problem."

"Phone for you, Matthew," Chuck called out from the front desk as he entered his office.

Matt picked up the phone on his desk, almost without thinking.

"Hello."

"Matthew Cubley?" said a gruff voice.

"Yes, it is," answered Matt.

He recognized the voice as he heard, "Big John McCulloch here."

"Hello, Mr. McCulloch, I hope you're having a good afternoon?" Matt asked, frowning.

"Cubley, we need to talk. You free for dinner?"

"Yes, I'm free tonight," responded Matt, his frown deepening.

"Meet me at the Alpine Restaurant tonight at seven o'clock for steaks."

"All right. Should I bring wine or anything?" inquired Matt, trying to be polite.

"Not necessary," came back the answer from Big John.

"No? Okay. I'll see you at seven, then. Thank you," but Matt wasn't sure Big John had heard him because the connection had been broken midway through his thank you.

"Chuck, you will never guess who just called."

"Mr. Big John McCulloch is asking you to meet over steaks for dinner. No wine, just you. Does that about cover it?" Chuck laughed.

"I've got to remember to close that damn pass-through. Have I no privacy around this hotel?" Matt jokingly feigned anger.

"Nope, not possible," said Chuck with a smirk as he continued with a flower arrangement he was starting for the entrance table in the lobby.

***

Tuesday afternoon dragged on and on for Matt. He was almost glad when it came time to change into a coat and tie for dinner. He returned to the lobby after dressing to tell Chuck that he was leaving.

"If you are not back by morning, I'll send out a posse," Chuck joked as he left.

Matt knew the man was trying to lighten his mood, but he felt uneasy.

"Don't think that will be necessary. Just call Mr. Koehler's hearse for a single pick up. I'm not sure if it'll be for him or me."

Getting into his Bel Air, he noticed the white top was dusty and made a mental note to get Billy and Kent to give it a rinse.

Matt drove slowly down the exit drive, looking at the valley view. The lake stretched out below him to his left, and when the road entered the trees, he caught only glimpses of the lake and river. He slowed and stopped at the foot of the hill at the three-way intersection.

Crossing the main road, he drove up the drive to the other hotel, passing below the western half of Green Mountain. The car eased up the gradual rise effortlessly until it crested the hill and coasted into the parking area. Green Mountain rose majestically to his left.

I own an entire mountain, he thought suddenly. He was still trying to get used to the extent of his inheritance.

He parked in the guest lot for the Alpine Restaurant, an impressive stone building with a European-style steep roof, and noticed Big John's 1955 Fleetwood Cadillac was parked in a reserved space by the front door.

His host was waiting for him at a table in a private room. Based on the empty glasses on the table, it was clear Big John McCulloch was on his third drink, having not bothered to wait for his guest. Matt expected that Big John's wife might join them, but it quickly became obvious that this was a men's only business meeting.

Matt greeted his host. "Good evening, Mr. McCulloch."

"Cubley, I'm three up on you. What will you have?"

A waiter arrived to take Matt's drink order. Big John ordered his fourth rum and coke, heavy on the rum, and Matt ordered a draft beer.

"Cubley, you follow the stock market?"

"No. I might start, however. My uncle left me a few shares," Matt replied, trying to hold up his end of the conversation.

"Too bad. A smart man can make a lot of money in the market."

Salads arrived without any order being taken. Fifteen minutes later, thick steaks with baked potatoes and green beans were deposited in front of them. Again, this was done without the intervention of their waiter.

Matt's steak was medium-well, just the way he liked it.

"Hope you like your steak? I had my cook call Maddie and find out your preference," Big John said with a flourish of his left hand.

"Looks great," Matt replied.

After a few minutes of enjoying their steaks, his host jumped right into the subject at hand.

"I figure you know why I asked you here. I want to consolidate my holdings."

"Yes, I suspected it was something like that," said Matt.

"How would you like to live the life of leisure?"

"I'm not sure."

"Well, I'm going to make you an offer. No need to answer now; just look over these figures and give me a call in a day or two. No pressure, but I'm sure you'll see how generous my offer is. I can have the money in your account by the end of the week."

Big John was talking and eating at the same time as if this conversation was of little importance. Yes, not of sufficient importance to allow his steak to cool. He reached over and dropped a thick envelope on the table between their two plates.

"How is business, by the way?" the larger man asked out of the blue while cutting off a large piece of meat.

"What? It's fine. My uncle really knew how to run a country lodge, and the regulars just stay regular," Matt responded, trying to make a little joke. He put down his fork, giving Big John his full attention.

Suddenly, Big John stopped eating, put down his cutlery, and spoke in a whisper, "The resort business can be tricky. One summer, you're booked to capacity, and the next, you know, things just dry up for no apparent reason. It's hard to figure."

Giving Matt a smile, his host motioned to the waiter to bring a fresh drink. The waiter looked at Matt, but Matt declined a second drink.

"Well, I'm new at this business. I hope I don't hit a dry spell," Matt said while he studied the other man's face.

"I'm happy to take the worry off your hands. I'll even cover all the closing costs. That'll save you a bundle. Think it over." Big John looked back at the bar for his drink with a frown.

Matt returned to his meal but noticed Big John was not a patient man. Not for a drink, and certainly not for business.

Supper ended with no more talk of business. One thing that could be said about Big John, he could discuss politics, baseball, and golf with the best of them. The dinner hour passed quickly, and after blueberry pie for dessert (not homemade but decent), Matt took his leave and drove back to Cubley's Coze, glad the outing was over.

Cliff Duffy was on the front desk when he returned, and Matt had a question he needed answering. First, he looked around to be sure they were alone.

"Cliff, tell me how you get the names over to your contact at the Green Mountain Resort without being obvious," Matt inquired.

"Easy, Mr. Cubley. I take a lunchbox they gave me, put the papers inside, and place it in the old Early Dawn Dairy milk box by the big sign for the Green Mountain Resort. Today, the Early Dawn Dairy trucks deliver the milk right to our kitchen, but in the old days when your grandfather ran the place, milk was delivered to those boxes. Each resort had its own box. Don't know what happened to the Cubley's Coze box, but the one for the other resort is still there. They built stuff to last in the old days."

Matt leaned against the front desk and checked again for guests. There were none in the lobby at the moment. Cliff continued with his explanation.

"I drop the lunchbox off when I go home each morning. When I come back to work, I pick it up empty.

"Did Chuck give you the fake list?" asked Matt.

"He did, and it'll be delivered first thing in the morning."

"Good, thanks, and goodnight," Matt said, waving as he walked across the lobby and took the elevator to the second floor.

CHAPTER 22

A RESORT WAR
Wednesday, June 15, 1955

I t was a dreary day with clouds, fog, and rain. The crackle of a fire in the lobby fireplace lightened the mood of both staff and guests, despite the temperature not requiring one. Chuck considered it a decoration, not a necessity.

Matt passed the fireplace without even noticing the fire. He missed having Billy and Kent at breakfast since no cars would be washed today and his general focus was turned inward on matters of the heart, some wonderful and others worrisome.

Polecat arrived on time to breakfast on the loading dock and lingered over a second cup of coffee. It was clear he was in no hurry to suffer his final wet ride over to the other resort to deliver his papers. Matt could smell that the rain may have enhanced, rather than reduced, his guest's odor problem. The wily old fox conned the loan of a dollar off Matt without providing him any news bulletins. They discussed the local's reaction to Chief Smith's bragging that he had solved the sniper case.

Matt returned to finish a final cup of coffee in his office, quietly reflect on life, and eventually read the previous day's mail. He was also half-listening to Boo manning the front desk, talking to a guest. The pass-through was open, making for excellent acoustics. When it was quiet, he even noticed the pop and sputter coming from the lobby fireplace.

It was somewhat unusual for Boo to handle the front desk, and he was realizing just how versatile she was. He heard Boo greet Chuck and there followed a sharp knock on his door.

"Come in."

He looked up as Chuck entered, picked a chair, moved it to a center position, and slumped into it.

"Morning, Chuck, sleep in this morning?" Matt joked and smiled to let his hotel manager know that he was kidding. This employee was such a hard worker; Matt found it necessary to order him to take more time off.

Chuck sat up a little straighter. "No, in fact, I didn't sleep at all last night. I heard you come in around eight, but I didn't want to bother you until this morning."

"Okay, what's the problem?" Matt asked, growing concerned.

"Where shall I start?" Chuck began and paused to gather his thoughts. "We had three cancellations last night. Two said they needed to make other plans, thanked me for canceling the reservation, and hung up. The third guest wasn't as abrupt. This guest told me flat out that he was going to the Green Mountain Resort because they were giving him a free night. I tried to talk him out of it and even offered his family a free night here, but my offer just made him mad. I found out why, when he continued our conversation: he was required to mail a non-refundable deposit to the other resort for the free-night guarantee. Since we didn't require a deposit, he was committed and we lost out, but he still got mad at me."

Chuck's retelling got faster and faster as he spoke until his words seemed to be racing each other. When he finally stopped talking, he needed to take a deep breath to avoid passing out.

Matt relaxed slightly and decided it wise to divert to a positive subject. He was certain that the hotel had plenty of guests. "What's the *house count* for next week?" he asked, feeling proud of himself for speaking hotel.

"We were at seventy-five percent until these three canceled. That will put us down, but we'll still make a small profit." Chuck was starting to fidget. A habit that caused Matt to know his manager wasn't completely finished.

Chuck blurted out, "What happened at your meeting with Big John?"

Matt decided to confide in Chuck. "He wants to buy me out. I told him I would give it some thought, just to stall him, but that's never gonna to happen. I'm hoping if he thinks he's going to buy the place, he'll back off trying to run us out of business."

"I knew it had to be that. Big John would never have you for dinner out of kindness," Chuck responded, but he was still clearly uneasy.

"You know, last night he warned me that the resort business could have dry spells and said he'd be doing me a favor by taking Cubley's Coze off my hands. What a nice guy, looking after my welfare." The frown on Matt's face told the real story.

"Nice, like a snake in the grass," Chuck replied.

"Funny you say that. Last night, when he told me that line of his, the same thought popped into my head."

Chuck nodded but didn't laugh.

"Any other problems?" he asked as he put down the guest book.

Chuck was still looking disturbed. "While you were out last night, Mrs. Longwood called and said her brother has had complications from the surgery. She needs to stay on with him and wants to talk to you about it. She was very distraught, knowing this is our busy season."

Chuck tugged his collar, pulling it away from his neck.

"What should we do?" Matt asked.

"You're asking me?"

"Well, yeah. I want your opinion since you know the staff. Her position as Maître D' of the dining room is critical," Matt stated, waiting a few moments for an answer.

"Mrs. Longwood has been very loyal. She has vacation time that normally she would not use now, but with these extenuating circumstances, I think her request is appropriate. I would let her have time off."

Chuck sat back a little in his chair and took a deep breath. Matt waited about fifteen-seconds to mull it over, looked over at him, and replied, "Done."

"Oh," Chuck squeaked. "Of course, this means Boo will have to continue to fill in for her. I mean, if that's okay with you?"

"Isn't Boo outside working the front desk?" Matt asked.

"Yes, I had her fill in for me this morning."

"Ask her to come in."

Chuck stepped over to the door and asked Boo to come into the office.

"Good morning, Boo. How are you doing this morning?" Matt asked with a smile that he didn't quite feel with all the bad news. He was trying not to let the morning go down the sewer or show his feelings to the staff.

"Fine."

She looked like she was also trying to put on a happy face, but Matt noticed that she was not her usual bubbly self.

"Please, sit down. We have a problem that you may be able to solve," Matt said and motioned her to a chair.

"I will if I can."

"Mrs. Longwood called and needs more time off for her brother. She doesn't know how long for sure, but Chuck and I think we should grant her request."

"Oh, I agree, Mr. Cubley. She's very worried about him. She called me last night at home to tell me all about his complications. How can I help?"

"Well, Boo, we need you to continue to run the dining room in her absence. I know it's a lot to ask, but you've been doing a good job. Would you consider it?" Matt asked and was hoping for a yes.

"If you think I'm doing the job to your satisfaction, I'll help out any way I can. I have to tell you, though, the receipts are running behind Mrs. Longwood's projections for the summer. I'm trying to learn the job and keep up with the books, but the income is slipping. So, if you need someone older with more experience, I understand." Boo looked anxious.

"Boo, you're doing fine. The problem is me."

"You? I'm not sure I understand?" Boo asked, but her expression said otherwise.

"Well, after reviewing the ledger from last year to this year, it's obvious that we're running too many meals off the books. We should be charging employees, except for the dining room and kitchen staff, a fee of half the normal price. Right?"

"Yes," Boo responded and looked very concerned. "Mr. Cubley, I didn't mean...I shouldn't have...you're the owner...it's not my place..."

Matt interrupted her and continued while shaking his head no. "Boo, stop worrying. I didn't know Uncle TJ's rules when I told Kent and Billy to help themselves to meals. I should have talked to you or Chuck and had them pay the employee rate. On the other hand, those kids aren't earning a lot, even being busy. I doubt if they could even afford to eat here, even at the half rate. I know Kent and his mom have it rough."

Boo nodded in agreement.

"I have also given free meals to the Bondurant family, and those two young ladies the other day. Polecat is a regular freeloader, although my uncle approved him because he performs a valuable service. It's best that we leave him on the list for free breakfasts."

"Yes, sir," Boo said with a smile.

"Send me a bill for all the free meals I've handed out since my arrival, plus, bill me for any I grant in the future. Oh, don't forget to bill me for my own meals."

"You, Mr. Cubley?"

"Yep, all of mine at the half rate. That way, when Mrs. Longwood returns, the books will be in order. You're right, I'm the owner, but I must be certain the profit and loss ledger reflects a true picture. Be sure Billy and Kent continue with meal privileges on me, and say nothing to them. Those two boys keep me sane. Will that be okay with you?"

"Yes, sir, of course," Boo responded, but Matt noticed she was still not herself. He thought he might know the problem or hoped he did.

"Now, Boo, that does leave one matter unresolved."

"Yes?" Boo asked with a blank look on her face.

"While you've been filling in for Mrs. Longwood, your pay has remained the same as the other waitresses, right? A dollar a day, plus your tips, and any meals at no cost?"

"Yes, sir," Boo answered.

"Have your tips dropped since you're not working tables?"

"Sir, I hope to make that up just as soon as Mrs. Longwood gets back."

"How is that fair? No, that will never do. The hotel will pay you the same salary that Mrs. Longwood was getting from the time you took over her job until she returns. This next payday, I'll have Chuck add what we owe you to your check," Matt announced with a firm look at Chuck, who had just raised an eyebrow.

"You can do that?" Boo asked.

"Well, I don't know. I thought you said I was the owner?" Matt chuckled and looked at his manager.

"He is the owner," Chuck agreed with a smile.

"Mr. Cubley, did my dad call you?" Boo leaned forward as she asked the question.

"Your dad? No, I haven't had the pleasure of meeting your dad. Why do you ask?"

"I got a letter from the business office of the university, and they raised my tuition for this fall. I was having a difficult time coming up with the extra money despite extra hours and good tips here. I want to finish this year, and with this salary, I might have just enough."

"I agree. You need to finish school. If it looks like Mrs. Longwood will not be back before you leave for school, will you help me hire someone to look after the dining room after you leave us?"

"Oh, yes, sir. Thank you so much. I need to call my dad and let him know. Oh, thank you!"

Boo excused herself from the office, looking much happier than when she had arrived, and returned to the front desk to call her dad.

"What else do you have for me?" Matt asked as he closed the office door. Chuck pointed to the pass-through, and Matt closed it, too.

"Matt, I think Big John is behind this next problem, as well. The company that supplies our paper products wrote to us that they are not able to complete our order. I called them first thing this morning but got nowhere." Chuck's left eyelid twitched. Not a good sign.

"This just gets better and better. If I'd known this last night, I might have poisoned the old scoundrel at his own restaurant." A burst of anger filled him, but he tried to calm himself. "What about Lynchburg if the Waynesboro people won't deal with us? Yes, let's reach out," advised Matt.

"I'll make some calls and let you know. We may have to go to Roanoke and pay the extra freight. We're low on paper because Waynesboro was supposed to send us a large shipment for the summer, but they dropped us like a hot potato. Can you sue them?"

"Not really. We placed an order, but don't have an exclusive contract with them. We might have a suit against Big John if we could prove he's interfering with our paper supplier, but even if we could prove it, by the time we'd get a judgment, it would be this time next year. Big John's pockets are deep enough that he can hire the legal talent to delay our case for one year, if not two. We need to start keeping all our suppliers secret; I'm just not sure how."

Matt stood up, walked over to his office window, and looked out in thought. Chuck waited to hear his plan. Matt turned and sat back down.

"Chuck, tell our suppliers that we want deliveries by out-of-town freight companies. I want them to stop using their trucks. If Big John and his cronies don't see their logos, they won't know the names of our suppliers, and it'll make it much harder for him to interrupt our deliveries. Also, we have plenty of storage space; let's order in larger quantities and ask for a volume discount. Tell me if you need more funds. Big John's not going to best us if I can help it."

Matt started tapping a pencil on the desk nervously.

"Matt, you may have solved my next problem with your last solution. Our meat packing supplier got stopped on the edge of town by the Highland Police; they inspected his truck from the front bumper to the rear mud flaps. When they didn't find a violation, they demanded he unload it. Well, he got angry, refused, and told them he was going to call his boss and the state police. They backed off on making him unload the truck, but they let him know they would be watching him. I think the phrase the officer used was, 'you better mind your *p's and q's*.'"

"Chuck, our old friend, Sergeant Little John McCulloch, said the same thing to me in my office recently. I bet you a slice of spice cake that I know which of the local cops is harassing our delivery truck." Matt frowned.

"Sounds about right." Chuck mimicked Matt's frown.

"That gives me more than one reason to use unrecognizable delivery trucks. Gosh, this is beginning to sound like Russia. Did my uncle have this much trouble with Big John?"

"Big John caused trouble from time to time, but not like this. I think he's testing you, or he's made up his mind that he's forcing you out and buying Cubley's Coze one way or another."

Chuck and Matt spent another half hour going over figures and how much damage Big John might be able to do. Strangely, they realized he would probably be at the meeting of the Highland Business Owners Association tonight. Matt was planning on attending that meeting, and Chuck suggested putting poison in all the tea and coffee pots, but Matt concluded it might scare off business if they killed Big John and all his cronies on the premises. Also, it would be difficult to cover up—too many bodies. Despite the attempt at levity, Matt had joined Chuck in the worry department.

A short time after lunch, Sergeant Barry Oliver and Trooper Bobby Giles dropped by Cubley's Coze to talk. Surprised, Matt offered them coffee or tea, which they declined.

"Thank you for seeing us without an appointment," Trooper Giles said in his almost too-polite manner.

"You guys are welcome anytime; you don't need an appointment. How can I help?"

"We need to ask you about the two boys you have working here washing cars. William Gunn and Kent Clark, both age twelve." Sergeant Oliver read from a small pocket notebook.

"Holy cow, I hope this isn't serious," Matt said with a surprised look.

"We need to know if they're trustworthy. Would they make reliable witnesses?" asked Sergeant Oliver.

"I would say yes to both questions. While I've not known them long, I have seen enough to know you can trust their word. They're very honest. Why do you ask if you're at liberty to tell me?"

"They were at the hotel on the day of the shooting at the courthouse. Mr. Gunn and Mr. Clark, out of the presence of each other, both gave consistent statements to the effect that the Beamis brothers were here that afternoon looking for you. According to them, the two brothers waited in the lot until no more than five minutes before the shooting. If that's true, the Beamis brothers would not have had time to drive from here to town, set up a sniper post, and begin shooting at the courthouse. It's not possible," Sergeant Oliver stated.

"Are you sure?"

"I'm sure. I had Trooper Giles and Trooper Quinn both time the drive to town from here. They couldn't make it in that time, even exceeding the speed limit. Trooper Giles did it at three this morning, and I'm convinced he drove the fastest possible time. Anyone driving that fast on Friday afternoon would have been noticed, but we have had no such reports. Mr. Tolliver confirms the time he saw them asking for you in the lobby but can't confirm when the brothers left. The two boys, however, seem certain of the time they left the hotel lot. So, our question to you is, do we have credible witnesses?" Sergeant Oliver looked at Matt expectantly.

"Yes, you do. I'm curious, did you tell them not to discuss this?"

"Not beyond what we tell any witness. Why?"

"I gave those boys a lecture on how a promise to keep a secret is a serious promise because they heard something here at the hotel that needed to remain a secret. To my knowledge, they kept that secret, and I can sure tell you they've had plenty of opportunities to tell other staff members and me about their talk with you. They have not uttered one word, so, I'd trust them if I were you. I have to ask, though: why did Chief Smith arrest the Beamis brothers? This doesn't make any sense."

Trooper Giles replied as his sergeant frowned. "Trooper Quinn tried to tell the chief what he'd found out, but Chief Smith refused to listen. I think he referred to Trooper Quinn as 'sonny boy.' Anyway, Chief Smith said he'd solved the case and the file was closed, so Trooper Quinn took a walk to prevent bloodshed. Isn't that how it went?"

Matt came to the rescue of the trooper. "Yeah, I can imagine how Trooper Quinn might react to that insult. Does the Beamis lawyer, Mr. Charles Parks, know about this?"

"He does now. He asked the prosecutor for any exculpatory evidence on the case and was given an open file privilege. He also got permission to talk to all the officers. When he called the office, we filled him in on our investigation and asked him to hold off telling the parents of Clark and Gunn. We thought it wise to make personal contact to inform them," said Oliver.

"That was wise," replied Matt.

"We've just come from both residences, and all the parents now know the boys will have to testify. They're not happy, but they seem to have accepted it. Anyway, we wanted a third party to verify the credibility of the two boys, and you've done that, so I guess we're finished here." Sergeant Oliver stood first, then Trooper Giles.

Walking with them out of the hotel, Trooper Giles thanked Matt again for seeing them.

While the sergeant got in his Ford and drove away, Trooper Giles lingered.

"Matt, can I ask you something?"

"Go ahead."

"Were you in the Marine Corps? Perhaps served as a gunny down at their sniper school?"

"How the hell do you know that? That was years ago, and I don't talk about it for reasons of my own," Matt responded, shocked.

"One of the troopers at HQ in Richmond was trained by you. He bragged about you being a good instructor. We've hit a dead end on this sniper case. The brass is leaning on us, hard, and our sniper expert wanted to know if you might be available to help him? I understand and will pass on your regrets."

Trooper Giles' caring manner often drew people into sharing confidences with him. Matt felt a strange compulsion to speak.

"Trooper, let me share this with you. I tried several times to transfer to a combat company, got turned down because my boss, a captain, wanted me where I was, and two other officers stopped me, a lieutenant and a general. The lieutenant was the general's secretary. She and I started seeing each other on the sly. Gunnies aren't allowed to date officers and marriage is a whole bigger problem. She went to the general before word got out and got special permission for us to marry. The catch was I had to stop asking for transfers. I feel guilty about missing combat. But, I'll help your trooper if he needs help. By the way, who is the trooper you say I trained?" Matt asked.

"His name is Benjamin Anthony Lusk. He was awarded a silver star and a purple heart," Trooper Giles said.

"I do remember him. Lusk the Tusk, he was called because his two eye teeth were a little out of line, larger than normal. They looked like tusks on a walrus when he smiled. He had trouble with windage calculations, as I remember, but once he slowed down and started calculating the crosswind properly, he got pretty darn good. I didn't know he was a trooper. Small world. I'm glad he made it back; many didn't." Matt turned, waved, and walked back into the hotel; his steps were slow, and his thoughts were of times past.

CHAPTER 23

BILLY AND CHANGES AT THE GARAGE
Wednesday, June 15, 1955

"Ouch," I grunted as something poked me in the back. I looked over my shoulder, and it was Scotty, poking me with his cap pistol.

"Scotty, do you know what today is?" I asked and moved to launch an attack.

"No?" Scotty said with a puzzled look.

"It's the day you die if you poke me again with that cap gun. Now get!" I made a quick movement like I was coming for Scotty and away he ran.

"Mommy, Billy's hitting me! Make him stop!"

"William Boyer Gunn, you stop that this instant! Don't make me come up there."

I was mouthing the words along with Mom since I knew the response by heart. "I'm not touching him; he's poking me with his cap pistol," I called back.

It was a rainy Wednesday, so I was in no hurry to get up, until the aroma of breakfast wafted up from the kitchen. I was the last one to the table. Even Mom had a plate in front of her. I grabbed mine from the stove, where it was sitting between the burners to keep my plate warm without cracking it, and sat down.

Breakfast was scrambled eggs, biscuits, and sausage gravy. Mom and Maddie were both great cooks, and I thought I might be putting on a little weight.

"Mom, this is the best breakfast ever!" I said, still chewing.

"Don't talk with your mouth full," Mom reminded me, but I knew she was pleased with the compliment because of the smile she was trying to hide.

I thought about all the cars Kent and I had washed this week. Even just getting to keep half the money because of the college fund tax had left us flush with cash.

There was one dark cloud over my piggy bank, though. Just when I thought I had it all my way, Dad cut my allowance back from a dollar to fifty cents a week and informed me that reduction was because I was working a steady job. It had been terrible news because fifty cents of allowance was equal to four washes at the hotel, plus I didn't have to save any of my allowance for college.

Breakfast ended with no family fights, and I tried to slip up to my room for some serious comic book reading, but Dad put a halt to that. He caught me and sent me to the garage to sweep it out. After I finished that chore and thought I was finished for the day—nothing doing—he told me to use a file and sharpen the blades on our rotary reel push mower.

Dad instructed, "Next sunny day, I want the grass trimmed up, and while you're at it, be sure you pick up all the rocks and old busted car parts that may be in the grass."

The rocks came from Scotty. When he gets a little older, if Dad catches him throwing rocks near customers' cars, even the wrecked ones, he'll be in for a whipping with a belt. I know all about Dad's belt. The whippings don't hurt that much if Mom or Grandma are home, but when Dad gets mad and they're not around, well, a certain little Scotty better look out.

I put a dent in an expensive car that Dad had parked, waiting for parts. I was throwing rocks and one went sideways. I swear it was an accident, but still, I hit it smack in the driver's door. That day was one of his quiet days. Mom and Grandma had taken Scotty to the doctor, so I was home alone with him. I tried to hide my wounds, but Mom saw the blood leaking through my t-shirt and shorts.

"Your dad came back from the war a different person; he just doesn't know his own strength," Mom told me. Well, he might not, but I sure found out.

Mom and Dad had a big fight over it. She put me in her bed and told Dad to go sleep on the couch. I thought he'd fuss or whip me again, but he didn't. He just left and didn't come home until the next afternoon. I felt horrible, 'cause it was all my fault. That was the last time he had two quiet days in a row. Mom stopped leaving Scotty alone with Dad after that.

I began filing the blades on the reel mower. I also oiled the gears and axle to make it easier to push.

While I was working, Dad got into a conversation with me about Boo Skelton.

"How did Mr. Skelton know I was looking for another mechanic?" asked Dad.

"Boo's nice. We talk at the hotel all the time. I told her about you looking for another mechanic. I was telling her how you were short of help since I don't work here all that much anymore, working at the hotel and all."

"Oh, so I'm having to replace you since you changed jobs from being my chief mechanic to washing cars at the big hotel on the hill," Dad said like he was cross, but I knew he was teasing me.

"Well, you did say you needed help, right?" I asked defensively.

"Yeah, I did. So, you and she talk at the hotel, huh? She's nice, is she? And pretty, I bet!" Dad was back to teasing me.

"Dad, she's all grown up and goes to a university. Just 'cause I said she was nice; you don't have to…"

"Don't get all worked up, son. Just kidding. Actually, thanks for putting him on to me. He's a good mechanic, but I wonder why he wants a change? Something must be going on at the dealership," Dad said, getting serious. "And someday soon, sooner than I would like, you'll be after those bobbysoxers." He rolled back under the car on his crawler.

Dad seemed to have a thing for feet. White bucks and now bobby socks. Well, give me a pair of black Keds with white laces, or my favorites, my Roy Rogers cowboy boots, and I'll be just fine. I began thinking about cowboys as we worked in the garage for the next thirty minutes.

"Billy, finish up. I have a tow job this morning," Dad called out from under the car. No way he could see me.

I had been looking out the window at some dogs chasing a cat across the road. I jumped. How does he know when I'm goofing off? I started back filing those darn blades while trying not to slice up my fingers on the sharpened edges.

The tow job was in a residential district. A car wouldn't start and, this time, the battery was good. Blacky pulled her in with no problem, other than the rain getting us wet. Dad got a lot of "town business," as he called it. The Chevrolet dealership got the company work and work from the plant's "bigwigs," like foremen, the plant superintendent, the rich people in town who run businesses for Big John and make big money. The bigwigs all go to the Chevrolet dealership.

Dad got normal people's business. That's what Kent called them. Normal people were generally much nicer, and according to my dad, paid their bills on time. Dad told Mom that the "bigwigs" could pay, but hold up paying, sometimes for a month or two. No reason other than to hold onto their money. A few of Dad's customers ask for credit, but not as often as you might think. Some barter or trade things, like my bike.

After we returned from the tow job, I finished up filing the reel mower, and Kent and his mom dropped by. We retreated to my room so we could hear Mom and Mrs. Clark talking about their concerns regarding Kent and me testifying in court. Grandma started telling Mrs. Clark that, on the news, witnesses were quite often killed before they could testify.

We laughed about it, but I was a little scared because I had never been to court before. Kent was talking about running away to miss court, and I asked, "Where would we go where those troopers couldn't find us? Besides, it's raining,"

He shrugged and announced, "Superman can fly above the rain."

I laughed at his nutitude.

Mom started telling Mrs. Clark that she had heard at the beauty shop—that place was almost as good for news as Polecat—that Mr. Cubley was lying about how the wreck happened. She had heard he was going to sue for the Beamis family, ruin the plant, throw a lot of people out of work, and just to get rich off the backs of the employees.

Kent got mad; he started downstairs to tell them Mr. Cubley would never do such a thing, but I grabbed his arm and told him to wait and listen.

Sure thing, Mom then said she didn't believe it. Both Mom and Mrs. Clark were saying it was that horrible Big John McCulloch just trying to get out of having to pay for his truck running over poor old Mr. Beamis.

The ladies moved on to the topic of new dresses in the window of the dress shop downtown, and Kent and I started talking about cowboys and who had the fastest horse. It was Roy Rogers' Trigger versus the Lone Ranger's Silver. I knew Trigger had it by a mile, but couldn't convince Kent. He got stubborn, sometimes.

A little while later, we heard a car pull up and looked out to see a deputy sheriff's car by the garage. I had seen the deputy before but didn't know his name. He and Dad ran from the garage to the house, trying unsuccessfully not to get wet. They barged into the kitchen, and Mom, Grandma, and Mrs. Clark moved to the living room. Kent and I read comics and listened at the vent. This new conversation had to be better than dress-talk.

"So, break-ins, huh?" We heard Dad ask as he started to bang on our coffee pot.

"Yeah, the 'B&E's' recently haven't been run of the mill. Odd stuff is being stolen; valuables are being left alone. In one house, a coat was taken; in another, a pair of hunting boots; then, there was a box of shells, but the gun they went to was left in the unlocked gun cabinet. Crazy! Food's missing from the church pantry, but only canned food. The hardware store lost a tent and sleeping bag. Another tent and bag were stolen from the Boy Scout leader. The drug store—now this is a puzzlement—had cold medicine and aspirin stolen, but all the strong painkillers were left untouched." We heard a chair scrape on the floor, and the deputy said, "I'll take mine black."

I heard Dad's voice from the vent. "Since it's too early for hunters and the stuff stolen's too nutty for hikers, what about some teenagers who are setting up a camp or planning on running away? On the other hand,…two snipers, yeah, getting supplies to hide out and lay low, makes sense. Especially the ammo stealing," Dad concluded with, "Ouch, that's hot!"

He sometimes thinks out loud and argues with himself, taking both sides of an argument and then coming to a conclusion. I sometimes laugh at how he does it, but he seldom gets stuck without finding an answer and, sometimes, I find myself doing the same thing.

"John, we think alike. I think we either have two older kids or two former soldiers who know the town and are using it as a supply base. Those North Koreans did it to us all the time. They stole us blind. Hell, we equipped their army better than our own. Catching the current thieves won't be easy. The sheriff has several of us working on these 'B&E's.' He's not leaving it to Chief Smith and his bunch, but the problem is, we're stuck as well."

"So, what can I do for you. I know you didn't stop by for the joe or my sparkling wit," Dad said with a snort.

"No, John. I came to ask you if you had noticed anyone new in town, seen anyone suspicious, or had a stranger calling you for a tow?" The deputy was talking a little softer like he was afraid someone might hear him.

"No new faces. The only new face in town is the new owner up at Cubley's Coze, but he's a former prosecutor and strikes me as honest."

Good for Dad.

"Judge Harland speaks highly of him. Sheriff Lawrence called the sheriff down in Roanoke. We were told Mr. Cubley should not be a suspect, despite Big John's bad-mouthing of him. We don't have to believe that puffed up asshole, but no one in the department can say anything bad about Big John that could cause the sheriff a problem with the election."

The deputy then went into the same details about Big John bad-mouthing Mr. Cubley that Kent and I had just heard from Mom and Mrs. Clark. It really was all over town.

Bored, Kent and I decided to see what we could find to do in the garage. The rain was down to a damp mist, and we got to talking about making slingshots from some old elastic we found, and where we might buy some firecrackers for the Fourth of July—got to have firecrackers for the Fourth. It was only a short time later that the deputy came out, waved at us, and drove off. Mrs. Clark, Mom, and Dad came out together, and Kent had to leave with his mom. They were going to the dress shop. Poor Kent. He begged to stay here, but his mom said no.

The phone in the garage rang as they pulled into the road. Dad answered it and just listened for a while. Finally, I heard him say, "Come on over, and let's talk."

"Dad, we got a tow, or is someone bringing in a car?" I knew it was neither, but with adults, the dumber the question, the more information you got out of them. Unless it was too foolish, and then you just made them mad and got nothing, or got whacked.

"What did you say, son?" Dad asked. I knew he was thinking about the call and answering me out of habit, rather than thinking about what I had asked.

"Who was that?" I asked. Now I was curious.

"That was Dan Skelton. He wants to come right over. Don't know what is going on, but something sure is. I guess we'll find out... strange... mighty strange."

Dad was talking to himself and thinking. I drifted back into the back of the garage and made out like I was busy doing something. Ten minutes later, a 1950 Kaiser, Deluxe Virginia, with a canvas roof pulled into the garage parking lot. Actually, it was a hardtop, but that canvas cover made it look like a ragtop. A large man wearing bib coveralls got out and walked into the garage.

"Hey, John, thanks for seeing me." The man was Boo's dad, and he held out his hand to my dad.

"Dan, good to see you, though I didn't expect it to be this soon." Dad held out his hand for a handshake after he wiped some grease off.

"Well, John, I just got fired. After five years working for the Chevy dealership, they fired me, just like that. I want to be upfront with you and not hide it." Mr. Skelton sighed and just stood there, shaking his head.

"When you said you were thinking about a change, I figured something was up. Want to tell me about it?" Dad asked and motioned for Dan to sit down on one of the four chairs that Dad kept in the garage near the woodstove. Of course, there was no fire today.

"Well, this all started with my daughter, Beverly. She told me your boy worked at the hotel, washing cars. That's how she heard you might need some help at the garage."

"Yeah, my boy was telling me just this morning about how he told her that I needed extra help. Glad he passed along the message." Dad looked around for me.

I was trying to be invisible, but Dad spotted me inside the parts cage and called to me, "Billy, come on out here. I want you to meet Mr. Skelton."

I walked up to Mr. Skelton, held out my hand, and looked him in the eyes. I was hoping I might get to stay and hear why Boo's dad got fired. Mr. Skelton shook my hand and said Beverly was saying nice things about me. She was getting better and better, in my opinion.

"Do you know Mr. Cubley, the new owner, very well?" Mr. Skelton asked my dad.

"I met him when he first came to town. My wife told me about him losing his family and some of his history. He knows Frank Dalton, who speaks highly of him, and I respect him enough to let Billy work for him. My knowledge is limited, but he appears to be OK."

I was surprised about the good things Dad said about Mr. Cubley since he wasn't one to hand out praise. I quietly walked around and took a seat in the third chair behind Dad. I noticed Dad stayed off the white shoe topic.

"Well, I don't know him, but Beverly thinks the world of him. He helped her and he didn't have to. He's good people in my book. In fact, Mr. Cubley has put Beverly in charge of the dining room because Mrs. Longwood is out with her sick brother. He was concerned enough to ask her about her not getting her tips since she wasn't working tables. I was surprised a new owner would know or care. Anyway, he's paying Beverly the same salary he was paying Mrs. Longwood, which is enough for her to go back and finish university. We thought she was going to have to drop out a semester." Mr. Skelton shifted again in his chair, either because he was nervous, or the seat was hard.

"So I have nothing but good things to say about him, and so does my Beverly. Our dreams were that she would finish at the university next spring. When my wife died a few years ago, her last wish was for our daughter to get a good education and have opportunities beyond Green Mountain County." Mr. Skelton finished with a quiver in his voice.

"That's good to hear that Beverly is going back to finish," Dad agreed.

"We thought our troubles were over. That's when I found out if Beverly didn't quit her job at Cubley's Coze, I might not have a job at the dealership," Mr. Skelton said in an angry voice.

"Hold on, what does one thing have to do with the other?" Dad asked. It was the same question I was thinking.

"The boss called me in and sat me down yesterday before I came over to see you. He and the shop foreman knew all about Beverly getting the promotion at the hotel. I was told Beverly needed to refuse the job and quit. They said she could come over to the Green Mountain Resort and hire on as a part-time waitress. Otherwise, I might need to find other employment."

"What was his reason, other than the one that makes no sense?"

"He claimed business was slow. The boss was going to have to lay off one or two." Mr. Skelton wiggled around in his chair and settled back down into a more comfortable position, before concluding with a shake of his head, "I'm not a new hire, far from it."

"Well, why in the world would they care where your daughter worked? What did you tell them?"

"I told them I had to ask Beverly to stall for time. It was a miracle that I heard about this job when I did. I didn't want to make her quit her job. We both have to work this summer and save every penny for her to return to the university."

I saw both men just sit, looking at the floor for half a minute.

"What about her raise? Wouldn't Green Mountain match it?" Dad asked, starting the conversation back up.

"Those cheapskates! They refused. Like I said, they told me she could sign on as a part-time waitress. It was up to her what tips she got, which put me in a bad position. Beverly and I talked about it last night. I told her she was keeping her job, and I was not breaking my promise to her mom. She was going to finish school. She cried, I have to say I got a little misty myself." Mr. Skelton wiped his nose with a red bandana from his pocket.

"So, today, I'm up against it. I have to have a job, or the wheels come off. When I went into work today, I honestly thought they would back down. I was in the middle of replacing an engine on a company truck. I knew business wasn't slow. We're covered up. I thought my job was safe. Boy, was I wrong. They cornered me, demanded an answer, and refused to give me any more time. When they pushed me into a corner, I told them if they didn't match her salary, the answer was no. Then they up and fired me on the spot. John, I'm here with my hat in my hand. I need this job in the worst way." Mr. Skelton sat and waited for Dad to say something.

My dad was not one to make quick decisions. I knew that. The silence dragged on and on. Even when Dad spoke, he didn't give him an answer, right off.

"Dan, the town is talking about how Big John is going to buy out Mr. Cubley. Billy, do you think Mr. Cubley is going to sell out?" Dad asked me, turning in his chair and looking at me.

That took me by surprise, but Dad sat looking at me, waiting for an answer. "Dad, Mr. Cubley is giving raises and talking to guests all the time, so I think he's going to stay. The guests all seem happy. He hired Kent and me for the whole summer," I said.

"I think you're right," Dad concluded. I don't think Dad needed my answer, but who knows?

"Well, there you have it from my boy, my former chief mechanic. My own flesh and blood quit me and went to work for Mr. Cubley, and I need to replace him right away. So, if he thinks the hotel's not being sold, I doubt I'll be getting him back. Can you start tomorrow?" Dad laughed and gave me a wink.

Wow, I wasn't sure what Mr. Skelton thought after that long path around the barn for Dad's bombshell. He shook Dad's hand and thanked him at least six or seven times, and promised to start whenever Dad wanted him to start. He had his tools in the car and was ready. Dad repeated that first thing tomorrow was soon enough, and they would start on a brake job. He had him bring his toolbox into the shop and store it with Dad's in the cage. He told him they would have to mark the tools to keep them straight, but Mr. Skelton said his were already marked.

Changes were taking place—big changes.

CHAPTER 24

THE HIGHLAND BUSINESS OWNERS ASSOCIATION MEETING
Wednesday, June 15, 1955

M att and Chuck spent the afternoon calling suppliers, putting in large orders, and making arrangements for rental
trucks to handle the deliveries. All the bother was to keep the local
police from interrupting their supplies. Matt was starting to worry
that he was involved in a hotel war he might lose.

It would devastate him if that happened. He was growing
fond of the place, its staff, and its regular guests. Since his arrival,
his respect for the employees had grown, seeing their hard work and
dedication. The staff had welcomed him and shown him the same
loyalty as they had shown his uncle with one exception, and Matt
hoped Cliff Duffy was the only example of disloyalty, though he
thought that had now been repaired.

He was realizing that he needed the hotel and its people
needed him because there were only a few employment opportunities in the valley not controlled by Big John McCulloch.

Meanwhile, Polecat continued to be invaluable. While his
informant had no breaking news at the moment, Matt asked him a
question that had troubled him since the Beamis brothers' arrest.
Why the Commonwealth's Attorney, a Mr. Albert Winston Brown,
was allowing Chief Smith to charge and prosecute the Beamis brothers with little to no evidence. After all, Matt knew the staff in his old
Roanoke office would have dismissed those charges before the ink
was dry on them. Under Virginia law, it was the Commonwealth's
Attorney's duty to see that no innocent man should ever be convicted and that the court received the truth at all times.

Polecat cleared that up quickly: "Mr. Albert Winston Brown
works for McCulloch Wood Products as their local attorney and
only serves as the Commonwealth's Attorney for the county part-
time. While Big John's important legal work goes to a Richmond
law firm to whom he pays a large retainer, McCulloch Wood Prod-

ucts pays Mr. Brown quite well to handle local matters. Small things like avoiding civil suits when the company fails to pay legitimate bills, prosecuting workers on trumped-up charges, and writing up eviction papers to illegally remove fired workers and their families from company houses."

"And Big John gets away with all that?" asked Matt.

Polecat smiled. "When you own the local special police, most of the businesses, and the Commonwealth's Attorney, it's not hard to get your way."

Matt sure didn't like it but he had to agree. Once again, Polecat had provided the answer that made the most sense.

"Tell me, Mr. Smith, why did the governor get involved in the Beamis traffic accident?"

"Mr. Cubley, I shouldn't need to pontificate on the lucrative arrangement Big John enjoys with the former lead partner of that Richmond firm I mentioned. The identification of that particular partner should be self-evident."

When Matt asked, "Our governor?"

Polecat flashed his yellow teeth with a big smile. Matt noticed one of the front ones had a green cast to it. Polecat really was a study in contradictions, but, oh, so accurate with his facts.

Polecat carried on, explaining that, when an employee was fired, the special police made sure the family left the rental house owned by the company before the required legal notice had run its course. The cops helped the tenant leave almost every time. It was not unusual for the former employee to end up on the wrong end of a nightstick during the move.

Usually, Chief Smith let Sergeant McCulloch and the town officers handle the relocation of tenants. That's what they called it: "the relocation of tenants." Sometimes, Chief Smith was present reading the eviction notice. What Polecat heard from station scuttlebutt was that Chief Smith even took pleasure in roughing up the ladies, which would cause the husband to charge in and end up with him getting a free ride to the hospital courtesy of the Highland PD.

According to Polecat, during the most recent "tenant relocation," an employee by the name of Doc Hathaway had gotten framed for stealing payroll checks, resulting in his family being thrown out on the street. One of Doc's friends had gotten the family out of town to safety, but few of their belongings survived with workers ordered to pile the family's possessions onto the back of a company truck so the load could be taken to the dump. The family had ended up being helped by a church in Waynesboro until Doc got out of jail.

Matt was beginning to see that this was a typical factory town with a "big boss" in charge of everything. Even as an attorney and former prosecutor, he was illegally outgunned and sinking in a swamp of corruption.

A part of him wanted to close it all down, fold up his tent, collect his rent from Big John, and crawl in a hole somewhere. He thought to himself, *if only Janet were here. She always fought for the underdog. She'd be able to keep going.*

Later on, Matt sat in his office, staring out of the window for an unproductive twenty minutes. After a while, he started to hear Boo and Maddie talking about dinner plans for the Highland Business Owners Association Meeting scheduled that evening, which brought Matt back to the present. He stood up and looked around the office that Uncle TJ had used to beat off Big John and all his pals for so many years. He felt disgust over his previous desire to cave. Someday, he would be with Uncle TJ, Jack, and Janet, and he realized he wouldn't be able to face them if he let someone like Big John McCulloch ruin Cubley's Coze.

At six-thirty, Matt went up to his room and put on a coat and tie. When he came down, men had already arrived for the meeting and were climbing the stairs to the second-floor banquet room. He hurried across the dining room, wanting to see if they would invite him to join them for dinner or exclude him—a little test to see who controlled the Highland Business Owners Association.

He approached Richard Lockhart, whom he already knew from having shopped in the hardware store, and extended his hand. "Mr. Lockhart, good to see you, and welcome. I hope you're ready for an enjoyable dinner."

"Good evening, Mr. Cubley. Nice to see you again." Mr. Lockhart shook Matt's hand, but that was all. No mention of Matt staying for the meeting or even his position with the group, which was telling, since Chuck had informed him that Mr. Lockhart was the president of the association.

Several other men joined them in the banquet room, greeting Matt if they knew him, or being introduced to him. All were friendly, but not a single one invited him to the meeting.

Promptly at seven, several of the waitresses arrived with salads and began taking drink orders. Big John arrived at ten past seven with three or four more members on his coattails. He was jovial and greeted Matt with a vigorous handshake.

"Hey, listen up," shouted Big John. "I want to introduce my good friend, Matt Cubley, our host, and wish him the best in his taking over this fine hotel."

He then held up both hands over his head like goalposts on a football field and called out, "Let's get started, dinner is served."

When they all sat down, Matt was left standing. After waiting for no more than five seconds, he left the room, leaving the waitresses working the recent arrivals for their drink orders.

He approached Chuck, who was working the front desk. After looking around the lobby and seeing no one present, he said, "Well, that was the warmest greeting and coldest shoulder I have ever gotten."

"What did you expect?" was Chuck's response.

"Oh, I guess that's exactly what I expected. Did Uncle TJ ever get invited to their dinner and meeting?"

"He was invited to eat with them on one occasion when an offer had been made by Big John to buy out your uncle. After that offer was rejected, he was never invited again. Even on that one occasion, they informed your uncle, after dinner was concluded, that the association had a financial matter to discuss, so the business session of the meeting was a closed meeting. He was asked if he would mind allowing them their privacy. Everyone knew the financial matter involved your uncle," Chuck concluded.

"Did Uncle TJ listen in that time?" asked Matt in a whisper.

"I'm not sure, but I don't think he cared enough to go upstairs to listen."

"Chuck, if anyone asks, I've gone for a walk."

The hotel manager leaned in close to whisper into his boss's ear, "Matt, I anticipated this. I oiled the slides on that little section of the wall, put wax on the floor so the bottom won't drag, and placed a small chair in your special room to make you a little more comfortable. There's a pad with an ink pen on the chair for notes."

"Thanks. Do you read minds, or are you just very good at predicting the future?"

"Both," Chuck said with a smile and went back to making up bills for guests.

The meeting lasted an hour and a half. Matt was back in the lobby, standing at the front desk when the first of the men crossed the lobby to leave. He smiled at each one and wished them all a good night. Big John even made it a point to come over to him and shake his hand.

"Hope you enjoyed your dinner, and your meeting went well," Matt commented, feigning ignorance.

"Like always, the food is great. Maddie knows how to kiss a steak with fire and not ruin it. And the meeting was productive. I expect to hear a positive answer from you soon. Have a good night," Big John concluded. He walked out of the building with the two plant guards that he had brought with him and posted outside the meeting room door.

Matt noticed Big John had parked his Cadillac in the guest check-in space.

What a pompous ass.

Matt went to the kitchen to check-in with Boo and Maddie. They said all went well, and Boo reported Mr. Lockhart, who usually left a small tip for the association, gave a little extra. He had also made it a point to ask Boo what her plans were for the summer, which she noted was an odd question. Her answer to the question had been, "As far as I know, right here."

Mr. Lockhart had ended the conversation with, "It's always good to keep an open mind. Does your dad still work at the Chevrolet place?"

She told Matt she had opened her mouth to answer, but Mr. Lockhart did not even give her a chance; he had just walked off.

"That is odd, Boo. I hope it's nothing, but you better tell your dad what happened tonight. He might need to know."

"I will, Mr. Cubley. Goodnight. Oh, by the way, I'll come in late tomorrow since I had the duty tonight. Teresa Long will cover for me until noon."

The rest of the evening passed quietly, and when Cliff Duffy arrived to take over from Chuck, Matt invited his employee to come up to his room for a drink.

"There are some things we need to discuss," he explained.

Once in Matt's room with drinks in hand, Matt gave Chuck a report of the meeting.

"Big John reported that business at the plant was good with plenty of orders for the fall and winter. Employee wages would remain at the present rate with a little Christmas bonus if profits remained strong."

"Was anything mentioned about Cubley's Coze? What could you hear?" asked Chuck.

"It's too bad that I have to resort to spying, but darn, if that organization isn't something. Mr. Lockhart might be the president, but Big John runs those meetings and the town with an iron fist. I think he has ego problems, and from what I heard tonight, he has most of the business owners in his grasp. He told them he was going to buy me out or run me out, and that that was a promise they could take to the bank." Matt stopped and sipped some Sloe gin over ice.

Chuck was having a tumbler of Bacardi's Gold rum with lots of Coke. "Between chats with Big John, Polecat's intel, and his own observations, your uncle knew Big John's intentions."

"Well, it gets worse: Big John told the group that I was a real troublemaker and to spread it around that I can't be trusted. He said it was a fact that Mr. Beamis had pulled out in front of the log truck, making the accident the old farmer's fault, and he defended getting the governor to pull the state police off the case to keep them from dragging out the investigation. His boy knew the facts. No need for any state interference."

Matt lowered his voice to just above a whisper, although they were alone. "What he told them next was incredible: he said Little John and Frank Younger heard me change my story when I found out it was a McCulloch truck. He said I was a two-bit lawyer from the big city who couldn't have even seen the accident, since I was too high up on the mountain. According to him, I'm just trying to make a ton of money off the Beamis wreck and even his driver would put the fault on Beamis. He warned them if the plant gets hit with a big lawsuit, then the town gets hit." Matt waited for a response.

"Matt, do you always make these wonderful first impressions when you arrive in a new town?" Chuck joked, trying to lighten the mood.

"Don't know. But after I get run out of this one, I could practice my technique and try to get better at it for the next one," Matt countered. He was determined not to let Chuck best him.

"Why did the meeting last so long tonight?" Chuck then asked, getting up to add more Coke to his rum.

"They talked about the courthouse shooting. Big John told the association the Beamis brothers did it. He went on to report on a Bible verse threat the brothers made to kill Chief Smith. The Commonwealth's Attorney will push for no bond at the bond hearing and petition for a delayed trial."

"Why no bond and a delayed trial?" Chuck asked as he sat back down with his drink, now more Coke than rum.

"The prosecution lacks evidence. If they delay the trial, keep the brothers in jail as long as possible, then it helps Big John in a couple of ways. It gives Chief Smith more time to find the gun used in the shooting. He hasn't found it, and I doubt he ever will if he thinks the Beamis brothers are the shooters. Based on what Billy and Kent saw, they couldn't have done it. Chief Smith is hunting for a rabbit in a bear's cave. He might stumble onto a bear if he's not careful."

"Let me guess: by keeping them in jail, they'll be too busy defending themselves to sue McCulloch Wood Products over their dad's death. You think Big John planned that all out?" Chuck asked.

"No, he's good, but not that good. He just saw Chief Smith's blunder into the arrests as an opportunity to avoid or postpone a civil suit against his company. Having the police and prosecutor in your pocket is a big advantage. I mean the police and prosecutor generally have immunity, but this crowd may step over the line and lose their immunity. Charlie Parks, the Beamis' lawyer, is no fool; he will push back hard. The brothers are in good hands with him. Plus, I've only heard good things about Judge Harland and Judge Carlton. A quick trial with an honest judge is the last thing Big John wants."

"Did anyone speak out against what's going on?" Chuck asked, shaking his head.

"No one argued with Big John, at least not tonight." Matt rose and looked at the clock in his room.

"Chuck, the rest of the evening, was spent talking about business, keeping out the competitors, but there wasn't anything else about the hotel. Honestly, it was boring as hell—I can see why Uncle TJ didn't spy on them—but I'm glad I took the time tonight; I at least learned what Big John is trying to do to my reputation. We're in a real fight to hold on to Cubley's Coze."

CHAPTER 25

BAD TO WORSE FOR BILLY
Thursday, June 16, 1955

The day was a summer paradise with blue skies and fresh air that had been scrubbed clean by the rain, and the southwest wind meant no smell from the plant. Kent and I were pedaling our bikes up Green Mountain Avenue toward Cubley's Coze when a delivery van with a big fish on the side honked and passed us. We both tooted our bike horns, though I doubted he heard it.

Suddenly, a siren screeched behind us, and I swerved. The police car that passed us was going much faster than the van, its siren wailing and red light flashing. It pulled the van over right in front of us about a half-block down the street, and I saw Officer Frank Younger get out of his patrol car with his ticket book. He walked toward the rear of the seafood van as we passed.

When Kent and I reached the hotel, we stashed our bikes behind the shed near the loading dock. Collecting our breakfasts from the hotel kitchen, we were sitting in chairs on the dock, enjoying the food, when Mr. Cubley came out with a plate. Kent told him about the excitement down on Green Mountain Avenue.

Mr. Cubley frowned and exclaimed, "Darn, the seafood company was one of the few who had to use their own delivery van." He got up, returned his plate to the kitchen, walked back out with his car keys and drove off in his Chevrolet.

Polecat rode up on his bike, not a minute later. He joined us with a plate of food. Kent and I were finishing up when Mr. Cubley returned. The fish van was not following him.

Mr. Cubley asked Polecat if he saw the van pulled over.

"I missed the initial detainment, but witnessed the aftermath," he answered. "I also acquired some disturbing news from behind the Highland Police Department as I listened to the officers at their shift change."

"I'm afraid to ask, but I better—what?"

I knew this was going to be important; Polecat stopped eating to speak.

"Mr. Cubley, I'm afraid that some of the constabularies are planning on stopping and inspecting every delivery vehicle bound here while providing as much irritation to your delivery people as they can manage, subject to their limited resources. Officer Roger Younger has managed to disable two police vehicles, backing one into a tree, and shooting the other. He exceeds all expectations of incompetence, according to Chief Smith, leaving his twin, Frank, to patrol while the sibling is confined to desk duty, unarmed for the time being, according to the town gossipers."

Kent and I smiled over that last comment as Polecat continued to speak and chew.

"Today, Frank's sole obligation to his department is to stop every delivery van bound for your tourist trap—the chief's words not mine—and not return until his ticket book is full. The chief wanted more cars assigned to this duty, but Roger's recent acts have left the department depleted of vehicles." Polecat gathered in a mouthful as Mr. Cubley spoke.

"Most interesting, Mr. Smith, but there are quite a few delivery vehicles on Green Mountain Avenue, some bound for here, some downtown, and some to the Green Mountain Resort. How are they sorting out the ones for here?" Mr. Cubley asked, trying to get Polecat back on track with some useful details.

"Elementary. Chief Smith has issued a proclamation for them to stop every delivery vehicle traveling south on Green Mountain Avenue. The officers are to question and ascertain the destination of each. If it is this locus, the vehicle is to be detained and searched with as much offensive inconvenience as they can manage. Every possible infraction will be written up with abandon. Meanwhile, vehicles bound for Green Mountain Resort or other businesses are to be expedited along their journey." Polecat said all that without missing a single bite or interrupting the chewing of his breakfast. Quite a remarkable feat.

Mr. Cubley just sat there, thinking. Then, he went into the hotel. Mr. Tolliver happened to be in the kitchen talking to Boo, and we heard Mr. Cubley tell him, "I'm going downtown to see

Frank Dalton about our fish delivery being delayed this morning." Mr. Cubley left for the second time.

Kent and I finished breakfast and went on to work on a Dodge. It was later in the morning when the seafood delivery van finally showed up and unloaded. Mr. Tolliver, who was quite talkative when he was nervous, later told us that the van driver verified what Polecat had already told us. The man was fuming over three citations and being held in a cell for over an hour.

Mr. Cubley came back a little later from the police department and met with Mr. Tolliver in the office. The window was open, allowing us to hear all about how Mr. Cubley got pulled over by Officer Younger as he left the station, but there was nothing wrong with his car or license. Then, right in front of Mr. Cubley, Officer Younger had stopped the seafood van a second time as the truck tried to leave town. Mr. Cubley began making calls to his suppliers. We could hear him telling them the police had changed tactics and to say they were making a delivery to the Green Mountain Resort. Any more problems and they were to call him as he was getting his attorney involved.

After we washed the Dodge, we were through for the day. When we picked up our pay, Mr. Cubley stopped us as we were getting ready to introduce ourselves to this cute girl on the veranda. She had just checked in with her parents, so we were going to try to talk to her while the parents were busy unloading their car.

"Hey, boys, if you're finished for the day, how would you like to go with Richard and me up to the hunting lodge. Have you ever seen it?" Mr. Cubley asked.

"I have heard Dad talk about it, but I've never seen it.

"Neither have I, but I think that would be fun. What do you think, BB?" Kent asked.

"Sure, let's go," I said.

Richard Baker drove with Mr. Cubley in the front seat while Kent and I rode in the back of the hotel wagon. Richard drove down the entrance driveway and made a right toward the two houses where he and Rose, and Maddie Johnson lived. We followed that road as it ran parallel to the Smith River in front of the hotel. Past Maddie's house, Richard turned right onto a gravel road. We stopped to open a gate with a big sign on it that said, "No Trespassing." I asked Superman if he was a "tea passer?" We both broke up, and I imagine Mr. Cubley thought we had gone totally nuts.

The road climbed up the mountain—first, one way, then around a sharp curve, and back the opposite direction. Mr. Cubley told us these turns and up-hill sections were called switchbacks, which was how they were able to build the road up such a steep mountain. We must have gone three miles in a zig-zag to climb up the mountain for one mile. We eventually came to a big meadow with a two-story, brown lodge on the other side. It had a stone porch and was constructed of the largest logs I had ever seen. It looked every inch a hunting lodge built for bigwigs. Off to the left side was a big, solid-looking rock storage building built right into the side of the mountain. Green Mountain continued to rise behind the lodge. If I had to guess, I think we were only about halfway up it.

Kent and I helped Richard unload the wagon. After five minutes of us helping him, Mr. Cubley said he and Richard would have to do the rest of the work because they were going to put out dangerous chemicals for bugs and mice. He told us we could go exploring, not beyond calling distance. We explored the big meadow, but after finding no signs of bears or coyotes, we returned to the lodge.

Mr. Cubley pulled out a big key from his back pocket. He used it to open a large lock on the rock storage building, which could oddly be unlocked from both sides.

The stone walls of this storage building were at least two feet thick with shelves in the back and cabinets on the side walls. Richard stored the leftover chemicals in the corner, then removed several things to be cleaned.

I became curious about hunting trails that my dad had mentioned, so I asked Mr. Cublem about them.

"Boys, they're two main hunting trails which go past the lodge and one goes all the way up to the top of Green Mountain. There are some side hunting trails off these two main trails. Deer stands are in some of the trees up higher, built for the hunters by my grandfather and Uncle TJ."

The woods above the lodge sounded like a great place to build a fort, Kent and I agreed.

"I bet you could hold off an entire army up there, and the deer stands could be secret observation posts for scouts. We need to check it out," I announced.

Kent suggested we could pretend the rock storage building was a bunker, and we were surrounded by Nazis.

Mr. Cubley cut in, saying that he hoped there were no more Nazis and we should pick a better game. When we picked cowboys and Indians, he said he wasn't sure that was much better and hoped our war games were always just games. Mr. Cubley was funny like that. So was my dad.

We decided we'd check out the woods above the lodge on our next visit and left shortly after. Going down the mountain, the road looked and felt steeper, and we both grabbed a handhold once or twice, but neither of us yelled. It sure felt good to be back on level ground.

When we got back, we looked, but the pretty girl was long gone. Mr. Charles Parks, the attorney for the Beamis brothers, however, was waiting in the lobby for Mr. Cubley. They greeted each other and went into the hotel office, and Kent and I walked around to the wash area to listen in. However, as we rounded the corner, I heard Mr. Cubley tell Mr. Parks that Mr. Dalton was on his way before closing the office window.

With no more cars to wash and nothing to hear on the sly, Kent and I decided to check out what or who might be over at the Green Mountain Resort. If nothing was going on and no girls were over there, we figured we could ride to the park.

Pedaling down the hill and then up the other hill, we arrived at the parking area in front of the other resort, where Kent spotted the Lockhart brothers and Lou McCulloch. He skidded to a sudden stop, and I almost ran into him but stopped myself just in time.

The three bullies had seen us too. They came out from between two bushes and pushed Kent off his bike. I hopped off my bike, leaning it on its kickstand, and helped Kent back onto his feet. There we stood, two against three.

"Well, if it isn't stupor man and little buh, buh, Billy, dumbass," Carl said with a smile that was anything but friendly.

"What are you two doing trespassing on Green Mountain Resort property? This is private property, you know." Lou snarled and took a step toward me.

"We got passes to be here," Kent said as he reached for his wallet to get out his employee pass. Mr. Cubley had given one to each of us.

Dickie Lockhart, however, did not give him a chance. He swung hard in a roundhouse swing that connected with the side of Kent's head, right beside his left eye., throwing him backward onto his bike. Lou drew a fist back to swing at me, but I managed to punch him in the nose as hard as I could, and his hands flew to his face. I could see blood start to flow.

Carl slammed me from the side and we both went down in the road. Dickie then landed on top of us. We all three were punching as fast as we could when several of the workers from the resort ran up and pulled Carl and Dickie off of me. Lou was still holding his nose. Kent was still over his bike, not aware of what was going on.

I got up and went to Kent.

"Kent, Kent, wake up. Are you all right?" I gently shook his shoulder but received no response.

The resort manager ran up, furiously demanding to know what was going on.

Carl answered him, "We caught a couple of trespassers. The three of us are teaching them to stay off Green Mountain Resort property," as if he had any authority to be there himself.

"Lou, are you hurt?" the manager asked Lou McCulloch. He was ignoring Kent, who was out cold.

"I think he broke my nose," Lou whined. His words were a little hard to understand; his nose was stuffed up like he had a bad cold.

"Well, we'll take care of these two. No one trespasses on our resort and starts a fight. No one," the manager yelled at Kent and me.

Kent's eyes started to focus as he came to his senses, and he sat up, wiping the blood from his cheek.

Realizing that Kent was not going to die on me, I stood up, reached into my back pocket, took out my wallet, and pulled out my pass from Mr. Cubley.

"Sir, we aren't trespassers. We're employees of Cubley's Coze Hotel. Mr. Matthew Cubley gave Kent and me these passes. See! He told us we could come over here and use the facilities anytime we wanted for free, but these guys stopped us. When Kent tried to show them his pass, Dickie sucker-punched him and knocked him out. Lou, Dickie, and Carl came at me, but all I did was defend myself. They started it!" My voice grew louder, the angrier I got.

"What he's saying is true. Here's my pass," Kent said, slowly standing up while holding the side of his head with his left hand. He shakily handed the pass over to the manager.

"All you boys, come with me!" exclaimed the manager, putting our passes in his coat pocket.

"What about our bikes?" Kent demanded.

"Sam, Pete, take the bikes and put them in the shed. Be sure to lock them up. We'll hold on to them until this is sorted out," the manager ordered. The workers who had pulled the bullies off me picked up the bikes and rolled them away.

My right hand was starting to hurt. I could only imagine how Lou's nose felt. *A little pain in my hand was worth it if it's true that I broke Lou's nose.*

Kent and I were escorted into the manager's office behind the front desk as he wasted no time telephoning Cubley's Coze. I heard him speak to Mr. Tolliver before it sounded like Mr. Cubley came on the line. The next thing I heard was, "Yes, sir. Of course, sir. In a few minutes? Yes, sir." It sounded like the connection was cut off from the other end. The manager looked at the phone like he had never seen a telephone before. Then he placed it back on its base.

"What are your names?"

"I'm William Boyer Gunn. My full name's on my pass—the one you took."

The manager pulled out the two passes and looked them over.

"And you're Kent Farnsworth Clark?" the manager asked Kent.

"Yes, sir," Kent said frowning. I knew how much he hated his middle name. If the bullies heard it, he would never hear the end of it.

"Well, Mr. Cubley is coming over here. Have a seat. I'll be right back." As he left the room, he asked the front desk clerk, "Misty, would you watch these young men. Please have someone bring an ice pack for Mr. Clark's eye."

"Could I have one too?" I asked, holding up my right hand, my middle two knuckles having started to swell and turn blue. The outside two knuckles were also beginning to hurt and turn red.

"Make that two."

"Yes, sir," the front desk clerk replied, smiling at us. "You boys tangle with older boys who outnumber you all the time, or was today special?" She asked in a whisper without giving us a chance to answer before she picked up the phone and ordered up two ice packs.

"Those three gave us no choice?" I answered and smiled back at her.

"Oh, I see. Perhaps not," she agreed.

Things got quiet as we waited for the two ice packs to arrive. In the movies, they always put a piece of raw steak on a black eye, but I guess the manager figured Kent was not worth wasting a good steak. It was then that we heard the manager's voice coming across the lobby.

"Did you think to look? Big John? Of course, I have to call your grandfather and your dad. Now sit there and keep holding that rag to your nose." I heard some more, but his voice grew quieter, and I couldn't make it all out. Then the ice packs arrived.

We heard a car pull up and stop right in front of the lobby door, and Mr. Cubley quickly came into the lobby with Mr. Dalton in tow. Someone was about to be in trouble—I just hoped it was not going to be Kent and me.

The manager greeted Mr. Cubley and Mr. Dalton; then, all three men came into the manager's office. The nice desk clerk went back to the front desk and softly closed the door behind her.

"Kent, are you okay?" Mr. Cubley asked, but before Kent could answer, he spotted me with an ice pack on my hand. "Billy, you, too? What in the world is going on?"

The manager started to say something, but Mr. Cubley stopped him. "Billy, you first."

"Well, sir, Kent and I were on our way over here after work. We were going to check out the marina since we had some time to kill and we thought we'd use the passes you gave us. We had just gotten to the front of the hotel when Lou, Carl, and Dickie stopped us. They called us trespassers, so Kent started to show them his pass, and that's when Dickie sucker-punched him in the side of the head so hard it knocked him out cold and he fell backward over his bike. I thought they might have killed him. Then Carl, Dickie, and Lou started getting ready to hit me. I tried to back up, but it was three against one, so I had no choice; I had to punch Lou in the nose to stop him from knocking me out like they did Kent. Then Dickie and Carl knocked me down, and I was trying to fight them when some guys pulled them off me," I said in a rush.

"Did you show him your pass?" Mr. Cubley asked me as he pointed to the manager.

"Yes, sir," I said.

Kent spoke up, "We both did; he still has them. He took our bikes, too!"

"So, they threw the first punch?" Mr. Dalton asked us.

We nodded.

"Aren't these the same three I saw giving you trouble at the hardware in town?" Mr. Cubley asked next.

We nodded again. Mr. Dalton then asked the manager if anything I said wasn't true.

"No. Nothing worth mentioning."

Mr. Dalton then said, "I seem to recall you were the manager when Uncle TJ had that little problem over the lease and his guests using the facilities. I thought we had this all cleared up: Big John promised the pass holders of Cubley's Coze that they were not going to have any more trouble. Was that last suit not expensive enough for Big John? Do we need to raise the amount high enough to get his attention? Since the law and facts were established in the first suit, the second suit will only be a matter of establishing the damages—both actual and punitive, since your resort was given a warning by the judge not to violate the lease a second time. I think you better have Mr. Albert Winston Brown give me a call today."

225

"We'll be going now. Would you be so kind as to have the boys' bikes placed in my wagon? Mr. Dalton will be in touch with Mr. Brown about damages to personal property, and of course, full compensation for the severe personal injuries suffered by my employees," Mr. Cubley added sternly.

The manager retrieved our bikes from the shed and placed them in the back of the wagon. The remainder of our visit to the Green Mountain Resort was a lot of bowing and scraping by the staff. We heard several apologies from the manager. I waved good-bye to the desk clerk, and she smiled and waved back. I saw the manager frown, but he didn't say anything to her.

Mr. Cubley drove us back to Cubley's Coze, where he and Mr. Dalton finished the meeting they were having with Mr. Charles Parks. Superman and I waited in the kitchen with our ice packs on, and when Mr. Cubley came out of his office, we told him we were sorry and volunteered to stay away from Green Mountain Resort.

Mr. Cubley agreed that, for the next few days, it might be a good idea to do just that. He clarified that he was angry, but not at us, and promised to tell us when it would be safe for us to go back there.

Richard drove us home. Poor Kent had to tell his mom how he got the black eye, and, before I got home, my mom already knew all about the fight. Dad didn't say much, but Mom and Grandma made a big to-do over it. I spent the rest of the evening up in my room, trying to stay out of sight and clear of Scotty. I tried not to think about how much my hand was hurting and daydreamed, instead, about the pretty desk clerk.

CHAPTER 26
BILLY GOES TO COURT
Thursday through Monday, June 16-20, 1955

Kent and I rode our bikes to the hotel on the morning after the fight. Superman's black eye was turning into a nice shiner, a little blood showing in the white part. Several adults commented on it, and he was really embarrassed.

The swelling of my knuckles had gone down, but my hand was still sore. I rode on the flats with one hand and only used my sore hand when I had to pedal uphill.

While we were waiting for our breakfast, I noticed Boo glancing at us and then writing a notation in the book she used to keep track of dining room charges. I asked her if we needed to pay something, but she said no, she was just making a note for Mr. Cubley. I knew employees, except the cooks and waitresses, paid something, so I guessed we were considered kitchen staff.

Mr. Tolliver entered the kitchen and asked Boo if she had seen Mr. Cubley.

"He's in the storage room," she advised. "I saw him go in about ten minutes ago."

When Mr. Tolliver looked in the storage room off the kitchen, but no one was in there. He walked out, saying nothing to Boo.

I went over, peeked in the storage room, and saw that a bag of sugar had fallen off a shelf, broken, and spilled. I got a broom, Kent got the dustpan, and we cleaned it up. Our good deed done, we collected our breakfasts and walked out to the loading dock to join Polecat, who was almost finished.

"Good morning, Mr. Smith," I said to Polecat.

"A fine morning for an ambulatory excursion into the wilds," he replied.

"I guess it is," I responded, but I had no clue what he had just said. I hadn't seen a single ambulance that morning.

"How are your injuries?" Polecat asked between sips of coffee.

"I guess you heard about our scrape? Not too bad. I got one good lick in on Lou McCulloch. I hope he's feeling it this morning."

Kent joined in with, "BB punched him a good one on his nose."

Polecat announced, "It's my understanding, based on what I heard, that young Master McCulloch suffers from bilateral sub-orbital hematomas, a nasal bone fracture, and a sore posterior from the whipping his father gave him with a cincture." Polecat ended with a grin that made him look just like a crocodile about to snatch a waterfowl.

"Gosh, he won't die from a hema-what's it's, will he?" Kent asked, all worried.

"Not from two black eyes, a broken nose, and a sore butt from getting spanked with his father's belt," laughed Polecat, who was talking like a normal person for once. "I heard Little John tell Officer Roger Younger that after the whipping I gave that boy, he won't sit for a week. I can't believe the little snot let a kid half his size get the best of him. Now his grandfather wants to kill him for maybe wrecking his deal to purchase Cubley's Coze.'"

Superman looked at me and mouthed, "Half his size?" He grinned that goofy grin, and I decided to get him for that later.

We returned to the kitchen for seconds when a door slammed and Mr. Cubley walked out of the storage room. He had dust on his boots and a flashlight in his hand. Maddie informed him that Mr. Tolliver was looking for him.

Boo asked, "Mr. Cubley, were you in the storage room?"

"Just now?"

"Yes, sir. I saw you go in this morning when I arrived, but when we looked a few minutes ago, the storage room was empty. I didn't see you leave or go back in. Just wondering."

"Guess you missed me when I came out and went back in. I've been around the hotel checking things and looking over our inventory. We don't want to run out since our deliveries are being harassed by Highland's finest."

"Me and Kent cleaned up the sugar," I said.

"Kent and I." Mr. Cubley corrected, looking puzzled. "And what sugar?"

Kent spoke up first. "The bag of sugar that fell off the shelf in the storage room," He then added, "BB and I cleaned it up for you. We even put the rest of the sugar in a paper bag we got from the kitchen."

"Thanks," Mr. Cubley said as I looked at Kent with an "I will kill you" look for being a brown nose. I was still mad about the "half his size" insult.

Mr. Cubley left in search of Mr. Tolliver. Kent and I went to work on our first car of the day. We worked until noon, then rode our bikes straight home. We were under strict orders from our parents: straight home with no detours. How was that fair? We didn't start the fight, but we were getting punished all the same.

When I got home, Mom and Dad told me that the sheriff had stopped by with a witness subpoena. I had to be in court on Monday at 11:30 a.m. for something called a bond hearing. Mom had my Sunday suit laid out with a white shirt and blue tie. I hated that white shirt 'cause it was itchy when it got hot, but wearing a tie was worse because it made the collar tight.

"Mom, it's Friday. I don't have to go to court until Monday. Why is my suit out now?" I asked.

"I'm putting it in my closet until you need it," she answered, like that made perfect sense. She took it and hung it in her bedroom closet.

The rest of the afternoon was spent mowing the yard with the reel mower and helping Dad in the garage. I got to talk to Mr. Skelton some, and he seemed just as nice as Boo. He asked me about the fight but didn't press the issue, which was good, because I was trying to keep quiet about it around my parents.

On Saturday, Dad and I were working in the garage when Trooper Quinn came by, told me he was going to court on Monday and asked if I had gotten my witness subpoena from the sheriff. I told him Mom had it, and I would be there along with Kent. I asked what I should say.

"Just tell the truth, Billy. Keep to the facts and you'll be fine. Court is easy if you just stick to the facts." The trooper smiled at me.

It was rare to see Trooper Quinn smile, so I took a chance and began talking.

"I promise to tell the truth. Besides, everyone already knows what I'm going to say. Mr. Parks came by again last night around five and talked to me. I told him the same thing I told him the other day. Funny, he said the same thing you just told me. Just tell the truth. I told him if I didn't tell the truth, I knew what would happen."

"And what would happen?" Trooper Quinn asked.

"My Dad would whip me black and blue."

I suddenly got worried. I had said too much. I was afraid the trooper might ask what I meant.

"Well, we wouldn't want that, so just stick to the facts," the trooper responded. *That was a close one.*

Trooper Quinn waved as he got back in his car and drove out of the lot. As he left, I saw my dad looking at me from the parts cage. He didn't say anything, just stared at me. I got busy, and he went on back to work, pulling replacement rings for a cylinder.

Monday morning was cloudy but with no rain. We needed rain, honestly, but it didn't look like there was any in the forecast. Mom got out my good suit to wear. I hadn't been allowed to wear it to church on Sunday, which was a good thing; Mom said she didn't want me to get it dirty. I wore one of my school shirts with a pair of dark pants to church. Today, I was scrubbed, dressed, and standing in the living room by ten-thirty.

I started to go outside, but Mom stopped me with a, "Don't you even think about going out of this house. I told you, you are not getting your clothes dirty."

That put a stop to that, so I talked with Grandma, instead. She made me feel a little less nervous. I asked her if she was going to court with us, but she said someone had to stay home and look after Scotty.

I agreed that Scotty would not do well in court. Church was bad enough. Going to court would be a disaster.

Finally, it was time to go. Mom drove over to Kent's house to pick him up. Kent's mom had to work, so it was just the three of us. When we got to the courthouse, I saw Chief Smith in the front of the courtroom and Officer Little John McCulloch in the back, checking people as they came in. Officer Frank Younger and his twin brother, Roger, were also in the courtroom. Mr. Cubley came in, greeted us, and took a seat right behind Mom, Kent, and me. A few other people, who I didn't recognize, were in the courtroom.

Finally, Trooper Mike Quinn and state police sergeant, Barry Oliver, came into the courtroom. They went down front, spoke to Chief Smith, and then sat in the front row.

Judge Carlton opened a door behind the judge's bench, and a deputy sheriff immediately called out in a loud voice, "All rise. The Green Mountain County Court is now in session. The Honorable Kenneth W. Carlton, Judge, presiding. All those who have business before this court come forth to be heard. Silence is commanded. Be seated."

This was nuts. First, the deputy says, "come forward," then he tells everyone to "sit down and shut up." Court rules were worse than school rules.

Mr. Parks came in from a side door with the two Beamis brothers, who wore strange coveralls with stripes. They had silver handcuffs on their wrists. They sat down with their attorney, Mr. Parks, at a table to the left of the judge. A deputy sheriff, who must have weighed three hundred pounds, stood behind the two defendants.

On the other side of the courtroom was Mr. Albert Winston Brown, the Commonwealth's Attorney for Green Mountain County. I knew his full name because whenever he introduced himself, he used all of his names. It was like he was afraid if he didn't say them all the time, he might forget one of them.

"Mr. Parks, do you have a motion for this court?" Judge Carlton inquired, knowing the answer.

"We do, Your Honor. I request bond in the amount of five hundred dollars on behalf of my clients, Mr. Jacob Beamis and Mr. Joash Beamis."

"Five hundred for both, or is that for each of them?" asked Judge Carlton.

"That would be each, your Honor. They are well-respected citizens of this Commonwealth and proffer those amounts in good faith. We are eager to set this matter for a preliminary hearing on the court's earliest date," Mr. Parks responded.

"What is the response of the Commonwealth?" asked the judge, turning in his big chair to look at Mr. Albert Winston Brown.

"Your Honor, we object to any bo...."

A siren from outside the courthouse drowned out what he was saying, so the Commonwealth's Attorney just stopped and stood there looking irritated.

"Your Honor, we object to any bond for either of the two defendants on the grounds that they are dangerous criminals of the most violent nature. They came to the chief's office in the Highland Police Department and caused a disturbance. When they were asked to leave, they made a threat against the chief. Then, shots were fired at this very courthouse, and lives were put in grave danger, including the young life of the secretary of Judge Harland. Yes, sir, a bullet just missed Mrs. Carlisle. We feel that to release these two on bond would place the community and this court in danger. The Commonwealth also needs additional time to investigate these matters. We ask for at least a six months delay on the preliminary hearing." Mr. Albert Winston Brown sat down and looked over at Mr. Parks, who immediately stood.

"Your Honor, I strongly object to any delay, and a delay of six months is outside the bounds of due process. Such a delay violates the speedy trial provisions of the Constitution. I fear the Commonwealth has no real evidence, and, in fact, I can produce evidence showing it would have been impossible for my clients to have committed the crimes for which they are charged." Mr. Parks took a breath, and before he could resume, Mr. Brown began to speak.

"Your Honor, Mr. Parks is not..."

A second siren was heard passing the courthouse with tires squealing and horns blowing. All of this noise was louder than before and very disruptive to the proceedings. You got to learn stuff like this to be a trooper.

"Bailiff, what is going on out there?" Judge Carlton asked the bailiff who was looking just as puzzled as was Mr. Parks and Mr. Albert Winston Brown.

"I don't know, Your Honor. Maybe the chief knows?" the bailiff suggested. He turned to look at Chief Smith.

"Your Honor. My day shift is in court, and I called in my two night shift officers to standby at the office. They must have gotten a call because I think both of them just responded to something."

Just then, a deputy threw open the door of the courtroom and shouted, "Judge, we need every officer to respond to a shooting at the plant! People are dead! There's a sniper killing police officers out there! We have officers calling code ten thirty-three!"

With that, every officer in the courtroom, except the bailiff and Chief Obie Smith, ran for the door of the courtroom. Within seconds, the courtroom was quiet, and Mr. Parks was looking first at Mr. Brown, then at the judge.

"Gentlemen, this case will have to be continued. I think we just lost most of our witnesses." Judge Carlton asked, looking first at Mr. Brown and then Mr. Parks.

"Yes, Your Honor. I need my Highland town officers; isn't that correct, Chief Smith?" Mr. Albert Winston Brown asked.

The chief just stood there, almost like he didn't hear the question. He was looking first at Mr. Jacob Beamis and then at Mr. Joash Beamis. He realized he had been asked a question and stated, "Judge, this town is under attack. These men are responsible."

"I object to this outrage!" Mr. Parks yelled. "I request Chief Smith be held in contempt for such an outrageous statement! It was not even in response to the question put to him!"

"All right, that's enough. First, Chief Smith, let's not be making accusations when you have not been called as a witness. Second, this disruption is sufficient to require me to continue this hearing, but I will set it for a date in the near future. Now, gentlemen, I will declare the court in recess for the remainder of the day. Chief Smith, I think you need to check on your men. All witnesses are excused." The judge stood up and turned to leave.

The bailiff called out, "All rise. This court is now in recess."

We all stood as the judge left the courtroom. Then, the bailiff took the Beamis brothers out with Mr. Parks following behind. I noticed Chief Smith started to walk out and then hesitated. He did not seem to be in much of a hurry to leave. All of a sudden, no one could speak or hear because five or six sirens started up and tires started squealing for half a minute. Clearly, every available trooper, officer, and deputy sheriff were all headed to the plant.

Kent turned to me and said, "Wow, my mom said court would be boring. Was she ever wrong."

"What is this about the town being under attack?" Mom asked no one in particular.

"Mrs. Gunn, I doubt the town is under attack. Something is going on though, so boys, you best go back to the garage with Billy's mother. I'll see you home," Mr. Cubley said to Mom.

"Thank you, Mr. Cubley. I would feel much better if you would follow us," Mom agreed. Now we heard one lone siren go past the courthouse. That was the chief answering the call. He didn't seem to be in much of a hurry—no squealing tires.

"I sure wish I could see what was going on out at the plant. Gosh, a shootout, just like on Roy Rogers or the Lone Ranger. This court business is exciting," I exclaimed and got a poke from Mom.

"Boys, you stay right with me to the car. Now move!" Mom ordered in her stern voice. I saw Mr. Cubley smile, but not so Mom could see.

CHAPTER 27

TOO MANY DEATHS FOR BILLY
Tuesday, June 21, 1955

I *was in a ditch, face-up, near the McCulloch plant. People were getting shot, and I felt blood dripping on my face. Was I shot? Whose blood was it?*

The dream faded as I opened my eyes. Scotty was dipping his fingers in a glass of water and dripping drops onto my face. When he saw my eyes pop open, he took off. I knew he was going down the stairs, much too fast, especially with a glass in his hand. He was headed for trouble and was too dumb to know it.

"Scott Robert Gunn, stop running with a glass in your hand!" Mom yelled.

I knew what was next. He dropped his glass on the kitchen floor, and I could hear it break all the way upstairs.

Now, both Dad and Mom started yelling at him. I loved it. Even Grandma joined in. The little ape got it from three sides. I listened for a swat, but if he got one, I missed it.

Last night, people called the house until late. Both Mom and Dad talked on the phone at different times with their friends. Scotty and I had been banished upstairs, but I still heard a lot through the vent.

I learned that the plant superintendent, Wesley Spencer, had been leaving the plant with a foreman by the name of Pete Franklin. They were on their way to meet with Big John McCulloch at the Green Mountain Resort for a business lunch to talk over something going on at the plant. They never made it to the meeting.

The plant superintendent was shot first. I heard Dad repeat it back to the caller, "Hit in the head, right through the eye. That sounds like a sniper to me, too. Yeah, I bet he did drop like a rock."

A cousin of the second guy shot called Mom, and she reminded Dad about a bill never paid.

"You remember Mr. Franklin? He was the one who refused to pay us for the jump start."

"The dead battery at the plant?" Dad asked.

"Yes, the one who told you to bill the plant. I billed the plant, but Mr. Spencer refused the bill because the Chevrolet dealership was under contract to handle service calls at the plant. When I billed Mr. Franklin a second time, he told me it wasn't his problem. We never did get paid. Guess we never will now. You know that's the way Mr. Franklin treated everybody. He had a reputation of being mean to workers at the plant, according to the girls at the beauty shop."

I heard Mom and Dad talking about how Mr. Franklin got shot once in the chest and a second shot in the back when he tried to run back into the plant. He made it to the plant door and collapsed, falling half inside and half outside the main entrance. He died right there in front of a line of people punching out on the time clock.

Over the evening, as calls had gone back and forth, I learned even more. Pete Franklin was a foreman over the rough end. I had no idea what that was until later, but at the time, it didn't sound like a job I wanted. Washing cars, at least, wasn't rough. Anyway, the people trying to clock out were afraid to go outside after those two men got shot. It must have been bad because Mr. Franklin had made it almost back inside. There he was, just dead, right on the floor in front of all those people. People kept saying, "We need to pull Mr. Franklin inside," and "Someone needs to go out there to check on Mr. Spencer," but no one tried. Then, the first police officer had arrived.

Both Mom and Dad heard from different friends what happened next. Watching through the main door, but staying back to avoid getting shot, several people saw the first police car pull in. It was Officer Larry Sparrow. He had stopped in the parking lot near the main entrance to the plant and got out of his car and walked over to Mr. Spencer, who was lying face down in a pool of blood. The people in the plant were yelling at Officer Sparrow to get down, but he ignored them. He rolled Mr. Spencer over and threw up when he saw the face. That's when he'd got shot in the back of the head.

When my parents were about ready to go to bed, Mom asked, "John, are we safe? The chief gets fired upon, right in front of the courthouse. Now, three men are gunned down at the main entrance to the plant. What's going on?" Mom sounded like she was about to cry.

That's when Grandma joined the conversation, "Laura Jane, I told you we needed to get out of here."

"Mother, we can't go off and leave the business, besides, there's no reason for us to be worried, is there, John?"

"I don't think so, but I'll talk to Trooper Giles first thing in the morning. If he thinks we're in any danger, we'll pack up and go. So far, it's the town police and the bigwigs in danger.

Grandma butted in with, "Well, I guess we'll be safe when we're all dead and in our graves. Yes, dead and in our graves." Then, she retreated into the living room.

"John, if this is an attack aimed at Big John, why didn't they shoot him? Wasn't he at the plant yesterday?" Mom asked Dad after Grandma had left the kitchen.

"No, he was at the Green Mountain Resort all day. That's why Mr. Spencer and Mr. Franklin were coming out together. They were both going to meet him."

"Those men might have been mean, but they didn't deserve to die. I hope someone is helping the families," Mom said sadly.

"When they called Big John, he, at least, did one decent thing: he ordered the Alpine Restaurant to prepare a bunch of food for the families of the victims."

One thing about this shooting, a ton of police came to Highland. Police cars were driving all around town—more troopers than I had ever seen in one place in my entire life.

The day after the shootings, I was grounded, and Kent was coming to stay with us while his mom worked because she didn't want him home alone. I suspected Dad would put us both to work for no pay.

"Billy, come down to breakfast right now!" Mom called, and that interrupted my cogitation. *Cogitation*, well, that was a new word that I had learned from Polecat. It means thinking deeply about something. I do that to figure stuff out.

Downstairs, breakfast smelled super for a Tuesday. Usually, Mom just put out a bowl of cereal on Tuesdays. Since I had started working at the hotel, I knew I had gotten spoiled. Maddie knew how to put together a breakfast. Today, though, Mom handed me a plate of eggs and sausage as Kent and his mom arrived. Both came into the kitchen.

"Hey, Superman, Howdy Doody?" I asked and smiled at my own joke.

"Who are you, Clarabell or the Peanut Gallery?" Kent shot back, interrupting my mom's greeting to Mrs. Clark.

"Now, boys, settle down. Kent, would you like some breakfast?" Mom asked Kent.

"He had breakfast at home," Mrs. Clark said to Mom as Kent grabbed one of my link sausages.

"Kent, behave! You mind Mrs. Gunn today. Don't leave the garage! It's much too dangerous for you boys to be off gallivanting around. Is that clear?" Mrs. Clark said to both of us.

"Yes, ma'am," we answered in unison.

Mrs. Kent told Mom to call her if there was any trouble, but Mom assured her she would see there was none.

I heard Grandma in the living room mutter, "Dead and in our graves, that's the trouble headed for this family. Dead and in our graves." I hoped no one else heard her.

After breakfast, Trooper Giles dropped by the garage. He looked tired and his uniform was muddy all around the bottom of his pants.

"Hard night?" Dad asked him.

"Not the easiest one I've had lately. We can't seem to get a break. We think we found the sniper's hide, but he didn't leave so much as a gum wrapper. Looks like he tied pine branches to his boots because his tracks were hard to follow, even for the dogs. Two of them got pepper up their noses, and the handler's ready to kill this scoundrel. When the handler tried to flush that dog's nose, it bit him."

"That's terrible," Dad said.

"The whole night went that way. A deputy got his car stuck in a mud hole, and Chief Smith ran into a ditch when a deer jumped in front of him. When we asked Chief Smith to go home and get some rest, he got mad and cussed us for trying to get rid of him,"

Trooper Giles sighed, leaning back against the fender of his blue and gray.

"How about some coffee? My wife might even have a little breakfast, still." Dad asked, seeing how tired he looked.

"If it's not too much trouble, I would love some. The sergeant has been running us so hard, none of us have had time to even eat. You ask your wife first, see if it's okay—I don't want to trouble her none."

Kent and I began to follow when Dad pointed to the garage and told us to wash off the trooper's car. Trooper Giles said to leave it, but Dad insisted.

When they came back out, Dad said, "Thanks for putting Laura Jane's mind at ease. She was thinking about packing up and heading for the hills of West Virginia."

"Grandma Harris didn't believe a word I said. Between us, she and Chief Smith are two of a kind. We can talk until we're blue in the face, but not one word sinks in. John, I didn't mean that about Grandma Harris. Now, don't you go repeating that about the chief, either. Shoot it all. I'm too tired to be out in public," Trooper Giles said with a tired laugh.

He was so exhausted that he was saying things he shouldn't and starting to ramble.

Mr. Skelton pulled up right then with a box of parts that Dad had ordered and had shipped to the bus depot.

"Well, well, Dan Skelton, I never expected to see you here at Gunn's Garage. Are you visiting or moving up in the world?" Trooper Giles chuckled, too tired to give it a full laugh.

"I'm lucky to be working here," Mr. Skelton answered as he passed by the trooper carrying the box of parts into the garage.

"I'll tell you about it later. Dan is a benefit of McCulloch's business plan on how to treat employees," Dad said in a whisper.

"Hey, boys, you've done a fine job on my car. I hear you are professionals, washing the cars of the rich up at Cubley's Coze. Here's a fifty-cent piece, can you get change and split it?" Trooper Giles asked as he tried to hand me a fifty-cent piece.

"Trooper Giles, we can't take your money," I answered. I saw Kent shaking his head in agreement.

"Won't take the money, but can I blow the siren?" asked Kent.

"Not today. Heck, half the officers in town might come in shooting. How about a rain check?"

"Yeah, a rain check would be great," Kent responded, looking at me.

"How about a test drive? We could ease her up to around, say, a hundred?" I fished, not expecting a bite.

"John, you got to keep your boy away from those rich folks up at that hotel. He's turning into a Wall Street negotiator or worse yet, a banker."

Trooper Giles pulled out into the road and turned on his redlight. He stayed off the siren.

After the trooper had left, Dad put us back to doing chores, but all in all, it was not that bad. Working on one of the chores, I was near Mr. Skelton, and I found it might be a good time to ask him a question.

"Mr. Skelton, may I ask you something about the plant?"

"Sure, Billy, what do you want to know?"

"What's the rough end?" I asked, knowing Mr. Skelton knew a lot of men who worked there.

"You mean the Rough End Department?" Mr. Skelton asked me back.

"Yes, sir. I heard that Mr. Franklin was the foreman over the Rough End Department. I was wondering what they did there?"

"Well, the Rough End Department does a bunch of things. When logs come into the plant, they're stored in the log yard until needed. Then, some logs are dragged to a debarker where the bark is removed. That log is put in a machine that rolls the log against a big knife they call the lathe, which cuts off thin layers of wood called veneer. The veneer is dried in the Kiln Department and used as a thin face cover on furniture. A pine or poplar board will get cherry or mahogany veneer glued to its face to make it look more expensive."

"Isn't that cheating?" asked Kent, who had also stopped working to listen.

"No, they don't keep it a secret from the customer; it's just a way to keep the furniture priced to sell to us working stiffs."

I thought he might be done, but there was more.

"The Rough End Department is also where the sawmill saws logs into lumber for furniture, homes, fence posts, or railroad ties," Mr. Skelton ended and counted on his fingers. He thought and decided he was done.

"They do a lot there," said Kent. "But why do they call it the Rough End Department?"

"I guess because the wood is not dressed but is rough, not sanded, and not quite ready to be made into furniture. Also, working there is hard work and rough on the hands—lots of splinters. Does that answer your question?"

"It does, Mr. Skelton. Thanks."

I now knew what a Rough End Department was. I was glad to settle that question, so Kent and I could move on to more important stuff. We began to argue over who had the best sidekick of all the cowboys. That argument was going to take some time.

CHAPTER 28
AVE ATQUE VALE
Wednesday, June 22, 1955

M att was worried. Things were spiraling out of control because of the trouble in town. Though the Highland Police were too busy to bother with his deliveries, his suppliers had started calling to say they wouldn't be making deliveries until things settled down.

Chuck was a nervous wreck, jumping at every noise, and barely sleeping. He had huge bags under his eyes and kept insisting that everyone was going to cancel their reservations, though Matt was not so sure.

This week had been one for the record books—three men dead and the shooter gone without a trace. The police had thoroughly searched the woods around the plant and tried to set up roadblocks quickly, but their efforts had netted no arrests. With this and the courthouse shooting, the town was in a panic.

Matt decided to enjoy his breakfast on the loading dock and eased into a chair with coffee, a plate of eggs over easy, and toast. Polecat was ahead of him by only a couple of minutes.

Meanwhile, Billy and Kent were being kept home by their mothers, which suited Matt. Until this sniper was caught, he didn't want the responsibility of the boys washing cars out in the open. Plus, if they were home, he also would not have to worry about them sneaking off. They were good boys, but they were still twelve-years-old.

"Mr. Smith, good morning," Matt greeted Polecat, having sat down upwind, but not so far from Polecat that his choice of seating was noticeable.

"Ave atque vale," Polecat said with a flourish of his left hand that left the plate on his knee teetering. His hand returned just in time to save the dish from falling. Matt noticed the plate was full of eggs, two more than Maddie had served him, plus a stack of

toast with a double bacon order, and crisp link sausages on top of the eggs. Maddie was really looking after the old boy this morning.

"I'm sorry, what did you say?" Matt asked in consternation.

"I said, '*ave atque vale,*' which means 'hail and farewell.' This is easy first-year Latin. Everyone knows what *ave atque vale* means, right? That's exactly how I feel this morning. I greet you with pleasure, but I'm most saddened by all the death brought by these odious assassinations, which makes me want to wander this earth alone. An evil wind blows into the nostrils of the just and the unjust at present."

"What news have you picked up on your rounds today?" Matt inquired as he dug into his lighter fare before his eggs got cold.

"None. The police are without direction or evidence. I suspect that this has all been done by one person—the strange thefts, the murders, everything. One actor, a black-hearted rogue, playing two parts, both thief and assassin." Polecat spoke with a voice of authority.

Matt was stunned. He stopped eating; his fork suspended in midair. Directing his next question to Polecat, he kept the beat with his fork as he spoke.

"You're ahead of me here. What makes you think it's all one person? I mean, whoever shot at the chief was a bad shot, but not so at the plant, and the thieves have been stealing from stores and houses all over town. Now we have the killing of three people in a single event. Where's your proof?"

"Highland is a small town with few crimes despite being the county seat. Now, all of a sudden, we have all of this happening in a short span of time. The courthouse is a bit confusing since those shots were not accurate, but the thefts, I believe, were preparatory to a predatory plan against Big John and the McCulloch Wood Products operation. Cut off the head, and the snake dies." Polecat paused, eating his breakfast before he set his plate on the ground and picked up his coffee.

"Tell me, why shoot at the chief?"

"You assume the target was the chief?" Polecat answered his question with a question.

"Point taken, I suppose, but there's no hard evidence to support your theory. The shooter at the courthouse was way outside of even a mediocre sniper's proper zone. Why was his shooting so poor then, but so accurate yesterday?"

"Again, I'm not sure, but relegate that point to a minor level."

"You say minor, but the answer to that question would help solve the motive, the next target, our number of shooters, and, perhaps, even the identity of the shooter. If for some reason, the sniper's aim was off at the courthouse, then the target wasn't the chief—holy smoke from the Pope's pipe, that means the target was Big John! That changes things! It'd make taking out the plant superintendent and the foreman a logical, secondary goal. If the sniper or snipers missed Big John at the courthouse, then Big John avoided being shot at the plant by being at the Green Mountain Resort all day. If that's true, he's in even more danger."

Matt gazed up at the mountain, paused, and then continued. "But we're back to the same question: who is the shooter, or shooters? And I'm still not convinced it's one person rather than several."

"A single person with sniper training can slip in and out of an area with less risk of notice than several. Remember, Highland is not a metropolis. Small town people notice anything out of the ordinary. The greater the number of snipers, the harder it would be to disappear." Polecat paused to let this item sink in and, then, continued.

"Let's look at the break-ins: one person could easily carry away what was stolen. If it were more than one thief, why wouldn't they steal at once and risk fewer break-ins? Four sleeping bags and two tents were available at the hardware, yet only one bag and one tent were taken. The second sleeping bag and tent were taken *later* in a separate break-in. Of course, my current theory is mere conjecture and no more."

Polecat was making sense, but the evidence was thin.

Matt added his thoughts. "Well, we know it can't be the Beamis brothers. Not only were they both in jail during this last shooting, but Kent and Billy cleared them on the shooting at the courthouse. There's only one way they could be involved, and that's if they hired a sniper to do the work for them."

Polecat's response was a quick one: "Honestly, I would begin to peruse the list of employees recently discharged from the plant, especially those who were either abused or devastated by the firing. I speculate it's a man, but a woman is possible. This list is interminable."

"The police have their work cut out for them," responded Matt.

"Sir, might I trouble you for two dollars until Tuesday next?" asked Polecat. "I shall, of course, repay you on that date."

Matt dug into his left front pocket, where he had stashed some quarters for this very reason. He pulled out eight quarters and handed them over. Polecat shoved them into his coat pocket, picked up his plate, and departed for the kitchen. His discussion of the matter ended.

Matt sat on the dock, sipping his coffee deep in thought. Polecat returned from the kitchen and passed by Matt with a farewell.

After a few minutes, Chuck came out onto the loading dock.

"Matt, two troopers—Lusk and Quinn—are here, asking for you." Chuck's left eye had a twitch. "They wouldn't tell me what they wanted."

"I'm sure it's nothing to worry about. I'll be right there."

Matt carried his dishes into the kitchen as Polecat rode his bike towards the Green Mountain Resort. He found the two troopers seated in the lobby. When they saw him, they both rose, and Trooper Quinn greeted him first.

"Mr. Cubley, I believe you know Ben, correct?" Trooper Quinn asked Matt with a turn to the other trooper.

"Ben, it's good to see you again. Are you still keeping ahead of the wind?" Matt asked with a smile and a handshake.

"Gunnery Sergeant, you cured that problem for good. I'm holding slow and tracking true. The years are catching up with me, but my shots are still within the zone. I hope you're well?" Trooper Lusk remarked as they shook hands.

"Well, running a hotel is a bit like kicking the butt of a bunch of wet-behind-the-ears Marines. I have to be kind and gentle, the same as I was with your sniper class. You do remember my kind and gentle nature, right?" Matt joked, giving him the evil gunny stare.

"I received a head wound along my path in the Pacific, even got a Purple Heart for my trouble, so maybe that's why I don't remember kind and gentle. Of course, I would never contradict you, Gunny Cubley," Lusk responded and looked at Quinn for some help.

"Could we have a word in private, Mr. Cubley?" Quinn asked; though he enjoyed Matt's ribbing, he wanted to get on with business.

"Only if you stop the 'Mr. Cubley' crap. Let's do an about-face and reverse our conversational direction. How about Matt, unless, of course, I'm being placed under arrest?" Matt decided to drop the Marine Corps jargon. It was bringing up too many memories.

"No, sir, we're here to ask your help. Ben and I think the Beamis brothers are clean. Sergeant Oliver, Ben here, and even the sheriff all think we might have a group with a grudge against the town," Quinn said.

"Gunny—er, Matt, would you be willing to take a look at the sniper's hide we found? You might pick up on something we missed," Lusk asked.

"Well, it's been years since the Corps, but if I can help out, I'd be glad to take a look."

"I would welcome your expertise, Gunny. I want to clear this up and get back home to Richmond." Lusk sounded relieved.

"Ben, again, it's Matt, and speaking of home, where are you staying while you're on assignment in our little town?"

"Well, I'm not sure. Sergeant Oliver is trying to work something out for those of us who are too far away to drive home at night. We have a temporary command post in the local elementary school since the kids are out for the summer and there's no summer school. He's talking about putting us all up in a cheap hotel over in Waynesboro. They have a deal at seven dollars per room per night. It's a dump, and the drive over and back will waste time, but he can't afford here or the Green Mountain Resort. No offense, but this place is way over his budget."

"Well, I happen to know the owner of one of the local establishments and he just might be able to help y'all out," Matt joked.

"In fact, we have vacant rooms available for troopers to use right now, and we might have a few more of them if this sniper runs off any more of our guests. Tell your sergeant that I'll charge the same rate as that cheap hotel over in Waynesboro; I only ask that he not spread my special price around. I'll even throw in employee rates for meals, which is half the regular rate. You guys just need to make reservations a couple of hours in advance."

"Thank you so much. We'll surely forward your offer along to the sergeant," Trooper Quinn spoke right up before Trooper Lusk could answer.

"Thanks," Lusk echoed. "If you're willing, we can run you out to the plant and let you do a quick recon. I don't think it should take more than an hour. The sergeant is also requesting a briefing after you look-see. So far, we don't have much to go on. If you're game, ride with me."

"I'm game. Let's go. Chuck, I'll be with the troopers for about an hour." Matt then informed Chuck about his offer to the troopers. When Chuck looked puzzled at the price, Matt whispered to him that with troopers present, it would assure the remaining guests that the hotel was a safe place to stay.

"This may just keep us from losing more guests," Matt added.

Chuck nodded. The news seemed to help his mood because he started working on one of the flower arrangements for the lobby, which was a good sign.

The silence on the ride to the plant was broken by Trooper Lusk asking Matt, "What's the purpose of the stick you put in the back seat?"

Matt's answer was odd. "Do you remember Sergeant Barking Dog from B Company?"

"Who doesn't? He won ten dollars off Gunny Bolton on the pistol range—that Injun beat the gunny with a bow and quiver of arrows against a sidearm. We all laughed for a month, of course, never around Bolton."

"Well, Barking Dog showed me how to track a man through the woods using what I call my stride stick. He called it by a Cherokee name that I never could pronounce. You measure the stride distance from heel to heel of a set of footprints that you know belong to your man, woman, or child. You mark the stick with that stride distance and it tells you where the next heel mark should land. It reduces the area one has to search to inches and makes tracking easier. Barking Dog was so good, he could track a man through the woods at a fast walk."

When they arrived at the plant, they found it shut down for the day, almost deserted. After they parked, Ben told Matt where the three victims had been standing when they had been shot and, based on the angle of the wounds, he pointed across the road to where the sniper's hide should be.

Matt leaned against the hood of the trooper's car for five or six minutes, just looking at the terrain across the highway from the plant. Then he spoke, "I see three possible spots from here. I figure the shooter would have come in and left from our left, so let's approach that hill from the right side."

Matt led Ben across the road, but when he got to the shoulder, he stopped so suddenly that Ben almost bumped him.

Ben asked, "What do you see?"

"Darn, it looks like two platoons of raw recruits charged across this road and up that hill. If there were any footprints left by the sniper, they're trampled. Who did this?"

"Sorry, Gunny. Between the town police, deputies, and several new troopers that responded, they charged up that hill like it was Mount Suribachi."

Matt threw down his guide stick in disgust. "So much for finding any tracks. We might as well head straight on up the hill and see what's left."

Ben showed him where they thought the sniper had hidden to fire down on the victims, and Matt agreed. The plants were mashed down over an area the size of a prone man. Ben informed him that no spent brass casings had been found, no gum wrappers, cigarette butts, nothing.

Matt got down on his hands and knees and moved slowly, an inch at a time, over the ground. He reached out and plucked a leaf off a small plant.

"Ben, our man used this spot all right. He was prone; the muzzle of his rifle was beside this Sassafras sucker."

"How can you tell?"

"See how the leaf has been shredded? He fired from here once, maybe twice, and the muzzle blast shredded it. This spot would have been my second choice, but it isn't bad. A better one is over there."

"Why is it better?"

"Easier to come and go with more concealment. Just better."

The two men looked over the lay of the remaining land, walking all over the slight rise, looking for clues. No luck. They went down the hill, circled the creek, which flowed past the hide and plant, and Matt waded up and down the creek twice after taking off his shoes. A small bridge allowed State Route 22 to cross this shallow creek.

Matt found what he thought might be the tracks of the sniper, but he had tied pine boughs to the bottom of his shoes, making the tracks almost impossible to see and preventing the dogs from getting much of a scent.

Afterward, Matt and Ben drove over to the elementary school with Trooper Quinn following. There were at least ten police cars parked at the school. Sergeant Oliver was inside talking to Chief Obie Smith and the sheriff of Green Mountain County, Richard T. Lawrence. Matt was introduced around until Chief Smith spotted him and demanded to know what a civilian was doing in the restricted area of the command center.

Sergeant Oliver explained, "Matt is a consultant and is present at our invitation. Matt, what did you learn by looking at the hide?"

"Sergeant, not much. No tracks that did me any good. My best guess is the sniper arrived by car. He probably stashed it on the dirt road, just northwest of the little bridge near the plant. I think he probably went down the creek bed from where he parked, climbed up the creek bank, and low-walked up the rise to the hide your people found. I saw where some pine boughs had been cut, and I bet he used those as foot cushions to hide his tracks and scent. The hide was high enough and was in a good position to allow him to keep a check to his rear and both flanks while having a good field of fire on the front entrance of the plant. The target objectives were the first two kills, in my opinion. The third kill was likely a target of opportunity, either to create confusion or because the sniper may have recognized the police officer. Hell, maybe the man was just in the wrong place at the worst possible time. Regardless, there's no way the shooter could have predicted that third kill ahead of time," Matt concluded.

Chief Smith had drifted back over to listen to Matt as he reported to the sergeant. He butted into the conversation. "What do you mean, he didn't plan to kill Officer Sparrow? All my men and I are under that Bible threat."

"Chief, I'm not one hundred percent sure you were the target at the courthouse," Matt said.

"Are you insane? Those damn Beamis brothers are out to get me! First, they threatened me, then they shot at me, and now they've killed one of my men. Besides, what in the hell is a hotel clerk doing running a state police investigation?" Chief Smith's voice was growing louder.

"Chief, Mr. Cubley is more than a hotel clerk. Trooper Benjamin Lusk is a former Marine; Gunnery Sergeant Cubley trained him. Trooper Lusk requested his assistance, and I agreed. Mr. Cubley is a valued expert on snipers, and we damn sure have a sniper problem. The state police will use all resources available to catch this person."

Sergeant Oliver was trying his best to hold his temper in check, but Chief Smith was not making it easy.

"Those Beamis brothers had this done. It's that cousin or some other bunch of their Bible-thumping relatives."

Chief Smith walked over to Little John, who also had been listening, and the two of them began to confer in low voices. They looked over at Matt several times as they spoke.

"Sergeant, may I suggest you obtain a list of all the people fired from McCulloch Wood Products over the last year or two?"

"That's already on our list of things to do as soon as we get our command post set up," Sergeant Oliver said with a nod.

"Okay, and how about checking the complaints filed against Officer Larry Sparrow? Hopefully, this list will be short."

The sergeant lowered his voice. "Well, I wish I could get my hands on the complaints filed against Sparrow, but the Highland Police Department doesn't allow complaints to be filed against its officers. Chief Smith takes them, folds them, and deposits them in the trash."

"This just gets more and more difficult. I'm convinced the Beamis brothers were not the snipers at the courthouse, although they do have a strong motive. Billy Gunn and Kent Clark will clear them from direct responsibility. The only other possibility is the brothers hired someone, which I doubt. They just don't seem to be the type to hire assassins," Matt stated.

Oliver wasn't done. "One question I have for you is this: if this is a trained sniper, why did he mess up the first shooting at the courthouse? Those shots showed poor marksmanship."

"That puzzles me as well. The sniper at the courthouse may have been a different person," responded Matt.

"Maybe he deliberately fired wild the first time to throw us off his trail," added Lusk.

"Maybe, but doubtful because it's too risky to deliberately miss for a little confusion, right in the center of town. I chalk that up as nuts rather than shrewd.

"Thanks, Mr. Cubley. Our chat's definitely been interesting and confirms some of my thinking. Lusk will drive you back. Quinn told me about your offer. I'll ask my lieutenant for permission to use your facilities. Your special price does fit our budget, and I also know how good the food is at your hotel. My concern is getting my men out of your dining room and back to work. Thanks again, and I'll be in touch."

Matt left, thinking. *A tough crime to solve, coupled with interdepartmental non-cooperation, was making a challenging investigation much more difficult.*

CHAPTER 29
POLICE, PRESS, AND PREACHERS
Thursday, June 23, 1955

"**M**att, we're at full capacity," Chuck reported to his boss.

"Are you sure?" Matt asked as he leaned back in his office chair and looked up from the bills he was checking.

"Yes, there were six new cancellations: two because of the campaign that Green Mountain Resort is waging against us with their free night's offer, and four because of the recent shootings."

"So, the troopers helped some, but not that much. What else?"

"We checked six troopers into three regular rooms and put Trooper Lusk in your old room in the attic at no charge. Reporters snatched up our remaining vacancies because the little town of Highland is making the national news. Having the troopers around has calmed the remaining guests." Chuck looked pleased as he went on with his report.

"I hate to tell it, but several newsmen had to be turned away. I sent them over to Green Mountain Resort, but their rooms are now ten dollars a night higher than normal. Plus, no troopers are handy for them to interview and they are clamoring to get rooms with us. I'm making a waiting list," Chuck finished with a smile. This was as happy as he had been in three days. Matt suspected he might have even slept last night.

Matt had learned from Polecat that the Highland Police thought the Beamis brothers were the masterminds behind the shootings. Chief Smith had sent requests to Roanoke and out-of-state to Charleston, West Virginia, for searches to be done at the homes and businesses of the two brothers, but all they turned up were scathing responses from the brother's wives.

Polecat said that Charles Parks had filed a petition with the Green Mountain County Court against the chief of police and the entire roster of Highland Police Department officers to cease and desist their harassment of the wives. The petition included a long-detailed description of the indignities the women had suffered when their husbands had been arrested, including being handcuffed and roughly thrown into the back of a police car, while their husbands were beaten. Some of the out-of-town papers were now investigating the treatment of the women, and one or two had begun to print articles about it.

Polecat had gathered a bit here and a piece there from eavesdropping on the sheriff's deputies, the Highland Police, and a news reporter arguing with the *Gazette* editor about what he was refusing to print. Apparently, the editor was afraid that Big John might drop ads if he published an article about the mistreatment of the wives. When the reporter had asked about printing a story about how the Highland Police had shot up their own police car, the editor had thrown him out of his office. The reporter might have been fired had he not been the editor's son-in-law.

"Mr. Cubley, rest assured, the gossip mill of the Town of Highland is, however, not so discriminating. Reports from the beauty shop and the barbershop are replete with juicy details. One can't censor gossip. It appears that the censor's pen has run out of ink." Polecat reared back and laughed so loudly Maddie came to the door of the kitchen to check on things.

After breakfast, Trooper Lusk told Matt that Big John McCulloch had tried to block his department from obtaining the list of firings at the plant. The request had then gone up the state police chain of command from Sergeant Oliver to the lieutenant and finally to a captain who had threatened to get a search warrant if the list was not given over voluntarily. Big John had eventually backed down and provided a list of fifteen names. The list was to be cross-checked against former military service with the troopers having a particular interest in any sharpshooters and trained snipers from World War II or the Korean War. It would take days, or perhaps, a week for the military to send them the information requested, and, in the meantime, the names were being divided up for interviews.

Sadly, Billy and Kent were still being kept at home. Billy's mom had even complained that, if they didn't catch this criminal soon, she would go nuts, having to keep certain children inside.

The town looked normal to someone just passing through. However, after ten minutes in a restaurant or store, the shootings surfaced as the primary topic of discussion.

At about ten o'clock, Sergeant Barry Oliver arrived at the hotel to deliver the fired workers' names to the troopers who were staying at the hotel. He also gave Matt an update on the firearm's report he had just received: unsurprisingly, all of the recovered bullets, which were 30.06 calibers, had been fired from the same rifle.

Sergeant Barry Oliver asked Matt, "Any thoughts about the rifle used?"

"A military rifle is my guess. I'm betting it's the M1C or M1D with the M84 telescope. That would give the average sniper a range of six hundred yards. The misses on the first shooting indicated inferior performance. Every one of them missed by a mile. If this is a single shooter, a trained sniper, either there was some type of interference as the sniper prepared to fire or an equipment malfunction occurred. Two trained snipers, though, would seldom use one rifle. The weapon has to be matched to the man."

The sergeant added, "We calculated that the sniper's position for the courthouse shooting had to be from a roof about five hundred yards away. That matched the report of a couple of witnesses who heard pops coming from there. The hide at the plant was around three hundred and fifty yards away, so being closer might be why the accuracy was improved. Obviously, we aren't sure if we have one or two shooters using the same rifle."

"I keep coming back to the same problem, Sergeant. Something changed. I just don't know what."

"Well, in better news, we think we might have a new prime suspect. His name's Maynard Donald Hathaway. Goes by 'Doc.' Many at the plant think he was framed for stealing. Framed or not, he pulled time on the charge. His family was treated pretty rough by the Highland Police when they evicted them from the company house, and they had a rougher time while he was in jail. We think he might be our man. No military service because of flat feet, but he's a good shot. He cleans up at the local turkey shoots, plus he has a 30.06, a 30-30, and an old over-and-under 12 gauge. The wife claims his guns were stolen when the police evicted him from the house, but I'm not buying that. No one reported them stolen. When I asked Chief Smith about it, he blew up and made it very clear his men do not steal tenants' guns. Anyway, Lusk is assigned to tracking him down and bringing him in." Sergeant Oliver concluded his report, turned to listen, and looked at the door of the kitchen.

Maddie was threatening to stab Connell Washington, her assistant cook if he didn't hurry up with some soup stock. A pot clattered into a sink.

Matt smiled at the sergeant and said, "All bark and no bite, sergeant. We think!"

"Well, I need to be moving along. Thanks again for the rooms: can we book six for lunch?"

"Sure, I'll tell Boo," Matt promised.

"What's a Boo?" asked Sergeant Oliver.

Matt related how Boo got her name. "Heck, everyone here calls her Boo. Even some of our regulars. One could not ask for a sweeter young lady." Matt rose as the sergeant stood.

"I have often seen her when my family dines here, but for some reason, I never knew about her nickname," claimed the sergeant.

"Well, I try not to let the guests know about it and hope they don't use it, but I have about decided that there are several things about this hotel over which I have no control."

Matt grinned as Maddie launched into another threat to fillet a waitress if she didn't pick up her ready order.

"One more thing: I have to run a firearm's report over to Mr. Albert Winston Brown at the courthouse. Here's a copy for you. Let's not tell Brown you got your copy before he got his," the sergeant whispered as he handed the copy over to Matt.

Matt placed it in a file folder that he had labeled, "Green Mountain County Sniper."

When the sergeant walked outside to meet Trooper Lusk, a reporter from the *Richmond Times-Dispatch* approached Matt with some questions. Since he was a guest at the hotel, Matt tried to sound friendly but made sure to give him no new information. The reporter did provide Matt with some information, though, as he confirmed what Polecat told Matt at breakfast about Chief Smith's certitude regarding the Beamis brothers' guilt.

Matt tried to convince the reporter until the facts were all in, assumptions could be dangerous.

Lunch was busy for the hotel staff. Among the extras were six troopers plus four pastors from local churches who were dining and discussing the upcoming funerals.

Matt learned from the preachers that the plant superintendent would have a funeral service at the First Baptist Church of Highland, and the burial would take place at the Highland Cemetery. Koehler Funeral Home would be handling the details. Officer Sparrow's funeral would be on Tuesday at the Methodist Church. The last funeral scheduled was for the plant foreman on Wednesday at the Catholic Church in Waynesboro.

Each pastor tried to invite Matt to Sunday service, for which he thanked them and promised to attend. He was relieved no one invited him to any of the funerals. Janet and Jack's funeral was too recent. He thought of how they were buried together in the same extra-large coffin, his boy now resting in the arms of his mother, as it should be. He had to wipe a tear from one eye, forcing his thoughts away from Janet and Jack and re-focused on the hotel.

Carol Martin and Linda Carlisle arrived at the stroke of one and were seated by Boo at a table in the corner. When Matt finished with the guests at table two, Carol motioned him over.

"Ladies, it is so nice to have you for lunch again."

Matt smiled at Carol and Linda. He flashed to a thought of Janet, but then rebuked himself. It was his duty to greet the guests.

"Matt, we want to thank you for buying us lunch the other day. That was much too kind. Linda and I must repay you," Carol said with a smile and turned her head toward Linda.

"Thank you very much." Linda gave him a smile that caused his face to feel warm.

"Oh, the pleasure was mine. I often treat favored guests to encourage return business. See it worked," Matt responded, trying to make it sound like a business decision.

"Favored guests, are we?" Carol giggled with another glance at Linda.

Matt noticed it was Linda who blushed.

"Oh, Matt, Mr. Dalton needs you to come by the office tomorrow and sign off on the hotel inventory for the estate. He said your detail on the work papers you sent saved him a lot of time with getting things ready for the court, so he has them early," Carol said, turning to business.

"What time would be convenient?" Matt asked, focusing on her and away from Linda.

"How about eleven-thirty? Then we could be finished by noon," Carol responded and gave Linda a conspiratorial glance. He noticed a frown flash across Linda's face.

"Sure, if that suits you. Eleven thirty sharp."

"I'll see you then. Don't be late." Carol grinned.

Matt retreated more than departed with a, "Here comes your lunch. I hope you enjoy it."

What was it that had him so flustered? He should have mentioned Linda's close call at the courthouse.

Matt made a circuit of the dining room and strolled into the lobby. He started passing the time at the front desk with Chuck, who had prepared a second list of bogus names for Cliff's second delivery that night. Matt had not heard of any results from their counter-spy operation, but it was bound to happen.

The troopers ambled out of the dining room, full and content. The pastors were lingering over dessert and coffee, clearly in no hurry to leave.

Carol and Linda entered the lobby, smiling. When they were halfway across the room, Carol veered off to the ladies' room, and Linda hesitated before approaching Matt.

"Matt, may I ask you something?"

He sensed she wanted to ask him something in private. "Let's step out onto the veranda where we can enjoy the view," he suggested.

"That would be perfect," she answered, following him outside.

"Matt, Carol is trying to get us together. I wanted to warn you that tomorrow, when you come to the office, she's going to ask you to lunch at the Black Panther Grill. I'm supposed to meet you two there by 'accident.' Since you and I have something in common—a very sad something, I wanted to warn you."

"Oh? Oh. Oh, my!" He flushed.

That was probably a little less of an answer than what she had been expecting, but it was all he could get out.

"Matt, my Frank died in Korea three years ago, this October sixth, and I know you lost your wife last fall. I also know all about the good intentions of friends. Mine have been trying to fix me up with dates for the last year, but I'm just not ready. I've had a lot longer to grieve than you, but I know how matchmaking can open wounds you want to keep closed. I don't want to be the one to cause you more pain."

As Linda said all of this, she averted her eyes from his.

When Matt struggled to answer, she offered, "I wanted to give you the opportunity to avoid a bad experience."

"I don't think anyone could call lunch with you a bad experience," Matt managed just as Carol came onto the veranda.

She called to them, "Sorry! I love the tea here, but too much sends me to the ladies' room. Linda, are you ready to head back to work?"

"No, but I guess I better. We have so much going on the judge will be wondering if I've been kidnapped," Linda joked, smiling, before giving Matt a quick concerned glance that she hid from Carol.

"Thanks," Matt mouthed. He watched them—more Linda than Carol—walk to their car. He remained on the veranda and waved again as they drove toward town.

He then retired to his office to think and remained there until around five, when Trooper Lusk returned and asked to speak to him.

"Sergeant Oliver asked me to give you an update."

"Great, shoot—sorry, Ben, bad choice of words."

"That's okay. I need a joke or two with this case. Anyway, I tracked down the Hathaway family and got nowhere. The wife was at home but said she didn't know where her husband was. She also said that if I had any questions, I should ask him, because she had no use for crooked cops. The two boys, especially the older one, were sullen. As I was leaving, I heard him tell his mom he hoped the sniper killed me along with the other scum cops. She fussed at him for wanting anyone killed, but that family hates the police." Lusk frowned.

"Do you know about the allegation that the husband was framed?" Matt asked.

"Yeah, Bobby Giles told me all about it. The husband was framed, and his family was tossed out of their house, lost a lot of possessions, and had it tough until he got out of jail. If any of that's true, I can see why they hate us. I was told not to expect much, but I have a job to do. Next time I go, I'm taking backup. Getting shot is not in my job description."

"Well, be careful. Getting shot shouldn't be in anyone's job description," Matt agreed as he watched the trooper leave.

CHAPTER 30
MEETINGS WITH MATT
Friday, June 24, 1955

A red sunrise painted the sky in the east, and Matt hoped it was not a harbinger of something other than a colorful day. It was going to be a hot one by mid-afternoon unless a storm cooled things off.

His troubles had prevented him from getting much sleep. He had gotten up at about one in the morning to think, ended up talking to Janet, and fell asleep in his easy chair. Linda Carlisle had been the problem.

He was fascinated by her smile and her honesty. Should he go to lunch with Carol? How should he react to Linda?

She understood his depression, his grief, and was thoughtful enough to warn him. He could heed her warning and not go to lunch with Carol, which would avoid the whole issue entirely. What should he do? What would Janet want him to do?

He was not ready to move on; he knew that. He was just not prepared. He had gone over and over this all night, and it was time to reach a decision... it had to be no lunch with Carol. He eased himself upright to face the day, tired.

During breakfast, Polecat had nothing new to share about the sniper situation. The town seemed frozen in place from fear. Matt went over the list of potential suspects from the plant records he had received from the state police, but, without knowing the people, he had no conclusions to draw. When any military information was added to the list of names, that might provide some answers.

The town was crowded with police, and Matt hoped their numbers alone would dissuade another shooting.

After breakfast, John Gunn called to tell Matt his wife was keeping Billy home and Kent's mom would be doing the same.

John also complained that Billy was a handful for both his mother and himself, so he hoped the police hurried up and made an arrest before the boys drove their parents nuts. Matt invited the families to come up to the resort for a meal out as a sort of a break. He reminded John that Billy and Kent got meals at half-price, as their discount remained in place because he still considered the two employees. John thanked him, saying he might take Matt up on his offer for a Saturday night outing.

Chuck informed Matt that Duffy had dropped off the latest "special list" of names and addresses at the milk-box drop off. Chuck whispered how the shootings were good for business, at least until the excitement wore off and the reporters left. Then, his face clouded over with his worried, nervous look. He launched into a doom and gloom narration on how bad business would be if they didn't catch the shooter. Matt tried to reassure him that with this many police working the case, they should be able to solve it before they had to close their doors, but he saw that Chuck was not convinced.

Sitting in his office, Matt kept nodding off, so he decided to go for a walk. Chuck had warned him that he was sure the sniper was hiding in the woods behind the hotel and begged him not to hike the main trail.

"Chuck, you worry too much."

Hiking up the main trail, he found himself a quarter way up the mountain, deep in thought. He had returned to thinking about Carol and her plans for lunch. He didn't want to hurt Carol's feelings, but his wife, his love, was foremost in his thoughts, and he was back trying to decide whether or not to go. He spooked a rabbit and it gave him a start.

Gazing at the quiet woods, he sat down on a flat-topped rock that provided a seat at the right height.

What would Janet want him to do? If the situation was reversed, what would he say to her? He would tell Janet to move forward, live her life, and honor him in her memories. The problem was he was not ready to move forward. It was just too soon.

Linda had also confided in him that she was not ready to move on with any kind of romantic relationship, either. He should respect her wishes and not go.

That was the correct answer. She understood what he was going through. She had been there. She was farther along this lonely road of grief than was he, but if lunch with her was a bad idea, he would heed her warning.

On the other hand, she might be able to help him with advice. Could he ask her to just talk from time to time? No attachments, but only as a friend? Was that a rationalization? A betrayal of Janet?

He got up from the rock. He thought he heard a faint click. He turned but only saw the forest and only heard a breeze in the trees.

Chuck was getting to him with his talk of snipers in the woods. He stood motionless for a few seconds and thought, if the sniper killed him here, it would be an act of kindness.

He gave the area one more look, stood tall, and took a measured step. No shot; all was quiet. He walked with no attempt to be quiet. Back down the path to the hotel, he went in disappointment.

Just before he left the woods at the hotel grounds, he resolved the question that was causing him so much concern. He decided to avoid lunch in town.

Perhaps he should call and tell Carol he would come by next week to sign those papers. That way, he would avoid having to face her. Maybe he should call Linda; no, better not.

When Matt returned to the hotel, he learned that Carol had called to remind him of his appointment. Yes, she was persistent. Chuck also had some good news, though: the deliveries were up to date, as the massive police presence was giving people a little peace of mind.

A county resident had even told Chuck that Chief Smith was bragging it was only a matter of time before he captured the Beamis' hired sniper because the shooter had nowhere to run. It was amazing how quickly people reacted, how quickly they decided to return to normal, or at least, partially to normal. Those things that caused the most inconvenience returned to normal first. The daily activities that one could put off without difficulty came back a little more slowly. Only one cancellation had come in for the coming week, and Chuck was not sure of the reason.

Matt arrived at the law firm about ten minutes early. He looked over at the courthouse, where workers were making repairs. The broken window had been replaced earlier. Now the bullet holes were being puttied and new paint to cover up all evidence was waiting in pails.

"Good morning, Matt," Carol greeted him as he entered.

"Good morning, Carol. Are you ready for me? I'm a little early," Matt asked and tried to put a pleasant smile on his face.

"We're all ready. Here are the sheets you need to check. Initial each page at the bottom. The final page is the signature page, and I will notarize it." Carol handed Matt the ten pages of data destined for the court.

Matt was familiar with the information. It didn't take him long to read and initial each page. When he finished, he took the papers back to Carol, who watched him sign the final page. She notarized her signature by placing her notary seal over it with a large seal stamper. The cast-iron device looked like it weighed three or four pounds.

"All done. Mr. Dalton, do you need to see Matt?" Carol called toward the closed office door. Frank Dalton came out immediately.

"Thanks for coming in, Matt. I have no question; how about you?" Frank asked Matt.

"No, looks fine to me."

Now, the moment of decision had arrived. Matt knew what was coming next. Yes, or no, to the next question?

"Matt, my goodness, look at the time. It's almost time for lunch. Would you please escort me over to the Black Panther Grill? I simply must repay you for lunch."

"Uh, isn't Frank eating at the Black Panther today?" Matt asked, trying to get out of the invitation gracefully by passing Carol off to Frank.

Frank spoke up as he shook his head, "Would love to, but I have to take Sam to get her eyes checked. She has to have drops and won't be able to see to drive home. Carol, I'll be back around two for my two-thirty. Matt, you're in for a treat. The cheeseburgers at the Black Panther are the best around. Have a nice lunch." Frank disappeared into his office.

Carol got up and picked up her purse, smiling. "Ready?"

"Well, maybe..." Matt started to say some excuse that would not hurt her feelings and sound plausible.

"Matt, I owe you a meal, and it won't take a minute, then you can be on your way. You do like cheeseburgers, don't you?" she asked with a tone of voice that said that anyone who didn't like cheeseburgers might be headed for a stay in a mental hospital.

"Well, yeah, I like cheeseburgers," Matt confessed and was about to add something about a meeting when Carol plowed ahead.

"Good, let's go. We need to get there before twelve. Sometimes the place fills up, and we don't want to have to wait for a seat." Carol locked onto Matt's arm and pulled him toward the office door.

And with that, Carol towed Matt to the Black Panther Grill, talking a mile a minute as they headed down the street. Matt never got to say a word.

There were still three booths empty when they entered the grill, and Carol pulled him toward one. She waited for him to be seated first and slid in beside him. The trap was closed.

She waved to the waitress near the fountain drink machine who hurried over with menus. A black panther was drawn on the cover in gold ink on a black background.

"Matt, you have to try a cheeseburger with fries or onion rings. These cheeseburgers are the best around, no kidding."

Matt heard the door open and looked up. Linda Carlisle was wearing a summer dress with flowers in pale yellow on a white background. Her face changed when she spotted Carol and Matt from curious to a repressed smile directed at Matt, or so he felt as he watched her approach.

"Matt, I'm pleased you were able to make it," Linda said, letting slip the secret that this was an accidental meeting. Linda took a seat beside Carol, who had moved from beside Matt to the other side of the table.

Carol tried to shush Linda, but it was too late. It was Matt's turn to say something.

"It's nice to see you," Matt said, feeling a blush creep up his neck.

The waitress arrived, chewing hard on bubble gum, and wrote down their cheeseburger orders on a pad with grease stains across the cardboard backing.

"There goes my diet," Carol laughed.

An awkward silence extended for a few moments before Matt decided he better begin a conversation.

"So, Linda, how's work?" Matt asked and thought to himself, pretty lame.

"Well, it seems the Beamis brothers are still the focus of Mr. Albert Winston Brown. He and Mr. Parks are at each other's throats. It looks like Mr. Parks has won an early date for the bond hearing," she said softly. She waited.

He was caught looking into her eyes and looked away.

"Oh, so when is it set? I might want to attend to see the two of them fight it out."

"This Thursday, right after the last funeral. Mr. Brown wanted it set off for at least sixty days, but Judge Carlton talked it over with Judge Harland, and they both decided there was no reason for a sixty-day postponement."

The talk changed to lighter topics, as Linda began telling about recent funny events that had occurred in the courtroom. She had both Carol and Matt laughing by the time the food arrived.

Matt enjoyed the meal, and it ended with the three chatting like old friends.

After the meal, the ladies picked up the tab, their debt to him now one-half paid. They reminded him that they owed him the other meal. Linda smiled and promised the next meal was on her. He thanked them both for a most delightful lunch, and Carol rushed off, leaving him with Linda on the sidewalk in front of the restaurant.

"Matt, lunch with you was nice. I'm glad you joined us. We must do this again," Linda said in parting.

"I would like that."

Linda was different from his late wife, but like Janet, she had the ability to reach Matt and change his mood. Talking with Linda had been friendly and pleasant and without pressure.

Matt returned to the hotel to find a message from Big John. The man wanted a two o'clock meeting, which was fine with Matt.

Big John arrived at the hotel in his black Cadillac at two minutes to two, and like before, he parked right in front. He walked into the lobby with a swagger and announced to Chuck that he was there to meet with Cubley. Chuck showed Big John into Matt's office and closed the door. Matt smiled when he saw the pass-through was open a crack on each side.

"Cubley, I'm here for your answer. I'm sure you now realize how generous I'm being."

"Good afternoon to you too, Mr. McCulloch," Matt said and extended his hand to his standing guest.

"I believe in coming to the point," Big John said and gave Matt's extended hand a cursory shake. "My banker has the funds ready. Soon as you sign, you can dump this problem and be on your way with a handsome sum."

Big John took a thick stack of papers out of his briefcase and placed the stack on Matt's desk. He stepped back and sat down.

"Well?" Big John said to Matt.

"Mr. McCulloch, I want to thank you for your generous offer, but this problem, as you call it, is the business my family built up over three generations. After much thought and soul searching, I'm not going to sell and must decline your generous offer."

Matt picked up the stack of papers, leaned over his desk, and tried to hand them back to Big John.

"Cubley, if you don't sell now, in six months to a year, I'll buy this place at the bankruptcy sale for ten cents on the dollar. I thought, being a lawyer, you had some business sense. I see now, you don't!"

Big John stood up with a look of hatred more than anger. He picked up his briefcase without taking back his papers from Matt and walked out of the office, slamming the door as he left. After a few moments, Matt heard the Cadillac startup. It spun gravel as the driver accelerated.

"Well, Chuck, like father like son. Neither one knows how to leave the hotel without throwing gravel all over the lawn," Matt said, eyeing the stack of papers that remained on his desk.

Chuck opened the pass-through fully and peeked through. "I'll have Richard go around and clean up the mess again," Chuck said with a smile.

Matt got up and walked out of his office to the front desk. He gazed around the lobby. He saw cut flowers on every table—fresh flowers. That other resort had fake flowers if they bothered with any at all.

"Chuck, I've had several meetings today. One legal, one pleasant, and the last one, which was just plain fun. I hope our bogus list of guests is about to cause Mr. Big John McCulloch some serious heartburn. And, by the way, I think I just taught Big John a new vocabulary word. One, he may never have heard before; the word: no!"

In the distance, Matt heard a siren, then a second, and then more joined-in. He remembered the red sky of this morning. He hoped the storm it foretold had not arrived.

CHAPTER 31
NOT A GOOD FRIDAY FOR BILLY
Friday, June 24, 1955

Friday was usually a day for a little work and a little fun, but Saturday was for a full measure of fun. Saturdays were for riding bikes or going to see a good monster movie at the Top Hat Theater. Sometimes it included baseball, fishing, or going over to Cubley's Coze or Green Mountain Resort to check out the new arrivals—girls, of course.

But this Saturday was different. All these shootings were ruining my summer, hurting people, and giving me nightmares.

Even teasing Scotty was getting old. If I didn't get out of this house soon, I was going to start shooting people myself. Well, not for real. I got up to report to the warden.

Downstairs, I walked past Mom, the warden, and Grandma without a word. I heard Dad in his bathroom, making weird sounds.

"What's up with Dad?" I asked, ending my silence. She was trying to flip eggs without breaking the yokes. I waited for my answer until after she was done. However, Grandma jumped into our conversation.

"John has a sore throat. That's him, gargling. If I've told him once, I've told him a thousand times, he needs to take better care of himself. All that smoking and staying out all hours of the night is leading him to an early grave."

"If he's sick, can I go over to Kent's house or up to Cubley's Coze on my bike?" I asked Mom with the hope of getting a temporary furlough. I waited for the warden's answer as she flipped another egg.

"No, you may not. Don't you start with your nonsense. I'll not have you getting shot unless I do it myself. I'm close, and my patience is wearing thin. Now sit down, or I might just give you a taste of Lash LaRue's kind of justice."

How did she know about his bullwhip? She must have seen *Mark of the Lash* or *King of the Bullwhip,* but when and where? My mom was full of surprises. Mom had been cross for as long as I had been shut up at home, and that last threat proved it.

"When I was your age, I was satisfied to stay home. I'm just amazed we're not all dead with the police doing nothing to get these killers off the streets." Grandma added dramatically.

"Grandma, when you were my age, did you have to fight Indians and cattle rustlers?" I asked. I knew Grandma was old. While she had never said much about her younger days, I was hoping for a good story to break the monotony. My mom fixed that.

"Billy, you stop that right now. No, your Grandma did not fight Indians or anybody else. What a terrible thing to say. Now, eat your breakfast."

Mom deposited several fried eggs with the yolks intact on everyone's plates.

Scotty was in his high chair, eating glop. He was eating it like it didn't taste like mud mixed with library glue. I knew what it tasted like because I had tried it once when Mom wasn't looking. I had gagged.

Dad came into the kitchen, all hunched over, wearing his pajamas and bathrobe. He looked sick. "Billy, you can stay out from underfoot by helping Mr. Skelton put away parts and tools. Mind what he says, and you better not make me come out there, understand?" His voice sounded like a busted muffler on a Harley Davidson.

"Yes, sir. If I get all my chores done, can I go over to Kent's?" I asked Dad, but Mom answered.

"Billy, it's may I, not can I. Since a crazy sniper is on the loose, you may not. I do not want you shot. Gosh, what do they teach kids in school these days?" Mom was obviously tired, frustrated, and worried.

I knew with Dad sick, Mom's lousy mood could only get worse. I finished up with breakfast and hurried out to the garage, where I heard Mr. Skelton banging on a piece of metal. I got busy and soon had all the tools and parts in order. I even swept out the garage. After a dull morning that felt like it lasted for at least twenty hours, we ate lunch. Dad did not come to lunch but stayed in bed.

Now it was time to pace my cell and read some of my old comics for the hundredth time.

Scotty followed me upstairs. He was quiet for ten minutes, playing with his toys, but then he grabbed the comic I was reading, and we got into it. Mom had to come upstairs. She told me that if I got into one more thing, she would take my bike away for the rest of the summer. She picked up Scotty and took him downstairs—a move that saved his little life.

Around two o'clock, the phone rang. I wandered out to the garage to see if anything interesting was happening. I knew Mr. Skelton would be answering all the calls since Dad was sick.

Hallelujah, we had a tow job! It was called in by the sheriff's office. Sheriff Lawrence's cousin had found a car with a flat tire blocking his pasture gate. A note on the windshield had explained that the driver would return tomorrow after he fixed his spare, but the farmer needed to get into the pasture to fix the fence before his cows got out. A deputy was coming to copy the information off the car's registration for dispatch to locate the owner. All we had to do was tow it.

Mr. Skelton started to leave with Blacky, but I asked him to wait. I said I needed to ask Mom if I could go.

"Ask your dad, son. He was listening in on the extension and knows the details. If he says it's okay, then it's fine with me, but you have to mind me," Mr. Skelton insisted.

"I sure will."

Off I went to ask Dad. It was a good thing I asked him since Mom was busy with Scotty, who had just dumped a glass of milk down his front and all over the kitchen floor. Dad was in bed, sipping iced tea, and Grandma was in her room napping.

"Dad, can I go with Mr. Skelton?" I asked from the hall.

"Yeah, it's just a flat tire near Cub Creek Road, and a deputy will be there," Dad croaked as he took a sip of hot tea and leaned back on his bed pillow.

I ran outside and told Mr. Skelton that I could go, climbed up into the cab, and we started off. I asked Mr. Skelton if I could blow the air horn.

"Sure, give her two blasts," he said as we started up.

I gave two blasts to let Mom know we were leaving. Then I remembered Grandma was napping, but it was too late. Oh well, at least I was getting out of the house. Maybe by the time I got back, she would have forgotten I woke her from her nap.

When we turned left at the Liberty Bell Gas Station, I saw the old bell was sitting all secure in its lot, but the grass had grown high. Someone was not mowing the lawn inside the fence. This sniper was causing a lot of things to be left undone.

Mr. Skelton drove to the farm road and had to back Blacky up the gravel road with the truck being almost as wide as it. I hoped we didn't meet another car and we didn't. Mr. Skelton backed Blacky almost as good as my dad.

Past the last pasture and to our left, going backward, was a narrow farm lane. This lane led through the woods. We backed to a stop near the pasture gate. There, in the middle of that lane and blocking the entrance, was a 1950 Kaiser DeLuxe sedan. It was green with a darker shade of green on the roof. I liked the color. There was a small dent in the door, but otherwise, it was in good shape, save for the flat tire. There was a white rag tied to the radio antennae and a note under the wiper blade. No one was around.

"I thought you said the sheriff called in this tow?" I asked Mr. Skelton.

"Yep. The sheriff's cousin reported it and wants us to tow it out of here. A deputy was supposed to meet us here to authorize the tow and write down the info. I wonder where he could be?" Mr. Skelton and I opened our doors. We both climbed down from the cab at the same time, walked to the rear of Blacky, and waited.

Mr. Skelton looked over the car as I threw a couple of rocks at some trees in the woods. I was cautious not to hit the Kaiser or Blacky. I knew what Dad would do to me. I would get whacked despite his being sick.

"Well, I'm sure glad the flat is on the back. I think there's just enough room to hook it up. If it had been on the front, this tow would have gotten interesting."

Mr. Skelton talked to me like I was an adult, which I appreciated.

We heard a car turn off the farm road and start driving on the lane to where we were parked. A Green Mountain County deputy sheriff's car pulled up about fifteen yards from where we had stopped Blacky. A deputy got out with a notepad and threw up his free hand at us.

"Mr. Skelton, are you working for John now?" asked the deputy.

"Yeah, thought a change might do me good. Is this the tow?" Mr. Skelton answered and asked in the same breath.

"It is. We got the call this morning, but I had to run over to Staunton to pick up a prisoner. It took me longer than I expected. When a prisoner has court, you would think they would have him ready—not a chance." The deputy was frowning. "The driver left a note that he went to fix his spare, but the sheriff's cousin, Dale, wants it out of here like yesterday. I bet he went back to his house to give Sheriff Lawrence a piece of his mind because I'm running late. Let me check the registration, and you can get this thing out of here. I want to be gone before Dale gets back."

As the deputy walked around to the passenger side of the car to get to the glove box, I heard a shot.

"Billy, get down! Get behind Blacky!" Mr. Skelton started screaming.

"What did you say?" I asked and turned to see Mr. Skelton crawling behind a log.

"Dammit, Billy, get down now!" Mr. Skelton was even louder than before.

Then I suddenly realized what was happening. I dropped down on my hands and knees and crawled like a bug on a hot road alongside Blacky. I hid behind the big, rear tandem wheels.

"Who's shooting at us, Mr. Skelton?" I yelled, now that I had come to my senses.

"Billy, shut up and stay down. Deputy, are you okay?" Mr. Skelton called out.

"Deputy, are you okay?" Mr. Skelton yelled louder.

There was no response.

This wasn't good. I panicked. This was real and not like the movies. Someone might have just shot a deputy. Here I was in the gravel, hiding behind Blacky's rear tires without my BB gun. I always thought they were big tires, but now, I wished they were bigger.

Mr. Skelton crawled behind his log until he was even with me. I hoped the Kaiser and Blacky were between the shooter and us.

Was the killer walking up on me?

It sounded like the shot had come from the far side of the Kaiser and deeper in the woods. Mr. Skelton suddenly rolled over the log and into the ditch beside the road. That put him nearer to me. Then, he crawled over to where I was hiding.

"You shot anywhere?" he asked me.

"No! But I want to go home!" I whispered frantically.

"Billy, you stay put. Blacky will stop anything. I'm going to try and make it over to the deputy's car to call for help. Now, that should be easy, but if anything happens, you see that log I just hid behind?" Mr. Skelton whispered in my ear. "If anything happens, you crawl over to that log and get on the other side. Stay on your belly and crawl to where it ends by the creek. You see that little creek?" he asked.

"Yes."

"Crawl up that creek until you get deep into the woods. Then you get up and run as fast as you can over to the first house you come to. You tell who you see that you need help."

Mr. Skelton finished whispering and crawled to where he was able to peek around the front end of the tow truck. He looked back at me.

"I'd rather you stayed here," I told him in a loud whisper.

"You stay put. I got to get to that deputy's car and call for help. If I don't make it, you gotta get out of here. Promise?"

He stared me in the eye and took another peek at the woods.

"I promise," I said, but wished I didn't have to. My voice was trembling and my mouth was as dry as a cotton ball.

Mr. Skelton took a last look and was off running for that deputy's car as fast as he could run. When he got to the front of the police car, he slid like he was sliding into home plate with the third baseman throwing hard to the catcher.

No shots.

I watched him call on the radio, lying across the seat. He finished and flopped out of the car and down on the ground beside the driver's door. He crawled partially under the vehicle. He gave me an okay sign with his finger and thumb.

It felt like we were left waiting for hours. I was all alone and shaking like a leaf. I wanted to cry, but I wanted to go home most of all because all the cops must have left the county. Then in the distance, I heard a siren. Then another and suddenly it sounded like all the police in the world were coming.

Just when I thought we were going to be saved, the police cars stopped way down the road from us. I saw a deputy sheriff's car slide sideways across it.

"Mr. Skelton, why don't they come help us?"

"Billy, you stay where you are. They're not going to come rushing up here and get shot. They'll work their way up through the woods. You stay still until I tell you to get up. You hear?"

"Yes, sir. I won't move until I hear you tell me to." I promised, but I wanted to run down the road to where those police cars had stopped. I next heard a farm tractor coming up the road, but it also stopped by the police cars.

Later, I would learn that the first police car had actually arrived within ten minutes of Mr. Skelton's call. It took another twenty for them "to clear the woods," which was fast, according to Sergeant Oliver, but by then, the shooter was gone.

When Mr. Skelton finally said it was okay, I got up and looked around on the far side of the Kaiser before someone noticed me looking. There was a bloody sheet over the body of the deputy.

I had this urge to go over and wake the deputy up. I wanted to fix things. That's when one of the deputies noticed me staring at the body and made me go with him back to his car, which was at the very end of the long line of police cars. They were turned every which way on the road with that tractor at the very end of the line. This deputy checked me over for gunshots. I thought doing that was silly.

When I got home, I was afraid my mom was going to suffocate me with all the hugs she gave me. I tried to act cool, but I was sure glad to be home. I didn't even protest when Grandma started hugging me. Grandma didn't even fuss at me for waking her up from her nap.

The deputy talked to Dad the whole time that Mom and Grandma were hugging on me and gave him all the details. Dad still looked sick but was up and dressed.

"Laura Jane," Grandma stated, "I told you this would happen. Did you listen to me? No, and here we sit in this awful town with bullets whizzing by our heads and death waiting at our elbow! Billy could have been killed! Shot dead on the side of the road!"

Grandma had just about wound down when Dad told Mom he was going back with the deputy to see about Mr. Skelton and get Blacky, which set off another round of arguments, but he had made up his mind. He got in the deputy's car with Grandma still going on about how she would carve on his tombstone, "Here lies a man who was warned but wouldn't listen."

When Dad returned about two hours later, he was towing the Kaiser and put it in the back lot. Mr. Skelton rode back in a police car, then he got in his car and drove home without saying anything.

Three state police cars drove into the lot, and the troopers went over that 1950 Kaiser with all kinds of equipment. I wanted to watch, but Mom said I had had enough excitement for one day. I noticed she was wearing her "I mean it" frown, so I knew not to argue when she said, "Not one more word, young man. Don't come down until I call you."

I heard Dad finally come in from outside; he sounded awful. He didn't go back to bed but stayed up with Mom in the kitchen, talking about what had happened. He said the police had located another sniper's hide, and he was certain Mr. Skelton and I hadn't been shot because we weren't the targets.

However, he confessed that he had gotten the shakes at the scene, and had had to lean up against Blacky. He promised Mom I was not going on any more tow jobs.

Then they got all mushy. Dad told her if she wanted to go to West Virginia, we would leave tonight, but he would have to come back home because of the business. Mom said he was too sick to leave tonight and demanded he hold her.

"Laura Jane, I'll give you this sore throat."

"John, you hush and hold me."

I wanted to call Kent and tell him about my scrape; he would understand.

That's when I heard more cars pull into the garage lot. I looked out my bedroom window and saw Mr. Cubley get out of his car and begin talking with several troopers. After a few minutes, Sergeant Barry Oliver knocked on the kitchen door. I could hear him and Mr. Cubley talking to my mom and dad.

Dad called me downstairs. I noticed he was back to wearing his goofy bathrobe. He announced that the sergeant wanted to tell the family something.

"Billy, I know just had a scary afternoon, but I want you and your folks to know we're going to catch this sniper. The governor is calling in more Virginia State Troopers for me to put to work on this case, and the Green Mountain County Sheriff has been given deputies from three other counties. Everyone's going to work together on this. We'll have patrols checking on your dad's garage all night and all day tomorrow."

Then he turned to Dad and said, "Mr. Gunn if any tow jobs come in, we'll send a police escort along to ensure your safety. We'll lock this county down if we have to. You have my word." He ended by patting Dad on the shoulder.

"What about us? Are we going to be safe?" Mom asked.

"Mrs. Gunn, if there's anything you need, you can call us and we'll be there."

Mr. Cubley asked Dad, "John, why don't you bring the family over to the hotel for dinner tomorrow night, on me. Maddie plans to put on quite a spread for our state police guests, and I can't think of a safer place for you to be than the main dining room at Cubley's Coze. How about it?"

Mom spoke up. "Mr. Cubley, we would be delighted, but we insist on paying. John and I don't like to impose."

"No, ma'am. My treat."

"May we bring my mother? She'd be afraid to stay here alone."

"Of course, she's invited." Mr. Cubley smiled. "I didn't mention it, but I will certainly be including the Clarks in my invitation."

"My men will escort all of you to dinner and back after what happened today," Sergeant Oliver promised.

"That's a relief." Mom seemed much calmer, and Dad hugged her.

"Laura Jane, you know we're all going to…" Grandma started to say.

"Mother, I am not going to be run out of my own home. We'll stay here through the weekend, at least. I trust the sergeant, and Sergeant, I'm holding you to your word."

"Yes, Ma'am. I'll see to it," responded the sergeant.

I relaxed slightly. Maybe, I thought, things were finally over. I couldn't have been more wrong.

CHAPTER 32
A DIFFERENCE OF OPINIONS
Saturday, June 25, 1955

P olecat was eating his breakfast on the dock when Matt came out to join him. Both of their plates were loaded, and Matt was starting to have trouble with his pants being too tight.

"Morning, Mr. Smith, thanks for the extra special edition papers. Is this the first time the *Highland Gazette* has put specials out on Saturday?" Matt asked.

"No, there have been nine. Past wars caused seven, one when the elementary school caught fire, and the ninth after Black Friday when the stock market crashed."

"Any news about the shootings that's not in the paper?" Matt asked as he cut up a link sausage and stabbed it with his fork.

"There are conflicting opinions among the constabulary," Polecat replied.

"What kind of conflicting opinions?"

Polecat lit up a cigarette that Matt knew from experience heralded a lengthy report. His newsman took a long drag, puffed out a smoke ring that hung suspended over his head, and started.

"The Virginia State Police are conducting a manhunt for Mr. Maynard Donald Hathaway, also known as Doc Hathaway. The search is focused on the Waynesboro area, especially at the residence of Mr. Hathaway."

Polecat skewered a small piece of sausage with his knife, stuck it into his mouth, removed the meat with his teeth without harming himself, and chewed. He burped and continued.

"The family refuses to cooperate. Official reports indicate the fourteen-year-old son even struck one of the troopers with a broom. He was restrained with manacles for his belligerence, but the troopers did not arrest him. When they departed the residence, they turned him over to his mother with a warning. So far, they believe Hathaway has been stealing cars from Waynesboro or Staunton and using them to commute to Highland for nefarious purposes. The car that was used to lure the deputy into the most recent ambush was stolen from a vehicle repair facility in Waynesboro. It was not noticed missing nor reported stolen until after the deputy was killed."

"Any evidence of value recovered from the car?" asked Matt.

"Negative. It was wiped clean of fingerprints. The flat tire was instituted by the sniper to fool the police into believing it was an innocent situation. Officials speculate the trap may have been set for the sheriff."

Polecat paused and inquired if Matt was going to finish his last sausage. Matt indicated he was, but he called Boo to bring Mr. Smith a piece of toast and one more sausage link. Polecat smiled as he continued.

"Now, the investigative focus of the state police centers on round-the-clock surveillance of the Hathaway residence. The troopers are trying to determine if he's currently living with his wife or if he has a hideout at another location."

The second order of food arrived, and Polecat dug in. He continued talking as he chewed, "The perpetrator of the latest crime scene left behind a dose of pepper to distract the tracking dogs and covered his tracks by putting cedar branches on his feet. This matches the *modus operandi* that was used at the factory."

"How in the world did you find all that out?"

"I merely appear with my papers at the state police command post. I sell them one and bestow two more gratis. This gives me access to the building when their six a.m. shift change is occurring. While I sort my papers in the hall, I can listen to the troopers going off duty catching their replacements up to speed. Little notice is taken of my presence," Polecat said with that crocodile smile.

"And do they let you stay and listen to the official briefing?"

"No, the sergeant clears the room of all civilians for that, though his use of that term is in error as civilians are non-military, and the troopers are not federalized."

"So how do you listen when they kick you out? You seem to know so much."

"My uncle is the school janitor, and sometimes I pay him a visit in the boiler room. It's amazing what one can hear down there. You see, the boiler room is beneath the school, and a recent repair of the hot water pipes has left voids through which we can hear. Of my eavesdropping, I am sure they are unaware."

"I understand that the state police are after Doc Hathaway. Do you know why he's called Doc? Is he a doctor of some kind?"

"His initials are MD," Polecat said with that quirky smile again.

"Oh, I see," Matt nodded. "Town gossips are saying Chief Smith remains convinced the Beamis brothers are behind all the recent shootings. Has he dug up any hard evidence?"

"Chief Smith believes that because the deputy was shot two or three miles from the Beamis farm. He mistakenly believes he has all the proof he needs. He thinks the cousin, who is now running the farm, is the sniper. Although the tracks, such as they were, led to a mountain gap and over it to a logging road on the Waynesboro side of that singular mountain, Chief Smith insists that trail is of little importance."

"Does he really?" replied Matt.

"In opposition, the state police believe the Waynesboro side of the gap is where a getaway car was stashed, and that fact to them is quite relevant. The chief and Little John think, however, that the trail up to the gap is a false trail, laid down earlier in the day to mislead police canines. The chief is convinced, without hard evidence, that the sniper ran from the hide across two miles of thick woods to the Beamis farm without leaving a trail for the dogs. He claims the cousin managed this by skillful woodsman-ship, so the Highland Police have now arrested the cousin. Another search of the farm turned up nothing. There is little left of the place, I am told. Officer Frank Younger bragged about how they searched the Beamis house and barn down to the studs in the walls." Polecat rose and appeared as though he might leave.

"Mr. Smith, what about the sheriff of Green Mountain County? What does he think?" Matt asked.

Polecat took out another cigarette, sat back down, and lit it. Blowing a smoke ring inside of another smoke ring, he continued as the rings drifted with some permanence over the loading dock. "The sheriff seems to think the state police are closer to the solution of this criminal activity than Chief Smith. However, he is also supporting Chief Smith in his arrest of the Beamis brothers and the cousin. He has an election to think about and does not want to exclude any solution or alienate either side."

Polecat rose to take his dishes back into the kitchen.

"Thanks, I appreciate all the information. Is there anything you've not covered?" Matt asked with a grin.

"No. You may, however, expect Trooper Bobby Giles to visit you this morning. He's going to request you accompany him to inspect the latest crime scene. Expect him around nine-thirty. I recommend you take a pair of boots for vipers. Also, may I trouble you for a small loan of say, four dollars, until next Wednesday?"

These loans were starting to add up, but Matt paid it without voicing a complaint. Polecat delivered his dishes to the kitchen and thanked Maddie over the noise.

Matt visited Chuck at the front desk soon after. His manager was anxious over additional cancellations by several regular guests, though this provided needed space for their new category of guests: troopers and reporters. The hotel was full. Plus, the extra meals being sold to the reporters, who were generally big eaters, were helping. The maids and dining room staff were happy and everyone was working all the hours they wanted.

Chuck reminded Matt that the dining room was still showing a slight loss since Matt was feeding the troopers at employee rates. Matt told Chuck to have Boo bill him for the difference.

Trooper Bobby Giles showed up at nine thirty-five a.m., and Matt noted that he would have to tell Polecat he was off by five minutes. He consented to go with the officer without a pause, and the trooper noticed Matt was wearing hiking boots upon his arrival but did not ask any questions.

Giles gave the same report as Polecat during the ride out to the scene, but with fewer details.

Matt examined the scene in the woods, just as he had done for the hide by the plant, and found this hide to be even more elaborate with a better, more secluded exit off to the rear. The hide was also a little closer to the bait car. A necessity, he concluded, due to the trees. The shorter the distance, the fewer the trees to block the sniper from his target.

Only one shot was fired to kill the deputy. No brass was found in the hide, and Matt concluded the sniper was policing up his ejected brass. Another sign that this was a trained military sniper.

Matt asked Giles to show him where Blacky had been parked and where Billy and Mr. Skelton had been standing when the deputy was shot. Seeing how close the two were to the deputy and even the sniper gave Matt a cold, cold feeling. It was abundantly clear that neither Billy nor Boo's dad had been a target as they each would have been an easy kill.

Giles then informed Matt that the medical examiner and the lab had worked all night on the evidence. They reported that the bullet recovered from the body was a 30-06 caliber and the markings on it matched the bullets recovered from both the courthouse and the factory.

While Matt was searching the hide for clues, there must have been twenty police officers going through the woods searching for evidence. They were using grid lines to cover the crime scene, up the mountain to the gap. A second group with dogs was searching the ground from the hide to the Beamis farm. If anything had been buried or hidden, the men and dogs were sure to find it. The searchers were almost done by the time Matt was ready to go. To the dismay of both groups, nothing of value had been located. Every piece of trash had been picked up, cataloged, and put into evidence bags. Matt had never seen so much effort put into a single crime scene, and he guessed that with two fellow officers killed, plus two civilians, no effort was being spared.

He also learned from several troopers that the governor had demanded three troopers be assigned to Big John McCulloch's home, and the town boss was to have a police escort whenever he went out. The police were talking about how he had better protection than the governor with a lead car to block traffic at intersections, a second lead car in front, and a trailing car to cover the rear.

Even with this protection, though, Big John was not making many road trips for the present. He was content to stay secluded at home.

The funerals would also be assigned full protection. In addition to a large police security detail, the troopers expected police officials from all over the state to attend the funerals of the slain officers. News agencies were coming in by the truckload and Highland was going to be crowded for at least a week.

Trooper Lusk had a detail of six men searching for Doc Hathaway. Eight other officers were hunting down the fifteen other former employees who had been fired at the plant.

The sergeant drove up and greeted Matt, just as he and Giles were preparing to depart. "Matt, my men are taking too long for meals. I'm ordering them to eat on the road."

"Sergeant, I might have a solution. How about I have the hotel kitchen fix box lunches? We can even deliver them to the command post at the school. Would that help?"

Matt didn't wait for a response but continued with, "You tell me the number, we will send them over. Same price. You can just put the money in a shoebox. Richard will collect it as he makes his deliveries. Boxed meals can shorten meal time for men on the go. You'll be doing me a favor by keeping all my kitchen staff employed."

The sergeant's face softened the more he thought about the offer. "This might work. It certainly should stop the griping. Thanks. I'll get the word out. Can we start right away?"

"Sure, not a problem."

The sergeant pulled out his wallet and counted out several bills. Send over thirty lunches for the day shift and twelve for the night shift. Here's the money. I'll treat the men to one meal and hope the complaining stops. If this gets to be too much of a drain on you or your kitchen, though, let me know."

"Sergeant, if this goes on for a month, I might have to cry uncle, but for now, things are okay. Your troopers are making the guests that are staying with us feel a lot safer."

"If this thing lasts a month, I may be applying for a job at your hotel," the sergeant replied without a trace of a smile. He continued with, "What did your inspection of the hide tell you?"

Matt filled him in on the few additional details he'd noticed. He repeated his initial theory of two snipers with a single gun. However, the more he saw, the more he was inclined to change his mind. Now, Matt was leaning toward the conclusion that there was only one sniper. He surmised the one sniper, who experienced some kind of difficulty on the first incident, had gotten his act together for the next two ambushes.

"How are you coming along with finding Mr. Hathaway?" Matt asked.

"Not good. His boy gave us some trouble. The whole family hates the police, *any* police. We have a large detail searching for him, but so far, nothing. I think with his hiding from us; he's looking more and more like our man."

"But the chief remains convinced the Beamis brothers are behind all of this?"

"Yeah. The chief just arrested the cousin. He thinks the farmhand's behind it all. The fellow claims he might have heard the shot in the distance but denies having a gun and being the killer."

"What's his background?" asked Matt.

"He's just a farmhand. Despite being roughed up a bit by the Highland Police, he's sticking to his story. One of the sheriff's jailers had to pull Little John off him and got punched for his effort by Little John. That started a fight in the jail between the two. It was finally broken up, but, now, the sheriff and chief are at each other's throats over it. It's a shame. I hate it when interdepartmental cooperation breaks down."

"We have got to solve this fast for all kinds of reasons," Matt said, shaking his head.

"Bobby, why don't you run Mr. Cubley back up to the hotel and then report in with Quinn. He's going to try and pick up a guy on the factory list by the name of Daryl Dean Shiflett."

"Sure will. Do we have a picture on file for Shiflett?" Trooper Giles asked the sergeant.

"Yeah, Quinn has one, but he's easy to spot. Shiflett lost two fingers in a table saw accident at the plant," the sergeant replied.

"Which hand and which hand is dominant?" asked Giles.

"I'm sorry, which hand is what?"

"Well, is he right or left-handed, and which hand is missing the two fingers?"

"Oh, he lost the pointer and middle finger off his right hand. You'll have to ask him if he's right or left-handed. The plant doesn't care if you're a lefty or not, so it's not in his personnel records. I don't know."

Matt and Trooper Giles walked down the lane to the trooper's car.

"Your sergeant is not having a good day, is he?" Matt commented to Giles.

"Sergeant Oliver is probably the best sergeant in the state, but Big John took the governor to task over the plant killings, so between the governor getting all riled and the press screaming, stuff has flowed downhill and landed on Sergeant Oliver big time. One thing I can say for the sarge, though: the stuff stopped with him. Oh, he's been a bit grumpy, sure, but not bad, and he doesn't pass it down to the troops. The men respect him for that. Some of our other sergeants would... well, I'll leave it at that."

"Bobby, you're too nice. We had the same thing in the Corps. We used to say, major assholes drop it, and the troops have to shovel it. The trouble was it was more than the majors doing the dumping. No matter who it came from, shit shovels the same and ends up at the same place." Matt smiled like he was joking, but his tone was serious.

"Well, we're lucky. The sarge buying us all a meal, puts him right up on top in my book. I can afford to miss a meal now and then, but darn, I'm starting to miss too many. I'm hungry. I've been hungry all morning."

"When we get back, I'll have Maddie fix you something quick to go."

The trooper and Matt made it back to Green Mountain Avenue and had not gone but a couple of blocks when a Highland patrol car with lights flashing and siren wailing passed them. It did a sliding turn into the drive to Green Mountain Resort.

"Hold on, Matt. Let's go see if they need any help," Giles said.

Matt soon found out why the other troopers called Giles the best wheelman in the district. His car was fast.

Upon arriving at the Green Mountain Resort Hotel in short order, Matt stood by the patrol car as the trooper and the officer, who turned out to be Officer Frank Younger, ran into the resort office.

It was only five minutes later when they emerged with a man in handcuffs. Officer Younger drove off with the prisoner, and Giles came back to the car, where Matt was waiting.

"Some idiot by the name of Marvin Kingsley rented a room, and then he tried to leave without paying the bill. He even tried to take the towels, bedclothes, and a lamp. A maid saw him loading up his car, and there you have it. She told the desk clerk, who called the police. The crook was walking through the lobby, getting ready to leave, just as big as you please, when Younger nabbed him. This county is swarming with police, and this nut tries to steal. Go figure," Giles reported in amazement.

"Yeah, go figure," Matt said with a knowing smile on his face. He recognized the name as one of the names on the first bogus list Cliff Duffy had delivered to the drop. *Yeah, go figure.*

CHAPTER 33

BILLY'S WEEK OF FUNERALS
Saturday - Thursday, June 25-30, 1955

D ad was feeling better by Saturday. Grandma kept Scotty while Mrs. Clark drove Kent, Mom, and me over to Waynesboro. Dad's birthday was July tenth, so I took my money to buy him a new hat for church because Scotty spilled food on his old one.

Kent and I sat in the back while our moms talked and we whispered about the shooting on Friday.

"BB, I sure wish I could have been with you," he whispered in my ear. "Weren't you scared?"

"Me scared? Heck, I wasn't scared a bit. But it's probably better you missed it. You can never tell where a ricochet might end up."

He wanted to know if I got to see the deputy all shot up, but I told him there was only one shot, and the police covered up the body before I got a good look at it. I did see some blood that had leaked through the sheet.

"They tend to cover bodies first thing," I told Kent. I was quickly becoming an expert on dead bodies. First, Mr. Beamis, now, the deputy. I was glad they covered up the dead bodies, but I sure wouldn't tell Kent that.

When we got to town, I picked out a medium, felt dress hat for two dollars and eighty-five cents at White's Department Store. Mom asked if she could pay for part of it, but I reminded her that I was a working man, though it did cut into my savings. I wanted my dad to have the best.

I knew that I would have to hide it from Scotty, the snoop.

Mom and Mrs. Clark treated Superman and me to cheeseburgers at the Fishburne Drug Store, which left me enough to buy a Peppermint Patty for later and a Zero for my little brother. Mom said it was nice to include Scotty, which made me feel good.

That evening, Trooper Giles showed up to escort us to Cubley's Coze, letting Kent and me ride with him. We ran the red lights down Green Mountain Avenue, and he even let us blow the siren going up the driveway to the hotel. It was neat. All the other cars pulled over to the curb to let us pass.

Grandma refused to go with us and kept repeating that we were going to be killed, fussing about how there wasn't a train from Highland to West Virginia. I reminded her there were no trains from Highland to anywhere because the closest train station was in Waynesboro.

She replied, "Horsefeathers!" which is Grandmother for, "I have reached the end of my rope, I don't care to hear anything else you say, and you better watch out." I knew not to say anything more.

Sunday, we all went to church, including Grandma. The sermon was about the evil that men do. I figured it would be a humdinger, but, about half-way through, I lost interest. The preacher never told us about any good killings—not one shooting, stabbing, or scalping—he just went on and on about the definition of evil.

He needs to watch Roy or Hoppy. He could learn some better stories for church.

A few of my friends were at the service, but none of us got to talk to each other because everyone went straight from the church to their cars in a big hurry. The pastor didn't stand outside on the steps, and I could tell he was nervous. He kept peeking around the door frame, keeping an eye on the street.

The Lockharts and Lou's family were not in church. In fact, the church was half empty. It looked like the week of summer vacation with everyone gone. The Lockhart boys and Lou McCulloch were big chickens as far as I was concerned for being too afraid to come to church.

As soon as we got outside, Dad told Mom to look at the five police cars sitting around the church to show her that we were safe. That's when Grandma cranked up. She told everyone she could grab that we had all better get out of town before we all ended up dead and in our graves. Mom tried her best to get Grandma to be quiet, but there was no stopping her. Luckily, the congregation was in a big hurry to leave, and no one paid her much mind.

That afternoon, Dad drove me over to Superman's house to read comics. When we finished all his new comics, we tried to sneak out to ride his bike.

"Kent, where do you two think you're going?" called his mom from the living room.

"Mom, BB, and I are just going to take turns riding in the backyard."

"When billy goats wear satin trousers. You either entertain yourselves in the house, or I'll call Billy's mom to come pick him up."

Around two o'clock, though, things took a turn. A new Presbyterian preacher had come to town and had the misfortune of looking a little like Doc Hathaway. The police had put up "wanted posters" all over town, and everyone was on the lookout for public enemy number one.

This new preacher knocked on the Clarks" door and, when Kent's mom peeked out to see who it was, she was terrified to see who she believed to be the town's most wanted man. Too scared to open the door, she retreated to the back hall for her phone. Superman and I heard him say through the door, "Ma'am, I would like to invite you and your family to church," but Mrs. Clark was too busy dialing the police to notice.

When he left a pamphlet inside the screen door, she thought he was trying to force his way inside. Kent and I watched him walk across the street as Kent's Mom yelled upstairs for us to go into the bathroom and lock the door.

Kent tried to stop her and yelled, "Mom… Mom!" but she wouldn't listen.

Now, as we found out later, while Mrs. Clark was talking to the police, old Mrs. O'Grady, the widow who lived alone across the street, had also seen the posters and was phoning the sheriff's office, as well. She was hysterical, screaming that the killer was trying to break into her house and shoot her.

In our town, before all the trouble, when someone knocked on your front door, it was no big deal. Now, though, it felt like everything was dangerous.

Superman and I heard the sirens five blocks away. We snuck out of the bathroom, looked out his bedroom window, and saw ten policemen pull up. Every one of them rushed the preacher, who was still across the street holding a pack of flyers.

He was run over by two big policemen, who we had never seen before, and the poor preacher went flying backward into Mrs. O'Grady's rose bushes. The cops then dragged him out of the rose bushes by his feet, picked him up, and marched him over to a squad car, where they slapped handcuffs on his wrists.

He was limping and bloody from the thorns. His little papers had been scattered all over the yard, and a gust of wind blew them into the street.

Things got worse because those big policemen were not from Highland, so they had no idea that he was just a Presbyterian preacher. The out-of-town officers thought they had arrested Doc Hathaway and were taking no chances. They punched him a couple of times for good measure, rendering him breathless, and demanded his name, and, when he failed to answer, they punched him some more.

Finally, Officers Little John McCulloch and Frank Younger arrived with the second wave of cops, though it was a little late for the poor preacher. He ended up with a split lip that required a couple of stitches, a minor concussion, two bruised ribs, and rose bush thorns all over his backside.

The policeman, who talked to Kent's mom afterward, told her a concussion was not serious, but I bet you couldn't convince the preacher that. He looked worse than Kent when he had gotten clobbered at the Green Mountain Resort.

After the neighbors saw the big commotion, phone calls started coming into Kent's house from all around town. It was not long before we found out that the Sunday night service had to be canceled at the Presbyterian Church.

Police stayed in front of Kent's house for a while, even after discovering who they had captured. One policeman told Kent's mom that he doubted if anyone would have gone to church after dark, anyway. I started to tell him it didn't get dark until way after church let out, but I thought better of it. They were all still looking like they wanted to pound somebody.

Mom and Dad came over after all the excitement and made me go home. I tried to tell them it was just a preacher, but they didn't want to listen.

Mr. Wesley Spencer, the plant superintendent, was buried the following Monday. Mom and Dad went to his funeral, but I got to stay home with Scotty and Grandma. A trooper I had not seen before came by the garage during the funeral to check on us. I think Dad must have asked him to because he even checked around the back of the garage.

Before he left, he asked me about the rifle locked up in the cab of Blacky. I told him right out, "My dad put it in there after he got back from towing in the Kaiser on Friday." Then, he asked me where the deputy's car was, and I replied, "Sheriff Lawrence let McCulloch Chevrolet tow it and not my dad." The trooper grinned and told me that he thought the sheriff was being extra careful since an election was coming up.

After the trooper left, I saw a long line of cars going from the church out to the cemetery. There were police at the intersections, and there must have been thirty cars in a line. All of them had on their headlights. Big John McCulloch was conspicuous because he had a police escort when he went past.

Tuesday was the funeral for Officer Larry Sparrow. Dad said no one in town liked him, but he still got a bigger funeral than Mr. Spencer. Police from all over the state came to his funeral, but we all stayed home.

Dad and I watched the Sparrow funeral go past the garage. The town cemetery where they buried Mr. Spencer and Officer Sparrow was on the hill across from the Liberty Bell Gas Station. If dead people can see things, I guess they put Mr. Sparrow and Mr. Spencer where they could watch over the plant.

Wednesday, we all stayed home again. This was the day for the funeral of the plant foreman, Mr. Franklin. I knew his youngest daughter from school. She was two years below me, and some of the kids had given her a rough time because her father had been mean to their dads. The teachers had to watch out for her because one of the older girls, whose dad had just been let go, poured Clorox over her head. It ruined her dress and turned her skin all red. The Clorox hurt her eyes, and I remember hearing her scream. They ran water from the hose over her for a long time. I had bad dreams about it for several weeks. Mom tried to find out why I was having nightmares, but I wouldn't tell her.

The little girl finally got well, but she became timid and wouldn't play with the other kids. Each day a different teacher would let her color pictures in her classroom during recess. The older girl, who poured the bleach, was expelled, which was sad because her father got fired from the plant, and he couldn't find work with anyone in the county. Several months later, the bank kicked them out of their home, and the family left town.

It became clear to me then how the McCulloch family ran things, with misfortune befalling anyone who crossed them. I knew I should stay away from Lou.

Thursday, June 30, 1955, was the last day of June on my calendar. The next day would bring a new picture and month. July had three fast cars at the top of the page, and I wondered if Trooper Giles could catch them.

The funeral for the dead deputy was conducted that Thursday. I was on edge. I was mean to Scotty without even knowing why and loud noises made me jump. To make matters worse, the night prior, I dreamt that someone was shooting at me. I woke up in a sweat and must have been crying because Scotty sat up screaming, which got Mom and Dad up. He got to sleep with Mom and Dad in their bed, and I had to stay in my room all alone. I hid under my covers, holding the pocket knife Dad had given me the previous year.

I couldn't get back to sleep for a long, long time, and shadows in my room looked like men with guns stalking me. When I finally woke up, it was late, and I was tired. Scotty grabbed my sock as I tried to put it on. I smacked him hard.

He cried, and I suddenly felt terrible that I had hurt him until I got a whipping from Dad. He used a belt but not like that other time, so I was glad I got one whack in on Scotty.

Kent and I had been begging to go back to work at Cubley's Coze for ages. Mr. Cubley said we could wash police cars, which sounded more like fun than sitting around here all day getting whippings.

Mom and Dad were tired of me. I was tired of me.

After my whipping, I figured I better let things rest. I would wait to ask if I could go to the movies on Saturday with Superman. If my folks said no, I would begin looking for a good spot to dig an escape tunnel from my house to the street.

Troopers had been telling Dad stuff, but so far, Doc Hathaway had not been caught. The police were claiming that either some of the factory workers were hiding him out, or he had left the area. I began to pray for the police to catch him and put an end to all this violence.

Mom let me know that since the funeral for the deputy sheriff was today, the bond hearing for the Beamis brothers had to be postponed because all the deputies were going to the funeral.

Before lunch, Mom and I watched the deputy sheriff's long funeral, with lots of police cars going past the garage. I was growing tired of police cars.

I overheard Mom talking to another mother about how kids all over town were getting into trouble because they couldn't go anywhere. It hadn't been this bad even when the polio epidemic had broken out. I remember how the mothers had scrubbed and scrubbed the school, kids, toys, pencils, school desks, school rooms, even the cars, but the parents couldn't wash this trouble away.

"Billy, where are you?" Mom called from the kitchen.

"In the yard, Mom. Same place I've been all week."

"Don't you sass me, young man. You want your father to give you another whipping?"

"I think I'll just run away."

I said it, but not loud enough for her to hear me. I couldn't afford two whippings in one day. My butt couldn't, anyway.

"What did you say?" I heard Mom ask. She came to the kitchen door.

"Mom, can Kent and I please, please, go up to the hotel tomorrow? We'll stay right by the hotel. With all the troopers staying there, it's gotta be safe," I begged.

"Let me talk to your father."

Mom and Mrs. Clark ultimately agreed, that before they killed us, Dad could drive us to the hotel on Friday. And, if we both decided to quit fussing, we might even be allowed to go to the Top Hat Theater on Saturday.

So, Kent and I put on our angel wings and halos and tried to be perfect. Perhaps a pardon was in the works, and we would be released from prison.

CHAPTER 34

DOC IS CAPTURED
Friday, July 1, 1955

Afte r Matt checked the calendar behind the front desk, he realized to his surprise that it was no longer June, and he headed to the kitchen. He heard Maddie fussing at Connell Washington, her assistant cook. She was tearing into him for coming to work late and looking like a bantamweight fighter after three rounds with Joe E. Lewis, "The Brown Bomber."

"Connell, *mon Dieu*! I'm tired of your drinking and fighting. You smell like a brewery. If the guests see that face, they'll think we're running a flophouse."

Maddie was advancing on poor Connell with a butcher knife that was at least eight inches long, not counting the handle. Connell had lumps and bruises all over his face. The lid of one eye was puffy.

"Mrs. Johnson, I'm stone-cold sober. I've had nothing to drink, well, not today. I was mugged last night! They took all my money, my face is killing me, and now you're yelling at me! Please, have mercy!" His lament was pitiful as he backed away from her.

The hotel's fruit and vegetable buyer was returning from picking up an order. And, seeing the ruckus, almost dropped the box of Silver Queen corn she was carrying.

"Connell, have you been fighting again?" she exclaimed as she carefully put the heavy box down on the kitchen counter. Boo hurried into the kitchen to investigate the noise.

Seeing the problem, Boo walked right between Maddie and Connell with her back to Maddie.

Matt cringed. *I sure wouldn't stand there.*

Maddie stopped when she saw Boo blocking her approach to Connell.

Boo showed no concern. "Hand me a dishcloth from the drawer. I need to clean up Connell, so he looks more like a cook and less like ground beef for tonight's stroganoff," Boo joked with the hotel pastry chef.

The pastry chef, who was trying to protect a pan of rolls he was letting rise, quickly grabbed a clean dish towel from the drawer next to him and tossed it to her.

Maddie threw the knife she was threatening to use on Connell into the metal sink. It made a loud clatter, and Connell jumped. Boo, however, didn't flinch as she began working on Connell's face.

Maddie threw up her hands as if she was offering a prayer to the gods of the kitchen and stormed outside, letting the screen door to the loading dock slam shut. Matt and the rest of the kitchen staff hoped she was leaving to cool off and was not going home to get her dad's squirrel gun.

Matt heard water splash and looked over at Toby Stanley, the cleaner. Toby appeared not to have noticed the disturbance. He was washing a plate as if it were the most crucial task ever assigned to a mere mortal.

Toby had never learned to read or write, despite going to the third-grade five times. The town's gentry referred to Toby as "very slow," while the roughnecks referred to him as "the retard."

Uncle TJ hired Toby a year after he was tossed out of school because his third-grade teacher decided he was unable to learn. The school board reviewed the matter, unanimously decided he was wasting space in the classroom, declared him unteachable, and excused him from school attendance.

Toby's family tried to find work for him, but he only lasted twenty minutes at the plant. After he had been fired from three more places, word got around that he was hopeless. No one would even consider hiring him. The boy sat on his front porch, whittling sticks with an old knife. He never made anything except slivers of wood but spent hours and hours carving.

Uncle TJ heard about Toby and, after talking with his dad, offered the poor boy an outside job at the hotel. Working for the groundskeeper turned out to be way too complicated for Toby. It seemed that no matter what work they gave him, after ten minutes, he would wander off. They regularly found him hiding in the woods behind the maintenance shed, just sitting on an old stump, whittling sticks. Uncle TJ thought he would have to let Toby go.

It was Maddie, the no-nonsense boss of the kitchen, who saved him. She had shown him how to wash a plate, and for a month, that was all he did; he cleaned plates—no silverware, no glasses, only plates. Then for two months, she added glasses to the plates. After a year and a half, Toby could clean all the dishes, plus the pots and pans.

He was slow, but he never allowed an item to leave his cleaning station without it being spotless. By the time Toby had been fully trained, the kitchen never got another complaint about a plate or anything else not being clean. Thus, the staff started calling Toby "the Cleaner." Now when a pot was burned, a cook would say, "Give it to the Cleaner," and it would come back like new. With this one talent, Toby Stanley earned the respect of the kitchen staff.

Boo passed by Matt, interrupting his thoughts about Toby when she whispered, "Typical morning after." She strolled out to the loading dock, and within a minute, Boo and Maddie came back into the kitchen arm-in-arm, talking and laughing as if there had never been a conflict at all.

Matt picked up the morning *Gazette,* and there was no mention of Connell being mugged. There was an article stating that Doc Hathaway had not been arrested despite the police being deluged with calls from citizens claiming to have spotted this phantom. A quote from Chief Smith revealed that he now thought that Doc Hathaway had joined the Beamis gang to accomplish their goal of exacting revenge.

As Matt finished the article, Billy and Kent arrived late for work, having been dropped off by Billy's mom after a severe and lengthy lecture on what might befall them if they failed to stay within ten feet of the hotel. Matt was so glad to see them that he didn't mention their being late.

The boys complained that an adult would be driving them to and from work. No bike riding allowed, and thus, only a portion of their sentence had been lifted.

Matt told the boys that there were three trooper's cars parked in the wash area, waiting for wash jobs. Under no circumstances were they to open a trooper's car door or trunk because the equipment inside was dangerous and very expensive.

Trooper Lusk arrived at the hotel an hour later and asked Matt for advice about how best to use his old Marine Corps Ghillie suit. The suit was nothing more than a set of coveralls with shaggy strings and leaf shapes sewn all over it to hide the wearer from view, and Matt agreed to take a look at it. They went out to the trooper's car, where Lusk pulled the suit from an old Marine Corps bivy bag. The suit was old and in bad shape.

"Gunny, what should I do to make this blend in with the terrain of Green Mountain County?" Lusk asked.

"Burn it," Matt responded.

"What? It's no good at all?"

"Where are you going to use it?"

"Well, I'm gonna use it around here to hide. We used them in training that way."

"Yeah, in training, you picked a hide and waited for your target to come to you. Our sniper prefers hit and run tactics, which gives him the advantage. You have to guess where he might strike over an entire county of real estate. How do you propose to lure him to your hide?"

"Good point."

"What did I teach you about movement? You use terrain features, not the suit. Using terrain will do a much better job of keeping you safe. A Ghillie suit makes you look like a stationary bush and not a person. Even a rookie is going to spot a moving bush, and this sniper is no rookie," Matt tried to explain without crushing the feelings of his student.

"Are you serious? Burn it?" Lusk repeated Matt's earlier response.

"No, it might be useful under the right circumstances, but how many times did you use it in combat?"

"Never."

"It's a good way to hide if you know the path of ingress or egress of the enemy ahead of time, but not if you need to be mobile," Matt instructed.

"Gunny, point taken. Do you think our sniper is using one of these?" the trooper asked.

"No, there's no evidence of it."

"Yeah, forget I asked about the suit."

"Don't take it too hard. Come on in for a cup of joe."

"Wish I could, but the sergeant wanted me to ask you to look around Big John's house and the plant for possible hides. He thinks Big John will be the sniper's next target."

"I agree. My best guess is that he'll hit Big John at his house. Though he could surprise us and strike the same place twice. Let's check the plant, as well. Are there any other places that Big John frequents?"

"His escort troopers report he still visits the Green Mountain Resort daily, and he goes over to Charlottesville every Saturday for a game of golf," said Lusk

"Since he's making trips to his resort, we better check it out, although, with all the activity around the place and the lake in front not providing a good area for a hide, it wouldn't be a sniper's top choice," Matt concluded.

"And the golf course?"

"The golf course in Charlottesville, I played with my uncle a bunch. I place it low on my worry list. It's too open for a quick escape. There is no way to hide on the fairways and greens. It doesn't have high weeds in the roughs or thick woods in which to hide. You might tell them to do a hasty search before Big John tees off, but that should clear it easily."

Trooper Lusk and Matt left in the trooper's car and drove over to the Green Mountain Resort. They both agreed they didn't see any good spots for a sniper in front of the hotel, and the land between the buildings and the lake was too short a distance and too open.

They both decided that the rear of the hotel was a whole other story. It was a bonanza of good hiding places among the wooded hiking and hunting trails and agreed it was imperative to warn Big John not to venture out the back of the hotel for any reason.

They proceeded over to the plant when a call came over the radio that Rockbridge County deputies and troopers were in pursuit of a 1953 Ford flathead V-8 pickup truck headed north at a high rate of speed. As they listened, the chase had crossed over the Blue Ridge Parkway, dropped down the Tye River Highway, and the Ford pickup was headed east on State Route 22. The pickup was coming their way.

"Matt, can I drop you off at the Liberty Bell Gas Station?" Trooper Lusk asked as they arrived at the intersection.

"Not on your life. Here he comes!" Matt responded and pointed to the Ford pickup as it raced towards them at a hundred miles an hour. It was now driving through the straights, picking up even more speed, and not a trooper was in sight behind it.

Trooper Lusk flipped on his red light atop the car, backed up thirty feet, and waited for the pickup driver to decide if he was going straight on toward the plant or try to turn right into the Town of Highland. When it was clear that the pickup was going straight, Lusk started his car rolling toward the intersection, and once the pickup passed the intersection, he floored it. The police car swerved into State Route 22 with the rear tires just starting to screech. This trooper knew how to get the most out of his car. Although he was in a hard right turn, going after the pickup, he was achieving maximum speed without losing traction.

Passing the plant, Trooper Lusk was going close to a hundred, and the pickup was no longer pulling away. The trooper drove his car over East Gap about as fast as Matt would care to go. The pickup was taking the insides of the curves—the crazy driver paying no attention to drifting into the wrong lane. So far, there had not been a head-on collision, but Matt did not think the pickup driver's luck would continue to hold. The trooper was flying, but he was at least staying on his side of the road.

Once over the pass, the road was straight. All of a sudden, Trooper Giles appeared, passing them as if Lusk's car had lost power. Giles was going at least a hundred and thirty or forty. Slowly, he was catching the flathead Ford.

"What's in Giles's car?" Matt asked with both hands on the dash and both feet pushing against the floorboard to keep himself snug on the front seat.

The trooper spoke except when he had to fight the wheel or pass someone, "John Gunn works on his car. He won't let our mechanics near it. The lieutenant wouldn't let anyone else get by with that, but Bobby Giles... has earned the privilege. The official monthly reports on his car…, come on, move over…, all bogus… but the mechanics file them, the sergeant signs them, and the lieutenant ignores them."

Lusk went silent as he fought his car through a series of sharper curves; though Matt was sure they were about to wreck, he held it on the road. The pursuit entered another straight stretch, and Lusk accelerated his car to its limit. The other two vehicles were pulling away from him.

The Ford pickup and Trooper Giles were about to enter into a right-hand curve. Suddenly, Lusk slammed on the brakes for about three-seconds as he neared the entrance to the curve, which threw Matt forward. Matt used his hands on the dash and his feet on the floorboard to keep from hitting the windshield. Then, Lusk accelerated through the curve, and the police car drifted closer and closer to the centerline until he passed the apex of the curve. Now, he floored it and rocketed out of the back end of the first curve and into the front end of the second to their left. The side forces as they entered the left-hand bend pushed the car right up to the outside of the road with only a few inches to spare before scraping the guardrail. The patrol car came out of the curve at full power. Matt noticed both his feet and hands were shaking.

"Watch this!" shouted Lusk, "This next sharp curve will require them to slow down. Giles is going to tap the pickup on the quarter panel coming out of the next curve. He's going to spin him out. I bet you a dollar."

Trooper Lusk was telling him this as relaxed as if he was watching a pitcher getting ready to strike out an opposing player. Matt noticed Trooper Lusk had started to slow for the curve ahead.

The pickup and Giles both hit their brakes hard at the same instant and slowed violently. They entered into the next curve to their left much slower, with Giles no more than four feet off the pickup's rear and was still closing gradually. When the pickup came out of the other side of the curve, Matt was able to see smoke from the exhaust of the pickup as it tried to add speed to get away from the trooper.

The trooper's car slowly advanced until it reached a mark about one-fourth up the driver's side of the other vehicle, and Matt could see that tapping the left rear quarter panel of the pickup at this point would, indeed, spin the vehicle out. That thought must have also occurred to the pickup driver because he hit his brakes and cut left into the trooper's cruiser.

They were going fifty as they collided side-by-side. The pickup driver had misjudged the maneuver because of the weight of the load in the back. He had thought he would bounce off the trooper's car and continue down the road while the trooper would be knocked off. Instead, both the trooper's car and the heavy pickup shot off the left side of the road, both vehicles dropping down an embankment.

Matt felt hard pressure on his hands and feet as Lusk locked down all four tires. The trooper fought to hold his car straight in the road as it slid to a stop.

Suddenly, there was a loud crash, followed by an explosion. The pickup had hit a tree as it slid down the embankment. A hundred, one-gallon glass jugs shot straight up into the air from the bed of the pickup then crashed to earth. Steam and smoke exploded from the front end of the truck.

Trooper Giles was luckier. He flew on past the pickup, missing two pines and a large oak. That was when the trooper's luck ran out. His car caught a large rock under its front axle. A terrible sound of metal shearing was heard as the undercarriage and oil pan were ripped off. A tree took off the left side mirror, and the trooper's car slammed into a large hickory that caved in the front bumper and grill.

"What the hell was that?" Matt asked, hearing the sounds but not being able to see much over the bank or through the smoke and steam boiling up.

"That's how Giles stops a load of moonshine!" Lusk exclaimed as he jumped out of his car, unholstered his pistol, and ran toward the two-vehicle wreck. Matt hopped out and ran to catch up, not bothering to consider that he had no weapon. He heard but was not fully aware that more police cars were arriving as he followed Lusk down the steep bank and into the woods.

Just then, he lost his footing, slid on the seat of his pants, and stopped near the rear of the pickup. He looked around the woods and was amazed at the number of one-gallon jugs he saw. Most were smashed, some were whole, and broken glass was all over the place. The pungent odor of moonshine filled the air. Matt stood and checked the seat of his pants, which was muddy but intact.

He was relieved to see Giles open the passenger door of his wrecked car and climb out. Taking a look at his wrecked cruiser, Giles shook his head and kicked a small rock, sending it flying off into the woods. Gazing back up through the trees and the path he had just plowed, he pulled his pistol and ran over a carpet of broken glass toward the pickup.

Matt looked through the passenger window at the pickup's driver. There was no glass left in the side window. The driver was out cold with his blood all over the cracked windshield and dashboard.

The troopers who had been in the pursuit and local deputies from Green Mountain and Albemarle were arriving. One of the deputies from Albemarle County pulled his handcuffs from his belt and, grabbing Matt by the arm, cuffed his right wrist.

"No, no! He's with me," Trooper Lusk called over to the deputy. "Matt's one of us."

"Oh, sorry," said the deputy as he freed Matt.

Suddenly, a voice rang out. "Trooper Giles, I don't know whether to write you a reprimand for destroying a perfectly good blue and gray or give you an accommodation for capturing Maynard Donald Hathaway!"

Matt and everyone then turned to see who was talking. There stood Sergeant Barry Oliver beside the driver's window of the pickup with a big smile on his face and his hands on his hips. Everyone took a closer look at the bloody driver. It began to dawn on each officer that despite the blood, this driver matched the picture on all the wanted posters. The search for Doc Hathaway was over. If he wasn't dead, he was certainly in custody.

Matt raced forward and rendered first aid to Doc, using supplies from Lusk's car. When the Koehler Funeral Home Ambulance arrived, Doc remained unconscious but was breathing with a good pulse. They carefully loaded him onto a gurney and into the ambulance. After the ambulance left, the officers began pounding each other on the back.

Giles, who was in the woods examining what remained of his blue and gray, was not joining the celebration, however. He knew it had been a long time coming, Doc's capture, but the cost had him worried. His vehicle was a total loss.

Giles was required by the sergeant to ride with one of the other troopers to get checked out at the hospital in Waynesboro. He was then ordered to report to the command post to begin writing the damage report on his car.

Luckily, Sergeant Oliver would see he got sole credit for the arrest of Doc Hathaway, and that might help him avoid trouble with headquarters. At least, he hoped it would.

The state police dispatcher sent for Gunn's Garage to come tow Trooper Giles' car over to state police headquarters at Appomattox. A nice tow and a nice fee for John since it had to be pulled up the bank and loaded onto the garage flatbed trailer in pieces. The dispatcher next called the Chevrolet dealership wrecker to come get the pickup and tow it over to headquarters to be held as evidence, at least until the owner could be located.

While the wreck scene was being cleaned up, the pickup was traced, and its owner located. Odd circumstances then surfaced; when the owner was notified by the state police that his pickup had just been in an accident, he remained silent for a few moments. Then, he asked where his truck was located and if he could drive it. When he was told how it had been apprehended and what cargo was on board, he then blurted out it was stolen, then hung up when the dispatcher asked when it was stolen.

The troopers picked up all the unbroken glass liquor jugs and emptied them, except two full jugs they were keeping for evidence. The remaining empty, whole jugs were taken to the dump, broken, and buried. A small test batch of the moonshine was burned in a tin cup supplied by the sergeant, making a pretty blaze as it proved to be good, high-quality hooch—blue flame stuff.

Matt was driven back to the hotel by one of the troopers in time to tell Billy and Kent about the capture of Doc Hathaway. They started jumping up and down, shouting about how the restrictions on kids would now be lifted, jubilant over everything could go back to normal.

While the boys were celebrating, Matt called Billy's mom. He told her he would be sure to send the boys home in the hotel van. Then he told the hotel staff to expect a bunch of happy troopers for dinner, after which Maddie got busy making her famous spice cake for dessert.

Half of the news reporters mobbed Matt to find out his version; the rest tore out of the parking lot, headed for the scene of the capture. When they arrived at the scene, they were too late: the cars had been towed. Those staying to talk to Matt did not fare any better, as he would only say, "Trooper Giles was a hero. His driving skill and the fact he risked his life for the citizens of this state resulted in the capture of Doc Hathaway."

One of the reporters asked Matt as the others drifted away to file their stories, "The sniper is behind bars. You, sir, were there to see it. How do you feel about that?"

"Well, Doc Hathaway has been arrested; I'm sure of that much."

The reporter raced off to find a telephone to file his story.

CHAPTER 35

BILLY IS FURIOUS
Saturday, July 2, 1955

"**M**r. Cubley, what's the idea?" I asked him with the meanest frown I could muster. I looked over at Kent with a look that clearly said, "Okay, say something."

"Yeah, what's the idea?" Kent joined in, finally figured out what was going on.

"What's the idea about what?" Mr. Cubley asked me right back.

I hated it when adults did that. Miss Jones seldom did that. If she didn't understand a question, she would say so, not give you a question back.

"Why did you call our moms and tell them not to let us ride our bikes to work today? Gosh, we can finish here by two, easy. Then, Superman and I could have enjoyed the town for a little fun. We ain't in prison no more." I was on a roll and tried to pile it on.

"We aren't sure it's safe yet."

I picked up the morning paper from a stack that Polecat had just dropped on the loading dock. He was eating little pancakes that had a funny French name and could be stuffed with sausage, cheese, or fruit. I began at the very top of the paper and read all the big-print headlines to Mr. Cubley.

"'Special Edition, Saturday, July 2, 1955, the *Highland Gazette*. SNIPER CAPTURED IN HIGH-SPEED CHASE. Sniper remains hospitalized. Green Mountain County citizens return to normal. Governor recalls task force.' See? The paper says they caught the sniper, so what's not safe?"

"Billy, I'm not so sure they got the sniper. I hope so, but no guns were found in Hathaway's pickup, and he remains in a coma. No one has been able to get a statement from him. The troopers who came back to the hotel late last night told me they found nothing of interest after searching the Hathaway house except a big roll of cash. If he's been running bootleg, that would explain the cash." Matt was trying to convince Kent and me, but when he saw he wasn't winning the argument, he gave up with a shake of his head.

That's when Polecat sank our ship.

"Gentlemen, you would be well advised to note the charges that the state police have lodged against Mr. Hathaway. Violations of the Alcohol Beverage Control Act do not support the conclusions you two and the newspaper are making."

Polecat smiled and returned to devouring another little pancake. Strawberry jelly was oozing out of one end onto the center of his shirt. This stain blended in with two others.

"Mr. Smith, this is the newspaper you work for. I think you just told me not to believe it," I exclaimed with both my hands up like I was asking for a handout from heaven. Moses did it, freed all his people, and got manna. All I wanted was a little good news and freedom for Kent and me. We had plenty of manna from the hotel kitchen.

"Mr. Gunn, believe nothing you hear and only half of what you read, and then you will know twice too much for your own good," replied Polecat.

Polecat said this almost exactly the way my grandma did. She used that same phrase except for the reading part; instead, she said, "What you see." I had heard her say it more than once.

"Billy, I don't want to take your fun away, but an afternoon of fun in exchange for getting hurt isn't worth it. The police should be able to figure this out. They just need more time."

"But what about the paper?" I pleaded.

"The press often jumps to publish. Sometimes what's first written proves later to be false." Mr. Cubley walked back into the hotel with a departing, "Those troopers' cars are waiting."

I sighed. At least Kent and I were out of the house. There was even a good movie on at the Top Hat, and Kent and I had money to go. It sure would be nice if Laura were there. Being grounded, I missed seeing all my classmates. While all the other kids in town were free, Superman and I were still prisoners, and we were going to have to beg Mom to drive us to the movies.

After we wolfed down our breakfast, Polecat gave us a funny warning. He told us to avoid the town cops because it was being said they beat up a drunk the other night from this hotel. "Don't trust those Highland cops," he said, "and you stay clear of 'em."

Then, he asked us to take the papers into the lobby. When we put them down on the front desk, we heard Mr. Tolliver telling Mr. Cubley that when the troopers checked out this afternoon, the hotel would have fifteen empty rooms. He was worried. Troopers, reporters, and guests were checking out, but only a few guests were checking in. He said the hotel was going to have a bad week.

Kent and I hunted up Boo and asked her about it.

"Well, boys, it's true, but don't you worry about it—Mr. Tolliver can do that for all of us. All the reporters checked out this morning. Half the troopers are gone, and the rest are the ones who had night duty. Once they get some sleep, they'll check out by suppertime. All that said, I know three who need their cars washed, so you better get busy."

Boo started to leave, but then she turned back around. "Now, don't you let Mr. Tolliver worry you. A lot of the guests canceled because of the sniper, but he's been caught. The Fourth of July is here, and I can't remember a time when the hotel wasn't full up for the Fourth. So, think you boys can get those police cars spiffy enough for a Fourth of July parade?" Boo asked with her special smile.

"We'll get them sparkling clean," I assured her.

"Yeah, if we clean them like wow, maybe we can talk a trooper into letting us blow his siren and turn on his bubblegum light," Kent told her with a wistful gaze.

"What's a bubblegum light?" Boo asked.

"Uh, you know, the red-light on top a trooper's car. It's like a bubblegum machine. They got them down at the dime store. You know?" Kent was all flustered because Boo was smiling at him.

"Oh, so that's what you call them. You are so smart."

I thought Kent was going to lose it. We both took off running to wash the cars before we embarrassed ourselves to the max.

Kent saw me grinning at him and he punched me in the arm. I had to punch him back twice. That led to a bunch of punches until we both decided to stop. Our arms were getting sore, and it was time to get to work.

The morning passed quickly. We finished cleaning up the second state car by lunch. The troopers, who checked out late after sleeping-in, were happy to be going home. They promised us fifty cents a car as we finished up on number three. The troopers were paying us too much, but we weren't complaining.

Mr. Cubley came out to inspect our work. Just as he arrived, Sergeant Oliver drove up with Trooper Giles in the passenger seat.

Kent and I knew Trooper Giles had captured the sniper but smashed his car in the process. Wow, and Mr. Cubley had been riding with Trooper Lusk and told us all about it. I wished I had been there.

Mr. Cubley greeted the two officers with, "Good morning, Sergeant Oliver, Trooper Giles. How are things this morning?"

"Fighting the press, Matt, fighting the press," responded the sergeant. "They got this whole thing solved, closed, and put to bed. Our problem, though, is we don't know if we got everybody. Is Doc the only sniper? The man is in a coma, and the doctors don't even know when or if he'll wake up."

"How bad is he?"

"That tree he hit didn't move. It left him with a fractured skull. At least he didn't break his neck. We're keeping our fingers crossed; we need to talk to him."

"How about the family? They any help?" Matt inquired.

"His wife and two boys, especially his older boy, are the most ill-mannered, uncooperative bunch I've ever run into." Sergeant Oliver threw up his hands. "This arrest has us puzzled. We found no guns in the house when we searched last night. That was probably a good thing. His fourteen-year-old boy... Well, if there had been a gun in the house, we might have had to shoot him. That family will not give us the time of day. I don't think they would talk to us even if it would help their old man," Sergeant Oliver finished, then looked a little ashamed like he had said too much.

After a moment, he added, "Sorry, Matt, I guess I'm tired and frustrated. You know the governor is pulling almost every extra trooper out of here today. I yelled and yelled until my boss let me keep Trooper Lusk. I convinced the brass I needed his expertise to get the case ready for court. But, between you and me, we may not even have the sniper in custody yet. I asked the lieutenant to keep at least one man assigned to Big John McCulloch, but that request has to be approved in Richmond."

"Typical," Mr. Cubley grumbled.

"Billy, Kent, did you guys clean up these three patrol cars?" Giles asked us.

"Yes, sir, we sure did," I answered.

"I've never seen a better job. Even that old forty-six looks brand new. Franklin better be careful, or they'll not replace that old wreck. I think he's scheduled to turn it in at the end of the month," Trooper Giles said with a smirk.

"Careful trooper, I might just recycle that car and give it to you, since you seem to be so hard on them." Sergeant Oliver gave Trooper Giles a stern look.

Trooper Giles stared right back at his sergeant. Then, speaking in a gruff voice, responded, "Yeah, well, if Franklin had been with me yesterday, I would have let him take the lead. Thing is, the only way he would have caught that pickup is to chase it until it ran out of gas. Even then, Doc Hathaway probably would've been able to outrun him."

Sergeant Oliver looked like he was going to blow a gasket. He took his finger, pointed it at Giles, and blurted out, "I think you may be right." Then they both started laughing.

Boy, that was a relief. I never knew when troopers were kidding or when bullets were about to fly. They seemed to know the difference, but I had a hard time figuring out when to laugh and when to duck. This was way better than watching a cowboy movie, though. Well, some better. Even Mr. Cubley was laughing. Once we knew it was okay, Kent and I joined in.

"Matt, I came by to thank you for housing my men. It was nice and close, saved us time, and the rates were good. The Virginia State Police appreciate it. Now, I got to go on a diet because I gained a couple of pounds this week. Those box lunches were a great idea."

"Glad to help out. You and your men are always welcome, and that special dining room price will always be available. I guess your men will be pulling out today?"

"All but Lusk. Is it permissible if he stays on?" Sergeant Oliver asked.

"Yes, Sergeant, we can accommodate Trooper Lusk for as long as he's needed. Either as a paying guest or in the free room on the fifth floor. It's been nice working with him again. I can now say with confidence, he's one good driver—not as good as Trooper Giles, mind you, but good. I wouldn't want either of those two after me." Mr. Cubley and the troopers smiled.

After the troopers left, Kent and I finished the last car for the last trooper. We cleaned up the supplies, and Mr. Cubley asked us into his office for a surprise.

This meeting ended up being about our scrape at the Green Mountain Resort. The other resort met Mr. Dalton's terms, our parents agreed, and they had settled the case. Kent got two hundred dollars for getting knocked out and a black eye. I got a hundred dollars for my hand and for suffering something called "emotional turmoil," whatever that was. We could not believe it. Kent and I were rich.

Cubley's Coze Resort got two thousand dollars to settle the breach of the lease part out of court. The best thing was that Big John McCulloch blamed the bullies for costing him all this money. He was so mad, Lou, Dickie, and Carl were not allowed to set foot on his resort without a parent.

Kent and I were handed back our passes, and Mr. Cubley told us we could visit and enjoy any of the recreational activities, all we wanted. If we had any problems, we just had to drop in and inform their resort manager. That was the good news. He next told us the bad news: our parents were to get the money so that they could put it into our college savings account. Kent and I only got to keep two whole dollars!

Kent and I had just finished three cars at fifty cents each. The troopers had also tipped us fifty cents, so that meant a total of three dollars. Half went to the bank, leaving us each seventy-five cents for all that work. So much for being rich. Having the adults put our hard-earned money in a savings account for college was like having it stolen right out from under our noses. Bank robbers had a better chance of seeing our money than we did.

Mom had more bad news when she picked us up: we had to go back to court to finish up that bond hearing. Mr. Charles Parks had convinced the judge that, with the capture of the sniper, it was time to hold a bond hearing for his clients, and the judge had set the case right after the Fourth of July holiday.

Kent and I would be going back to court. We fussed, we complained, but it did no good. We thought the best we could hope for was getting to see a jailbreak or a fight in the courtroom.

Mom drove us home to our garage. She took both envelopes containing our college money into the house, letting us keep the two dollars and seventy-five cents to go to the movie. She also reminded us that she or Kent's mom would drive us and pick us up, which we decided was better than nothing. The movies at the Top Hat Theater were *20,000 Leagues Under the Sea* and *Three Ring Circus* with Dean Martin and Jerry Lewis. Mom ended up being the one who dropped us off, and we were surprised when we only saw four members of our class at the show. Neither Laura nor Judy had made it.

Mom was a little late picking us up. While we were killing time, we spotted Lou and Carl. Dickie was not with them, but we were trapped, since the theater workers had locked the doors to clean up after the matinee. We backed up against the wall to get ready.

"Well, hello, stupid man. Look, it's BB, big butt Gunn. I'll clue you in: you're dead. You are so dead. We're gonna beat you to a pulp till your own mommies won't be able to recognize you." Lou McCulloch was so mad he was spitting as he talked. I noticed he stayed just outside of arm's reach, but he was closer than I would have liked. I also noticed a bump on his nose.

"You want another broken nose? Come on! I'll push it through your sorry face and out the back of your head. People won't know if you're coming or going," I said, hoping Mom would hurry up.

Lou was ready to kill me. That's when I heard a horn blow just up the street. It sounded familiar. Mom pulled up, right in front of the theater. She blew the horn again. Lou jumped, took a quick look, and the two bullies walked off like they didn't even know us.

"Wow, that was close," Kent said, breathing a sigh of relief as he got into the back seat.

"I would have put his nose through his face," I said all brave like, but I got quickly into the front seat, slamming the car door harder than normal and locking it.

"I guess I got here just in time," Mom said, frowning. "I'm going to talk to your father about this. Lou and those Lockhart boys better stay away from you two, or your father will settle their hash."

Mom was too mad for me to say anything, but I hoped my parents left things alone. Lou had stayed his distance. Maybe Kent and I had shown them that we weren't the babies they had thought we were. The threat still bothered me, though. Kent and I had better stick together. If those three caught either of us alone, things might not turn out so good.

CHAPTER 36

BILLY'S MORNING OF THE FOURTH
Monday, July 4, 1955

I drifted slowly awake with the feeling something was wrong. I opened one eye. Scotty was standing no more than six inches from my bed with his pointer finger up his nose. I opened both eyes and watched him working on getting a booger out while his other hand was scratching his butt. When he saw I was awake, he pulled his finger out of his nose and looked at the tip of his finger. He decided to forget the nose booger and wiped it on his shirt.

"Momma's gonna take us to the park to see fire workers," Scotty said, all excited.

"Scotty, it's fireworks, not fire workers."

"Nuh-uh. It's fire workers. Mommy said so. I'm gonna tell!" Scotty stuck out his tongue, and off he went to tattle on me. His favorite thing to do.

"What a shame the circus wasn't in town. I bet I could trade Scotty for a lion cub or clown suit." I said this out loud and then crossed my fingers and spit twice, 'cause I really didn't mean it. Well, not all of it. Not trade him away for good—just for a month or two.

Getting up was easy on a holiday, and Scotty was right. We were all going to the park that afternoon with fireworks provided by the plant this evening. Mom and Kent's mom were packing picnic baskets for the families to share, and Mom was bringing her deviled eggs. They were the best. I was hoping to see Laura and Judy today.

I hurried down to breakfast and remembered to tell Mom how good it smelled. That didn't stop her from giving me the bad news.

"Billy, you need a haircut. Right after breakfast, you and Scotty are getting one. The whole town will turn out, now that the troubles are over. Right after lunch, you both are going to get a good bath, too. I don't want to see either one of you getting dirty after I get you dressed for the picnic. You hear?" Mom announced in her, "I mean business" voice.

"Yes, Ma'am," I said, dreading the haircut. I hated how the hair tickled when it fell inside my collar. The barber used a cape to keep the hair off, but Mom claimed that was just silly. She would put a chair out in the drive and cut away without any regard for where loose hair fell.

I noticed in my mirror this morning that I needed a haircut. I wondered if I could talk Mom into a butch cut so I could use Hair Care Butch Wax to make it behave or even stand up.

"I want fire workers," Scotty yelled, waving around a piece of toast with jelly on it. He made a circle around his head like he was a cowboy with a lasso. There was a good chance that Mom would be cutting Scotty's hair with jelly in it. Grandma was trying to distract him but was not having much luck. He was going to be wild.

Mom served us a special breakfast. She had fixed cheese omelets, grits, toast, and country ham. This was one of Dad's favorites, and he wasted no time digging in. It was quiet except for Scotty until Dad pushed back his empty plate and stretched. The rest of us were still finishing our meals.

"Laura Jane, you remember that pickup truck? The one that the man from Waynesboro brought me to soup up?" Dad asked Mom.

"The one I worried about because I thought you were going to get arrested. I'll never forget it. Everyone knows that guy runs liquor," Mom ended and gave Dad a cross look.

I remembered the argument that she and Dad had over that particular job. It was something.

"Laura Jane, I told you then, and I'll tell you now: I fix cars! That's all I do. I don't ask, and they don't tell me what they're going to do with them after I fix them. Now, I'm trying to tell you something if you'll let me." Dad was starting to get irritated.

"Laura Jane is exactly right. You keep fooling around with these bootleggers, and you'll end up in prison with the rest of them: Mark my words, John Gunn. Off you'll go to prison, leaving my poor daughter and this family destitute and on the poor house dole," Grandma announced with finality.

"Oh, for gosh sakes—a man can't tell one simple, damn story without getting lambasted. Just forget it. I'm going out to the garage."

Dad pushed back his chair so hard it fell over backward with a clatter. He left it there, stomped out the back door, and slammed the screen door so hard it bounced back open about halfway.

"Laura Jane, why you married that man, I'll never know. His temper will be the death of us all."

Grandma was fussy. I could tell she was itching for a fight. Holidays and just before vacations, Grandma always picked a fight with Mom or Dad or both. Today was going to be no exception. I tried to hurry up and finish my breakfast. I knew what was coming next.

"Mother, for goodness sakes. You always have to jump in whenever John and I are talking. You're the one who gets him mad. For once, can't you just be quiet and let us talk?" Mom picked up her plate and scraped the rest of her uneaten breakfast into the trash. I could recite what Grandma was about to say.

"Stingers and bouquets, that's all I get. Here I try my best to get along with you and that ill-tempered husband of yours, and what do I get? I get stingers and bouquets. I guess you'll be happy when I'm dead and gone. That's what you want, to put your poor old mother in her grave." Grandma got up and stormed into the living room.

Scotty tuned up to cry, and Mom picked him up to walk him around and try to get him to stop. He would have none of it.

Now Grandma was mad, Mom was mad, Dad was mad, and Scotty was howling. Another happy holiday. I finished what was left on my plate, then gathered up all the dishes, washed and dried them. I quietly slipped out of the kitchen and eased the screen door shut as Mom continued to try to get Scotty under control.

Dad was in the garage, just looking at the motor under the open hood of one of the cars he was working on. He was not doing anything, just looking.

"So, Dad, what about that pickup you fixed?" I asked, trying to see if he would get over being mad and talk to me. I hated the fighting. Sometimes you just had to leave things alone, but sometimes if you talked to Mom or Dad after a fight, they weren't as mad as you might think.

"What?" Dad turned his head and stared at me. There goes the question to answer a question, again.

"The pickup, what were you going to tell us?" I asked my question again and stood beside my dad. Both of us were now staring at the motor.

"Oh, that. I souped up that pickup to run faster than any pickup I ever worked on. Do you remember that special carburetor I ordered from Detroit? The one that took a month for me to get?" Dad asked, and he didn't look so mad anymore.

"I 'member."

"Well, the truck that Doc Hathaway was driving was that very truck. That's what I was going to tell your mom. Hell, I knew it was a bootlegger's truck, but I did nothing wrong. I heard from some of the deputies about how they chased that truck all over creation but could never catch it. It was fast, even with a load of liquor on board. I bet the weight in the back made it track better through the curves. I even got a second job off that pickup: Trooper Giles asked me to fix up his car to run faster than the pickup. I promised him I would, and I did. I was going to tell Mom how I made that trooper's car so fast that it did the job," Dad finished with pride in his voice.

"You mean Trooper Giles knew you souped up that truck for the Waynesboro bootlegger?" I asked. "I knew you fixed it, but I never heard you say the police knew you were the one. Why didn't they arrest you?" I was starting to get nervous.

"There was nothing to arrest me for. If Mom and Grandma had been able to be quiet for thirty-seconds, I would have explained it. But no, your Mom takes after her mother sometimes. I get so mad I could... well... I just get angry." Dad was starting to get louder and angrier.

"Well, why was it okay for you to fix his truck?" I asked, trying to get him back on our conversation and off of the fight.

"Ford builds trucks and sells them, right?" Dad said to me.

"Well, sure, everyone knows that," I answered.

"If I buy one of their trucks and haul liquor or stolen property in it, do the police go over to the Ford dealership and arrest all
of the salesmen and the owner of the dealership for selling it to me?"

"No, that would be stupid. So, if they can't arrest you just
for fixing a truck, why did Mom get all upset?" I asked, hoping for
an answer.

"Women, son. Just because you marry one doesn't mean you
ever understand them. Now, I got two living under my roof, which
makes it four times as bad." Dad shook his head, walked over to his
toolbox, picked up a wrench, and got his work light off the shelf.

I knew his math was off but didn't want to tell Dad about his
two's and four's tables. It was not worth the risk.

"How'd you know that guy was hauling moonshine on his
pickup?"

"I didn't. I mean, I suspected it but didn't know for sure, and
I wasn't about to ask. Several months after the job, the deputies and
troopers started telling me about how this sly old bootlegger was
picking up liquor from the Woody family down in Franklin County
and running it up to Waynesboro, Staunton, and Charlottesville to
the local nip joints. They knew about it but couldn't catch him. He
never ran the same route twice in a row, and they never knew when
he was going to make a run."

Dad gave a shrug, held his wrench down by his side, and
continued.

"Trooper Giles tried to catch him after I souped up his blue
and gray, but every time Giles would place a stakeout for an inter-
cept, that pickup would take a different route. It was starting to look
like someone was tipping him off. Everyone was surprised when
this time, Maynard Donald Hathaway turned up as the driver. All
the troopers on the chase thought it was going to be the Waynesboro
bootlegger. The police think the bootlegger who owned the pickup
believed the police were getting too close for comfort. Being pretty
sharp, he hired Doc Hathaway to drive for him since Doc was desperate for money for his family. The bootlegger knew if the police
caught a load, Doc would take the fall. That's exactly what happened, and now, the owner of the truck is off the hook. He's claiming
the truck was stolen."

"But Dad, when Mr. Hathaway wakes up from his coma, won't he tell the police he was just the driver?"

"No, the driver's in trouble no matter what. To tell on his boss would violate the code. Might even get him or his family killed. Bootlegging can be a rough business. I might fix up a vehicle or two if I don't know for sure what's going on, but I stay away from those people otherwise. I sure as hell stay way, far away from the business end of what they do. I'll work on anybody's car, but they all know I won't cross the line." Dad began taking off a water pump on the car he had been staring at when I arrived.

"So, Mom's afraid you might get hurt?" I asked.

"What? Hurtt?—Well, when you put it that way, maybe I shouldn't have gotten so angry. Your Mom doesn't understand business. The police do, and the bootleggers do, so, yeah, I guess she was afraid I might get in too close. I know how to keep my distance."

Just as I turned to go outside, Trooper Quinn drove into our lot with Trooper Giles riding shotgun. They both got out and walked into the garage where Dad was working.

"John, how goes it?" Quinn asked Dad.

"Doing fine, Mike. Hello, Bobby." Dad put down his tools.

"John, I need a favor," Giles said.

"Bobby, what can I do for you?" Dad leaned up against the fender of the car.

"Well, Richmond isn't going to send me one of the new cars. The one I thought I was in line to get is going to Sergeant Oliver instead. I think the sergeant is going to assign me the car he's driving now."

"Oh, I think I know what you're going to ask." Dad began to grin.

"Yeah, I need some work done on it to get her up to speed."

"When can I start?" Dad leaned forward away from the fender and stood without leaning against the car.

"I'm not sure. They'll have to process my report on the wreck. Then, if I don't get a reprimand or suspension, things should finish out in a week or two."

"You don't really think they would send down a reprimand, do you? A suspension? Are they idiots?"

"I hope not. It was my fault for not seeing that suicide move coming, though. I was too darn focused on tapping the sweet spot on his quarter panel. We've been after that pickup for so long that I got focused on putting him in the ditch and let him get the jump on me." Trooper Giles was shaking his head, embarrassed.

Quinn jumped into the conversation, angry. "Bobby, not one of us would have expected the suicide. That guy must have been crazy, and you see where it got him. It was lucky that both of you weren't killed. They don't call it the suicide maneuver for nothing. You don't have a fifty-fifty chance of pulling it off without wrecking both cars. Richmond knows that."

"Yeah, Mike, but Richmond's not going to reward one of us for wrecking a car. I know a quarter panel spin-out is risky, but I've done it so many times with both cars staying on the highway and no damage."

"This truck we were after was a major problem; turns out he might be the sniper," stated Trooper Quinn.

"Richmond isn't sure how to react, not even for a major problem. A bootlegger or sniper, both were major embarrassments to the department. But the man is in a coma...you know how they think." Trooper Giles spoke in an even tone, just like he was discussing the weather.

Dad broke in because things were getting awkward. "Well, Bobby, drop it off when you can, and I'll fix her up. Same modifications as last time? More importantly, what's your spending limit?"

My dad always got right down to business when it came to fixing a car. Finding out how much someone could spend on a repair gave him a good idea on how much he could work on it.

"Just like last time, except this time, the suspension needs more beefing up in back. We got some new heavy equipment we have to carry, and I don't want her fishtailing on me in a curve or bottoming out in the bumps. I plan on another hundred over what I paid you the last time. Will that cover it?"

"It should be plenty; if not, I'll let you know. Besides, your credit is good here," Dad said quietly. Mom fussed when he did work on credit.

"John, I gotta say, though, the work you did on that hooch wagon was something."

"I always do my best for my customers, whoever they might be. I just got your car to run faster because you weren't carrying a load of whiskey. You weren't, were you?" Dad laughed, so I knew he was joking.

"No, John, if Richmond thought I was running hooch, my blue and gray would turn quickly into a ball and chain." Giles laughed, too.

"John, when you get Bobby back on the road, I might let you take a look at my blue and gray, too. I don't have the same pull that he does with the sarge, but a little change here and there might help me keep up with certain other troopers in a chase. I'm tired of not leading the pack." Quinn gave Giles a fake scowl.

"Bring 'em by and line 'em up. I'll do what I can, but I can't promise the mechanics down at Appomattox won't notice it. You two have to be sure they don't report my little adjustments to Richmond. I don't want a visit from your lieutenant."

This was interesting, but Mom called me to come get my haircut, and, when I got back to the garage, the troopers were gone. I helped Dad until it was time to eat lunch and get my bath. Since I had hair down my shirt, taking a bath was not going to be such an awful thing. Our outing to the park would make up for it, or so I thought.

CHAPTER 37

BILLY AND THE FOURTH OF JULY CELEBRATION
Monday, July 4, 1955

Scotty was wearing new clothes and his face, knees, and hands were scrubbed clean. I had on a brand-new pair of blue jeans so stiff and so blue that they didn't look real. I was wearing them without complaint because I didn't want to hurt Mom's feelings since she bought them just for the Fourth. I preferred my old ones because when I sat down, the new ones felt like cardboard and itched.

Both Mom and Dad took me aside that morning for a family conference about the three bullies. I told them I could handle them, but Dad said three against one wasn't a fair fight. It was time for him to step in. He was going to have a little "heart-to-heart" with Little John and Richard Lockhart. At least he didn't say I wasn't as big as the bullies.

Dad warned me to stick with Kent and stay away from them that afternoon until he could talk to their fathers. Mom repeated his warning twice.

Adults always tell kids the obvious several times over. I just said, "Yes, sir. Yes, ma'am. I'll be careful. Can we go now?"

Meanwhile, Grandma had been in her room, refusing to come out. I heard her and Mom arguing. Finally, Mom came downstairs with Grandma in tow. At first, I thought Mom had won, but Grandma got in the last word.

"Laura Jane, I'll go, but I'm not going to have a good time. You have ruined my Fourth. You'll be sorry when I'm in my final resting place."

Grandma had been holding Scotty and playing with him like she didn't have a care in the world while she was piling it on. Mom had resorted to adding guilt.

"Mother, Scotty will be heartbroken if you don't go. There's no reason we all can't go and have a good time. You do this every time there's a holiday. You're not happy until you start a big fight."

Grandma walked out to the car with Scotty in silence, putting him in the back seat and climbing in beside him.

"John, it's time to go, and Mother can just sit in the park and sulk," Mom grumbled.

"I know. Let's not spoil it for Scotty. This will be the first Fourth of July where he'll know what's going on." Dad was trying to console Mom as he picked up our heavy picnic basket and fitted it into the trunk of our car. Life that summer would have been so much better if the adults hadn't fought so much.

Mom and I followed after she locked the kitchen door. We never locked the door before, even when we went on vacation. Otherwise, if the door was locked, Mrs. Clark couldn't come in and water the plants or check on the house while we were away.

When we got to the park, it looked like the whole town had turned out. It didn't take me long to find Kent. He and a bunch of kids had started a softball game at the ball field near the lake. I ran over and got picked for the same team as him. Roger Younger, our team captain, was nice, despite his dad being a mean cop.

Roger called out, "Superman, you're shortstop... BB, take second."

Judy Peterson was on our team as an outfielder, which made Kent happy. Laura got picked last for the other side. She had a fast swing, but she always missed the pitch, even slow ones. The other team had her as a fourth outfielder. We were loose with the rules back then; it was just us kids playing.

We had noticed two boys—strangers—standing off to the side, watching us. Roger asked them to join our game, but they refused. I was pretty sure they were brothers because they looked alike.

Lou McCulloch was standing near the men who were getting the fireworks ready. Roger didn't call out to him, and he hadn't offered to play, which was a relief, and I lost track of time during the game. The Lockharts weren't even at the park, at least not yet.

Scoring was usually high because the pitchers were pitching slow balls under-handed. Each side scoring five or six runs per inning wasn't unusual. Laura smiled at me a couple of times when the inning changed. She surprised everyone. She got a hit but was thrown out at first base. I yelled, "Way to go; nice hit!" and got punched by two of my teammates.

We were hot and thirsty by the end of the sixth inning and decided to end the game. Some kids had already quit to get a pop or go for a swim. Laura had left at the end of the fifth inning. Kent asked Judy to go with him to get a soda, and I walked with them to the concession stand. After we bought our pop, I walked back to the ball field with my Dr. Pepper to let Superman have some time alone with her.

I was also hoping to find Laura, but I didn't see her, so I sat down on the bleachers in the shade to enjoy my cold drink. That's when I felt something hit me in the back of my head.

"Ow!" I yelled, although it didn't hurt that much. I turned to see which of my friends was pulling a prank on me and found Lou McCulloch standing behind me under the bleachers.

"Well, if it isn't BB, big butt!" he mocked. I noticed he was holding a bat in his left hand. As I watched, he switched the bat to his right.

"Lou, leave me alone."

"Oh, the baby wants to be left alone. Well, isn't that too bad. I told you I was going to get you. Your time's up. You're dead meat, Gunn."

He spat on the ground and started toward me around the end of the bleachers. He began swinging the bat hard with both hands.

I left my drink sitting on the bleachers, jumped down, and started backing up toward the soft drink tent. I was looking for my friends, but I didn't see anyone nearby. Lou and I were the only ones on the ball field.

"Come on, BB, I got something for you." Lou took a full swing with the bat like a player does before advancing to the plate.

"Put the bat down, and I'll fight you. Do you want another busted nose? It'll only be an improvement."

I was hoping I could, at least, get him to drop the bat. He was bigger than me by twenty pounds as it was. That bat was scary.

324

"I'll put this bat down your throat and pull it out your ass." He took another swing. This one came close, and I felt the whoosh of air as the bat passed a couple of inches from my face.

I saw my chance and tried to rush him to get in close, so he wouldn't have room to swing the bat, but he was quicker and stronger and pushed me back with his left hand. My fist just missed his face.

Oh, no! I goofed! I thought with a sick feeling.

The bat was in his right hand, and he now had just enough distance to swing it one-handed. It caught me just above my left ear. *Crack!* I saw stars.

My vision got narrow. It was like I was looking through a pipe. I took a step back, trying not to stumble, but I think the ground was moving under me. I put my dukes up to protect my head when Lou just disappeared.

Darkness closed in on me. The pipe I thought I was looking through got smaller and smaller. I couldn't stand anymore. The ground tilted, and I sat down hard on my rear end.

I shook my head and took a deep breath. My vision cleared a little. It was fuzzy, but Lou was on the ground a few feet away. Those two boys, the strangers, were on Lou. The bigger one was punching him in the head with his fists. The smaller one was jumping up and down, yelling, "Hit him, hit him!"

Suddenly, the smaller one stopped jumping. He began kicking Lou in the nuts. I heard all the air go out of Lou, then he took a breath and screamed.

The bat was about five feet away, where it must have landed when the two brothers tackled him.

I felt blood running down over my left ear and jaw. I pulled out my handkerchief and shook it with one hand to unfold it, placing it over the wound, or, at least, where I thought it was.

My head started to hurt. Blood kept running into my left eye. I tried to wipe it off, but more ran into my eye as soon as I moved the handkerchief.

With my one good eye, I saw Lou balled up on the ground, moaning. The two brothers left him and came over to see how I was doing.

"Here," the older one said, taking my handkerchief. He put gentle pressure on the wound to stop the bleeding.

"Let's kill him," the smaller one said.

"No, we got him good enough. We need to get out of here before his father shows up. He might take it out on Dad."

"Who are you?" I asked. I was starting to make sense of things even though my headache was getting worse.

"My name's Skip. This is my little brother Barry."

"Thanks, but why did you help me? I don't know you, do I? Where do you go to school?" I asked my questions so fast they didn't have a chance to answer.

"No, you don't know us. We don't live here. Let's just leave it at that. So long." The brothers walked off toward town.

Several people had noticed me bleeding, and Lou on the ground all balled up. I saw a couple of adults running my way. The brothers cut left through some trees that grew beside Smith River, and, just like that, they were gone.

That's when Kent and Judy came running up.

"BB, what happened?" Kent asked, panicking.

"Gosh, you're bleeding. Are you okay?" Judy asked.

Kent began asking more questions, but my head hurt. I didn't want Judy to think I was a weakling, so I gave him short answers.

"Lou hit me with a bat."

"Did you beat up Lou?" asked Kent.

"No. A couple of kids did." I attempted to explain, but every time I talked, it made my head hurt.

A crowd had gathered around Lou, who was still on the ground moaning. Kent and Judy helped me get up. With one on each side, they walked me back to where my family was sitting on a big blanket. When Mom saw me, she jumped up and ran over.

"Billy, what happened?"

"Mrs. Gunn, Lou McCulloch hit him in the head with a ball bat," Kent blurted out.

"That's true, Mrs. Gunn; we found him bleeding. We thought we better bring him over here to get him fixed up." Judy was holding me by the shoulder.

My mom lifted the handkerchief for a look. "John, look what they've done. Billy, sit down. Let me get you cleaned up. Your shirt is just ruined."

Mom had taken charge. There was no use for me to try to do anything but sit down and let her go to work.

I knew my shirt was ruined, but my new blue jeans were blue so that they wouldn't show a gallon of blood. Grandma was fussing about how this town was going to the dogs. Scotty was screaming because he was afraid of blood. Dad looked angry. Things were going badly when they got worse.

We heard a siren. Little John McCulloch pulled into the parking lot of the park and he drove slowly right into the crowd until he had to stop because the people weren't able to get out of his way fast enough. He parked on the grass more than three car lengths into the park, yelling at a lady to move so he could open his door and get out of his patrol car. It was a miracle that he had not run over anyone.

I could see the top of his head as he ran through the crowd to the location where Lou had been rolling around on the ground in the infield. I figured the way today was going; I would join Doc and the Beamis brothers in jail before sundown.

Dad started asking me questions as Mom doctored me. I told them I felt fine, which was a lie. Neither bought it.

They led me into a park bathroom. I wasn't sure if it was the men's or women's until I saw a man clear out when he saw Mom, but they didn't seem to care. Mom cleaned me up while Dad put a bandage on my head that he had made from Mom's clean table cloth. I thought Mom would get mad, but she didn't say a thing. I looked like some foreign king wearing a turban.

Things began to calm down after the Koehler ambulance arrived. Several men carried Lou over to it on a stretcher, and the ambulance left with Lou's dad following in his patrol car. Both vehicles had on their lights and sirens. What a noise they made. My head was killing me.

It was then that Chief Smith walked over and spoke to my dad.

"John, I'm going to need to get some information from your boy. Lou's hurt bad," Chief Smith said.

"I want Lou McCulloch arrested for hitting my boy with a ball bat. He started it. Now, when are you going to do something?" Mom jumped in, furious.

"Is that right son, did Lou hit you with a ball bat?" Chief Smith asked while staring at my head, all wrapped up and blood all down my shirt.

"Yes, sir."

"Is that why you beat him up?" The chief said it like it had to be a fact.

"I never touched him."

"Well, if you didn't, then who did?"

"I don't know. Two strange guys rescued me. Don't think they're townies. If not for them, Lou might'a killed me." I then gave a little moan for effect.

Right then, Kent came up with Roger Younger, the town officer's son.

"Chief, BB is right," Roger spoke right up. "First, Lou hit BB with a ball bat. Then, these two kids came out of nowhere and beat the snot out of Lou. BB was staggering around and fell down after he got hit. He never hit Lou once."

I was sure glad that Roger was taking up for me. That's when Dad got right up in the chief's face.

"Chief, this isn't the first time Lou McCulloch has attacked my son. I'm sure you know about the incident over at the Green Mountain Resort. That was the first time. The second time was when my wife picked Kent and Billy up at the movies. Lou and one of those two Lockhart boys were right on top of the boys, threatening them. Now Lou hits Billy with a ball bat. I want it stopped, and if you won't do it, I will!"

The chief got red in the face and I saw his hand move toward his gun. Dad got even closer.

"Now, John, don't you go telling me how to do my job. Once I'm satisfied that I have all the facts, then I'll do what I have to do. You just better hope that Lou doesn't press charges against your boy. I would be worried more about that if I were you."

I thought Dad was going to hit the chief. Mom put a hand on his arm and he looked at her for an instant.

"I see how it's going to be. Chief, I suggest you get the hell away from me before I do something we both might regret." Dad was staring at the chief in the eyes and not moving.

"Roger, you come along with me. You need to go talk to your dad," Chief Smith said as he walked off with Roger, holding his left arm like he was under arrest.

"John, what are we going to do? That man is not going to do a thing," Mom said, and it looked like she was ready to cry.

"Laura Jane, I'll handle this. I'll handle this the Army way," Dad whispered the last part with his voice cold, scary cold. He stood a moment, then turned to me and asked me if I wanted to go home.

I answered, "Heck, no, but a Dr. Pepper for my headache would sure help. It makes you feel better at ten, two, and four. You know it's almost four."

Neither of my parents laughed. I thought Kent was going to lose it. Judy giggled. Mom sent Dad to get three Dr. Peppers, one each for Kent, Judy, and me. He went without any argument.

The rest of the afternoon, my classmates checked on me. Laura sat with me for half an hour. We talked about getting cooped up during the time of the sniper and how great it was that things were back to normal. She wanted to know about me getting shot at and even called me brave. I left out telling her how scared I was and continued to be.

We also talked about Mr. Cubley and the high-speed chase. I bragged about how my Dad souped-up Trooper Giles' blue and gray so he could capture Mr. Hathaway. Despite my headache, it was a glorious afternoon. Grandma never said one fussy word after Chief Smith left.

Supper was fun because Mom insisted I take an extra piece of fried chicken as if that would cure a bop on the head. Kent kept up with the amount of chicken I ate. Grandma stayed on her best behavior.

The sun was setting when word came around that Lou was back home. The medical report was nothing serious. He was in bed with a big ice pack on his southern region and a smaller one on his face. I hoped he was in agony.

A man came by who acted all concerned about poor Lou. He

was telling Dad about Lou's injuries and was trying to get Dad to admit to something that he could take to Lou's dad or grandfather to get in good with them. Dad was smarter than that and just stared at the ground until he got the message and walked off.

After it got dark, there were fireworks over the lake. It was like watching double fireworks because they reflected in the water. Scotty kept saying, "Look at the pretty fire workers!" No amount of saying it right changed how he said it, so, finally, we all just gave up.

As we were leaving, a couple of honest men, who were Dad's former customers, came up to say that they had seen Lou hit me, and, if we had any trouble, to let them know since they had heard the chief trying to find someone who would say that I hit Lou first.

My family knew how this town worked. The chief would find someone who suddenly remembered seeing me hit Lou. Very likely, a factory worker would step forward with a version about how poor Lou was minding his own business and that Gunn boy attacked him from behind for no reason. The following week he would have a nickel raise.

That night, though, all the chief got was the truth. He left disappointed.

CHAPTER 38

BILLY GOES BACK TO COURT
Tuesday, July 5, 1955

The day of the bond hearing came much too soon after my Fourth of July scrape with Lou McCulloch. When I got up, there was blood on my pillow and a big lump on my head and my headache was hammering to get out .

Dad came upstairs to clean the wound and wrap my head with a four-inch compress and a roller bandage. Now I looked like Henry Fleming from the *Red Badge of Courage*. Before I knew it, I was back in court wearing my Sunday clothes. Mom kept checking to be sure I wasn't getting blood on my white shirt. Both Mom and Dad came with me this time.

When we picked up Kent, his mom left a note on her kitchen table, asking us to keep an eye on him. We were not to let him wander off. She knew Lou McCulloch was laid up, but the Lockhart brothers were loose.

We entered the courtroom, but today there was only one reporter present, a lady from the *Highland Gazette*. Sergeant Oliver and Trooper Giles were down front, near the judge's bench, talking with Sheriff Lawrence. Chief Smith was in the front right corner, huddled up with Sergeant McCulloch and Officer Frank Younger. The bailiff stood in front of the judge's bench, waiting for the judge.

"All rise. Oyez, Oyez, Oyez. Silence is hereby commanded in the County Court of Green Mountain County. The Honorable Kenneth W. Carlton presiding. Be seated and remain silent." Sheriff Lawrence had just called the court to order and not the bailiff. I wondered what that was about. Mr. Albert Winston Brown entered from the side with Mr. Charles Parks, the Beamis' attorney. Both of the lawyers stood to the side of the judge's bench, but I didn't see the two Beamis brothers nor the farmhand.

The door to the jail opened and in walked a man wearing handcuffs and leg irons with a chain around his waist that connected to the cuffs and the leg irons. He had a big bandage on his head—a lot bigger than mine—and was either drunk or dizzy because he was all wobbly. Two deputies escorted him, one on each side.

There was a noise in the back of the courtroom as some people came in late. I turned and saw a woman followed by the two boys from the park who attacked Lou McCulloch. Now I was curious.

"Your Honor. The first matter on the docket this morning is the arraignment of Maynard Donald Hathaway on various charges. The Commonwealth requests no bond on this criminal." Mr. Albert Winston Brown, I realized, was putting Doc Hathaway ahead of the Beamis brothers.

"Are you Maynard Donald Hathaway?" Judge Carlton asked the prisoner.

"Yes, your Honor. I'm not guilty," Doc Hathaway answered the judge.

"Mr. Hathaway, today is your arraignment. I read the charges to you and only determine if the bond is correct. Your case will not be tried today. There is no need for a plea at this time." The judge read the charges to himself slowly. He checked the pages of the warrant like he was looking for more pages.

"I see the charges are serious, but they are not the ones I expected. Do you understand what charges I have here, Mr. Commonwealth?" Judge Carlton looked up at the prosecutor. He waited for Mr. Albert Winston Brown to say something.

"Your Honor, the charges are preliminary at this time. These are the charges the Virginia State Police filed. We are not sure what additional charges my office will file." Mr. Albert Winston Brown spoke in a loud voice and looked at the state troopers seated behind him.

"In that case, Mr. Hathaway, here are your charges. A misdemeanor charge of reckless driving, a felony charge of attempted murder of State Trooper Robert Giles, a misdemeanor charge of failing to stop for a police officer, and a felony charge of theft of a motor vehicle. Do you understand the charges I have just read to you?"

"I understand. I'm not guilty," Doc Hathaway insisted.

"Based on the charges, I will set your trial on the misdemeanors and your preliminary hearings on the felonies in thirty days. I agree with the no bond provision as set by the justice of the peace. Now, Mr. Hathaway, I urge you to hire legal counsel. Sheriff, you may take charge of the prisoner."

Judge Carlton handed the stack of warrants to the bailiff when I heard a muffled cry from the back of the courtroom. The woman started crying, and the two boys helped her out through the main door.

"All rise. There will be a five-minute recess for a prisoner exchange to take place," Sheriff Lawrence called out as the judge exited the courtroom.

When Trooper Giles stood up to stretch, I motioned for him to come over.

"Billy, what happened to you?" Trooper Giles asked with some concern.

"Lou McCulloch attacked him yesterday in the park with a ball bat," Mom answered before I could say anything.

"Oh my! I heard about those three jumping you and Kent over at the Green Mountain Resort last week, but this is news to me. Looks like you boys have some serious enemies," Trooper Giles commented with Sergeant Oliver looking on.

"Uh, Trooper Giles, who was that in the back of the courtroom? You know, the lady and the two boys?" I asked, pointing to where they had been sitting.

"That was Doc Hathaway's wife and their two sons, Skip and Barry. Why?"

"Oh, I was just wondering. No real reason. Are we going to have the bond hearing today?" I said, trying to change the subject.

"It should start in—"

"All rise, this court's back in session. All of you be seated. Silence is commanded. Find a seat." Sheriff Lawrence was loud and sounded grumpy, probably from having a busy morning.

The heavy door to the jail opened with a creak, and Jacob and Joash Beamis walked in with a third younger man. All of them were in handcuffs, leg irons, and waist chains. The door opened in the back of the courtroom, and I turned to see Sarah Beamis, Jacob's wife, and Lucinda Beamis, the wife of Joash, walking in together. They came down front and sat in the audience part of the courtroom but near their husbands. Mr. Parks sat on a bench, just inside the bar.

The troopers told me in a court that only certain people could go inside that fence-like thing called the bar unless the judge said so. I knew better than to test that rule.

The judge began by asking each side if they were ready. The Commonwealth's Attorney stood. "Your Honor, the Commonwealth is not ready. Certain circumstances require us to have additional time to prepare."

This hearing was off and running with a heated argument between the two lawyers on who was ready, who was not, and what was going to happen or not happen. The judge finally said his mind was made up: he was going to hear the bond hearing this morning, and Mr. Parks could proceed.

For just a moment, I thought Mr. Albert Winston Brown was going to interrupt, but he must have thought better of it. Instead, he sat down and took some papers out of his briefcase.

Things happened quickly after that. Mr. Parks asked for all the witnesses to be sworn.

Mr. Albert Winston Brown called Chief Smith, Sergeant McCulloch, and Officer Frank Younger. He did not name any troopers.

Mr. Parks called Kent and me along with the two troopers and the two Beamis wives. When Kent and I stood, the judge held up his hand. He looked at Mr. Parks with a frown on his face. He asked him about our apparent injuries. Kent still had a nice shiner and my white bandage stood out.

Mr. Parks answered the judge before Kent or I could say a word. He announced how we had been attacked twice by Lou McCulloch, the son of one of the town officers. The two attacks were intended to interfere with and delay this bond hearing. He explained that Kent and I were crucial alibi witnesses for his clients and since that piece of information had been revealed to the prosecution in an effort to acquire a reasonable bond, the son of the ranking Sergeant had repeatedly attacked Kent and me to keep us from testifying. Mr. Parks laid it on thick. This was getting good, and the defense attorney wasn't done.

"Another less obvious reason for the attacks on these two boys is to prevent the Beamis heirs from pursuing a wrongful death action against the McCulloch Wood Products Company for the death

334

of their father. Stopping the civil suit from being filed is why the prosecution wants my clients in jail. It has nothing to do with their guilt or innocence, but a malicious attempt to circumvent justice."

Mr. Albert Winston Brown jumped up and began to yell, "I object. This accusation is immaterial. This court has no business hearing anything about a civil suit. I demand …."

Judge Carlton didn't say a word, but he pointed his finger at Mr. Brown, who stopped talking.

"Mr. Commonwealth, I will decide what I hear and what I don't hear when I'm asking my own questions at a bond hearing. I rule this information is material. Now, I'm going to hear Mr. Parks out. If you interrupt again except to make a valid objection on a different topic, then you and I will retire to my chambers. Understood?"

Mr. Brown sat down without responding to the judge. Mr. Parks stood back up. He took a drink of water and cleared his throat.

"Furthermore, in proof of the conspiracy to prevent my clients from being able to exercise their right to have access to the civil court, I ask the court to focus on the day of the accident. Sergeant McCulloch intruded into the state police investigation in the fatal death of Jacob Beamis. This town sergeant, being second in command and not even the chief of police, demanded the state police yield to his department and halt their inquiries. When the state police rightfully refused, since they had appropriate jurisdiction, Sergeant McCulloch called his daddy, Big John McCulloch, the president of McCulloch Wood Products, who, in turn, called the governor. The governor ordered the state police not to investigate the accident in violation of the duties of his office."

Mr. Parks cleared his throat, took another sip of water from a glass on his table, and paused to stare at the now noticeable argument going on at the prosecutor's table. During his speech, Sergeant Little John McCulloch had been arguing with Mr. Albert Winston Brown. What started as a whispered conversation was getting louder and louder until they saw the judge frowning at them. They wisely stopped their discussion. Mr. Parks waited for the disruption to cease, cleared his throat again, and resumed speaking to the judge.

"Now, the very department which derives its sole income from the owner and operator of the log truck responsible for the accident is covering up the company's liability for this terrible accident. I further state, as a fact, that every one of the officers who are investigating the Beamis fatality is on the payroll of McCulloch Wood Products. The governor has the company, in effect, investigating itself. We all know where that will end. Your Honor, the sniper has been caught according to every newspaper in the area. The arrest and detention of my clients on the charges before you are not based on any evidence because there is none. No! Their arrests are only to prevent my clients from suing civilly. To make this case a total mockery of our judicial system, the prosecutor draws a salary from this same corrupt corporation."

There was no way for the judge to be heard as Mr. Albert Winston Brown jumped to his feet and began screaming. Chief Smith and Little John McCulloch joined him. Officer Younger was the only one of the town officers in his seat and obeying the command to keep silent.

The sheriff finally got everyone to shut up and sit down, which was not an easy task nor done quickly. Kent and I tried to get as small as we could. We sure did not want to be noticed.

The court called another recess. Kent was leaking a giggle. I started to whisper to Kent, but Mom poked me with her elbow and gave me her famous frown. I got quiet as a mouse.

The judge took Mr. Parks and Mr. Albert Winston Brown into his chambers along with the sheriff and the two troopers. Chief Smith tried to follow them, but he came right back outside, red-faced and mumbling under his breath. Sergeant Little John McCulloch and Officer Frank Younger hurried into the men's room. The prisoners were led back out to the jail.

"Wow, is court always this much fun?" Kent asked no one in particular.

"If it is, I think I want to be a lawyer or a state trooper," I said.

We heard the main door to the courtroom open. Mr. Cubley walked in, looked around, and spotted us. He came right over to Mom and Dad and smiled at Kent and me.

"Hey, sorry, I got held up at the hotel. Glad I didn't miss anything."

We all started laughing. Mom explained what he had just missed. Chief Smith, Sergeant McCulloch, and Officer Younger returned to the courtroom but sat on the prosecution side, which was on the other side of the courtroom from our group.

After about ten minutes and some loud voices coming from the judge's chambers, everyone filed back out into the courtroom, the judge being the last to enter. The sheriff skipped the "all rise" part.

The judge pointed and said, "Sheriff, please return the prisoners to the courtroom." The prisoner escorts must have been listening just outside the door because the door opened at once and all three prisoners were led back inside.

"Mr. Parks, do you have a motion to make to this court?" Judge Carlton asked, looking first at Mr. Parks, then giving Mr. Albert Winston Brown a frown when the other man started to rise, before thinking better of it and sitting back down.

"Your Honor, I move my clients be released on a fifty-dollar bond each, pending the preliminary hearings on these matters."

"Motions granted. The bond amounts are so ordered."

"I also request the court admonish the Highland Police Department, their officers, and the underage members of their immediate families to refrain from any further violence toward the witnesses in this case, to wit: William Boyer Gunn and Kent Farnsworth Clark."

Judge Carlton pointed at Chief Smith and Officer Little John McCulloch. He motioned for them to come forward with his forefinger.

I looked over at Kent. His face turned beet red over the Farnsworth part. He shook his head and put his head down in his hands. A more despondent sight was never to be seen.

I looked back at Chief Smith and Sergeant Little John McCulloch, who were shaking their heads like they were going to refuse to come up to the judge's bench. Mr. Albert Winston Brown leaned over to them and, after ten or fifteen-seconds of conversation and some finger shaking, the two officers rose and approached the judge's bench. He said some words, and they raised their hands. They were sworn to obey the witness order of protection.

When the judge left the courtroom, all kinds of noise erupted. Chief Smith and the sergeant left cussing, but my dad stood and caught up with the chief and Sergeant McCulloch. I heard Dad say over the other noise in the courtroom, "One more thing and the least of your worries will be going to jail for violating the judge's order, I promise you that."

As Dad walked back to where Mom was standing, I was afraid Sergeant McCulloch was going to come after him. Mr. Albert Winston Brown and Sheriff Lawrence both took hold of him and said something I couldn't hear. Then, the chief and the sergeant left the courtroom with Officer Frank Younger following. I don't think he wanted to be near them. I heard a few more cuss words from the chief as he neared the exit. I had never expected to hear anyone cuss in a courtroom. *Dragnet* was never like this.

The three prisoners were taken back to jail. When the two wives asked Mr. Parks what was going on and why their husbands were not being released, he told them that the jail had to process them out first. It would take about fifteen minutes.

Mr. Parks got hugs from the ladies, which also surprised me. Who would have thought people would be cussing and hugging in court?

The troopers came up to Kent and me to say that if we got bothered again, we could call on one of them for help. Dad said something about the troopers needing to pick up the pieces. Both Mom and I held onto Dad's arms 'cause we didn't want Dad to get into trouble.

Giles said, "John, you know you're the only one I would let work on my patrol car. Don't you go and get yourself locked up when you have good friends that can help." He gave Dad a light punch on his arm.

Dad patted Mom on the hand and said, "I'll consider it."

She hugged his arm in return, and we slowly moved out of the courtroom. I let go of Dad at the door, and Mr. Cubley asked me how I liked court. I told him it had a lot more action than I'd expected.

"Was it like this every day when you were a prosecutor down in Roanoke?" Kent asked him.

"Oh, no. Some days there was a ruckus but never as much as this. You and Billy seem to stir up trouble wherever you go," he said with a laugh.

"You have no idea," Mom agreed as she hugged Dad's arm even tighter.

When we got outside, Mr. Cubley told us he would be sure to call when we had our next wash job at the hotel.

"Right now, the hotel is only half full, but Chuck is starting to get calls from people wanting to book again. We think things will pick up soon."

Kent and I were shocked when he added if Mom and Dad couldn't drive us to work, he would be happy to send the hotel wagon.

"I thought things were back to normal?" I interrupted.

"Yeah, we want to ride our bikes," Kent joined in.

"We shall see, but for now, you boys are going to be driven or picked up. Even if the sniper is behind bars, you've still got those bullies to worry about. I want you safe. No sneaking off or you'll be grounded for the summer. Do you understand?" Mom gave us both her stare.

I guess the Beamis brothers were out on bond, but Superman and I couldn't say the same.

CHAPTER 39

POLECAT GETS KICKED
Thursday, July 7, 1955

Matt had slept in. He had been up late the previous night, exploring certain secret parts of the hotel. The boots and clothes he had worn were in the middle of his bedroom floor covered in dust, stained with rust, and spotted with oil from his servicing a particular piece of equipment. Lucky for Matt, Uncle TJ had left him instructions and the service manual in the safe. He had finished around five a.m. and fallen into bed wearing only his underwear.

When he roused, he looked outside to see it was raining, which matched the gloomy outlook for business at the hotel. The month of July, which was usually the month that carried them through the winter, had not been good, according to Chuck. Part of the problem had been the sniper attacks, but the campaign being waged by Big John against him had been more successful than he had predicted.

Chuck had billed the state police, but the state was slow to pay. At least the dining room was busy, allowing him to switch several of the maids to waitress duty. Their base pay was less, but the tips made up the difference, and other jobs in the area were scarce. He was going to have to make some hard decisions unless business got better.

He rolled out of bed, tossed his discarded clothes in the hamper, washed, and put on fresh clothes. He felt a lot better after his hot shower.

Chuck was working on a flower arrangement for the lobby when he came down for breakfast. The lobby was deserted, but Matt heard activity in the dining room. That was good. No troopers except Lusk and no reporters, but the dining room was still half full.

Chuck quietly informed him they were only forty percent occupied but might get up to eighty percent occupancy by the weekend. The guests were slowly coming back. This good news improved Matt's mood.

Chuck also informed him that Cliff Duffy had delivered a third bogus list to the drop off point. Green Mountain Resort would likely begin to suffer since this latest list contained the names of three check forgers and a guest who had gotten drunk and demolished a room. How he broke the sink and the bed was a mystery, but he managed to put that room out of service for two weeks, and Chuck had enjoyed adding this name to the bogus list.

"Matt, the Hartfords booked the hunting lodge for the last week in July and the first week of August."

"Who are the Hartfords?"

"He's a University of Virginia biology professor, who's bringing his family and two graduate students for two weeks of scientific study and fun. He's booked the lodge for the past several summers. I need you to ride up to the lodge with Richard and make a list of what's needed to be repaired, resupplied, and cleaned. In addition, tell me what food you want me to order for the lodge pantry."

"I'll take Richard and do it this morning. This rental would bring in a boost to our ledger ahead of the regular hunting season."

Matt checked the kitchen to see if he was too late for breakfast. He was in luck. Usually, arriving this late would land him on Maddie's list of the unfavored, but today, Maddie was in a good mood. She gave him a plate of breakfast leftovers.

Boo asked Matt if he knew why Polecat had not arrived, which was very odd. The man was never late for breakfast, even when it was raining. It certainly wasn't pouring rain, and there had been no reports that local roads were flooded. Matt hoped Polecat wasn't sick or injured.

While Matt enjoyed his stack of leftover pancakes with link sausages, Polecat rode up on his bike. The newsman had tied three empty feed bags together to fashion himself a homemade rain suit. He slowly climbed the steps onto the dock, shook himself like a dog, and untied the feed bags from his body, draping them over two empty chairs to dry. Next, he went back to his bike, pulled two papers out of his newspaper bag, and carefully placed them on the dock.

One of them was wet, which was unusual because Polecat protected his papers more than himself.

"Mr. Smith, what a rainy day that's only good for a duck," Matt commented, hoping to lighten the mood for a troubled Polecat.

"I know one of God's creatures that I would like to disembowel and roast, and he's no duck," Polecat grumbled, limping into the kitchen.

Matt heard Boo greet him cordially, and, though he usually spent several moments in a pleasant conversation with her over the day's news, today he was taciturn. When he came back out, he eased himself into one of the chairs, sighed, and began to eat, but not with his normal gusto. His bites were small, and he chewed very slowly. His demeanor was that of someone with a heavy burden.

"You seem troubled. Anything I can do?" Matt tried to say this in a cheery voice to draw him out.

"Mr. Cubley, some of the inhabitants of this valley, are an abomination to all mankind and should be exterminated."

"Anyone in particular?"

"The son of the patriarch of this valley is a rogue and a scoundrel. A low life of the lowest order of flagellates," Polecat exclaimed and ended his sentence with a snort.

"What's Little John done now?"

"He has one of your delivery trucks stopped in your driveway after waiting for it to make the turn. He's not brilliant, but he's not stupid when he wants to focus his efforts only on you."

"I was wondering when the Highland Police were going to get back to harassing me. I guess I was lucky it took them this long. Is that what's angered you?"

"No, although you have my sympathy," Polecat said with indignation. "Sergeant McCulloch saw me sorting papers in the corner of the lobby of the Highland Police Department, just like I do most mornings, especially when we have rain. He yelled at me to get out and said I stank like a wet dog."

"Oh, dear!" Matt responded.

"Well, if that wasn't an insult sufficient to warrant a plague upon his house, he picked up my stack of newspapers and threw them outside in the rain. They landed in a mud puddle. Ten of them were ruined! Now I must account for the loss from my personal resources. It just so happens that the ruined newspapers were Green Mountain Resort papers." Polecat waved his fork toward the other resort.

"I'm sorry. The McCulloch family is causing all kinds of trouble. I guess you know what Lou did to little Billy at the Fourth of July celebration?" Matt's voice was full of disgust.

Polecat wasn't finished and didn't seem to hear him. "He kicked me! When I tried to save my papers, he kicked me in the buttocks as I exited the lobby area. I landed on my hands and knees in the same puddle as my papers." Polecat held up his hands, and while the dirt did not seem worse than normal, there were bloody abrasions as well.

"Why would he do that?" Matt asked, feeling sorry for Polecat.

"He was mad; the chief was mad; all the officers were mad about what happened in court at the Beamis bond hearing. People better steer clear of them for the next several days. I pity the next person who gets arrested in this locality."

"Why don't you let me bandage your hands?"

"It's not necessary. I'll do it when I return to the newspaper office. I have some supplies in the shed behind the press room."

"Any news about Doc Hathaway?" Matt asked, thinking a change of subject might help his guest.

"Well, I have some history. Mr. Hathaway was discharged from the hospital on Sunday evening after he regained his faculties. His wife and two boys tried to see him at the hospital, but the sheriff refused and made them wait until Monday, the Fourth, for visiting hours, as they do every holiday. When the family arrived, a deputy told them that the sheriff would only allow the wife to visit. She sent the boys over to the park to watch the celebration to keep them busy."

"How old are those boys?"

"Near the age of Kent and Billy, why?" asked Polecat.

"I wonder if the two strangers who beat up Lou were the Hathaway boys?" Matt said to Polecat.

"I would wager they are. They would have spent most of the afternoon over at the park waiting on their mom. The sheriff made her wait for the last visitation slot, claiming they had to remove all other visitors from the area for safety. When she left, the commotion at the park was over." Polecat rose to take his dishes into the kitchen.

"Well, that explains a lot. The enemy of my enemy is my friend, and Billy was the beneficiary," Matt said with a laugh.

CHAPTER 40
BILLY AND THE ONE THAT GOT AWAY
Friday, July 8, 1955

"Mom, it's time to go," I called from beside the car. I was eager to get to the Coze because the day was clear, and two cars were waiting to be washed. It had rained the day before, but now the sun was shining.

It was going to be a great weekend with the *Bowery Boys Meet the Monsters, Them,* and *The Snow Creature* playing at the Topp Hat Theater. There was nothing better than a good monster movie. It was fun getting scared. I just hoped they wouldn't cause bad dreams. They never had before this summer.

"I'm coming," Mom said, coming out of the kitchen door with her car keys.

After picking up Kent, we drove to the hotel, where we saw Mr. Tolliver on the veranda. Waving to him, we wasted no time walking to the kitchen, greeting Boo and Maddie, picking up our food, and exiting onto the loading dock to eat. Mr. Cubley and Polecat were about half finished with their food.

Mr. Cubley invited us to ride up to the lodge with him if we got through our work by eleven-thirty, so Kent and I went into high gear.

Polecat complained that Lou McCulloch passed him on his bike last night, swerved at him, and yelled, "Get out of my way," causing him to almost wreck.

"Guess those two strangers need to teach Lou another lesson," remarked Kent.

Then, Mr. Cubley shocked us with, "You mean Skip and Barry Hathaway. They'll be keeping out of sight for a while."

Mr. Cubley told us how he and Polecat had figured it out but promised that the secret was going to remain a secret. Kent was surprised as well.

"Do you think Doc Hathaway is the sniper?" Kent asked Mr. Cubley.

"No, I don't," Mr. Cubley said.

"What makes you sure?"

"Well, Doc Hathaway was probably framed for the payroll theft, which landed him in jail. He certainly has a motive for shooting plant officials and the police. That's for sure! But many people, at least those on the list of fifteen, have the same motive—a hatred for Big John."

"So, why not Doc Hathaway?" I asked, beating Kent to the punch.

"When this man got out of jail, his family needed money. He chose the wrong path by running moonshine, but three things tell me that he's not the sniper. First, he needed to earn money for his family. Running moonshine is a way to earn quick cash, but it also means keeping quiet and not being noticed by the police. Shooting up a town isn't a good way to do that. Second, he was making moonshine runs, clear down to Franklin County and back. Running moonshine all night, then setting up hides, and shooting people during the day doesn't exactly give someone time to sleep or see their family. Third, he was never in the military. He's familiar with guns, but our man, I feel certain, has actual sniper training."

"What now?" Kent asked.

"The 'what now' boys, is why I don't want you running around town. So, until all these murders are solved, you get rides with Richard, me, or your parents. Promise?"

We both promised and Mr. Cubley seemed satisfied with that.

We finished with the two guests' cars just before eleven, picked up our money, and waited for Mr. Cubley and Richard. It wasn't long before Richard came out carrying four lunches in a big basket plus four cold Dr. Peppers in a bag of ice to the wagon.

We arrived at the lodge after what seemed like a shorter trip than our first trip up the mountain, and Mr. Cubley set out the picnic basket and drinks on the porch. We all sat down to dig in.

After lunch, Mr. Cubley told Kent and me we were free to look around, but we shouldn't go too far. He and Richard only had a couple of things to do, so we had to stay within shouting distance. We hiked up the mountain on the main trail and noticed a big boulder all by itself not far from the lodge. Climbing on top of it, the trees were too thick to see very far, but looking down the backside of the boulder, we saw some dead bushes covering something. We climbed down and pulled back the branches to find a piece of plywood. When we tried to lift it, though, we found it wouldn't budge.

"This plywood is stuck. Why do you suppose that is?" Kent asked like I would know.

"It's not old, maybe leftover from last hunting season. I bet a hunter buried stuff here. It's a box with a plywood top."

We got some sticks and worked and worked, but no matter how hard we pried, we could not get the top to come loose. It was stuck tight.

"Kent, let's get tools from the hotel and come back another day. Come on, let's go higher up the trail. I think I see a place for an observation post on top of those other rocks. We can use this plywood to build us a real lookout if we can get this dumb thing unstuck."

The rocks that were a little higher were big and flat on top. Once you climbed on top of them, it was possible to see for miles. We could see the plant, the town, and everything. We heard Mr. Cubley calling, so we immediately climbed down and ran back to the lodge.

"Did you boys find anything?" Mr. Cubley asked.

Kent answered with a big smile on his face, "Yeah, there's a neat lookout up on those big rocks, way up above the lodge."

"Yeah, I used to play on those big rocks when I was your age. You can see across the valley, all the way over to State Route 22, on a clear day."

"We think we found something buried, too. There's a plywood box buried up on the mountain, near those big rocks. We tried to get it open, but it's stuck. Can we get tools from the hotel to dig it up?" I asked, trying to be polite.

"Sure," Mr. Cubley said.

Richard cautioned. "Be careful when you pick up stuff like that. There are rattlesnakes and copperheads all over this mountain. Watch where you put your hands."

"Oh, we'll be careful. Do we get to keep whatever's buried there?" Kent asked, and he sounded certain that we had found buried treasure.

Richard laughed. "I bet you found an empty box. Some hunter probably used it to store supplies. It would save him from lugging them up and down the mountain. Anyway, it's time to go, boys."

After we piled in, we started for the hotel in the Ford wagon. Going down was scary, but we made it without wrecking. Trooper Lusk was waiting for us when we got back to the hotel. I figured he was the reason that Mr. Cubley had to get back. He probably wanted to tell him the latest on the case.

Kent and I asked to stay to listen, and, when Mr. Cubley looked at Trooper Lusk, he smiled and said he thought it would be alright—nothing confidential.

"We found and cleared everyone on our list of suspects with military records but two. The local troopers will have to finish up with the final two suspects. My work here is almost finished, at least according to my lieutenant."

"So, these final two suspects, are they high on your list?" Mr. Cubley asked, and he was showing a considerable measure of curiosity.

"Perhaps. The first one was roughed up when he got fired. Then, he moved to Arizona the day after someone broke out the windshield of Pete Franklin's car. Nothing connects him to the vandalism, but it's a mighty curious coincidence. I sent an official request asking Arizona to track him down, but they can't seem to locate him. His name is Bert Casey, and he was in the infantry. He wasn't a sniper, but he did get his expert marksman certification. I asked Arizona to put a team on him and said that finding him was important. I hope to get an answer back in a day or two. This guy could have returned for a little more payback."

"Matt, Casey's local relatives have joined the crowd of people who are not being cooperative. A neighbor reported seeing Bert on the road near his father's house a week ago, but two other neighbors claimed not to have seen him since he left for Arizona. We don't know where he might be."

Trooper Lusk moved on to the second suspect. "The last guy on the list was a former sniper, but he's now a cripple. Not sure just how much of a threat he might be. He trained under Captain Walter Walsh, so you may not have run into him. He lost two fingers at the plant and got fired because of it. Some kind of equipment problem caused the accident. The foreman made a big deal of him being a cripple, and guess what? That foreman was Pete Franklin. The list of people that hated that foreman seems to be a long one. After the firing, the family was forced to move out of the company house by the plant police. He, his wife, and kids moved back in with her parents. No one at the plant heard much after that."

"Is that all on him?" Mr. Cubley asked.

"A trooper, two counties over, tracked down the in-laws, and he did find a little more on him. There was some trouble between the husband and the wife's father. The father-in-law ran him off, and the wife claims she doesn't know where he is. Sergeant Oliver wants this guy kept on our list of suspects, just if it turns out Doc Hathaway is not our man. Richmond has closed down this investigation and sent everyone home, but Sergeant Oliver is saying he's not sold on Hathaway."

"I think I remember the sergeant mentioning this crippled fellow before. What's his name?"

"Shiflett, Daryl Dean Shiflett. Lost his pointer and middle fingers on his right hand, his shooting hand. Tracking him is hard since he's cut off from his family. He has two cute little girls: Karen, age eight, and Betty, age five. I could see him having a grudge. He might be our man, although I doubt it—not with a crippled hand. A sniper buddy of mine mashed his fingers when the bolt of a fifty cal machine gun slammed down on two of them. He was never any good after that. They discharged him on a medical."

"Those fifty calibers always gave me the willies," Mr. Cubley added.

"The sergeant has gotten permission for me to stay on for a few more days, but they'll send me home first of the week. Giles and Quinn are good men. They'll take over from here."

"It's a real shame no one can get Doc Hathaway to give us a confession. That would allow us to close out these murders. I wonder if we're missing anyone else." Mr. Cubley put his hand on my shoulder.

"No person, but if we can ever find it, that sniper rifle is going to be the clue that solves this case." At that, Lusk turned and started back into the hotel.

I liked Trooper Lusk. As he went up the stairs of the hotel, he turned and told Kent and me, "You boys might make good troopers someday."

Richard drove Kent and me to my house. We told Mom and Dad about Trooper Lusk's compliment, and Mom said we would grow up soon enough, so we shouldn't rush it. She then told us that troopers had to have good grades, so we both needed to earn all A's. Dad didn't say anything; he was smart when it came to fixing things, I knew that, but perhaps not as good as Mom when it came to school grades. At least, that's what Grandma said about him after saying Mom was always the top of her class. She bragged that Mom was much smarter than Dad. I knew that hurt Dad's feelings, but he never said anything.

The phone rang and Mom handed it to Dad. Sheriff Lawrence was calling and asked Dad to pick up a 51 Plymouth that was broken-down on a side road over near the plant. Dad asked Kent and me if we wanted to go with him. When Mom fussed, claiming it was too dangerous, Dad said it was clearly a broken-down car.

"Laura Jane, the sheriff checked it himself. It's not stolen, and a Deputy will meet us there. The keys are in it, and the engine won't even turn over. The deputy walked all around it, and there's no place to hide. Besides, I've towed four cars over the last couple of days without any problems. Let the boys go... I'll be extra careful."

We all climbed into Blacky and drove over to the side road near the plant, where we waited until a deputy drove over from the plant to escort us. When we got to the location, the car was gone.

"See, just a dead battery or something. I guess whoever broke down got it fixed," Dad stated as he turned Blacky around and drove back to town. The deputy went back to the plant.

When we turned at the Liberty Bell Gas Station, I thought I saw a 51 Plymouth parked behind the bell, but I wasn't sure about the color, and we were going way too fast for me to see the license plate. A man was standing by the car, opening the driver's door with his left hand. I started to say something to Dad, but we had passed before I could.

It didn't matter much. If that was the car we were called to tow, we were too late. Dad wasn't allowed to charge the man. Dad always said that the towing business was like fishing. You try to get a hook on as many as you can, but some just get away.

CHAPTER 41
REVENGE IS SERVED
Saturday, July 9, 1955

Daryl Dean Shiflett awakened with a start. He listened but heard only the sounds of insects in the woods. The man watched and waited, trying to make out shapes in the woods by using his peripheral vision, which trick was his military training coming back to him. After several minutes, he was satisfied that it was only a bad dream and not someone sneaking up on him.

His attention changed to where his fingers used to be. Last night's liquor had dulled the pain, but now, the burning was back. The phantom pain where his fingers used to be was very real, despite what the doctors called it.

Striking a match, he checked his watch. He had spent the night in the woods, and it was at least a couple of hours before dawn. He was in no particular hurry, but today was the day. He was anxious to begin.

Shiflett started the stolen 1951 Plymouth and used the windshield wipers to get the dew off. It had been necessary to stab his wife's uncle to death to get the Plymouth. Like his father-in-law, the old man never liked him, and he put up a fight. Neither his wife's father nor her uncle thought he was good enough for Tawney Sue. Killing the uncle had to be done to be sure this car wasn't reported stolen for at least a day or two. Being a loner and living a mile back off the road, meant the body would not be found for days.

He drove from his hiding place over to the Liberty Bell Gas Station, turned toward town, and parked in a residential area. The streets were quiet, with no traffic when he parked. He quietly got the hose and gas can out of the trunk. Once he stole sufficient gas to fill his car, a gallon glass jug, and the five-gallon can, he threw the hose in some bushes. Then, he carefully placed the can of gas and the jug in the back seat floorboard of the Plymouth.

He was ready to get his revenge on Big John McCulloch. The man responsible for the loss of his fingers, his wife, and his two little girls. The bigwigs at McCulloch Wood Products took it all from him. Today was the day they would pay. Once done, he would escape to kill his father-in-law and reclaim his family. Anyone who got in his way would die.

Shiflett drove the Plymouth out of town and back into the original side road he had picked out and used the day before. It was very fortunate that he had seen that snoop of a farmer spot his car yesterday. He prided himself on how skillfully he had hidden inside a culvert while that dumb deputy thought he cleared the area. And removing the coil made it appear to that dumb deputy that the car was broken down. That cop had never noticed the missing coil.

Once the deputy left, Shiflett had moved the car over to the gas station. He hid it in plain sight before the tow truck had arrived. That big black tow truck had almost messed him up on the day he'd shot the deputy. Shiflett had hoped that Sergeant McCulloch would show up, but instead, it was just a deputy. Oh well, shooting one cop wasn't much different from shooting another, and he thought that deputy resembled the one that had been hanging around his wife.

The real bonus was killing Officer Larry Sparrow. Sparrow had shoved his little girl when the cops were forcing his family out of the company house. Sparrow had become a dead man at that moment; he just didn't know it.

Today, Shiflett would fix it so Big John could not resist rushing to the plant. The boss had had his chance to fix that saw blade, but the man had been too cheap.

Since it was Saturday, the plant should be empty except for the man who stoked the boiler and acted as a night watchman. That guy was a bigger joke than the town cops—he slept more than he watched.

Shiflett waited in the woods until the sun came up, then he drove right up to the plant to park near the side door that led to the finishing room. The wind was in his favor today. It was out of the northeast and would help spread the fire.

He carried a paper bag with his alarm clock timer, the jug, and the can into the plant, setting the full glass jug of gasoline down behind some barrels of finishing material—good flammable stuff with warning labels posted all over them. It took only a minute to pry off their lids.

The timer was a simple affair. At ten o'clock, the battery alarm would ignite the fuse with a spark, which would burn to the cherry bomb firecracker attached to the glass jug, breaking the glass and setting fire to the gasoline without much noise. The small fire would spread across the floor to the large can, which was uncapped and tilted at a forty-five-degree angle. It was held by one strand of twine tied to a post. On the post was a big no-smoking sign. When the fire burned the twine, the can would fall over, emptying its contents across the floor. The more massive gasoline fire would be quiet but was sure to ignite the finishing material. After that, the amount of noise would make no difference. The plant would burn.

He picked Saturday because the workers were off. There would be no eyes to call in an alarm until it was too late. And, besides, one or two of the men had been friends—he was no monster.

Having set up his timer and bomb, Shiflett returned to his car, drove across the highway and down the farm road, parking close to his new hide. He quietly sat in his car while he finished his bottle of whiskey and waited as the morning warmed. All remained quiet at the plant.

Shiflett checked his watch and saw that it was getting close to the time his bomb was set to go off. Once the fire got going, the police would be expecting him to make a run for it. He was smarter than that.

He knew going either east or west out of Hidden Valley on State Route 22 would get him caught. No, he planned to fool them, drive over to Cubley's Coze, and escape up the main hunting trail. Once he picked up his supplies, he could hike out of the county using the mountain as cover. After he put some miles and a day or two of time between himself and Highland, he would steal a car. That's when he would go after his no-good father-in-law.

He got his rifle, modified for a left-handed shooter, out of the trunk. His first try at the courthouse had been a disaster; the distance was too great. Also, trying to shoot right-handed without a trigger finger had compounded his mistake. He had missed Big John by a mile.

After botching his first try at the courthouse, it took him a thousand practice rounds, shooting left-handed, to return his skill level to an acceptable zone of marksmanship. He was below his normal skill level, but he was good enough to hit Big John at this current distance.

Shiflett hummed a tune to himself, perhaps the product of a little too much whiskey. He then began talking to himself as he sneaked over to his hide without so much as a passing car to cause him concern. His hide for today was better than his first one and nearer the plant. Actually, this one was perfect. It was close to a creek that led back to his car and gave him a closer and better field of fire over to the plant.

Through his scope, he saw the sign that read "Reserved" over Big John's parking spot. That sign would make a fitting grave marker for Mr. Big Shot. He planned on dropping the body next to that sign—nothing like knowing exactly where your target was going to park.

When the detonator went off, there was no big explosion, just as he had planned. He barely heard a pop. He saw a puff of smoke try to escape out the finishing room door, the one he had left partially open. Then, just as quickly, it got sucked back inside. That door provided an excellent draft to allow the fire to take off. Shiflett heard an audible whoosh, followed by two more massive whumps. Barrels of finishing material were cooking off. The finishing room was ablaze. Dark smoke was billowing out of the partially opened door. When the smoke got sucked back into the building a second time, the backdraft slammed the door shut. Shiflett knew the factory was doomed.

It only took ten minutes for the second floor to be engulfed in flames. As the fire advanced, the windows on the second floor blew out. The smoke and flames curled out, igniting the roof.

The wind blew the smoke and flames toward the main plant next door. Embers set the main plant roof and the lumber yard on fire like a line of dominos falling. The wind might even allow the fire to reach some of the houses of the factory supervisors, and perhaps, even Big John's mansion might burn.

He had mixed feelings about burning down the town, but if God wanted this town wiped off the face of the earth, well, it was out of his hands—totally out of his hands.

He saw the dope of a watchman run outside, stop, and then run back into the boiler room. There was a phone in the boiler room that the watchman could use to call the fire department.

The siren on top of the Highland Volunteer Fire Department began calling out the men. Two firemen arrived ahead of the fire trucks, and getting out of their private cars; they just stared dumbfounded at the fire until the first truck arrived.

The first truck was a pumper that parked near a fire hydrant. Then came a water wagon and utility van with all the coats and gear.

Every fire truck was a Chevrolet, ordered up special by Big John's dealership. Oh, he knocked down the price, but the dumb workers had raised money like crazy to pay the greater portion of the bill for this equipment. Those firemen were about to get a hard lesson in fire fighting today.

Shiflett saw Chief Danbury talking with Lieutenant Tom Daniels, who had just driven up in his car before he ran back to the pumper and climbed inside the cab to call for more help. He would need a lot more help. This fire was at least a five-alarm fire already and by the time help arrived from Lovingston, Waynesboro, Staunton, and Charlottesville, the plant would probably be too far gone to be saved.

More and more firefighters began arriving in their personal cars, and the last and oldest pumper from town pulled into the lot. Some men were hooking up smaller fire hoses directly to hydrants set around the plant, not to the firetrucks. The water pressure in these hoses would not be nearly as strong as the water pressure from the hoses connected directly to the pumper, but they might help some.

Shiflett considered firing on the fire crews. Not to kill anyone, just to disrupt their efforts, but he decided to wait for Big John to show up. The last thing he wanted was to give the man a warning and have him escape his punishment.

Shiflett had been smart and laid low since Doc Hathaway's arrest. The press had been the biggest help in making people believe that the sniper was behind bars, and Big John now had no reason to suspect that this fire was anything other than a terrible accident.

Just then, a Cadillac came tearing into the parking lot and almost ran over two firefighters. A Highland Police Car was trailing close behind. The Cadillac slid to a stop into Big John's reserved space.

Shiflett began his slow breathing regimen and tried to slow his heart rate. When Big John McCulloch got out of his car, it was clear that his only concern was the fire. He began to wave his arms and yell to Chief Danbury, who was still on the two-way radio in the pumper.

Shiflett calmly fired two bullets into Big John's back, sending the bossman's body violently forward to the ground. He then shifted his sights over to the town officer who was getting out of his police car. It was Chief Obie Smith. Shiflett almost smiled but stopped himself, so his aim would be true. He fired three evenly spaced shots. The first round hit the chief in the back of his left shoulder. The force of the high-powered bullet hitting bone spun him, so he was facing Shiflett as he began to fall backward. Shiflett tracked the body as it fell. He slowly let out his breath and fired a second shot for the chest, but it struck the officer in the forehead. A third shot caught the man, who was dead but not yet on the ground, under the chin. This third round took off most of the Chief's mouth, nose, and forehead.

It's a closed casket for you, Shiflett thought to himself.

Moving his sniper scope around the scene, he repeatedly fired at the windshields and windows of the fire trucks and private cars. The firemen began to shout warnings, drop hoses, and dive for cover. When the fire hoses connected to the pumper were dropped, the water pressure sent them whipping about. The loose hoses were shooting streams of water back and forth all over the place. This got the attention of more firefighters. Within moments, the Highland Volunteer Fire Department had stopped fighting the fire and were taking cover behind the nearest solid objects they could find.

The pump engineer on the new pumper, after seeing four loose hoses whip closer to some men, bravely crawled out from under the truck, reached up, and shut off the pump. The four hoses dropped like dead snakes. He dove back under the truck, fully expecting to be shot. His prayers to be spared joined several being offered by other men.

Shiflett left the empty brass this time, took his rifle, and crawled into the ravine. Standing bent over in a crouch, he ran down this ravine to the creek and waded up it to his hidden car. Reaching it, he threw the rifle on the back seat and slowly drove down the farm road like he had all the time in the world. When he reached State Route 22, he sat for a moment, looking over at the plant. Satisfied with his work, he drove to the Cubley's Coze Hotel. He crossed in front of the hotel to the guest parking lot and backed into a spot near the trees. He got out, looked around, and, with his rifle down beside his leg, he walked into the woods.

Chuck noticed the 1951 Plymouth pull into the guest lot, but when no one came to the lobby to check-in, he walked into Matt's office and looked out the window to see where the guest had gone. He just caught a glimpse of a man disappearing into the woods.

A hiker, he thought. This time of year, that was not an unusual occurrence. Chuck was much more interested in the fire sirens downtown.

Back at the plant, a couple of the braver firemen had determined that the shooting had stopped and resumed fighting the fire. Chief Danbury was still hunched down in the pumper's cab, calling for the police on his radio. Soon, five deputies arrived with Sergeant McCulloch in the lead and the Younger brothers following. Roger Younger was driving much slower than the others because he dared not wreck another police vehicle.

Little John spotted his dad on the ground and went straight to him, ignoring the body of the chief of police a short distance away. Not waiting for an ambulance, Little John began screaming for the Youngers to help him load his dad into his patrol car. A deputy offered to drive, seeing Little John's panic. He urged Little John to get in the back with his dad and start putting on bandages to staunch the bleeding. Little John jumped in the back with a first aid kit from the trunk, and they tore off for the Waynesboro hospital. It was going to be a swift ride.

Then, several firemen and a deputy checked on Chief Obie Smith. Finding no signs of life, a fireman threw his bunker coat over the body. Several more of the braver firemen roused everyone else to get up and start fighting the fire. A few got up, but others waited another minute. When no one got shot during this "wait and see" minute, they all jumped up and returned to fighting the fire.

A column of smoke was rising a thousand feet into the air. Another curtain of smoke was drifting toward Highland. After twenty minutes, fire trucks from Waynesboro began to arrive, having made a fast run over the mountain. Their hook and ladder would be a big help, its height allowing for water to be directed down onto the fire from above. The fact that the wind was blowing away from the main parking lot allowed this truck to pull in close, and the wind would keep the truck's ladder out of the thick smoke. Along with the ladder truck, Waynesboro sent another water wagon and two pumpers. Both pumpers were big, and each pumped a thousand gallons a minute.

Staunton's Fire Department arrived fifteen minutes behind Waynesboro. They brought an American LaFrance pumper, a rescue vehicle, and another utility van with a total of ten additional firemen. All the pumpers were now working the fire. However, the rough end department of the plant had caught fire and was an inferno. The finishing room roof, along with the second floor, had collapsed onto the first floor. The main plant was starting to burn. The office building might be able to be saved, but the lumber yard was ablaze on the end near the main parking lot. Considering the direction of the wind, it did not look good for saving much of the lumber.

To make matters worse, the water tank that served the plant was almost empty because the electricity to it was out. The fire had burned through the power lines to the plant. Without electricity to the pumps for the big water tank, there was no way to refill it.

A call had gone out for more pumpers. Two were on the way from Charlottesville and one from Lynchburg. When they arrived, they ran supply lines from the river to the pumpers fighting the fire. Putting the newly arrived pumpers into a tandem line allowed water to be pumped directly from the river with good pressure for the pumpers fighting the fire. The water wagons ran laps back and forth to the river, but the travel time and the time it took to fill and discharge them, made this process too slow to be much help.

This was a fire that was bound for the history books. Reporters were arriving from all the local newspapers. The Lovingston Fire Department from the adjacent county had moved equipment into the empty Highland firehouse in case of other fires. Other fires were quite possible with all the embers blowing downwind toward town.

Chief Danbury and his lieutenant had worked up several plans for major fires, but the real thing was so much worse than what they had thought possible. They had not planned for the factory water tank to run dry—an embarrassing surprise.

The chief was doing his best to save the boiler room since it sat apart from the main plant. This separation had been done on purpose, as everyone had expected a potential fire to start in the boiler room, then spread to the main plant. Reality and the wind blowing from opposite its normal direction had caused the reverse to be true.

There was truly no chance of saving the plant, and the Highland Fire Department was learning a hard lesson. Two pumpers were simply not sufficient to protect a large wood products plant. The chief had tried several times to get Big John to buy better equipment for the town, but the man had always been satisfied with the equipment they had.

The Highland Police Department and ten county deputies gathered to talk in the plant parking lot. All the town police were present, except for Little John and Chief Obie Smith. Few believed that Big John would make it, though such thinking was only whispered to fellow officers. It was dangerous to talk about Big John to the public, one way or the other. This town had too many gossips.

The state police had already sealed State Route 22 at both ends when reports of shots fired came over the police radio network. Now, other than dead-end farm roads inside the perimeter, they believed they had the sniper boxed-in, and more police were headed this way from all over the state. The state police were sending an armored car from Richmond, but it was heavy and slow and was not expected for two more hours.

Half the town drove out to see the fire, which required the sheriff to divert resources to start working the crowd. When word got around that the chief was dead, Big John had been shot, and bullet holes riddled the fire trucks and firemen's cars, the more cautious people went home and locked their doors.

Word quickly spread through the gossip grapevine that the sniper was still loose, and fear spread with it, like smoke from the fire.

CHAPTER 42

BILLY'S BURIED BOX
Saturday, July 9, 1955

We were looking for some tools to take up to the lodge to open the buried box. I found a great pry bar, but it was tangled in a garden hose some idiot had tossed into the maintenance shed.

"Hey, Superman, do you have the shovel? I think I have the pry bar if I can get it unstuck."

I pulled and pulled on the pry bar, but it was trapped.

"BB, I got the shovel. Do we need the hoe or just the shovel?" Kent questioned.

"Only the shovel. Ugh... Richard says there are two or three old axes at the lodge... darn... which they use for busting up firewood. We can use one of those for a hoe if we need to. He also said there's a toolbox with a hammer and some screwdrivers stored at the lodge."

I ended my last sentence with another grunt as I finally got the pry bar pulled loose. When it did, I almost fell on my rear end.

We loaded our tools into the hotel Ford Club Wagon and waited on Richard. He was holding us up while he fixed a light switch in the hotel.

Once we dug up the box, we didn't plan on telling our moms or dad if we found something. They were bad about wanting our money for useless stuff like college. No, we were going to hide what we found and live *The Life of Riley* just like on TV.

"We have to take a blood oath never to reveal our find," I said with conviction.

"Are we going to make Mr. Cubley and Mr. Baker promise not to tell, too?" Kent asked.

"Finally, here comes Richard," Kent announced, and we both hopped into the hotel wagon. Richard placed a basket with three sack lunches in the back beside a bunch of boxes that he was taking up to the lodge, and off we went.

Richard told us he had to rewire some stuff and replace a bunch of rusted light fixtures. He said he would rather do it alone, which meant Kent and I had one or two hours to dig up the box. About halfway up the mountain, we all heard the fire department siren on the roof of the firehouse. It kept sounding over and over. I guessed they had a big house fire or maybe even a fire in one of the stores in town.

Gosh, I hope it wasn't near the Top Hat, I thought at the time.

When we got closer to the lodge, we couldn't hear the siren anymore, and I assumed the fire department would have the fire out long before we got down off the mountain.

Richard drove up to the front of the lodge and parked. Once we were done unloading, Richard sat down on the porch to eat his lunch. When he opened a Dr. Pepper, Kent and I decided to join him, even though it was a little early. There's nothing better than a cold Dr. Pepper, and it was close to ten o'clock.

We opened our lunch sacks and wolfed down our sandwiches and fried chicken. Pimiento cheese sandwiches and fried chicken just go together. We also had a couple of pieces of white cake with light brown icing. Having had breakfast at the hotel, now an early lunch, Kent and I decided to save desserts. We were eager to get started.

Kent got the toolbox we needed out of the lodge closet. We checked to be sure Richard wouldn't need the hammer or the two largest screwdrivers. He told us we could take them.

I found an old rusty ax, so if we used it for a hoe, no one would fuss at us. I knew digging in the dirt with an ax would dull it. Dad taught me that certain things were not worth a whip'n. This was one of them.

We hiked up the main hunting trail loaded down with tools. I carried the old ax and the heavy pry bar, and Kent was carrying the shovel, with the two screwdrivers in his back pocket. The hammer was tucked under his belt.

Once we reached the spot where the wooden box was buried, we checked for snakes by poking the shovel and pry bar all around. It was all clear, not a snake anywhere. We pulled back the brush with our hands. The top of the box was now ready to be opened.

"Kent, do you see any screws?" I asked.

"Yeah, but only these two over here on the corner." Kent pointed to them and started to back out the screws with one of his screwdrivers.

The first one was hard, but he finally got it. The next one was harder, and we both had to grip the screwdriver to get the screw started. It finally came loose, and Kent backed it the rest of the way out. Once the screws were out of this end piece, we lifted it off the corner of the box.

"Now what? There aren't any more screws," Kent said as he searched around the edge of the box.

I began to see how the thing worked. "Here's a grove along the front edge of the box where that little piece of molding slides off the front, so the top can slide down the side grooves and off. Put your hands on this long piece of molding and help me push or pull it off."

Kent pushed and I pulled on the molding across one end of the box. At first, it only just moved a little, but as it slid sideways, it got easier, and finally, slid off the end of the box. Now we could see the top piece of plywood fitted into slots on three sides of the box. We pulled on the plywood lid; it slid down the side slots and off the end.

Inside the box were some big waterproof bags. The first one contained brand new clothes with store tags on them. The second bag held three knapsacks full of army stuff. We found a little camp stove, a small cast-iron skillet, a coffee pot, a dish with a spoon, a knife, and a compass. There were maps of the county and some medicine bottles from the drug store in town—all kinds of stuff to explore this mountain.

"BB, who do you think left all this stuff?"

"Probably some hunter from last deer season. I wonder why he left it?"

"Maybe he got shot in a hunting accident," Kent said, examining a brand new sleeping bag.

"Naw, that would have been all over the news. I think the guy who's breaking into the houses and stores in town is stashing the stuff up here," I said, picking up some of the shirts that had price tags on them, all from local stores.

"Should we turn it in? Maybe there's a reward."

"Yeah, I guess we better. Grab that knapsack. We can take some of this stuff to show the cops." I was getting a bad feeling that there would be no reward—a lot of work for nothing.

After we took some items and put them in one of the smaller knapsacks, we found a metal box; inside was a pistol wrapped in an oily cloth and boxes of bullets. I checked the pistol, and it wasn't loaded.

"Kent, this has got to belong to a robber. Let's beat feet."

We took the pistol, one box of bullets, a couple of items with store tags on them, and put our loot in one of the knapsacks. The rest of the stuff we put back just like we found it. The plywood top we refitted with only the corner piece left off. We figured the police would return in a day or two and get the rest of the stuff. They might even be able to catch the thief by hiding in the woods to see if he returned. The Lone Ranger had used that trick to catch thieves a couple of times.

"Hey, do you smell smoke?" I looked at Kent and sniffed the air again.

"Yeah. Look over yonder—I see some. Where do you think it's coming from?" Kent asked, and then suddenly, he sneezed.

"You know, we heard the fire siren going off when we were coming up here. Maybe something's on fire in town or out at the plant? The wind's coming from that direction."

"Let's go up to the lookout. We might be able to see what it is," Kent suggested and started off before I could answer. I sneezed twice from the smoke and ran to catch up with him.

"It sure stinks, whatever it is," I said, falling in behind him.

We left the bag of loot with our tools, so hiking up to the big rocks for a good view of the valley only took us a couple of minutes. I pushed Kent up, and then he pulled me onto the top of the biggest boulder. It was flat on top and made a great observation platform.

"Great Caesar's Ghost," Kent exclaimed, which he did whenever he got excited. He liked to quote the editor of the Daily Planet.

"The plant's on fire! I've never seen so much smoke. Half the county's on fire!" I remarked and added another sneeze.

"Let's get our stuff and go. Maybe your mom will take us to see it," said Kent, and I, too, wanted to watch all the firemen put out a fire this size.

We climbed down off the boulder, ran to where we found the box, and Kent grabbed the knapsack and the shovel. I got the ax and the pry bar and stuck the hammer in my belt. We ran down the trail and got to the lodge just as fast as we could go without falling. We were out of breath when we arrived. Both of us tried our best to tell Richard what was happening, but we were out of breath from running and the smoke.

"Did you get snake bit?" Richard asked, thinking something was wrong with one of us.

We both began shaking our heads.

Finally, Kent got out, "Fire!"

I added, "Plant!" Then, I took a deep breath and got out, "The Wood Products plant's burning!"

Kent added, "Mr. Baker, that's what the siren was for."

"We could see the plant from the lookout." I pointed up the mountain.

"Quick as a toad on a hot skillet, boys, get your stuff and load up. I'll close up the lodge. We better get back to the hotel," Richard said, shaking his head.

Making good time on our way down through the switchbacks, we were about halfway back when we saw a man near a tree. He had just stepped out from where one of the hunting trails crossed the road. It looked like we startled him, popping around the last bend, driving so fast. The hiker moved to the middle of the road, grinned, waved, and stood waiting. It was obvious he wanted us to stop. I thought he might be lost and needed directions. Richard quickly slowed to a stop. That's when I saw the man was carrying a rifle.

"Who's that?" Richard asked no one in particular.

The man walked toward us with his rifle pointed at the ground for safety. I wondered what he might be hunting since deer season was late fall. When he reached the driver's window, he spoke to Richard.

"Good morning. Are you coming from the lodge?"

As Richard began to answer, the hiker looked first at him, then me, and, finally, Kent. When he glanced in the back seat at Kent, his expression changed from a smile to a frown. He took his left hand, slid back the slide on the rifle, and released it. He suddenly pointed the cocked weapon right at Richard's face.

"You boys have been up to no good," he said to a stunned Richard.

"No, sir. We're workers from the hotel, just doing a little work at the lodge. We have permission to be here," Richard was showing as much respect as he could muster.

"You have what's mine, and I aim to get it back." He was speaking to Richard, but his glances kept going back to Kent.

"No, sir. We only have hotel tools—honest!" Richard was trying to convince the man as best he could without being a challenge to him.

"You're a liar! You've got my knapsack! The rest of my gear better be where I left it; otherwise, y'all are dead," his voice was almost a growl.

He opened the door beside Kent with his right hand, the one that had a glove on it. He had trouble with the door latch but finally got it.

"Move on over, boy, and give me my knapsack, now!"

He climbed into the back seat. He shoved the shovel and pry bar over onto Kent and switched the gun to point at him.

"Y...yes, sir. We didn't know it was yours. We just thought a hunter buried and forgot it. Here, I don't want it."

Kent had a quiver in his voice. I was plenty scared for Kent and me.

"What's your name?" The man bumped Richard in the back of the head with the barrel of the rifle. Richard gave his full name while he carefully turned the hotel wagon around on the narrow road. After three tries, we finally made it and started back up the hill to the lodge.

It took Richard a lot longer to slowly and carefully drive back up the hill. We both feared that if he hit a bump, that gun might take his head off. When he got to the lodge, the man forced Kent and me to stand on the porch facing the wall while he got Richard out of the driver's seat. He then marched him up to the door and ordered Richard to open it. Richard fumbled with the key, dropped it, but he finally got it unlocked.

Inside, the gunman made Kent find some rope. He warned him. "Boy, if you don't come back; first, I'll shoot Richard; second, I'll kill your little buddy. Then, I'll track you down and cut you up a piece at a time."

Kent started to shake.

"Get moving, kid!" yelled the man.

Superman hurried into the kitchen, and we could hear him slamming stuff open to find the rope. Richard finally spoke up. "Kent, look in the kitchen pantry."

Kent returned with a clothesline. This was getting serious, so I thought I better say something.

"Mister, the only thing we took is that knapsack. We only got the box open a little while ago. We didn't mean nothing. We thought somebody left it and forgot about it. If we had known it was yours..."

"Shut up! For your sake, it better be there. Now, Richard, you tie those boys up to these here chairs, and it better be good and tight. If I find out you tied them loose, I'll shoot them one at a time and make you watch. You hear me?"

That's when Kent raised his hand.

"What?"

"I need to go to the bathroom. Please don't tie me up until I use the bathroom. I truly gotta go." Kent was pointing to the bathroom, and I'm thinking, *Kent, I hope you got to pee and aren't trying something nuts.*

"Oh, for gosh sakes, all right, go pee, but you try anything, and your little buddy here gets a bullet right between the eyes. You don't want to see what a 30.06 would do to his pumpkin, do you?"

"No, sir! I'll be right back, I promise!"

Kent used the bathroom, and we heard the commode flush. I noticed Richard trying to get the clothesline out of its package as Kent came back into the room with his hands up like in a cowboy movie.

"You got a gun on you?" the man asked him.

"No, sir, I ain't got no gun," Kent responded.

"Well, put your damn hands down and sit." I noticed the man was holding the rifle with his left hand, and it seemed a little awkward for him.

That's when the man asked me, "You, boy, you got to pee?"

"No, sir. But if we gonna be here for a long time, I better," I said it just to see if he would let me. I figured if he were going to kill us, he wouldn't care if I had to pee or not.

"Okay. Go on, but hurry up!"

When I returned, Richard had Kent tied to one of the chairs. I saw there was no way he was going to get loose. Each arm and each leg was tied down separate. Richard left Kent, no wiggle room.

I sat down and got the same treatment. Each arm and each leg tied with no wiggle room. It was so tight, it hurt.

The man turned to Richard. "Boy, you might as well know who I am. My name's Daryl Dean Shiflett. I just killed Big John Mc-Culloch, your Chief of Police, and I burned down McCulloch Wood Products. You give me any trouble, any trouble at all, you're next." Mr. Shiflett's threat to Richard made me shiver. Kent and I gave each other a worried look.

Mr. Shiflett pulled the pistol out of the knapsack and loaded it. Then he put a handful of bullets into the left front pocket of his pants. Funny, the things you notice, tied to a chair.

He tossed the knapsack to Richard and motioned with the rifle for him to leave out the front door. Just then, the phone sitting on the table next to the kitchen door rang and kept on ringing.

Bang! I jumped.

Even tied up, I jumped. Looking over my shoulder at the phone, I saw that it had been blown to pieces, and portions were spread all over that side of the room.

Mr. Shiflett took the rifle off his left shoulder and pointed it at Richard's back. He told him to walk, and they walked outside, one behind the other.

I waited a moment and whispered, "Can you get loose?"

"I don't think even Superman could."

A visible cloud of smoke drifted through the open door of the lodge. I sneezed, and then Kent sneezed. We both needed to wipe our noses but couldn't.

"I hope Richard's going to be okay," I said.

"I hope *we're* going to be okay. BB, I don't want to burn up."

When Kent mentioned we might burn up, I started to pray.

CHAPTER 43

THE SNIPER IS IDENTIFIED
Saturday, July 9, 1955

After Matt got the boys and Richard safely off to the hunting lodge, he drove over to Gunn's Garage.

"Hey John, how's your Saturday going?" Matt asked with a smile.

"Just fine. I appreciate you and Richard Baker watching the boys this morning. Letting them work at the hotel is keeping them occupied. Being grounded, they keep trying to sneak off on their bikes," John said with a laugh.

"Billy's better for me than you. I'm not his parent."

"I guess that's true."

"Actually, they're digging up some old box that a hunter left, and they aren't on the clock?"

"More likely digging up an old deer carcass."

"No, I do think they found a buried box."

"I wondered why they were so all fired up about getting to Cubley's Coze this morning. I can't believe they got Richard talked into digging up an old box," John said with a shake of his head.

"He's not. He's replacing some wiring and light fixtures and keeping an eye on the boys. I promised to have them back by noon. I guess you know there's a triple feature on at the movie theater, all monster movies," Matt informed John.

"News to me, but hey, a triple feature of monsters should get them back. What brings you to town?" John put down a wrench and leaned against the fender of his customer's car.

"Well, the hotel wagon needs two back tires. We expect more trips up to the lodge, what with the fall hunting season, and good traction is a must for that road. Would you put in an order for me? I'll drop it off when they arrive."

Just then, the fire department siren began to wind up to full pitch. It was fairly loud even at the garage, which eleven blocks from the firehouse. The men waited for it to stop before continuing their conversation. One set of five cycles, and it usually stopped. When it wound down, John began again.

"Do you have the—" John started to ask, but the siren started up again and drowned him out. "Do you have the size written down?" John had to yell.

"I do. Wonder what's on fire?"

That was when the new pumper came by the garage with its siren wailing and air horn blasting. It was going at top speed toward the Liberty Bell Gas Station with the water wagon and fire department's utility van speeding close behind. Every truck was making the most of its siren and horn. No sooner than the trucks had gone by, then the siren started up for the third time.

"Hop in Blacky, and we'll see what's going on. I may have to drag some cars away from a pump at the gas station."

As John unhitched Blacky from a tow, the old Highland Fire Department pumper number one roared by, followed by ten or twelve firemen in their private cars. The racket was enough to wake the dead.

Finally, Matt and John jumped into Blacky, and as the tow truck left, John gave two blasts on the air horn to let Laura Jane know he was headed out. He saw her come out on the back stoop to see what was going on with all the sirens, and now Blacky leaving. She knew there was no scheduled order for a tow—no recent phone calls.

John started to pull out but stopped. He heard another siren coming up fast from his left. Big John's Cadillac sped past going eighty miles an hour with a Town of Highland police car close behind, siren wailing and red lights flashing.

"Either someone just stole Big John's Caddy or the plant's on fire. Let's get over there!" exclaimed Matt.

Blacky followed at a much slower speed. When they got within sight of the gas station, it clearly wasn't burning. The intersection confirmed which way the fire trucks and firemen had turned: the fire department's water wagon had sloshed out water onto the street, and there were five or six fresh black marks on the road, showing which way the vehicles had turned.

"Look!" John exclaimed, pointing down the road. "I see black smoke ahead!"

When they passed by cemetery hill to their right, a plume of black smoke over the plant came into view.

"Holy Mother of God, the main plant's on fire! There's no way they can save it!" John called out.

"Watch it!" Matt warned. A town police car came tearing out of the plant parking lot with a deputy driving. There was someone hunched over in the back seat. "Who was that?"

"Don't know, but look at him go. He's running flat out.".

John backed up and parked facing the road beside the plant driveway. One or two cars drove slowly past the plant on the highway, but neither Matt nor John took any notice of them. Their eyes were on the fire.

"I'll park Blacky here out of the way. Let's walk in. Fire trucks from all over will be headed our way, and I don't want to get blocked. This fire's going to burn for a long, long time."

Both men got out and hurried toward the plant and conflagration. They were about a hundred yards from the fire trucks when they heard small explosions going off inside the plant. Stranger still, no water was being put on the fire.

When they got closer, they found the area to be in chaos. Someone was lying on the ground with a fireman's coat thrown over him, and the firemen were cowering behind cover and under vehicles.

As they approached, the firemen were started to nervously creep back into the open. Two or three of them ran to pick up hoses that had been dropped. More police and firemen began to arrive as troopers, deputies, and town police assembled for a conference over the hood of one of the state cars. Matt and John couldn't hear what was being said, so they watched the fire. Now, the whole front of the plant was ablaze, the fire eating its way across the roof.

Trooper Lusk came over to Matt and laid a hand on his shoulder. "Our sniper just killed the chief and shot Big John. Help me with the sniper's hide."

Matt did not hesitate, and John also offered to help.

Lusk instructed them to stay in the rear of the search party until the area was found to be safe. The three crossed State Route 22, where a group of police had gathered on the far side of the highway in a skirmish line.

John asked, "Should I get my rifle out of Blacky?"

"No. I have two officers with high powered rifles and scopes that will flank the search party and provide protection. We better keep things simple. If you hear a shot, hit the ground until I give an all-clear. I'm betting this rascal has hit and run again." Lusk then raised a fist, made several circles with it over his head, and motioned the men forward.

The search party started across the field in a line, advancing away from the plant. Most of the men had their hands resting on their pistols, just in case.

The group halted at a place where the grass was mashed down on a rise. A deputy pointed to some brass casings in the grass, and Lusk took pictures before picking up the casings with a pencil and dropping them in envelopes that he pulled from his backpack. Each envelope was marked with a number, and a square piece of cardboard was marked with the same number. The numbered piece of cardboard was then tacked to the ground with a four-inch framing nail to mark the spot. This process was repeated for each shell casing the group located and recovered.

"Our sniper left his brass this time," Lusk said to the group of officers.

Meanwhile, Matt moved to his left. "Gentlemen, here's where he went down into that ravine."

Police fanned out and followed the ravine to the creek. They found the weeds were bent and broken. A few officers were sent down the creek toward the plant, and the rest proceeded in the opposite direction, checking both banks until they came upon fresh footprints that scaled the bank. The trail ended at fresh tire tracks in the dirt road that ran parallel to the creek.

John Gunn then called to the group, "Hey, I got a call from a deputy to come out to this very spot yesterday and tow in a 1951 Plymouth. A farmer reported it was parked here all morning, but when I got here, it was gone. I see these older tire tracks match these fresh ones."

Trooper Quinn spoke up, "Giles, didn't you get a request from the Amherst Police to be on the lookout for a stolen 1951 Plymouth when you came on duty?"

"I sure did," Giles answered. "A couple of neighbors found an old man stabbed to death when he failed to show up to go fishing. We need to get on the horn and ask dispatch to check with our roadblocks to see if anyone with that tag number has been seen."

Just then, Lusk spotted Sergeant Oliver driving up the farm road toward them. He stepped into the road and flagged him down.

After Sergeant Oliver called in the new information to the state police dispatcher, he received a response that there had been no 1951 Plymouths with that tag number seen going through any of the checkpoints. The sergeant asked his dispatcher to call Amherst and get all the details on the stabbing.

"Okay, guys, our sniper either got out before the roadblocks went up or he's hiding somewhere. If he tries to leave now, the roadblocks will stop him," Lusk explained.

"Lusk, organize some men and have them report to the Liberty Bell Gas Station. We can use the area by the bell as a command post to launch a county-wide search. I'm going to personally check each of our roadblocks," ordered Sergeant Oliver.

When the sergeant drove off, Lusk turned to face Matt. "Do you need a ride anywhere?"

"No, thanks. I'll ride back to the garage with John. I'll be at the hotel if you need anything. Good luck, capturing this guy."

"Thanks for helping, Gunny."

"Watch yourself, Ben, if you get him cornered.

Laura Jane met Matt and John as soon as Blacky pulled into the garage lot. Smoke was now visible over the town. When they gave her the news, she took it better than John had anticipated. She just said that she better be the one to tell her mother, as the woman was already fussing about all the smoke.

John drove Matt back to the hotel in the family car, and, since he planned on leaving right away, he parked out front. It was twelve-thirty. He had just enough time to get the boys to the Top Hat Theater. Both mothers thought that being next to the police department and the sheriff's office, that the theater was the best place for them.

Chuck was outside on the veranda, watching the smoke drifting up the mountain from the valley.

"Hey, Chuck, are the boys back? I didn't see the Ford wagon around back," Matt asked with surprise but not concerned.

Chuck was twitching nervously over the fire, and the fact smoke was creeping into some of the guest rooms and the lobby. "Richard's running late. I'm hoping it's not because of the thick smoke on the mountain."

Matt quickly caught Chuck up on the fire and the shootings. When he revealed the sniper might be driving a 1951 Plymouth, all of the color drained from Chuck's face.

"Call the police!" He shouted as he raced inside to the front desk and grabbed the phone. He looked at it but failed to dial any number. Everyone followed him into the lobby and over to the front desk.

"What's the number for the lodge? Somebody, please get me the number!"

"Chuck, slow down! Tell me what's wrong!" Matt gently shook Chuck's arm, trying to get his attention.

"There's a 1951 Plymouth parked in our guest lot! It arrived at about the same time as the fire, but no one came in to register. I saw the driver, I think, and he hiked up the mountain. He's on the mountain!" Chuck's eyes darted from Matt to John.

Without another word, John and Matt bolted out to the guest lot. When they saw the license plate number, they each had the same sick thought: the sniper was on his way up the mountain, probably headed towards the lodge or near it on one of the trails.

Matt ran back to his office and called the lodge, but the phone only rang five or six times before the line suddenly went dead. He redialed the lodge number, but when it didn't ring at all, he dialed the number for the sheriff's dispatcher and gave her the news instead.

"The sniper's on the mountain behind Cubley's Coze! We need help! He may have hostages!"

Within thirty-seconds, sirens could be heard coming their way, and the front of the hotel and guest lot quickly filled with troopers and deputies. Sergeant Oliver arrived and rapidly began to formulate a plan.

John started to drive to the lodge, and several deputies had to restrain him. Matt and Trooper Giles finally persuaded him to go with a deputy to get his wife. "She needs to be here, and you need to be the one to bring her."

After John left, more police arrived. Rifles, shotguns, tear gas guns, and even a machine gun was being readied. It was starting to look like preparations for a full-scale battle.

Sergeant Oliver and Trooper Lusk called Matt over to a table on the veranda, where they had a road map, though it didn't provide much information. Matt got several trail maps from the front desk and gave them to the sergeant, which contained more details about the trails and road up to the lodge.

He drew them the lodge floor plan. From the front, the lodge had a window on each side of the front door that opened into the main room with two bedrooms off to the left. Stairs, a gun case, and a fireplace were to the right with no windows on that side. To the rear of the main room were the kitchen and the pantry. He also showed them the shortest trail approaches. After his information was delivered and during the sergeant's conference, Matt learned some troubling facts.

"Men, I'm sure Daryl Dean Shiflett is our sniper. Also, the Amherst Police believe he stabbed his wife's uncle and stole his car. The stolen car shouldn't have been reported for days, but the old man missed a fishing trip. His fishing buddies got concerned when he didn't show up this morning and found his body shortly after daybreak."

Just then, Matt heard a commotion in the lobby and rushed inside to find that Chuck had fainted. Boo was trying to shake him awake gently. All the hotel employees had gathered just inside the dining room, watching. Maddie and Rose were in tears, and even Toby, the Cleaner, had left his station.

Matt felt death tugging at his elbow once again.

CHAPTER 44

DEATH ON THE MOUNTAIN
Saturday, July 9, 1955

Chuck Tolliver was passed out on a couch in the lobby. Boo brought him around with a cold compress on his forehead and a whiff of ammonia on a rag that she briefly placed near his nose. Maddie and Rose were seated in the dining room, sipping water while doing their best to remain calm. Both had red eyes.

All work in the kitchen had stopped. Lunch preparations were forgotten. Several guests were assembled in the lobby as the news spread about the two little wash boys and the yardman.

Sergeant Oliver, Sheriff Lawrence, and Trooper Lusk were going over one of Matt's trail maps spread out on the hood of the sergeant's car. Matt quickly approached them.

"Ben, I don't want to interrupt, but you might need to know this: Billy and Kent found a plywood box buried beside the main hunting trail that runs from the lodge to the top of the mountain. The box was near some big boulders above the lodge."

"You think that might have something to do with our sniper?" Ben turned the map around to show Matt.

"If our sniper intends to escape over Green Mountain, that might be his cache of supplies. Look, he can follow this trail from the lodge up to this notch on the eastern side of Green Mountain. He could slip through this gap and down the backside. He'd be in for a rough hike, but you guys would be in for an even rougher chase."

Matt pointed out the route with his finger on the map.

"I know that mountain, and chasing him over it will be a piece of work," said the sheriff.

"Plus, there are a lot of hides up there. Picking off pursuers one by one might be his plan. If he has plenty of supplies and ammo, he has the advantage."

"Matt, you really think that this box the boys found belongs to Shiflett?" Sergeant Oliver asked, worried.

"Not sure. Hunters have been known to hide stuff in buried boxes to keep from hauling supplies up and down the mountain during hunting season. We figured the boys had found an empty box left over from last deer season. It could be nothing. For the sake of the boys and Richard, I hope it is."

"Ben, call everyone together. We need to get up this mountain," ordered Sergeant Oliver as he folded up the map and started counting how many officers he had available.

Lusk rounded up all the troopers and deputies, and while he was waiting for the sergeant to get started, he began to check out the deputy with the machine gun. Matt walked over to the sergeant as he finished counting noses.

"Sergeant, if I may: I know this mountain, and I know how snipers think. Let me go first. A lone person can get in close where a group would be too noisy. If he's got them, he might try to use Richard, Billy, or Kent as a shield if he hears a posse."

"Any other ideas?" Sergeant Oliver leaned against his car and looked at Matt.

"Don't take this wrong, but seeing this many guns and at least one machine gun, I'm afraid of friendly fire. If I take a shot up there, I won't miss, and I'll make damn sure my employee and those two little boys are not in my line of fire."

"Look, I appreciate your offer, but there's no way in hell I can allow you to go up that mountain. I don't care if you're the best shot the world has ever seen; you're not a sworn officer. There's no way any supervisor in the state police would approve of me allowing this. I'm sorry." The sergeant looked pained as he apologized, but it did nothing to ease Matt's worry.

The sergeant returned to checking over his equipment, then started handing out walkie-talkies to the assault force.

Matt spotted Lusk talking to a group of deputies and Giles and eased over to ask him for a word. He told Ben the same thing he had just told the sergeant, adding, "Ben, I know a shortcut. I can beat the assault team up to the lodge by twenty minutes or more."

Lusk considered it for a moment before shaking his head. "Matt, stay off the mountain. It's just too dangerous. If one of this group sees you, a lone man ahead of us, hell, they'll shoot you and ask questions later. I promise we'll do everything we can to bring Billy, Kent, and Richard back safe."

Giles, who was nearby, asked Matt if he could impose on him for some soft drinks from the kitchen. Matt almost told him off for worrying about some damn soft drinks at a time like this but decided he needed to get away from the police to calm himself. Plus, taking Giles into the kitchen might help.

They walked into the deserted kitchen. "Matt, I'm sorry you have to stay behind," whispered the trooper as he took out a pistol and laid it on the kitchen counter.

"What's that?" asked Matt.

"This here six-shot, thirty-eight Smith and Wesson is a gun that belonged to my dad. I think it's one of the finest shooting guns I've ever used for close-up work. Dad always told me that a lawman needed an extra piece. You never know when it might come in handy, and best of all, it can't be traced."

"It's a nice gun, Bobby. What kind of soft drinks do you want?"

"A couple of Cokes would be great. I get mighty thirsty hiking up through these woods."

Matt put half a dozen drinks from the cooler in a sack and handed them to Bobby. The trooper took them, thanked him, and left.

He took a single step, and that's when he saw the thirty-eight pistol still lying there. He picked up the gun and found six rounds in the cylinder.

Matt checked the kitchen a final time for staff or guests, but he was all alone. Walking into the storage room, he cut on the light and closed the door. Bending down, he pulled on a spring-loaded pin that was located behind one of the legs of the storage shelves. Matt then tugged on a set of shelves. They were on four hidden hinges and swung open like a door. Behind the shelves was another wall with a standard door that opened into a tunnel. He flipped a switch located on the tunnel wall, and lights came on.

He slowly pulled on a rope handle attached to the shelves to close them. The last time he'd closed them from this side, he'd done it too quickly, and a bag of sugar had fallen off. Once he heard the locking pin click as it slid back into its hole, he softly closed the tunnel door on his side, and the entrance was now doubly sealed.

Matt jogged down the tunnel, being careful not to trip over the ore cart ties, going deeper into the abandoned copper mine. The electric lights glowed every forty or fifty feet along the way. The walls were stained from the old coal oil lanterns. Thankfully, Uncle TJ replaced them with electric lights. The mine location had been explained to him in the documents he had received from Frank Dalton when he had first come to town. What a surprise it was to Matt, who had no idea this tunnel existed. Even Chuck wasn't aware of it.

Deep inside the mountain, the tunnel came to a dead end. Thirty feet from the end was an electric elevator sitting in a large steel structure. The cage had once been able to hold twelve men or a loaded ore cart and sat on a wooden platform. This was the same elevator he had recently oiled and serviced according to the instruction manual Uncle TJ had left him. He thought it had been a fool's errand, but now, he was glad he had given into his whimsy. This elevator, deep inside the mountain, would get him to the lodge ahead of the police.

He stepped in, closed the outside gate, then the inside gate, and grabbed the wooden handle of the wheel installed on the side of the cage. He pulled back for up, and the cage began its ascent of nine hundred feet to the mine's top level. Halfway, the weights for the elevator slid past him, going down.

While it took the elevator five minutes to reach the top, he knew he would beat the troopers by at least thirty. When the elevator jerked to a stop, he pulled open the two gates and jogged up the incline, first, deeper into the mountain, then, a gradual turn to the surface.

Old mining tools were rusting and strewn about on the top level. Soon, he came to another wooden door set into a timbered wall, which opened inward. Beside this door was a cabinet, and from it, he removed a flashlight with new batteries he had recently installed. He turned off the tunnel lights and clicked on the flashlight. A cone of light illuminated the door in front of him.

Slowly and quietly, he lifted the latch and eased the door open. Behind this door was another set of shelves like the ones by the kitchen. He repeated the process to open the shelves and stepped into a storage room inside the rock bunker. He shined the flashlight on the wall and located the hidden, second big key for the bunker door lock.

He turned off his flashlight and placed it on the floor, opened a pinhole in the door, and looked out. He could see the hotel Ford, which meant Richard and the boys were still here. He hoped, yet again, that the sniper had taken another route, and they were just running late.

He watched for two or three minutes, hardly breathing. Everything was quiet. Well, it was now or never. He used the big key to unlock the bunker door. The lock clunked as it opened and sounded so loud to Matt that people in town could have heard it.

He eased open the bunker door, crept to his left, and slipped down the lodge sidewall to its rear, taking a quick peek in the kitchen window. Despite seeing no one, he was not about to enter through the front or even the rear door.

There was a crawl space door in the lodge's back wall, and he opened it, checking for snakes. There were none as far as he could see near the opening, but farther in where it was dark; he wasn't so sure. Thinking of touching a snake in the dark gave him the shakes, and kicking himself for leaving his flashlight behind, he took a breath and crawled inside. He felt over his head, found, and raised the trap door into the kitchen pantry. Someone had recently rummaged around and thrown things on the floor, which caused him to make more noise than he intended. Climbing into the pantry, he could hear muffled voices.

Very slowly, he opened the pantry door and, listening closely, only heard Kent talking. He checked the kitchen for the sniper, and when he found it was clear, he eased into the kitchen with his pistol cocked.

From the kitchen door, he could see into the bathroom, and most of the two downstairs bedrooms. They were clear. Kent and Billy were tied to two chairs in the main room and seemed calm. Matt took a chance because he was running out of time. He slipped behind the couch.

"Billy, where's the sniper?" Matt whispered very softly to Billy, but not loud enough for the sniper's ears—he hoped.

Matt brought up the pistol, knowing he would have only a split second to take the man out.

"Kent, did you say something?" Billy asked out loud.

"No, you're hearing things," Kent replied.

Matt stood up, confident that the sniper was not inside the lodge.

"You boys stay quiet while I cut you loose."

"Mr. Cubley! He took Richard!" Kent blurted out.

"Hush, and do exactly what I say!" Matt whispered harshly.

Matt quickly cut the boys loose with his pocket knife and rushed them out through the back door. He put them in the bunker, handed them the big key, and told them to lock the lock from the inside.

"The police are on the way, but don't open this door unless you hear me say, 'Billy the Kid.'"

Suddenly he heard Richard's voice. Matt ran from the front of the bunker and hid between it and the lodge. He was in an excellent position to see the lodge porch and beyond with a quick peek.

Richard was wearing two knapsacks and carrying a third, and behind him, Shiflett was prodding him with a rifle. Based on sounds, Matt knew both men had stepped up on the porch, and Richard deposited his load with a thump, thump, thump. Matt risked another peek, but unfortunately, Richard was in his line of fire.

"Mr. Shiflett, sir, please let the boys go. By the time they get down off this here mountain, you can be long gone. They're good boys. I'm beggin' you, *please*, don't hurt them none."

"Shut up, boy, and get back inside. I ain't gonna hurt them boys—I got kids of my own—but I won't hesitate none about shoot'n you, so, move!"

Richard took one step through the door but suddenly stopped. The boys weren't there.

Matt took that opportunity to jump onto the end of the porch, aim his thirty-eight pistol at Shiflett, and shout, "Drop it!"

This warning gave Shiflett time to bring his rifle up and around. The rifle was now aimed at Matt.

They both got off one shot.

A quarter second before Shiflett fired, a boot mule-kicked him on his right hand.

Matt felt a searing burn across his left upper arm, but he was able to fire three more times. The sniper's rifle also fired again, but he missed, striking a front porch plank.

Daryl Dean Shiflett started to say something, but his mouth was filling with blood. He turned toward Richard, coughed, and blood splattered all over the back and side of Richard's head and shoulders. Shiflett fell to the porch with four bullet holes in his chest, dead.

Matt, keeping his pistol on Shiflett, kicked the rifle off the porch and checked the body. He found and removed a pistol stuck in Shiflett's belt, tossing it beside the rifle. Finally, he checked for a pulse; there was none. That's when he saw that Richard was down on his knees, wiping blood off the back of his head.

"Mr. Cubley, where on earth did you come from? Is he dead?"

"He's dead."

"Mr. Cubley, sir, you're bleeding."

"It's only a graze. That mule kick of yours threw off his aim, or I might be down there beside him. Thanks."

"Are the boys safe?"

"Yeah, I got them into the bunker. I do seem to be leaking on the floor."

Matt sent Richard into the lodge for a towel to tie around his bleeding arm. Then, Matt pulled a yellow cotton blanket off one of the lodge beds and used it to cover the body. When blood started to seep through at one corner, he added a second wool blanket and put it over the cotton blanket. This was as good as he could manage. Finally, Matt walked over to the bunker to let the boys out.

"Billy the Kid, are you and Kent alright? You can open the door. It's safe."

The lock clicked, and the door opened a few inches. Billy was bent over, with Kent almost on top of his back, peeking over him.

"We heard a bunch of shooting. Are you shot, Mr. Cubley?" Kent asked first.

The door opened all the way, and they scrambled out into the sunshine. Billy was first to notice Richard still cleaning blood off himself.

"Kent, Richard's been shot," Billy cried.

"No, Billy, I'm fine. I just got blood on me, but it's not mine." Richard pointed to the body on the front porch.

They both caught sight of the covered body. The two blankets had helped, but there was still blood seeping through in several places. Blood had run in a little stream across the porch and off the end. Matt could have kicked himself for not walking them to the other side of the bunker.

Kent groaned, ran several steps into the yard, and threw up; next, Billy gagged. Matt grabbed the shaking boys by their arms and escorted them and Richard to the side yard to a picnic table. Here, they were out of sight of the body. He got them some water and made them sip it while they waited for the police.

After a moment, he slipped back around to the bunker and locked the door, sliding the key into his pocket. He would return it to its proper place later tonight when the kitchen was closed, and there would be no witnesses.

After what seemed like hours, Matt saw movement at the edge of the woods. He yelled and waved a white rag, beckoning the police to come on up to the lodge. Eighteen officers emerged from the woods and spread out in a skirmish line. One of the deputies had a large walkie-talkie and called down to the command post that everyone was safe. Sergeant Oliver replied and ordered the patrol cars to leave their parking spot halfway up the mountain and drive to the lodge.

Then, the sergeant ordered Giles to bring the boys to their parents at the hotel. The trooper offered to run the lights and siren for Kent and Billy, but to his surprise, the boys told him no.

One of the deputies asked Matt how he got up to the lodge so fast. Matt responded, "I'm a Marine; I ran and I know a shortcut."

CHAPTER 45
BILLY'S BIRTHDAY GIFT TO HIS DAD
Sunday, July 10, 1955

Sunday, the rest of the family slept late, but not me. I was awake before dawn. My night had been troubled with bad dreams, scary ones. I got out of bed when I heard my parents downstairs. Mom gave me a big hug as soon as I got to the kitchen. I thought that she might smother me, but I didn't mind.

She held me at arm's length and said, "No more excitement for you, even if I have to move this family to West Virginia!"

"Please don't! It's not my fault; besides, all my friends are here."

"I don't blame you. I blame this town."

Last night at first, Mom, Dad, and Grandma only had good things to say. They made a big to-do over Kent and me when we came down from the mountain. But inside the hotel lobby, Mom started crying over me in front of Mr. Tolliver, Boo, Trooper Giles, and everybody. She kept blubbering about how her baby could have been killed. All the hugs felt good, but not the fuss.

I tried to make her feel better when we got home by telling her how Mr. Cubley saved me, and I was never in any real danger. That's when Dad hugged me, and I thought I was convincing everybody until I noticed Mom crying again. I knew when it was time to shut up and go up to my room to bed.

Sitting in my room, I realized that I never got a chance to ask Kent not to tell anyone how I almost threw up. That's when I remembered Kent did throw up, so he had more to lose than me, telling our secrets. I also wanted to ask him if he had nightmares last night.

After breakfast, we had to get ready for church. I was brushing my hair and explaining to my bathroom mirror, "I've had enough, Mr. Mirror. This isn't a wish, but it would be nice if you stopped the adventures. You've done more than a person could want."

In church, the pastor preached how this community needed to turn to God in our time of trial and tribulation. Heck, everyone knew all about the town's troubles. Everyone was worried they might never get their jobs back with the plant burned up and Big John in the hospital all shot. If he didn't make it or decided not to rebuild the plant, this place was doomed. The preacher didn't need to remind us.

After his sermon, the preacher tried to calm the town by telling us he had visited the hospital, and Mr. McCulloch was still alive, and it was time for us to say a silent prayer. Just when I got going good on mine, he started up with his own prayer and drowned mine out. I bet God only heard a piece of my prayer.

Anyway, the pastor didn't pray for Mr. Shiflett, but I did. Mr. Shiflett could have shot me a bunch of times, but he didn't. So I put him in my prayer. I hope God heard it over all the nice things the preacher was saying about Big John McCulloch.

Getting out of church is always great, and it got even better because when we got home, we celebrated Dad's birthday. Mom had helped me wrap his present, and it looked beautiful. I wanted him to like it.

Mom made Dad a white cake with white icing, his favorite. We gave him his presents, and he opened mine first. Dad said that he liked his new hat, then he told me it was too expensive. I reminded him I was a working man. Mom gave him a wool scarf that matched his hat, and he was all ready for fall and cold weather.

There was another big party on Dad's birthday. Mr. Cubley had invited the staff, troopers, and us to the hotel for dinner. While the hotel's regular guests ate in the dining room, we all had a special party in the banquet room on the second floor.

Kent and his mom met us at the hotel because our car was full; Grandma had agreed to come. When we got there, I noticed a lot of cars in the parking lot. This was going to be a humdinger.

We walked in, and the first thing I saw was Kent in the lobby waiting for me. We hugged and started talking like it had been years since we last saw each other.

Boo walked through the lobby, telling everyone to come on up to the banquet room. When we got upstairs, Boo gave Kent and me a hug. I hugged her back. I waived to Richard Baker and his wife, Rose, and they both waved back. All the local troopers were there, even Trooper Lusk.

Mr. Cubley motioned for Kent and me to come over to where he was standing. He wanted us to meet some friends of his. Boy, was I surprised to see Skip and Barry Hathaway! Mr. Cubley introduced us to their mom, who seemed very nice. Skip and Barry said hello, but I didn't stay and chat. I was worried that someone might find out that they were the two boys who beat up Lou. I didn't want them to get into trouble over helping me.

Trooper Giles spoke to Matt. They walked off like they wanted to be in private, so I walked behind them, bent over, and pretended to tie my shoelace.

"Bobby, did you get the package? I was afraid the sergeant was going to keep it, but he decided he didn't need it."

"Thanks, Matt. Chuck gave it to me. I don't understand how I could have forgotten it. Guess I'm getting old." Trooper Giles was giving Matt the look I often gave to Kent.

"Think Sergeant Oliver will ever forgive me?" Matt asked.

"Since it turned out the way it did, give him forty or fifty years, and he might. I just can't ever let him lay eyes on it, or my goose is cooked." Trooper Giles laughed, but he was whispering.

I wasn't sure what this was about, but you know adults.

I was even more surprised when Trooper Giles walked right up and spoke to Skip and Barry. I noticed they didn't walk away when he approached them. Tonight, mighty strange things were going on. I edged closer to see what was happening. The trooper saw me and walked closer.

"Billy, I understand that Skip and Barry came to your rescue in the park," Trooper Giles said with a grin on his face.

"How in the world did you find out?" I blurted out.

"Troopers know everything. Actually, I've been asking around. It looks like most of the town of Highland knows. I also learned about Mr. Hathaway being framed for the trouble at the payroll office. I spoke to his wife about it, and I'm going to try to collect enough evidence to persuade the governor to pardon him."

"I thought you charged him with all those crimes over the wreck. He did bump you off the road." I was shocked that this trooper would do anything to help out a criminal.

"Billy, desperate people do desperate things. He was trying to help his family but was doing it all wrong. I think it's time he got a little justice. Every officer should be sure no innocent person ever gets convicted. If he was framed, it's time that injustice gets corrected."

"You can do that?" I asked.

"Well, a couple of us are going to try. I think we'll be able to get a couple of witnesses from the payroll office to talk, now that the plant's shut down."

"To answer your other question, you're correct. He'll have to pull some time for wrecking me, but I'm going to let the court know the whole story. Besides, his family did nothing wrong. Skip and Barry helped you out of a tough spot; you owe them."

"You're right about that. Although, I still get headaches from that scrape," I said.

I saw my mom motioning for me to come over to the table she had staked out. I excused myself and joined her.

I noticed Mr. Cubley was with Mrs. Carlisle, a beautiful lady. Also, I saw Mr. Dalton, his wife, and Miss Martin with a date. I looked around to see who else was at the party. Most of the hotel staff were present, even the coloreds, and no one was objecting. It was like we were all a family, sort of. The waitresses were taking turns downstairs and joining the party upstairs.

We all sat down to dinner, and Richard Baker said grace. Kent was seated at my table, and so was Boo and her dad. Kent and I talked to Boo the most because she had been so nice to us that summer.

When we were starting dessert, Mr. Cubley stood up and began to speak.

"Ladies and Gentlemen, I have some news from Sergeant Oliver. The state firearms expert has confirmed the rifle recovered from Mr. Shiflett was used in all of the shootings. The sniper has been identified, the threat is over, and the town is safe."

Everyone started clapping. Several people yelled. Boo's dad did a whistle with his fingers in his mouth that was louder than anyone. I was glad Kent and I were not going to have to worry about someone else being the sniper. I was jumping at loud noises and felt anxious every time I passed a stranger on the street. Mom wanted to know my every move, and even Dad was acting goofy. I wanted to be normal.

Mr. Cubley continued, "Regarding other news, while Big John McCulloch is in critical condition at Waynesboro Memorial, the report is he's doing better. He might lose a lung, but his other lung is strong, and the doctors are hopeful he will make it." No one clapped but only listened politely.

"The plant, of course, is closed. A fire crew remains there to ensure what's left doesn't reignite. We won't know if it will be rebuilt until Big John recovers. The town needs him, so let's keep him in our prayers."

There were a lot of nods but no outburst of applause.

"Now, let's thank Sergeant Oliver, Trooper Quinn, Trooper Giles, and Trooper Lusk for some great detective work. They stayed the course when there was a lot of pressure for them to jump to make a quick arrest, but they waited until they got solid evidence. A great job, guys!" Matt said and began clapping, which was followed by everyone joining in.

My Dad stood up, and I was surprised because he didn't like to speak in public.

"Yes, John?" Mr. Cubley said, and then, he sat down.

"Matt, Billy's mom and I want to thank you for saving our boy, Kent, and Richard. You deserve more than we can ever say in words. Today's my birthday, and you gave me the best present a father could have—you got my boy back, safe and sound. Thank you." When Dad sat down, I thought I saw water on his cheek.

The place went nuts. It started with clapping, then the four troopers shouted, and people were yelling. Suddenly Mrs. Carlisle leaned over and kissed Mr. Cubley on the cheek. Wow, right in front of everybody. Kent was banging a spoon on the table until it flipped and came down on Boo's plate. Slowly things calmed down. Matt got up and held up his hand.

"Happy Birthday, John. I'm sorry we don't have a birthday cake. A certain employee failed to tell me. I'll be sure to mark it on my calendar in case Billy forgets next year."

My face was red. Dad reached over and scrubbed the top of my head with his fist, but I didn't mind.

"John, thanks. I just wished it would have ended a little better. There's been too much death." Mr. Cubley was speaking softly, and things got quiet. After a pause, Mr. Cubley looked around and continued.

"Now, Mr. Parks called me, and the Beamis kin will have all their charges dismissed tomorrow. So, Mrs. Carlisle may expect him waiting when she opens the judge's office."

She gave Mr. Cubley a big smile.

"My final announcements are about the hotel. The guests have started to call and rebook their reservations. Chuck Tolliver and I think the rest of the summer may be back to normal. "

More cheering erupted, especially from the staff.

"I do have some sad news. Mrs. Longwood, our regular Maître D', has decided not to return to us. Her brother's sick, and she's decided to stay with him. Miss Beverly Olivia Skelton will…"

"Who?" yelled out Connell Washington and Maddie Johnson in unison.

"Okay… Boo!" Matt called out over the laughter. I thought Mr. Skelton was going to get mad, but he started laughing as well.

"Boo will continue as Maître D' until she leaves for school at the end of the summer. We all expect she'll finish and graduate with honors."

There was more applause and the stamping of feet. I could only imagine what the guests in the dining room below us thought was going on. I bet the lights were dancing on their chains with all the stamping.

"Now, that leaves us without a Maître D' for our dining room this fall and winter. We're looking for someone, hopefully with experience. If anyone has any ideas, come see me."

Mr. Cubley then thanked everyone for coming to the party. He sat down, and I saw Mrs. Carlisle pat his arm. It was the sore one, the one he got shot in, but he didn't seem to mind.

Grandma motioned for our waitress to come over. She told her she didn't like ice cream on her pie. Mom put both hands over her eyes. Just then, Scotty threw his cookie across the table. It landed in a glass of tea. The waitress smiled at me, left to get a piece of pie with no ice cream for Grandma, and a rag to clean up the tea. Mom smacked Scotty on his hand, and he started crying—nothing ever changes in my family.

After dinner, Kent and I talked with Barry and Skip, and I heard their mom telling Mr. Cubley how she had once run a restaurant. She asked him if she could come by and talk with him about working in the dining room? He told her that he would love to talk to her.

Mr. Cubley started to walk past Kent and me. I stopped him and asked, "Mr. Cubley, where's Polecat?"

"You know, funny, you ask. I did invite Mr. Smith to the party; he said he'd come, but only on one condition," Mr. Cubley gave me a grin, and I knew Polecat had done something goofy.

"What condition was that?" Kent beat me, asking the obvious question.

"He would only come if I let him eat dinner on the loading dock. That's what he did. He ate his dinner on the loading dock." Mr. Cubley laughed.

"Some people don't change," Kent said and laughed.

"Boys, are you ready to come back to work at our peaceful little hotel?" Mr. Cubley was teasing us.

"We sure are," Kent said, and his face broke into his crooked smile.

"I just hope for the rest of the summer our adventures are little ones. I'm tired of getting shot at by snipers, seeing dead bodies, and being kidnapped. Can you guarantee a little peace and quiet?" I teased him.

"Well, I don't see why not. Isn't that why this place is called Cubley's Coze?"

Mr. Cubley laughed and went over to Mrs. Carlisle, who was waiting patiently for him.

ABOUT THE AUTHOR

R. Morgan Armstrong, born in Martinsville, Virginia, was a prosecutor, trial attorney, and General District Court Judge there. He attended Virginia Military Institute, received his BA degree from Duke University, and his law degree from the University of Richmond. During law school, he worked summers as a park ranger for the Army Corps of Engineers at Philpott Dam and during the summer of 1972 as a police officer for the City of Virginia Beach.

While a prosecutor, he helped organize and supervise a special police unit composed of state troopers, county deputies, and town police. While a judge, he wrote the Unauthorized Practice of Law section of the Virginia District Court Judges Bench Book.

He joined the National Ski Patrol (NSP) in the fall of 1980. Armstrong served in every line officer position and most instructor positions. He was elected director of the Southern Division, then elected to two terms on the National Board of Directors for the NSP, chaired the Governance Committee, and in 2019 was inducted into the National Ski Patrol Hall of Fame.

Upon his retirement from the bench, he moved to Wintergreen Resort with his wife, Jo Ann, and their dog, Bailey. He enjoys working with the local ski patrol and writing.